Sarah's
FALL

A NOVEL

PAULA RIEHLE

Sarah's Fall
Published by Remedy Publishing
Lakewood Ranch, Florida

Publisher's Cataloging-in-Publication data

Names: Riehle, Paula, author.
Title: Sarah's fall / Paula Riehle.
Description: Lakewood Ranch, FL: Remedy Publishing, 2022.
Identifiers: ISBN 978-1-7356857-0-0 Subjects: LCSH Friendship--Fiction.
| Cheerleading--Fiction. | Chicago (Ill.)--20th century--Fiction. | Women--Fiction. | Bildungsroman. | BISAC FICTION / Women | FICTION / Coming of Age Classification: LCC PS3618 .I44 S27 2022 | DDC 813.6--dc23

Cover and Interior design by Victoria Wolf, wolfdesignandmarketing.com

REMEDY
PUBLISHING

To Max

1

IN HIGH SCHOOL, my friend Tori warned us that we all might lose touch one day. She was resigned to the possibility, stating it matter-of-factly as something we needed to consider. Her rationale was simply that once we graduate, "things just change."

At the time I'd dismissed her declaration because you don't let friendships like *ours* go. Yes, *things* change. We grow up, get married, have careers and kids, but we do those things *together*. And when that part's over, we grow old and wrinkly and laugh over cocktails as our daughters tell *their* daughters, "They've been friends since they were *thirteen*!" So, while things may change, friendships don't. At least not ours.

And now, twenty years later, I sit here asking myself how I'd been so quick to let them go. Hoping they can at least forgive me for everything I did—and didn't—do. Most of them, anyway. One I don't care about at all, and I hope she doesn't come today. But with everything that's happened, especially lately, it's become blisteringly clear that friendships are the best defense against this tumultuous world. I wish I'd recognized it sooner, pulled them closer. Instead, I pushed them away.

As I nervously smooth a lump in the white tablecloth, the waiter approaches. I wave him off because I'm not sure anyone will show up to a reunion we'd committed to as teenagers, especially given the circumstances. Most of us haven't even spoken in twenty years, so who knows if they remember—or care. And I'm the only one who *has* to be here. Well, we all have to be here because we made a promise that no matter where we were in our lives, we would meet here today. But I'm the only one who's truly obligated because I am in possession of the incentive we gave ourselves to show up. I take a deep breath as I put the tattered red duffel bag on the chair next to me and hope I'm not taking up this five-person table for nothing.

I check the time on my phone—ten more minutes. I wish my curiosity hadn't driven me to get here early because as the minutes tick by, my hopes of a successful reunion begin to fade. *Why would they remember? Why would they care?* And as the afternoon martini crowd fills in around me, I start to get restless, feeling irritated by their apparent zest for life, while mine is falling apart. I feel preemptively defeated and wonder if it's better to leave now before the loss is forced upon me—no one remembering, no one caring. I want to leave. But a deep need for connection, for forgiveness, for closure compels me to stay. I try to distract myself with some people-watching. But the beautiful people, swilling their cocktails, laughing in that celebratory way twenty-somethings do before life starts kicking them around, are making me feel worse. I sense my cynicism rising and look around the room for anything to stifle it. My eyes are drawn to the expansive view, so I rise from my chair, move to the window, and lean my forehead against the chill of the glass.

It's one of those perfect Midwestern fall days, where the sun touches everything just so. The sky is clear enough that I'm sure I can see my childhood home. So, I scan the cityscape for the northwesterly highway and follow it with my eyes. As I zero in on the blur of the general vicinity, I start wondering about the home I haven't even driven by in twenty years—wondering who lives there now. Wondering if they're happy. Wondering if they have a teenage daughter who will one day ruin their lives. This line of thinking isn't helping my nerves, so I sit back down.

As I child, I loved this time of year—the excitement of the new school year when you're actually happy to be there. The reuniting with friends, trading shorts and flip-flops for bulky sweaters and boots. The start of football season and cheerleading. The traditions—Homecoming, Halloween, apple picking. The sweetness of fall. The sweetness that now makes me sick to my stomach. I have a lot of wishes about that tragic day. I hate to admit that one of the bigger ones is that it would have happened in another season instead of permanently tainting my beloved fall.

My eyes wander to the entrance, and I am instantly relieved when a familiar face enters my view. It's Tori. She told me she was coming, but I still had my doubts. She's the only one I've kept in touch with since everything happened—if the occasional phone call and social media count. Even though we haven't seen each other in person, at least social media makes me feel like I still know her. I know her kids are ten, seven, and five, two boys and a girl. I know she likes to travel to exotic places and dine at trendy restaurants in New York City. And she seems to love her family and her job. I suppose her social media portrayal of her life could be a misrepresentation of the real thing, but I doubt it. She genuinely seems happy.

"Is it just us?" she asks, setting down her oversized Louis Vuitton bag. Tori has done very well for herself, so she's probably the most eager to attend the unveiling. She married a great guy, an entertainment attorney. She attended Syracuse University and majored in journalism. And she's established herself as a reporter on a major news network. I attribute at least some of that success to the fact that Tori's conscience is cleaner than the rest of ours. "I did *everything* I could with what I knew at the time," is the way she says it. That's mostly true. But I'm sure that despite her squeaky-clean conscience, part of her fears the story will come out someday and jeopardize her perfect life. As far as Tori is concerned, my conscience is clean too. But judging from the way my life has turned out, she should know better. The chilly scent of dried leaves lingers on her wool coat as she leans down to give me a hug.

"It's so good to see you, Sarah." She runs her fingers through her glossy, auburn hair. It falls perfectly into place as she takes the seat across from me. "How've you been?"

"Well, you know. It's been a little hard since Shawn and I separated."

"God, I'm sure. I'm so sorry. I should have called, but I've just been so—"

"Busy," I interrupt her. "I know. Everyone's busy. The kids are busy, my friends are busy . . ."

"And your parents, how are they? Are things better between you guys?"

Tori seems great, as if she hasn't given much thought at all to what happened twenty years ago today.

"I don't know . . . not really. They live in Florida and have ever since . . . well, you know . . ." I say, trailing off. "I mean how is anything supposed to get better if we never got the chance to fix it. I think about that a lot. It's like one day things were great, and one day they turned to shit, and then they moved. So, things just stayed . . . broken. It's like arrested development or something. And there's no way to go back and change anything. Excuse me," I shout to the waiter. "Can I get a sauvignon blanc please?"

"Just a Pellegrino for me," Tori adds. "And Kevin?"

"He's there too. He wasn't happy when they moved right before he was supposed to start high school, but it grew on him. He's married, two kids . . . and they live about a mile from my parents, which of course they love."

"It's got to be hard trying to keep your family together with no family of your own here. Who's keeping you together?"

I see the look of pity in her eyes for a millisecond before it turns to excitement.

"Look! Is that Stacey?"

I turn toward the hostess and see a tall woman dressed in all black. Jimmy Choo booties, coated leather pants, and a fitted cashmere sweater. Her wavy blond, lowlighted hair reaches just below her shoulders. She's still stunning, maybe even more so. Tori and I wave eagerly to get her attention. The scent of Coco Chanel announces her approach.

"Hi girls!" Stacey pulls out the chair next to me. She glances at the duffel bag occupying the seat and then opts to sit next to Tori. "Oh my god, I can't believe we're actually here. Honestly, I didn't think you guys were going to come. I wasn't sure I was going to come, but I live in the building. I decided I didn't have a good excuse not to."

"So, you didn't want to come?" I ask.

"Did you guys? I was thinking if we wanted to keep in touch, we would have. But it was too convenient for me not to at least pop in and say hi. If anyone showed up, that is. Or even remembered. Well, it is the day before your birthday, Sarah, and the anniversary of . . . well, it's been twenty years since all of the ugliness happened. I figured it would be good for us to cleanse our souls a bit."

"Well, we're glad you're here." Tori smiles warmly and puts her arm around her. "You look amazing."

"What's amazing is how much it costs to keep all this up," she says, running her hands from her face to her thighs. But you look *fantastic*." Stacey scans Tori from head to toe.

Tori's smooth forehead and full cheekbones make it clear she's no stranger to the dermatologist, but she looks natural. Beautiful. I'm sure whoever does her work has all sorts of celebrity clients. And writes a column somewhere. Or has a reality TV show.

"Do you even remember what it was like when we just had it, without having to go through all the effort?" Stacey raises her cheeks with her fingers.

"Right? Think about what I have to go through just to be on camera," Tori says.

"I cannot even imagine. Add that to the reasons I'm thankful I don't have to work. I'd never be able to handle that kind of pressure." Stacey lets her cheeks snap back into place and rests her hands on the table.

They know better than to include me in this conversation. There's no erasing the toll these years have taken on my face. I could live on green smoothies and spend my last nickel on plastic surgery, but my appearance would still scream guilt and failure. I notice the dirty blond split ends resting on my chest. I hate that I couldn't drag myself to the salon in time for today.

"So, marriage? Kids? I heard you got married," Tori says.

"Yes, Greg and I have been married for five years now. No kids. We're not sure we want them."

"Tick tock." I offer what I can.

"I know. Everyone keeps reminding me. But, you know, kids are just so much to worry about. I don't know that I could handle the enormity of the responsibility. I don't want to fuck them up, you know?"

"Well, I'm doing a very good job of fucking up my kids," I say, raising my glass.

"They will be fine, Sarah," Tori tries to reassure me, as she always has.

"Will they? Look at our childhoods. Some of our parents were great and some not so great. But no amount of good parenting could have stopped what happened."

"That's kind of my point. I think my kids have it pretty good, but I'm not naive enough to think that means they'll turn out okay.

There's only so much you can do. Sometimes I think you get what you get and all you really have to do is feed them until they can feed themselves." She laughs. "I can't tell you how happy I was the day Jasper learned to make mac and cheese by himself. I literally said out loud, 'my work here is done.'"

"So, you're saying my shitty parenting might mean they'll turn out just fine?" I ask pleadingly.

"What I'm saying is that you can't protect them from everything. But if you love and support them, like I know you do, odds are they'll be okay. Stronger even. Resilient."

"Well, thank you. I feel much better now!"

It suddenly hits me to my core how much I've missed her. Tori has always been so consistently who she is. Honest and intuitive. Empathic, yet emotionally practical. I love that even as a teenager, I could have predicted she would become the woman sitting across from me today.

"All right, I'm having wine. But just one. Stacey?"

"I won't be stopping at one. Did I mention I live in the building?"

The waiter brings a bottle of Kim Crawford. As we fill our glasses, I feel warmth and familiarity spilling over me, just like I did the day Ella moved back to Chicago. Ella.

I can't believe she's not here. I quickly push that thought deep inside, as it's threatening my ability to enjoy the moment.

With the help of the wine, we are right back into it, laughing as if not a day's gone by, when suddenly Stacey's laugh falls right off her face. "Oh my god." She nods toward the host stand. I look over and see Dalia scanning the crowd. From a distance, it appears that her life has turned out a lot more like mine than Stacey's and

Tori's. Her untamed amber waves look like they've been bleached and recolored countless times. She's rail thin, wearing tight, ripped jeans and a black moto jacket. I have to take a second look to be sure, but as she gets closer, I catch those unmistakable Mila Kunis eyes. She approaches nervously.

"Dalia." I stand up and hug her, sure I wouldn't have been so friendly two glasses ago. She smells exactly the same, and I'm struck by the range of emotions this evokes. Even though I'm ultimately responsible for what happened, Dalia had planted the seed. And I'd held that against her for twenty years. Yet somehow, it feels good to see her.

"Hey bitches." She greets us the way she did when we were seventeen, although with a little less enthusiasm. She hangs her jacket on the seat occupied by the duffel bag and sits on the other side of it. The empty space between us does not go unnoticed.

"You made it," Stacey says. "Has anyone talked to Jenny?"

"Yeah, sorry I'm late. I talked to her last night. She should be here." She fidgets with her phone before turning it on vibrate. "So, what did I miss?"

"Excuse me, another glass please." I flag down the waiter and motion to Dalia.

"No wine for me. I'm in the program. Three hundred eighty-five days, but who's counting," she says, playing with the triangle engraved sobriety token on her chain.

"Well, good for you." Stacey claps with the tips of her fingers.

"Yeah, more like fuck me. I wasn't going to come, to be honest. Part of me wanted to, but the other part, well, you know." She inspects her black polished nails to avoid making eye contact. She takes the drink stirrer out of Tori's Pellegrino and starts chewing on it. "But my sponsor said I have to work the steps. Steps eight and nine are about making amends, which she said is important if I'm serious about my sobriety. Which I am. I have to be. For my daughter." She takes a deep breath and leans back in her chair.

"Why don't we just catch you up before we get into all of that," Stacey suggests. "You missed a lot, so I'll give you the *CliffsNotes*. Me. Married for five years to Greg, an investment banker I met while staying at my parents' house in St. Bart's. No kids, no interest in having kids. And that's about it. I don't know, is there anything else?"

"Do you work? Of course you don't."

"Actually, I'm on the board at the Children's Hospital and the Museum of Contemporary Art. I also sit on the board at one of my father's companies, so between the three I'm pretty busy."

"Well, look at you," Dalia says. "Must be nice."

"It is, actually." Stacey rises above. "My work is very rewarding."

"Tori, I see you on the news. Looks like you're having a pretty good go of things."

"It's hard work, Dalia, but I really enjoy it."

"Sarah." She pauses, taking inventory of my face. "You look like you've seen better days. How's our friend Shawn?"

I guess I should have expected it, but I'm pissed she even mentions him. Or maybe just pissed at myself that I've failed. "We're separated," I offer. That is all she will get out of me.

"Well, that's too bad. Hey, tell him I said hi."

I shoot her a glare as we sit through an awkward silence, the feelings of warmth evaporating before our very eyes. Dalia ignores my obvious irritation.

"Doesn't anyone want to know about my life?" she asks.

"Go for it," Stacey says.

"Well, after high school, my mom moved in with her boyfriend, and that was about the last she wanted to do with me. They paid the rent on the apartment for a while, though, so I survived well enough. I waited tables to put myself through beauty school and got a job at a decent salon."

She goes on to tell us how she met a great guy, Tony, one of her clients, and that things were great in the beginning. They didn't have a lot of money, but they were in love. They married, and a few years later, she had her daughter, Frankie, now thirteen.

"But, one day I took Frankie to the park. I was just sitting there watching her play on the swings, and I felt happiness. Like the real thing. It was weird. I'd never felt that way even once in my entire life. And it lasted for about a minute. And then I couldn't breathe." She starts talking faster. "I started thinking that I didn't deserve all this, and one day it was going to be taken away from me, cuz who the fuck was I to have all this when Ella didn't get to. And the feeling wouldn't leave no matter what I did, so I started drinking. Just a little at first, to take the edge off." The beginnings of tears well up in her eyes. "Then I hurt my back, so I couldn't cut hair anymore, and this asshole doctor got me hooked on pain pills. Let me tell you, you don't ever want to be hooked on that shit."

I see a small tremor in her hand as she sips her water, as if the mere mention of her pain pill problem brought back all of the physical torment.

"It didn't happen overnight, but Tony warned me a million times that I'd better get it together or he was going to take Frankie and leave. And then one day, my back was really bothering me, so I took some pills. And I had just one vodka, because the pills weren't doing it." She pauses. "I'd totally forgotten I had to pick Frankie up from camp. They called looking for me, and I couldn't get a hold of Tony, so I had no choice. I had to go get her. So, I got in the car and barely made it to camp. Thank god, I opened the car door and fell flat on my face. I actually split my head open on the curb. See this?" She moves her hair aside to show us a scar on her forehead. "The camp counselor called the police, Tony came and got Frankie, and I've been fighting to get her back ever since."

"Dalia, that's terrible." Stacey touches her hand. "You know, I do some work with a sober living facility. I can try to get you hooked up with someone there, if you feel like you need to work some things out. They're really great."

"So, this is what I want to know. Are you supposed to suffer your *whole life* for something that happened when you were a teenager? *When does it stop?!*"

Dalia starts to sob. People start to stare. I'd spent the last twenty years suffering myself, so I'm surprised at how strong my urge is to comfort her. Maybe it's my maternal instinct. Or maybe it's the wine. But as I reach over the chair to hug her, I am overwhelmed with emotion and say something I would have never said an hour ago. "You don't have to suffer forever, Dalia. None of us do."

"You guys, it's a little awkward to break this up right now, but I don't have much time." Tori looks at her watch. "Chloe and I have a tea date at the Peninsula."

"Cute," Stacey says. The two of them have been remarkably unemotional during this whole scene. Maybe they're better at compartmentalizing. Or maybe they feel like it's between Dalia and me.

"Well, I think it's safe to say Jenny isn't coming." I reach for the duffel bag.

"I don't understand. Where the fuck is she?" Dalia checks her phone. "She said she was coming."

"Did you talk to her today?" Tori asks.

"No. She hasn't answered me all morning."

"She probably just changed her mind. Well, I guess we can't wait anymore. Everyone ready?" I reach into the bag and pull out the time capsule that's been sitting in a toy chest since October 28, 1995. It's finally time to see how the goals we set for ourselves twenty years ago have fared—if our lives have lived up to the hopes and dreams of our teenage selves. I don't have to open the time capsule to know that two of our teenage selves are going to be disappointed.

"I'm ready." Tori rubs her hands together.

I unscrew the circular cover and reach inside. We'd been careful to place our handwritten notes in individual Ziploc bags, so I'm surprised when the first thing I feel is a folded piece of paper.

"Huh. This must have fallen out of one of the bags. Okay, I guess we'll start here." I unfold the purple piece of monogrammed stationery and gasp. "*Oh my god.*" My voice trembles. My hands start to shake as I read the unmistakable handwriting.

Hello ladies . . .

2

THE SUN STREAMED DIRECTLY into Sarah's eyes through the top of her blinds, shaking her from a deep sleep. She glanced at the old-fashioned brushed bronze alarm clock with bells on top that, despite looking ancient, had reliably woken her up for two years. But not today. Even though her mom had given her the clock, she constantly warned Sarah not to depend on it in case she went too long without changing the batteries. *Eleven o'clock? How could I have slept this late?* She squinted at it and rubbed her eyes, seeing spots as she tried to make sense of the two hands. *Maybe it stopped at eleven last night. Maybe I can still get to school on time.* She jumped out of bed and hurried down the stairs to see that the microwave digitally displayed 11:00. *Did I forget to set my alarm?* As reason slowly crept in, so did a wave of sheer joy when she realized it was the first day of summer vacation, and she didn't have to be anywhere at all but on the couch.

She pulled off the ponytail holder that lived on her wrist, and she made a giant bun on top of her head as she relished the freedom the next eighty-two days would bring. Eighty-two days. She knew the exact number because she'd made a promise with her girlfriends to make each and every day of this summer count. Senior-year summer wouldn't be quite as long, and they'd all be leaving for school at different times. So, this was the one. The summer between junior and senior year was the one that really counted, and they were determined to make the most of it.

The house was silent and comfy as she opened the pantry, settling on a bag of Doritos and iced tea for breakfast. Happily crunching away, she curled up on the couch in her black sweats and Nirvana T-shirt. She had just started reading an article about how to create smoky bedroom eyes when she heard the garage door open.

"You're still in your pajamas?" her mom asked as she walked in. "It's just gorgeous outside. You really don't want to miss this one." Carrie Blake set her purse on the counter and hung her keys on the tiny brass hook next to the door going into the garage. On the wall, there were two hooks for keys that, clearly, one of her parents had eyeballed when they installed them, as evidenced by the half-inch height difference. Oddly enough, a pencil mark was on the wall where the hook should have gone. Sarah had always meant to ask them about that, but it was just one of many over-looked household issues. While the house was cute and clean, it would take an army of handymen to fix the small flaws they ignored. Those little details didn't seem to bother her parents like they did other people, though. Her parents viewed every paint chip, scratch, and ding as fond memories, signs that a home was loved and lived in.

While Sarah was in full-on relaxation mode, her mom wanted to talk. Carrie stood above her, breathless as if she had some news she just couldn't wait to share. So, Sarah wasn't exactly surprised when her mom said, "You'll never guess who I ran into today."

"Who?" she asked, certain she wouldn't be nearly as excited as her mom was.

"Ella Connor and her mom! She said they're in town house hunting. Apparently, Alan's transfer didn't work out quite the way they'd hoped, and they're moving back." She tsked and shook her head. "It's too bad for them, but I told her you'd be *so excited*."

"Yippee," Sarah barely responded, completely engrossed in her *Cosmopolitan* and chips.

"What. You're not happy about that?"

"Mom." She let the magazine fall into her knees. "I haven't seen her in years. Aside from a couple of letters, we haven't talked at all since before high school."

"I know it was hard for you guys to stay in touch, but she was your best friend for ten years. You were in diapers together. Dance classes, all those weeks of summer camp, doesn't that mean anything to you?" Carrie leaned across Sarah authoritatively and twisted the blinds open. "Aren't you at least curious to see how she's been?"

"I don't know. I mean, I guess. But I don't know if I want to hang out with her. What if it's weird? A lot's changed in five years." Sarah put a crease in the corner of the page and set it on the coffee table. "I don't hang around with anyone I did back then, and I'm pretty sure I wasn't even wearing a bra the last time I saw her." She glanced at her chest and realized she should probably have a bra on now. "What if we're totally different people now?"

"And what if you're not? I think it's safe to say that she, too, is now wearing a bra. Should give you *hours* of conversation material." Carrie laughed at her own joke and used her hands to sweep Dorito crumbs off the coffee table. "Make sure you clean all this up. And we're having dinner with them tonight, so don't make any plans."

"Mom, no. I already have plans. *Big* plans. We're all going to Jenny's to swim and then right to Stacey's house. It's her big summer party, and I'm *not* missing it."

"Well, you're just going to have to bring her then."

"Absolutely not." She sat up and crossed her legs. "I can't just bring whoever I want, and you can't just take away my night."

"Sarah, please don't give me a problem. I am thrilled to see my old friend, and I would love for you to come with me. But I will give you the option to skip dinner, on the condition that you take Ella with you to Stacey's. One or the other, your choice."

"God, Mom. *Fine!* I'll go to dinner. But I'm going to Stacey's afterward, and there is no way I'm taking her."

"Fair enough."

"Well, this was fun and all, but I have to get ready. Dalia is picking me up."

"Dalia." Carrie sighed. "I really wish you two didn't spend so much time together. She's just so . . . *mature*. And her mom is, well, not mature enough, I guess."

"That's cuz she's like thirty-four!"

"Exactly. I give her credit for raising Dalia on her own all these years, but she should at least try to set a good example for her impressionable daughter."

"Dalia is hardly impressionable. If anything, she does the opposite of what her mom does just to spite her."

"Oh, I feel better now." Carrie rolled her eyes. "If doing the opposite of what her mom does turns out to work in her favor, it would be a pretty amazing thing. But I'd say in my experience, more often than not, the bad habits of the parents rub off on the child, one way or another."

"In your experience? From your drama-filled childhood?" Sarah teased.

"No, from my many years of having no drama of my own, allowing me to observe and judge and draw conclusions from the drama of those around me," she said smugly.

"Well, at least you admit it. Thou shalt not judgeth, Mother. Isn't that what the Bible says?"

"I don't know, let me consult my Bible Expert, Sarah." She laughed as she grabbed her keys off the hook. "I'm running to the mall. Have fun swimming and be back by five."

As Sarah heard the door close, she laughed at the nickname she hadn't been called in years. *Bible Expert.* A title earned back in her church camp days when she'd arrive home and enthusiastically share the few things she'd learned. Her parents sent her every summer with Ella, whose extremely religious family introduced them to the concept. Sarah had told them she loved it, which she did. Though Sarah only loved church camp because she and Ella liked boys there.

3

"SARAH, DALIA'S HERE," her brother Kevin yelled up the stairs.

"Hurry up!" Dalia shouted up to her. "We're missing peak tanning hours."

"I'll be right down," Sarah yelled back as she slipped her ripped jean shorts over her black string bikini. She threw on a strappy black tank top, stepped into her Steve Madden slip-ons, and put on her favorite generic sunglasses. She'd called them "a find" when she bought them at a thrift store, but Dalia thought they looked cheap.

"When are you going to get a real pair of sunglasses?" Dalia asked the second the front door shut behind them. She pointed to the thick-rimmed, oval-cut Pradas resting on her head. Dalia and her mom didn't have money, but they always had designer accessories.

"As soon as *my* mom gets a rich boyfriend."

"Yeah, that's not gonna happen," she said as they stepped into what Dalia referred to as her "bullshit car." It *was* bad. No one even knew what kind it was, as all identifying markings had rusted away, but at least it got them from point A to point B. Dalia turned the ignition and glanced over to Sarah's empty lap. "Where are your clothes for tonight?"

"I'm not bringing them." she said, scowling. "I can't go to the party until *way* later."

"What the fuck, Sarah? Isn't Jake supposed to be there?"

"Yes! I'm *so* pissed. My mom just told me I *have* to go to dinner with her."

"Really." Dalia's tone changed. "So, you're *mad* that your mom is *making* you go to dinner with her? How about you just be happy you have a real mom who cares about you, unlike mine. Trudy's been a fucking nightmare," she said as she craned her head around and backed out of the driveway.

"Come on. You'd be pissed, too, if *Shawn* was going to be there and your mom wouldn't let *you* go."

"No. I wouldn't. You're lucky. You totally don't appreciate what you have."

"What. Just because I have good parents, I never get to complain?" Sarah asked as she cranked open the window. The handle broke off in her hand. She slid it under the seat when Dalia wasn't looking, as she could already tell she shouldn't add more fuel to Dalia's fire today.

"No. You don't. Your mom is a *good* mom. She *wants* to spend time with you, and you don't even appreciate it. You should really be nicer to her."

"Nicer? I'm always nice to her. It's not like I told her to fuck off, I only told *you* that I'm pissed."

"Yeah, and I told *you* you shouldn't be."

"Dalia, I am allowed to feel however I . . . why am I even bothering?"

Sarah closed her eyes for a moment and breathed slowly through her nose. It was the first day of summer. The weather was perfect. The *last* thing she wanted was to get drawn into a stupid argument just because Dalia was in a mood. Sarah had two choices. Take the bait and risk the afternoon being ruined or try to steer the conversation back to Dalia. It took everything she had not to take the bait.

"So, what's going on with Trudy?"

"Trudy," Dalia groaned. "So, I told you about the Italian. He's such an asshole. So, she's spending more time at his place, which, fine. Whatever. But three nights ago, she didn't come home at all. No note, no call, nothing. Can you believe that shit?"

"*Seriously?*" Sarah immediately softened toward her.

"*Yeah!* You'd think living in our white trash apartment complex, she'd at least check on me. I mean, she wouldn't even know if I were dead."

"Well, are you sure nothing happened to her?" Sarah asked. She wondered which would be worse in Dalia's eyes. Something bad happening to her mom or purposeful abandonment.

"You actually think I'm that lucky? I called her today. She said she just figured I'd call if I needed anything. She didn't even ask how I was doing."

"Oh my god. So, what's his deal?"

"*Total* asshole. Like he just drives some big *Mercedes* and wears gold *chains* and has a wad of *cash* all the time," she said, her arm flailing in sync with the tone of her voice.

As Sarah listened to Dalia complain about yet another one of her mom's boyfriends, she tried to picture what it would be like to come home to an empty apartment. To live with the knowledge that you're, at best, an afterthought in your own mother's eyes. She understood why Dalia hated these men, but it didn't necessarily mean they were bad guys. Though trying to convince Dalia of that was never worth the effort.

"Well, at least he has money," she offered.

"Yeah, but who knows how he got it. And he's a total perv. The last time I saw him, he brought me a necklace. And when I put it on, I caught him checking out my tits." Dalia took both hands off the steering wheel and cupped them proudly, like she always did when she talked about how great she thought they were, which was a total red flag. Even though Sarah felt bad that Dalia had to deal with these things, Dalia was definitely part of the problem.

"Are you *sure?*"

"*Of course I'm sure!* Who brings their girlfriend's daughter a necklace? He totally gave it to me so I'd put it on, and he could check out my tits."

"Dalia, is it possible he was just trying to be nice? I mean, if he's looking at the necklace, it's kind of close to your chest so . . ."

"That's *why* he bought it, Sarah!"

"So he could check out your tits when you tried it on. Got it. Total perv." She sighed. "Has your dad been around lately?"

"No, thank god. At least this one seems to be getting her over him."

"Well, that right there is worth giving him a little titty show," she joked.

They turned into Whitetail Estates and wound around the hilly, tree-lined roads. Whitetail Estates, also known as home to their best friends Jenny and Stacey, appealed to the richest of their suburban town, their houses tucked lavishly behind protective landscaping. Except for Jenny and Stacey, Dalia hated *those people.* But she especially hated them when she had to drive her bullshit car around their neighborhood. They reached the stop sign at the top of the hill, just beyond the entrance, when Dalia's stick shift car stalled.

"*What the fuck. Every fucking time.* Did they put this stop sign right at the top of this hill to keep people out who can't afford automatic fucking transmission? Look at her staring at me." She extended her arm out the window and pointed to a woman in tennis whites, holding a racquet in one hand and pulling two kids in a Radio Flyer wagon with the other. "Sorry I'm poor, lady," Dalia shouted and gave her the finger.

"Well, you're in a mood today."

"It's not *me*, Sarah. These assholes are all Neighborhood Watch every time they see my bullshit car."

"Let's just try to have fun," Sarah said as they pulled behind Jenny's BMW.

"Come on in, ladies," Jenny's mom greeted them through the speaker, a detectable slur lurking behind her perky welcome. They followed the voices of several adult women and found them standing around the kitchen island, day drinking mimosas out of crystal stemware. Jenny's mom was drinking a filled-to-the-rim martini that sloshed around and spilled over the edge as she raised her glass.

"We're just planning our annual fundraiser for the . . . which one is this?" She turned to the rest of the ladies. "Oh," she said, laughing. "For the *Opera House*. It's so hard to keep them all straight anymore. You wouldn't *believe* how much work goes into these things." She took the skewer of olives garnishing her martini and slid one off with her teeth, seeming to savor it as if she hadn't eaten in a week. Jenny's mom looked noticeably thinner every time Sarah saw her. The former Miss Teen Illinois was almost unrecognizable, as her gauntness had removed most traces of her former beauty. Her long blond hair had become wiry and brittle. The skin on her face hung from what little collagen she had left now that her food pyramid consisted mostly of vodka.

"Oh, it's *tons* of work," blond mom number three said as she topped off her mimosa with a generous pour of *Veuve Clicquot*. Their glasses united in a celebratory clink.

"You girls have to try these. Fresh squeezed orange juice is the secret to a good mimosa," Jenny's mom whispered and winked at them as she handed them each a glass.

"Pretentious bitches," Dalia said once they reached the solarium.

"Jenny's mom isn't like the rest of those women. She's so nice. And you know she grew up with nothing."

"*I know*. How did she ever land a hot, rich guy like that? She's like a real-life Cinderella story."

"You mean the one where the prince cheats on her and Cinderella drinks herself to death?" Sarah slipped her mimosa between two potted ferns. It was way too early for champagne.

"Boohoo. We've all got problems. Well, except for you."

"What do you mean, except for me?"

"Exactly what I said. You have *no* problems. It's so unfair." Dalia flung her hair back as she walked ahead of Sarah.

"I've had problems." Sarah picked up her pace to catch Dalia. "Remember that whole thing with Neil Spencer?"

"Oh, *the trauma*. A two-month high school relationship doesn't work out, and you lose five pounds. I'm talking *real* problems. You're like the only person I know that doesn't have any."

She was totally right. Sarah didn't have any problems but felt defensive to the point that she wished she did, just so she could win this one. She opened the double glass doors to the pool and found the rest of the girls sunning themselves on resort-style, cushioned lounge chairs.

"Tori's never had any problems," she said. Even if Dalia was right about her, Sarah could still prove that Dalia's *everyone* claim was wrong. The girls were all relaxing, tanning their fronts, when Tori promptly turned onto her side to face them.

"What kind of problems. Psychological problems? Money problems? Or like my dad dying kind of problems?"

Sarah envied Tori's brain, the way it could switch gears appropriately on a moment's notice. But sometimes it was annoying. Like right now when Sarah realized she'd just committed a major blunder. Tori's mom had been married to the same man for as long as Sarah had known her, so it never quite clicked that he wasn't her real dad.

"Oh my god, I'm sorry, Tori. We *were* talking about your dad kind of problems. I can't believe I forgot."

"It's fine, Sarah."

"I don't have any problems," Jenny said, sitting up. She took a long sip of her margarita and then dragged the sweaty glass across her forehead.

"Yes you do, your mom's a drunk and your dad's a cheater," Dalia said.

"Well, except for that, I meant." Jenny shrugged.

It was no secret that Jenny wasn't the most introspective person. She never dwelled much on anything going on in her house. Or anything else, for that matter. But even though she didn't seem bothered by Dalia's comment, Sarah was, on her behalf.

"Dalia, *enough*. Just because you've got some things going on right now doesn't mean you get to be an asshole," she charged. "How about you just stop talking until you have something nice to say."

While she felt a little bad for yelling, at least it did the trick. Dalia's mood lightened up, and they were finally able to shift into summer fun: working on their tans, catching up on gossip, and making plans for the twelve weeks of freedom ahead of them. As Sarah soaked up the Midwest sun, she wished it could last forever. But the dreaded dinner was rapidly approaching.

"If you want, you can leave your stuff here, and we'll walk to Stacey's." Jenny picked a chunk of lemon out of her long blond hair and flicked it onto the concrete. "Does my hair look lighter? I used a whole lemon this time."

"You guys, I have to go home first. I have this thing. I have to meet you at Stacey's," Sarah said. It pained her to even bring it up.

"*What?* What *thing?*" Stacey raised the back of her chair and took off her sunglasses.

All eyes were on Sarah, as no "thing" could ever be more

important than going to Stacey's tonight, especially to her. Everyone knew this was the first time in months she'd see Jake Crenshaw outside of school. They'd flirted in art class all year. And while sometimes they crossed paths socially, they hung in different crowds, so it was a crapshoot as to whether she'd run into him on a weekend night. But it was all but confirmed he was coming tonight, and she'd been desperately looking forward to it.

"I can't even believe this is happening, but there's this girl I was friends with—she moved in middle school, and now she's moving back, and my mom is *making me* go out to dinner with her and her mom. She just decided this *today*. But I will be there right after dinner."

"What friend? Who is she, and why have we never heard of her?" Tori pulled from the textbook of aspiring journalist questions—which was no surprise, considering she and Tori planned to study journalism together at Syracuse.

"Well, Tori, her name is Ella. We met when we were toddlers, at some mommy group thing, then our moms put us in all the same activities, and then she moved. Right after school started in seventh grade. Why you've never heard of her, I guess, is because I haven't heard *from* her since like two years before I met you guys. And by that time, it wasn't important to me. Does that cover it?"

"So, were you close friends?" Tori continued the inquisition.

Sarah felt a squeezing in her chest as she thought about why she didn't want to answer this question. For sure she wouldn't admit to being close to Ella until she found out how she'd turned out. But more importantly, she loved her life exactly as it was: problem-free. She loved her family and her friends. School and cheerleading. She also had a big crush on a great guy that she was pretty sure was interested in her too. As close as she had been to Ella, Ella was her past. And she didn't feel like dealing with someone who could screw with her present. But she wasn't interested in explaining that either.

"I mean, yes. We were good friends. But it was like forced." She dismissed ten years of friendship with a flick of her wrist.

"So, you're not excited to see her?" Stacey asked.

"I haven't spoken to her in *years,* so of course I'd rather be with *you* fuckers," she said, as she shoved her sunscreen into her beach bag.

"Are you gonna bring her to Stacey's?" Jenny asked.

"*No.* I'm going to dinner, then I'm meeting you guys. *All by myself.*"

"You should totally bring her. I want to meet this girl." Dalia's eyes flickered with excitement.

"*Stop.* I am *not* bringing her."

"Sarah, it's going to be really rude if you just ditch her to go to a party. Think about if the roles were reversed." Tori put on her *I expected more from you* face. "How would you feel if you were moving to *her* area, and she didn't help *you* get acclimated? I mean, come on."

On the surface, Sarah knew Tori was right, which she generally was about most things. But she'd thought about it all day, and she couldn't get past this feeling that Ella's return was a small threat, no matter *how* she'd turned out. There could be pressure to hang out with someone she didn't want to hang out with, or worse. She could march right into Sarah's life and take it over. What if she stole her friends? What if she set her sights on Jake? For someone who was fiercely protective of the status quo, this was extremely unsettling. No, Tori was not right about this one. Or if she was, Sarah didn't care. Nothing good could come from Ella's return. And no way was she going to bring her to Stacey's. But she would keep that to herself for now.

4

SARAH WALKED IN THE HOUSE at five o'clock, sunglasses resting on her oily hair, damp towel draped over her like her lack of enthusiasm for this dinner. She heard a voice from the past coming from their living room, the room normally reserved for company that magically brought out adults' phony voices. She had to catch her breath for a second. She'd assumed they were meeting at the restaurant and wasn't mentally prepared to make awkward small talk. After briefly debating whether to sneak up to shower first, she dug deep and found her phony voice.

"Hi Mrs. Connor, it's nice to see you."

"Honey, I was just about to call Jenny's to tell you to get your butt home. We decided to start the festivities early." Sarah's mom smiled, pouring a deep red into her glass.

Ella's mom, hiding her portly frame under a royal blue pantsuit, rose from the couch and walked toward her.

"Sarah, how nice to see you. *Look at you.*" Linda Connor grabbed Sarah's hands and spread them wide. While Linda inspected the *new Sarah,* Sarah inspected the stomach fat jiggling over Linda's tacky gold belt. "It is amazing the difference just a few years makes. *Isn't it amazing, Carrie?*" She turned toward Carrie while still holding Sarah's hands.

"I ask myself every day where the time has gone. Can you believe Kevin is thirteen now? He already sounds like a man." Sarah heard a sadness in her mom's voice for just a second before she *completely* changed direction. "And the tissues all over the place? *Disgusting.* I find them *everywhere.* I actually found some shoved in the couch cushions in the basement the other day."

"Mom, *gross,*" Sarah interrupted, covering her ears. "No one needs to hear about that, and now I can never sit on that couch again."

"I mean, my god. You can't even be bothered to do it privately? Or, at the very least, clean up after yourself? I love him, but teenage boys are about the most disgusting creatures on the planet."

"Are you talking about what I think you're talking about?" Linda's jowled face fell as she put her hand on her heart.

"You mean masturbation? It is nonstop. You're probably not there yet with Greg."

"You're telling me you allow that to go on?"

"Allow? What does that mean? Like you can stop a teenage boy, or girl for that matter, from exploring their bodies?" Carrie gripped her wine tightly and took a literal step back. Her elbow knocked over the table lamp. She caught it right before it fell to the floor.

"Masturbation is a sin, Carrie. We've told Greg, who is eleven, by the way, from a very early age that his body is for procreation in marriage only, and any other *activity* is a violation of his commitment to God. He wouldn't even consider it."

"Oh," Carrie responded as she nervously bit her lip. "I apologize, Linda, I guess I should have . . . I guess I didn't remember how serious your commitment to the Bible was."

Sarah was feeling somewhere between smug and in pain, watching her mom squirm.

"And what does Ella say about all this?" Carrie asked.

"Ella? Girls don't have the same urges as boys. I don't have to put her through any unnecessary, *awkward* conversations."

Carrie glanced over at Sarah and looked away before Sarah could telepathically tell her *I told you so*.

"So where is Ella?" Sarah asked.

"She's upstairs using your shower. I hope you don't mind. We had a busy day looking at houses. The last one was right up the street, so your mom told us we should just come on over and get ready here," Linda said.

Sarah ran upstairs, envisioning Ella going through her things. She flung open her door, expecting to find Ella reading her journal. Instead, Ella was sitting on her bed, hair wrapped in a towel, flipping through her *Cosmo*.

"Is she done yet?" Ella looked at Sarah with sad eyes.

"*Who?*" Sarah asked. It came out bitchier than intended, but she didn't know how to fix it.

"My mom. I tried to come down to ask for a blow-dryer when I heard her giving the dreaded masturbation lecture. I had to come back here and hide. She is so embarrassing."

"Yes she is." Sarah laughed. "I'm sorry, but she really believes all that?"

"Yes, and it's getting worse. They've always been religious, you know that. But as we've gotten older, they're so far into it I think they've gone insane. Well, my mom anyway. My dad's probably just going along with it to keep the peace."

"Maybe it's their way of keeping you on a leash."

"Probably. But how can they not see that it's totally backfiring? I used to like church and camp and all that. Now, she drags us to this cult. One of those big evangelist things in an auditorium. It's so different from our Catholic church; it's like not even real." She took the towel off her head, spilling damp, chestnut curls onto her tiny shoulders.

"How's Greg feel about it?"

"Oh, he hates her too. And she's crazy if she thinks he's not *pleasuring himself*."

Sarah laughed as Ella pretended to toss off.

"I found a *Hustler* magazine in the Monopoly box. And he's eleven."

"*Oh my god.*" Sarah slapped her hand over her mouth.

"He probably got it from some creepo preacher. I don't dare tell my parents, though. They'd probably send him away."

"Maybe it's time for a new church." Sarah smirked. "Do you need a blow-dryer?"

"Yeah," Ella answered, running her fingers through her hair. "I didn't want to go digging through your things."

Sarah wondered what she'd been so worried about now that they were connecting so easily.

"It's under my sink. And my brushes and curling iron are in the drawer on the right."

"Thank you, Sarah. Sorry to be invading your space," Ella

said as she stepped into the bathroom. "I wanted to go back to the hotel, but my mom insisted we come straight here. And I promise, when I'm done getting ready, I'll ask you how you've been," she said, smiling sweetly.

5

ELLA BARELY ACKNOWLEDGED her mom as they drove to dinner. Instead, she spent the ride aligning herself with Carrie and Sarah in an invisible battle against her mother. The dreaded masturbation lecture? Really? That was Linda's idea of a fresh start? It wasn't exactly a surprise she would sabotage any hope that they could just pick up where they'd left off, but within the first five minutes? At least Sarah was on her side. And Carrie was doing a really good job of acting like it had never happened. Ella wondered how some people could just let things go like that.

"So, if it's okay with you guys, I thought we'd try this new Italian restaurant in town. It's where El Hacienda used to be," Carrie said, pulling the visor down to shield her eyes from the sun.

"El Hacienda is gone? I loved that place," Ella said. She hadn't loved it that much, but its mere mention triggered fond memories of sitting next to twelve-year-old Sarah in this very car. "Remember how we'd eat all the chips and salsa, and they would get mad that we'd be too full to eat our dinner?" She turned toward Sarah.

"*Oh yeah.*" Sarah met her eyes and laughed. "It would be some *big surprise* every time that we didn't touch our meals."

"They were too busy drinking margaritas to notice." Ella made a googly-eyed drunk face that made Sarah laugh out loud.

"Well, it is now Trattoria 10. I hear they have a great patio and a fantastic wine selection—and probably all the *bread* you can eat. Is this the perfect night for it or what?" Carrie motioned toward the vivid blue sky.

"That sounds perfect," Linda said.

"Ella?"

"Sure, Mrs. Blake. Whatever you guys want to do is fine."

"Ella, you are way too old to be calling me Mrs. Blake. Please. Call me Carrie."

Ella hesitated. "Uh . . . okay," she said, her spine stiffening.

Linda turned around and shot Ella a frigid glance. Ella immediately looked down and stayed that way, even as they entered the restaurant.

"Right this way, ladies." The very tall host patted Ella's head as if she were a child. She turned around and swatted his hand away. He recoiled once he realized his mistake. Yes, she was barely five feet tall. But if he'd bothered to look at her face, or her boobs, for that matter, he would have known she wasn't a child. But then she caught a glimpse of herself in a mirrored wall and saw what he saw—the Kmart rainbow striped top, the two-inches-too-short jeans—and she couldn't blame him. As she walked next to Sarah, who was wearing a fitted black halter top and lacy shorts, the humiliation burned hot. If Linda would let her pick her own clothes, she wouldn't feel like this right now, she thought as they were seated in the ivy-covered courtyard. The waiter handed Carrie a bound wine list.

"Chianti, right?" Carrie asked Linda.

"Carrie, it's been so long since I've even bothered to read a label. If it's got alcohol in it, sign me up!"

"Okay! Well, to celebrate the Connor-Blake reunion, tonight's dinner is on us." Carrie clapped her hands together.

"Hi ladies, will you be ordering wine tonight?" The waiter pulled a gold pen from behind his ear.

"Absolutely." Carrie put on her reading glasses and dragged her pointer down the wine list. "We'll have the *Ruffino Chianti Classico Riserva.*"

"Excellent choice. Four glasses?" He winked at the girls.

"I'll just have lemonade," Ella said.

"Iced tea, please," Sarah said.

Linda and Carrie looked at each other and laughed. "Iced tea for Sarah and lemonade for Ella. Some things never change, I suppose." Linda's facial creases began to relax. And for the time being, so did Ella.

"I'm having déjà vu." Carrie reached across the table and squeezed Ella's hand. "This is so fun!"

The waiter returned. After presenting their wine selection, he filled their glasses. Ella steered her eyes toward Linda's glass and gave her a long look. Linda offered up a patronizing smile and raised her glass to her lips. Ella said a silent prayer.

She started to think her prayer was answered when, under the pink sky, Linda and Carrie began to talk like the old friends they'd been. She felt hopeful as she watched them find common ground. Venting about all things marriage, swapping helpless husband stories. From toilet seat battles to man flu, there wasn't a thing they didn't agree on when it came to husbands.

The whole thing started to feel right. As hands of all shapes and sizes delivered grilled calamari and creamy Caesar salads and tiny plates of roasted garlic, Linda seemed almost normal. And Sarah seemed happy to see her. And as the pink sky turned to midnight blue, the four of them talked and laughed, as if not a day had gone by when they were apart. An hour later, there were two private conversations going on at the same table. But just as Sarah and Ella were diving into their one-on-one catch-up, the mention of another bottle of wine caught Ella's attention. She tried to covertly point to the wine and made a throat-slitting motion. Charades was never Sarah's strong suit, so Ella had to come right out and say it. "Ixnay the Ineway," she whispered in pig Latin.

"Oh." Sarah laughed. "Don't worry. I can drive home."

"It's not that."

"What is it? Aren't you having fun? I hope you are because I'm having a *great* time."

So was Ella. And she felt a strong urge to protect it so she could have *more* great times. "No. I am too. It's her drinking. She's okay after a couple. But three or four? Forget it," she whispered. "She's a disaster. Can you ask your mom to not get any more?"

But it was too late. The waiter had already returned with the second bottle.

"Ella, it will be fine."

"You'll see."

She wasn't wrong. Somewhere between glass three and four, Linda's mood began to change. Her pupils were dilated, and her laugh wasn't genuine anymore. A chip grew on her shoulder before their very eyes, and they were no longer having fun. Any accomplishment or vacation story Carrie shared evoked "well, look at you's" and "aren't you lucky's." As Ella came to terms with the fact that even moving back to a place where life had once been peaceful wouldn't fix her problems, she debated lobbing a grenade that she knew would reveal to the world the crazy she'd been dealing with while everyone else had been living their perfect lives. It was risky. The Blakes could very well decide they'd want nothing to do with her. But if there was any chance they'd help, it was worth it.

"*Carrie,* are you still playing tennis?" Ella asked, placing special emphasis on Carrie's name.

"Not as much as I used to." She patted her stomach. "As I'm sure you can—"

"*Ella,*" Linda barked. "How many times have I told you, you are *not* to address adults by their first names? You are to address them by Mr. or Mrs. *You know this.*" She pointed her finger sharply at Ella's face.

"I'm sorry, Mom, she told me to call her *Carrie,* and—"

"Linda, it's fine." Carrie placed her hand on Linda's shoulder. "I prefer it that way."

"Oh, *you* prefer it that way." Linda yanked her shoulder back so aggressively that it caused her chair to wobble. "Did you consider that *I* might prefer that she address adults properly? Do you think you know how to raise a child better than I do?"

"I certainly do not, and of course I respect your wishes, but my feeling is that you gain the trust of your kids' friends if you get past some of these silly formalities. That they'll feel comfortable coming to us if there's ever an issue, if they can speak to us as peers."

"Oh, there it is. Everyone thinks they're best friends with their kids now. Where's the discipline? Where's the sense of order? Do you know what happens next? You lose complete control over them. You'll see." She shooed Carrie away with her fingers, spitting as she spoke.

"Well, Linda, we prefer supporting, not *controlling* our children. Jason and I parent based on mutual respect between parent and child."

"So, *you're* being respected? *Suuurrrre* you are," she slobbered. "That boy of yours spreading his seed all over your house. Very respectful, *Caarrrrie*. And nice shorts your daughter's wearing. Can they be any shorter? Why do you think that waiter offered them wine? Letting your daughter prance around with her vagina hanging out. Nice *vagina* shorts, Sarah. You're doing a *great* job, *Caarrrie*! You should be *so proud*! Parent of the year over here, folks." She clumsily pointed at Carrie, shouting to anyone who would listen. Her outsized gestures sent her long-stemmed wine glass crashing to the floor, burgundy drops spattering the woman's white blouse at the next table. The commotion sent the waiter hurrying to the table.

"Is everything okay, ladies?"

Ella stared directly at her mother and shot her a satisfied smile when no one was looking. Given the opportunity to show her true colors, Linda rarely disappointed.

Carrie scrambled to find her credit card. She leaned close to the waiter. "Please just close out our tab, tip yourself thirty percent, and I'll pick up my card tomorrow. I'm so sorry. Ladies, let's go." She grabbed Linda firmly by the arm and motioned for Sarah to do the same. A stumble into another table seemed to give Linda the wherewithal to realize she needed help getting out the door, but it wasn't enough for her to stop talking.

"And we don't need your charity, *Caarrrrieee. Dinner's on us tonight.*" She mimicked her in a bratty teenager voice. The number of onlookers grew as Linda fumbled around in her purse and threw some singles at Carrie that landed on the floor. Ella picked them up and tried to give them to Carrie, who shook her head. It took all three of them to get her in the car. "Sarah, you drive," Carrie said as she got in the back seat with Linda.

They managed to get a moaning Linda in the motel room and into bed without any issues. Carrie took off Linda's shoes and took the bedspread from the other bed to cover her up. The three of them tiptoed out the door, and Ella closed it behind them.

"Mrs. Blake, I am so sorry. I tried to warn Sarah, but . . ."

"This is *not* your fault," Carrie said.

"I know, but I know she gets like this, and I should have . . . well, she doesn't get like this every time. Only when she's really stressed. Which is a lot, so—"

"Stop," Carrie said firmly, yet lovingly. "This has nothing to do with you. But obviously, we're concerned, and we are here to help." She gave Ella a hug.

Ella felt safe in Carrie's arms. Maybe there was hope after all. "Thank you. Well, if you don't mind, I'm just going to go to bed, so—"

"Absolutely not, Ella, you're coming with us. We'll leave her a note."

Ella felt empowered as she watched Carrie rip a piece of paper from her planner and start scribbling against the hood of the car.

Linda, I'm not sure what's been going on in your life, but you made me worried for Ella, so she will be spending the night at our house. We will talk in the morning, when you've had a chance to sober up.

Carrie folded the paper. She paused, then unfolded the paper and began writing again.

P.S. Those "vagina shorts" Sarah was wearing? Those are mine.

6

THE GIRLS WENT STRAIGHT to Sarah's room. Ella sat on the carpet and rested her elbows on her knees. Sarah flopped onto her bed and looked at her watch. It was 9:05 then 9:07 then 9:08. She felt bad she couldn't stop thinking about Stacey's and bad she couldn't stop checking her watch. But she felt *really* bad for Ella. The whole thing was just too much, *especially* for the first day of summer. The last day of summer, fine. But not the first, when all she wanted was to just go to the damn party. And for Ella to feel better. *Arrgghhh*. She let out a silent groan as she wrestled with what to do. She pressed her palm firmly against her forehead. And then summoned her inner Tori that knew staying with Ella was the right thing to do.

"Do you want to talk about it?" Sarah asked.

"Not really," Ella said casually. "Do you have somewhere to be? If you do, don't let me keep you."

"No. I mean there is this party that I was supposed to go to, but it's no big deal. Just a bunch of drunks saying stupid shit. Sorry! Oh my god, I'm so sorry." Her face flushed.

Ella laughed out loud. "Sarah, tonight isn't anything I haven't seen a hundred times. I just feel bad *you* had to witness it!"

Sarah got up and checked her hair in the mirror. "Ella, she's a *total freak show!*" she said as she secured her breezy beach waves with a light mist of hairspray.

"Total freak show. Hey, do you wanna get high?"

"*What?!*"

In the mirror's reflection, Sarah saw Ella holding up a joint. "That is about the last thing I expected to hear from you right now, but *yes*." She laughed and eagerly motioned for Ella to pass it her way.

"*This* is how I survive. I don't know what I'd do if I didn't have my escape." Ella inspected it lovingly and then walked it over. "Can we go outside?"

The friendly neighborhood's no-fence rule meant everyone's yards were connected. While it was great for kids to play together, it was not so great for sneaking off to smoke a joint. But Sarah knew whose yards they could cut through and who was out of town, so it just took a bit of maneuvering. They walked through grassy knolls until they reached the shed in the Grahams' yard. A solid choice, considering the Grahams were in their eighties, mostly deaf, and never up past nine.

"Let's stop here." Sarah steered Ella into the tiny space between a nestle of trees and the shed wall.

"You sure?" Ella pointed to a light coming from the second floor.

"Trust me. We're fine."

Ella fired up her lighter, took the biggest girl hit ever, and then passed it to Sarah. "Here," she said, effortlessly holding it in and talking at the same time. Sarah tried to do the same and started coughing up a lung. Ella laughed hysterically.

"What was *that*? Haven't you ever smoked before?" She pressed her lips into a closed smile as her giant eyes morphed into tiny crescents.

"I have," Sarah coughed, "a few times." She passed it back to Ella's fingers. Ella took another huge hit, while Sarah tried to compose herself. "Apparently, you've got a little more experience than I do."

"Apparently." Ella exhaled a skunky, puffy cloud into the stars and then she laughed. "So, Sarah, tell me more about how *you've* been."

"There's not much more to tell. Things are great. I feel bad saying this to you, but everything is exactly how I want it to be. Steady. I would never survive your situation, or the things some of my other friends have to deal with. I'm just not cut out for . . . *uncertainty*." The word rolled pleasurably off her suddenly stoned tongue. "Wow, this is strong."

"You would adjust, if you had to."

Sarah found her attention glued to Ella's face, to the words that came out of her mouth, as if nothing and no one else existed in this moment.

"People don't know what they're made of until they're tested," Ella went on. "It's weird. It's like we lived here, and things were perfect. And we moved, and things started to change. *Reeeeally sloooooowly.* And then *reallyfast.* And I woke up one day and realized our family was just *gone.* It's like you know bad things happen, parents die or whatever. But I didn't know a normal family could just implode. I feel like if it happened to us, it could happen to anyone."

Sarah watched Ella's face bend with curiosity as she recounted the events of her life that created the unforeseen fork in the road. Where their perfectly parallel lives had split paths.

"Well, I don't want to be tested. And I'm gonna pretend you didn't say that. I don't want to jinx anything."

"Still superstitious, huh." Ella smiled.

"Absolutely." Sarah knocked three times on the side of the shed. "Let's finish up."

Ella put the joint out on the bottom of her shoe and tucked it in a piece of aluminum foil that had magically appeared in her hand. She spritzed them both with perfume, and they went on their way. Sarah's heart quickened as they heard adult voices coming from a patio nearby, so they left the grassy communal area and opted for the street.

"So, you were saying you have a party to go to?"

"Yeah, but I can stay with you. Unless, well," Sarah said, laughing. "I *really* thought the *last* thing you were going to want to do after tonight was go to a party. But I'm starting to rethink that." She was suddenly in hysterics, thinking about how far they'd come from Ella sitting on her bed with a towel on her head.

"You *are* a beginner! How about we get you off the street?" Ella wrapped her tiny fingers around Sarah's arm and pulled her into the Larsons' front yard. "Will there be any cute guys there?"

"Well, there's only one that I care about, but you can't have him."

"Oh right. Jack was it?"

"Jake. Crenshaw. Totally hot. Well, I think so. None of my friends do. He's a total grunge, Kurt Cobain lookalike. Skinny, blond, tattoos, goatee . . ." Sarah went weak at the thought of touching Jake's facial hair. "Not like the football player types they're into."

They tiptoed through a small patch of trees, the light of the moon streaming through the branches. The sounds of nature seemed to amplify around them, like they'd just walked into a mini magical forest. Sarah saw the silhouette of a frog right where she was about to step, which made her scream, which made Ella laugh so hard she fell to her knees. Ella stayed down while Sarah checked the sole of her shoe for frog guts, even though she could see that he was alive and well.

"Come down here and look at him. He's *so cute.*"

Sarah reluctantly got on the ground, and they stared at the ribiting frog, watching his chin bulge in and out. His beady eyes stared back at them as the dry grass tickled Sarah's chest.

"But I have to say, I'm worried because you are super hot, and I'm *slightly* threatened by that," Sarah said.

Ella tried to pet the frog, and he hopped off. She stood up, reached her hand out to help Sarah up, and they left the protection of the trees, continuing their walk down the dimly lit, quiet suburban street.

"Stop it. I would never go after your man. Besides, I like those football player types too. You can have Mr. Grunge all to yourself."

"Well, good. That was the last thing I needed to know before I decided if we could be friends again."

"Does that mean I can go to the party? Now that we've gotten this *man* situation sorted?" She stopped and batted her long lashes at Sarah as they reached her front yard.

"On one condition."

"Which is?"

"We get you out of those nasty clothes. What the hell are you wearing?!" Sarah finally purged herself of the question that had dogged her all night. Linda was a shit show, but Ella's outfit was the disaster. How could *anyone* their age wear an outfit like that, *especially* someone so pretty?

"Oh, you haven't seen this? It's Kmart, 1990. You really need to keep up on your fashion, Sarah. It's vintage, and it's about to be all the rage." Ella pranced around an imaginary runway. Sarah almost peed in her pants laughing, having no idea how high she was until then.

"Trust me, there's nothing I can do," Ella added. "But I don't want to talk about that now. Do you have anything I can wear?"

"Maybe." Sarah took a moment to look her up and down. "We do have this small height difference to think about. We can try, but there's no way I can face my parents right now, so *shhhhhh . . .*" She snorted as they reached the front door. Muffling her laughter through her nose, she tried to quietly open the door. After what seemed like twenty minutes, they managed to sneak back upstairs.

They opened the mirrored, sliding door to the closet and concluded they had no choice but to turn those awful jeans into cut-off shorts. Sarah took her sewing scissors and decimated Ella's jeans with an impressive fringy cut. Whether it *was* impressive or just the pot making it *seem* impressive, at least they showed off her perfect legs.

"How about this?" Ella had moved on to the dresser and pulled out a black tank top. It was small and tight, one that Sarah only wore under other shirts, but it fit Ella perfectly. Sarah rolled onto the bed and fought the gravitational pull to give her a thumbs-up.

"That's not half bad." Sarah nodded slowly at the ceiling. "Not half bad. What does that *mean*? Doesn't not half bad mean it's like half good? Or does it mean it's less than half bad. But it could mean that it's more than half bad, so it really doesn't tell us anything other than it doesn't fall on that exact line of *half bad*." She spread her fingers and looked at her hand, fascinated at how close she'd gotten her purple nail polish to her cuticles. "Because not half bad means it is *anything but* half bad, and that's like pretty much all of the rest of everything. Can you think of one single thing that is *exactly half bad*? Whatever that might be, your outfit is *not* that."

"*Sarah!* Focus. I still need shoes." Ella's tiny voice, coming seemingly from a distance, nudged her back to attention.

"My mom and I are both a size nine, so I'm not liking our chances."

"I saw some black flip-flops by the front door that looked like they might fit."

"You did? They must belong to one of Kevin's little friends, because they're not Kevin's. His feet are huge."

"Can we take them?"

For some reason, the thought sent Sarah into another fit of laughter, and she knew they needed to get out in a hurry before her mom came in to see what was so funny.

"Sure. Hand me that pen," she said, muffling her laughter with her hand. She scribbled a note and left it on the dresser.

Mom, Dad, went to Stacey's. Back by 1:00.

-S

They ran down the stairs, grabbed somebody's flip-flops, and got the hell outta there.

7

SARAH REACHED THE UNFRIENDLY stop sign at the entrance to Whitetail Estates for the second time in a day. But the Wagoneer had automatic fucking transmission, so they breezed right in.

"My friend Jenny lives in that house. That's whose pool I was at today," she said, pointing. "Jenny is super sweet, but she's not very smart, so we have to look out for her. Tori's the complete opposite. She's wicked smart, and she has your back one hundred percent. Well, unless you're doing something stupid. And Stacey's really cool. She's filthy rich, but totally down to earth. But she went through a bad breakup recently, so maybe don't ask her if she's dating anyone. And Dalia . . . Dalia is, well . . . there's Stacey's house." She changed her own subject. Dalia was too complicated to sum up in a sentence. She parked the car and pointed to the luxurious Tuscan-style estate. "Some people think Stacey's house is a little over the top, but—"

"Oh my god. You *know* these people?" Ella asked as they began their walk.

It had never occurred to Sarah that she should think she wasn't worthy of being in this neighborhood. That sentiment was reserved for people like Dalia; Sarah understood why *she* felt that way. As she took a closer look, though, she realized that these people probably spent more money lighting up their landscaping than her family spent on the entire cost of their house, and she wondered if Ella might have a point. But then she remembered she was stoned and crawled out of the rabbit hole.

"Ella, they're just people."

"People with a lot more money than we have."

Stacey lived only five doors down from Jenny, but the size of the yards made it feel like miles. While Stacey didn't have a pool, her house was just as fun. It had every game known to man. Air hockey, darts, a billiard room, stand-up video games—it even had an old-fashioned-looking jukebox that played actual CDs.

"*This really is where the party is? I can't believe it!*" Ella said as she took in her surroundings. "I didn't even know houses like this existed in this town."

"They didn't. This was still that horse farm when you lived here, and now it's like Beverly Hills. My parents say all the people who don't fit in on the North Shore took it over. *Nouveau riche*, they say. Whatever. Dalia, you'll meet her tonight, she hates coming here. Or, I should say, she hates driving her bullshit car here. That's what *she* calls it. She definitely loves being here, but she's got this major insecurity about the fact that she has no money. She always feels like everyone's judging her."

"I can see why." Ella glanced at the raggedy, faux suede, cross-body purse she was carrying, and tucked it behind her back.

They'd almost reached Stacey's house when Sarah saw it. Confirmation that she was going to see Jake tonight. She jumped around in a circle cheering and almost fell into Ella.

"What are you *doing?*" Ella stepped back from her.

"Jake is in the *hizzouse!* There's his Mustang. EKJ 5850. I have his license plate memorized. I know, I'm such a loser." She made an L with her fingers and put it against her forehead.

"You have to memorize their license plates. How can you stalk them if you don't?"

"*Totally.*" Sarah side-hugged her as they walked up the circular driveway. "Ready to go in and meet your new best friends?"

"I *think?* Wait. Is there *anyone* I know here?"

"Probably not. Except for Shawn Matlyn. You remember him."

The way Ella's eyes popped out of her skull jogged Sarah's memory. "Oh my god, you totally had a crush on him."

"A *crush?* More like an *obsession. Are you kidding me?* He was my *first kiss.* I thought he'd moved, or he would have been the *first* person I asked about. *How was that not the first thing you told me?*" Ella spilled so much excitement, Sarah thought Ella might need to change her shorts.

"*Oh yeah!* How did I forget about that?"

Sarah noticed that the clasp on her necklace had floated to the bottom. She pinched the horseshoe charm with one hand and the clasp with the other.

"Make a wish," Ella said. "I know what you're going to wish for."

"Yes you do," she said as she slid the clasp behind her neck. "I forgot Shawn was supposed to move. I wonder whatever happened with that. We're actually really good friends still."

"Shawn Matlyn. I *knew* this night would turn around!"

Something changed in Ella's gait the moment Shawn's name was mentioned. She walked taller. More confidently. Shoulders back and chin up. And then she asked for a mirror.

"Hold on." Sarah stopped, just as her thumb touched the door handle. "There is a small problem."

"What is it?"

"Dalia. She is completely obsessed with Shawn, like borderline psychotic. He's her Jake Crenshaw times a thousand, and she will not take kindly to a stranger walking in and setting their sights on Shawn. So, if I were you, I'd keep that first kiss situation to myself and play it cool with Shawn. Trust me, you do not want to start the year off on Dalia's shit list."

"Well, are they dating?" Ella asked, making Sarah think she wasn't comprehending the seriousness of the situation.

"In Dalia's mind, they are. So, for our purposes they are, and that's just how it is. We know not to question it."

"Well, what does Shawn think of all this?" Ella persisted.

Sarah motioned for her to move over and let two sophomore girls pass so she could get her full attention.

"Now hear me out. It's one of those things where they hook up pretty much every time they're at the same party, but they've never been out alone together. Neither of them hook up with anyone else, though, so it's kind of like they're dating. It's been going on for months—and she is *determined* to lose her virginity to Shawn the night of Homecoming, which is four months away. So, I am *very serious* when I say to not get excited about him. If you have any ideas about starting anything with him, you have to put them out of your head immediately and forever."

"Dalia's a good friend of yours?" Ella adjusted her bra strap and then used her finger to spread out her lip gloss.

"*Yes, Ella*. She for sure has her issues, and when you first meet her, you quite possibly will hate her. But that's because she's moody, so it really depends on the day. But she grows on you. She is absolutely one of my best friends, and she needs to be yours too," Sarah said protectively. She wasn't quite sure who she was protecting, though. Maybe herself.

"Well, it's not like anything serious ever happened between us. He was a total jerk everywhere but camp, so don't worry. Remember how he blew me off at the ice-skating rink? I was heartbroken. I'm sure he won't care that I'm back."

"Nothing serious happened? Ice-skating rink? Ella, it was *middle school*. You *have* to listen to me." Sarah grabbed her hand and looked her in the eye. "It's not just for me, it's for *you*. Fucking with Dalia Jacobs could possibly be the biggest mistake of your life. *Especially* when it comes to Shawn. Promise me you won't flirt with him, or I can't take you inside."

Ella hesitated and then grabbed Sarah's other hand. Holding them both, she said, "Sarah, I most solemnly promise I will not think about, flirt with, kiss, or otherwise fondle Shawn Matlyn for as long as we both shall live. Is that good enough?"

"Good enough," she said, wishing she felt like Ella really meant it. For the time being, though, she had no choice but to give her the benefit of the doubt.

"Just one question," Ella said. "How does he look?"

"Really hot, if you're into that star quarterback thing."

Ella put her head down in a way that made Sarah feel like she was weighing her options, but there was nothing more she could say.

8

SARAH OPENED THE DOOR to the biggest party she'd ever seen, *far* bigger than they'd planned for. Every square inch of the Italian marble floor was covered with shoes. And beyond the shoes, shoulder to shoulder people. Ella almost tripped and hopped on one foot to steady herself. "I didn't even need these." She tossed the flip-flops aside and inspected her toes. "Should have painted my toes, though."

"You're fine," Sarah said without even looking at her toes because she was sure she'd agree and didn't want to lie. The girls all had appearance things that were more or less important to them. Stacey would leave the house in sweats, but her hair and makeup had to be perfect. Jenny was fine with no makeup, but her hair and outfit had to be perfect. And Tori wouldn't leave the house unless she was "put together," as she called it. Sarah had much lower standards than the rest of them. But *none* of them ever left the house open-toed without polish, and she knew the girls would notice immediately.

"Just don't leave them here," Sarah instructed. "I don't want to be woken up early tomorrow when Carrie's losing her mind, wondering what happened to them."

The two-story foyer echoed chants from a crowd full of strangers in the kitchen. A stocky linebacker type deep-throated a monstrous beer bong held by two frat boys standing on the large stone island. Next to them, three skanky girls in half shirts showed off their professional stripper aspirations, while a creepy mullet man held up a boom box playing "Push It." Sarah sneered at all of them, feeling above this entire scene, mostly because she didn't know any of them.

"Who are these idiots?" she said as she peered through the jungle of legs dancing on stools. Sarah led Ella through sweaty elbows toward the back staircase and headed down. Before they even reached the bottom, she heard Dalia shouting.

"I win!" Dalia stood up and raised her arms into a V.

"What do you win?" Sarah asked. "And who are all those people upstairs? This is *insane!*"

Jenny, Tori, and Dalia were seated around the bend of a leather sectional surrounding a glass cocktail table covered with multiple bottles of liquor. The girls smiled politely at Ella from behind their red Solo cups.

"I bet Tori that you were going to show, and here you are. I *knew* you couldn't resist a chance to hang with Jake. Loser has to do two shots of the winner's choice." Dalia steered her mischievous smile toward Tori. "What's it going to be? Jagermeister or Jack Daniel's?"

Tori stood up and pointed her finger. "You did not, Dalia. There were two parts to the bet, and I won the second part. And nice you pick the two things you know I can't stand."

"What was the second part?" Ella asked. Her confidence seemed to catch everyone off guard, except for Tori. Tori liked confidence. She viewed it as a strength—a trait of the kind of people she liked being around, so she predictably embraced Ella right away.

"I said I didn't think Sarah would come at all, but if you did," she said, looking at Sarah, "you'd bring Ella. Hi Ella, I'm assuming you're Ella. It's so nice to meet you. I'm Tori." She extended her hand. A formality not typical for high schoolers, but a standard for Tori that the girls always teased her about, because sometimes it got awkward.

"It's so nice to meet you too," Ella smiled graciously and shook Tori's hand.

"Dalia bet me Sarah was going to come, but alone. So, we both won, one cancels the other, so no one does any shots," Tori said as she sat back down.

"No, *Tori*, that means we *each* do *two* shots." Dalia slid two shot glasses in front of her.

"Since when does that mean . . . oh my god, Dalia, just *stop!*" Tori glared at her. "She's been like this all night."

"She's been like that all *day*." Sarah emphasized, forming a timeout T with her hands. "Ella, this is Jenny, and you probably already figured out that *that* is Dalia. Everyone, this is Ella."

"Hi *everyone*," Ella gave a friendly wave and then sat with Sarah on the couch.

"So, Ella, what brings you back to the lovely suburbs of Chicago?" Dalia asked with a selfishly curious smile.

"Dalia . . ." Sarah started. She immediately recognized the motive behind that smile and thought about how to defang her. Tori and Sarah loved to talk about why people are the way they are, and Dalia was an easy go-to. "Novelty," Tori had said one day. "She constantly craves drama, so anything new stimulates her, because it is *potential* for drama." And here it was, front and center. A new person in the mix who could scratch Dalia's itch. In the pause between question and answer, Sarah felt the urge to bail Ella out with a vague synopsis. But then Ella crossed her legs. She had to lift her leg high to avoid knocking into the cocktail table, which put her bare foot on full display. Sarah caught the satisfied look of disapproval on Dalia's face when she noticed Ella's unkempt toes and knew that would tame her bite. No one who didn't polish her toes could ever be a threat to Dalia, so Sarah decided to let Ella fend for herself.

"Well, Dalia, I lived here until the beginning of seventh grade, when my dad got a big promotion. But the job was in Arizona, so they moved us all out there, which completely sucked. Then, my dad lost his job because of some *accounting irregularities* at the company. I didn't know this, though, because my parents are liars and told me he was just taking some time off. I got to hear the truth from a friend of mine whose dad also worked for the company, which was fun."

She picked up a clear bottle filled with golden brown liquid and inspected the label. She shrugged and filled the shot glass in front of her. "Is this okay?"

Sarah nodded. Ella sniffed it, and then downed it whole with a smile. The endorphins flowed through her so visibly it was contagious. The girls leaned in.

"We went from rich to poor really fast with all of the legal bills and, you know, no income. Then my mom started making us go to this crazy church where they told her we were all sinners, and she needed to save us, which, I don't know how religious any of *you* are, comes with *all sorts of* fun rules. Then she started drinking. Throw in some pills, and she went completely off the rails. My dad thought that a fresh start might be best for the family, so they decided to move us back here."

The girls, including Sarah, sat riveted. Ella hadn't told her this yet, and she was impressed. The way Ella just put it all out there? It took a lot of balls to spill her guts like that to girls she hardly knew.

"Sarah, I know my mom told you we were looking at houses, but actually we rented an apartment. I think it's a trial period to see if they can save their marriage." She turned back toward the group. "So, that's my story."

Sarah gave her knee a proud squeeze as Ella reached for her purse. "Does anyone want to get high?" she asked, pulling out a fresh joint.

Sarah's head swung in her direction. She didn't remember Ella being so *on full display*. And she kind of loved her for it. But it also made her think that Ella had a serious marijuana problem. Or maybe it was her go-to ice breaker with everyone she met. But who was she to judge? At this point, Ella was batting a thousand.

"I do!" Dalia raised her hand high and then grabbed it out of Ella's hand so fast that it cracked in the middle. She sheepishly dangled the white L shape and then tried to pinch it back together. "Oh my god, I am so sorry."

The girls moaned in disapproval, which sent Ella into a fit of laughter.

"I can reroll it, you guys." She reached in her purse and pulled out a pack of rolling papers. She took the mangled joint, and with surgical precision, spilled the contents into a new rolling paper and licked it closed. "Good as new."

"Where did you learn to roll a joint like that?" Dalia warmed. "We're gonna be best friends. Let's go out back."

Sarah was getting antsy to find Jake and thought she'd spent enough time situating Ella that she could leave her. But Tori was waving for her to follow them through the crowd to the back patio.

"Who are all these people, and where is Stacey?" Sarah kicked a plastic cup and a dirty T-shirt out of her way as they seated themselves around the stone fireplace.

"She's on damage control. Craig is home from school, and he invited all his friends without telling her. She'll be down soon," Tori said.

"That's so rude!" Dalia chimed in. "They're not even good-looking. You'd think with all their money that he'd at least bring some *hot* friends, instead of these assholes."

"What do you care if they're hot, Mrs. Matlyn?" Stacey said, sneaking up behind them, her white sundress billowing in the wind. Her blond hair was in a tight bun, wrapped in a perfect tiny braid. "But you're right. I don't know where he finds these people. We worked it out, though. He's replacing all the liquor, and he's paying to have it cleaned. Do we have a special guest?" She opened her arms to Ella.

Without saying a word, Ella greeted her with the lit joint. In her high wedge espadrilles, Stacey stood a full foot taller than Ella.

"Well, *it* is nice to *meet* you, Ella, I'm Stacey."

As she pinched it from Ella's fingers, she took a step back and bent down to look her in the eye. Which, in Sarah's mental state, looked like a Disney princess taking drugs from a little girl. She started laughing all over again and decided if she was going to see Jake tonight, she should take it easy.

While moths danced around the patio light, the girls passed the freshly rolled joint. Sarah sat back on the stone railing and watched Ella get to know the girls on her own. She fit in perfectly, no signs of feeling awkward about their private jokes, and contributed what she could without overstepping. Sarah was impressed with how Ella handled herself, especially when the conversation turned to Shawn.

Dalia went over their entire history, how they'd hooked up last fall at Joey Bennett's party, and eleven, no, ten other times after Homecoming, but before Prom, and how she'd been *sure* he was going to ask her to Prom, but he couldn't because he *had* to go with Julie Benson.

"Some family friend from his church. His parents *made* him take her." She gave the sky a hard middle finger. "Can you believe that shit? But he felt bad about it, so I know there's no way he won't ask me to Homecoming this year. Whatever. You'll meet him eventually, but he's not here tonight."

"He isn't?" Ella asked, barely hiding the disappointment in her voice.

"We went to grade school with Shawn," Sarah said quickly when she realized she probably should have mentioned it. "You guys know that."

"You *know* him?" Dalia gasped.

"Oh yeah. I know Shawn," Ella said. She raised her hand to the height of the top of her head. "He's about five feet tall, really skinny, braces . . . I hate to say it, Dalia, but I think you can do better."

The girls erupted in laughter.

"You're funny, Ella," Jenny said.

Ella handled it perfectly. And she was clearly having fun. Sarah started to feel good about the whole thing. Good about reconnecting with her. Good that she was able to help her. She was very close to conceding that she'd been wrong to worry at all about her return.

"This whole time, I've been trying not to laugh. I keep picturing you hooking up with a twelve-year-old!" Ella laughed with her hand on her chest. "So why isn't he here?"

"He got stuck working late at the restaurant we work at."

"Well, does the restaurant deliver?"

"Yes, but he waits tables. I like the way you think, though," Dalia said. She reached over and twirled a lock of Ella's hair around her bony finger. Looking her right in the eye, she said, "Ella, Sarah didn't tell us how pretty you are. Sarah, why didn't you tell us how pretty little Ella is? She's like my pretty little dolly." Dalia squeezed Ella's face.

"You should talk, Dalia," Ella mumbled, twisting her face until Dalia let go. "You're like a model," she said as she pulled out her perfume. "Who's on the cover of this month's *Cosmo*? Paulina? You look just like her. But prettier."

"I like this girl, Sarah." Dalia grabbed the perfume out of Ella's hand and spritzed everyone.

"Okay!" Sarah checked her watch. "Now that everyone is best friends, has anyone seen Jake?"

9

STACEY HAD SPOTTED JAKE in the billiard room, in the middle of an *intense* game of pool. Sarah loved the billiard room. It was right out of a 1920s gangster movie. Dark wood bookshelves, candle sconces, red velvet everywhere . . . it was over the top, but amazing, like everything else in Stacey's house. "See ya," she said to the girls and ran back inside.

Sarah's house didn't have much in the way of fun things to do, and it certainly didn't have a fancy billiard room. But it did have a pool table. A beautiful, red felt covered antique that sat, unlike Stacey's, surrounded by cement walls in their cold, dark basement. It was her dad's prized possession, inherited from his own dad. And the setting for many fatherly advice type conversations.

Her dad started teaching her to play pool from the moment a stepstool boosted her high enough to see over the table. And as his dad did with him, he used their pool-playing time to teach Sarah life lessons. But rather than say them directly, he wrapped them in stories from his own childhood that usually culminated into some weird *you know what they say* saying. And while she teased him about the weird sayings, she appreciated him now more than ever because she was an exceptional pool player. And she was excited she had a reason to naturally stumble upon Jake. She just wandered in, wanting to play some pool, and there he was, is how it would go in her mind. She knew she had to be careful, though. Jake didn't *seem* like the kind of guy whose ego would be bruised if a girl beat him at pool in front of his friends. *But you never know*, she thought, and then decided he didn't need to know that she had her own monogrammed cue at home.

"Hey you." She walked up behind him. "I didn't know you play."

"*Hey, Sarah.* Yeah, I have a table at home." He leaned his cue against the table and hugged her. It was their first hug, and it was great. Long and lingering. And she was pretty sure he sniffed her hair, which *had* to mean he was interested.

"Do you play?" he asked, his arms still around her waist.

"Sometimes." She lied.

Sarah's dad had a tally etched in pencil on the basement wall, counting every game they'd ever played. It was over a thousand at this point. If she and Jake ever actually started dating, he was going to find her out. Her dad's voice began to spring up in every corner of her mind . . . *big or small, lies are lies . . . trust is built over years and gone in seconds . . . if someone lies to you once, they'll do it again . . . always be yourself.* She had to come clean.

"Okay, that's not true. I play all the time. I'm really good," she blurted out. He got so close to her face, she thought he might kiss her. But no.

Instead, he said, "Were you gonna hustle me and then you felt guilty or something?"

"No! I . . ." She panicked.

What was she supposed to do? Share her mental tangent where she was afraid that if they started dating he would someday see the pool tally, catch her in a lie, decide he'd never be able to trust her, and break up with her? She certainly wasn't going to tell him *that* before they'd even started dating. He'd think she was a total psycho. *Well, which is it, Dad?* she wondered, and then decided her dad would have rightly pointed out that she shouldn't have lied in the first place.

"You were, weren't you? Sarah Blake, I'm gonna have to keep my eye on you."

"Caught me," she said, red-faced and smiling. "So, do you want to play?"

"Yeah. But you won't be getting any of *these* out of *me*." He picked up the three dollars he had sitting on the table.

Sarah racked the balls and broke hard, just as Metallica came on the jukebox. "It's about time. I put this song on forever ago," she said, even though she'd purposely played it right before she walked in to see him, knowing it was his favorite band, hoping he'd bring up the concert.

"You like Metallica? They're coming this summer," he said, leaning over the cue as he lined up his shot.

"Yeah! August second. I'm stuck in the lawn seats, though."

"Yeah, me too. We should meet up there," he said as he sunk a stripe and then scratched.

Sarah gripped the cue tightly, trying to contain her excitement. The whole thing went down exactly as she'd hoped. Except for the fact that he said it no differently than if he were suggesting she tie her shoe. No voice inflection or eye contact—which didn't stop the instant fireworks from exploding in her head, of course. But she wished at least one of the girls had witnessed it, so they could spend the rest of the night trying to figure out if it was a real date or not.

"For sure. That sounds fun."

She squeezed around him and let her hip ever so slightly brush against his. Just enough that he'd question whether it was on purpose or not. She cued up her next shot and then ran the table. He never had a chance.

"It's a good thing you're not a very good liar. I would've been out three bucks."

"Good for *you*," she said, flirting. She was hoping he'd ask her to go somewhere else and have a drink, just the two of them. But they were interrupted.

"*No way*, Sarah, that was *awesome*." An overserved Mike Shepard clumsily grabbed the cue out of Jake's hand. "I got next game."

So instead of running off with Jake, Sarah found herself trapped in a never-ending pool tournament. She beat Mike. And then Rob Glaser, and Josh Bailey, and Rick Fremont. And then Jeff Weiss and Kurt Pultz, all while Jake watched from the bar. And before she knew it, it was one thirty in the morning, and Jake said he had to get going. She died a little on the inside when she realized she'd missed their chance to hang out. She should have just stopped playing and sat with him at the bar, because maybe he'd been waiting for her to do that. Maybe. But it was too late. He just walked off without even asking for her number, which she hoped was because he didn't want to in front of his friends, which didn't make her feel much better, because now she didn't know when she'd see him again, other than their *maybe* date for Metallica at the *end* of the summer.

When she finally climbed out of that thought process, she realized that one thirty was late for her too. She hurried upstairs and found the girls in the kitchen. Stacey had broken out her strobe light. They were having a dance off on the stools as Digital Underground blasted over the speakers.

"We're so late, Ella. I said we'd be home at one!" she shouted, waving her over. Ella, who looked to be having the time of her life, glanced at Sarah. And then glanced just beyond her, quite obviously pretending not to see her. Sarah marched right up to her and tugged on her shorts. "*Now.*"

Ella detached herself from the barstool and took her time following Sarah out the door. That normally would have been the point where they started recapping the night and laughing about all the funny stories. But they didn't get to because the second Sarah closed the door, they saw him. Shawn Matlyn. He recognized Ella right away, and their eyes locked immediately. Ella started to glow. And she wasn't the only one glowing.

"Hey Shawn, this is Ella Connor. Remember *her?*" Sarah pretended not to notice what was going on right in front of her.

"How could I forget? Ella . . . *wow.* You look *great.* Sarah didn't tell me you two kept in touch. Are you in town visiting?"

Shawn looked good. He always did, being his tall, dark, and handsome self. But coming from work, he was looking a little less

GQ and a little more scruffy—more like her type, Sarah thought as she watched him rub his chin like he wished he had shaved.

"We haven't kept in touch. We're in town house-hunting, and we ran into Sarah's mom this morning."

"*You're moving back?*" he asked, far more enthusiastically than Sarah *ever* would've expected. The whole scene was making her very uneasy.

"Yes. She is." She grabbed Ella's wrist. "But we need to go. And Dalia's downstairs waiting for you." She said the first thing she could think of to try to stop whatever this was.

"I am. We're leaving tomorrow to pack up Tucson, but we'll be back next week for good." Ella looked like she was trying to suppress the fact that this just might be the happiest moment of her life. Her smile, if left to its own devices, would have split her face in two.

"You guys, we *have* to go," Sarah insisted.

"That's *great!* Yeah, so we should catch up. How do I get ahold of you?" Shawn talked over her. And then the dimple on just the left side of his face appeared.

Shawn's left dimple always reminded Sarah of the Asians at school who were missing an enzyme that breaks down alcohol. They could never drink because their faces would turn bright red at the first sip. A dead giveaway to their parents. That's what Sarah called Shawn's left dimple. His dead giveaway. There was something about the way he smiled when he was *really* excited about a girl that caused it to surface like the flushing faces of those poor enzyme-deficient Asians. As obvious as it was to her, though, she was the only one who noticed it. She also noticed that it never revealed itself when he was with Dalia. This wasn't good.

"Well, I don't know," Ella said with a perfectly executed, charming head tilt. "Maybe call Sarah in a week? She'll know where to find me."

"I will. It's *great to see you*," he said. And then he gave Ella a hug that was far too long for Sarah's liking.

"Have fun with *Dalia*," she shouted as she hurried Ella down the driveway. As soon as she heard Stacey's door shut, Sarah went off.

"What the fuck was that?"

"What was what?"

"I told you, he's hands off."

"What did I do?"

"Lead him on?"

"Sarah, I don't think I did anything wrong, but if you—"

"You agreed to see him."

"What was I supposed to say? Anything else would have been awkward. And rude."

"I know, but you were clearly sending him signals, and you promised to keep your distance," she reminded her.

For a second, she thought maybe she was being too hard on Ella. But when they got in the Wagoneer, Ella changed her tune. She clicked her seatbelt and turned toward Sarah.

"Does Dalia really have any right to claim him? I mean Shawn and I were together first, and who knows what would have happened if I hadn't moved. And you said they're not even dating."

"Okay, Ella. You are so overly romanticizing your little grade school crush. But if you pursue this, I will not be able to protect you from Dalia. So, don't expect me to get in the middle.

And I hope you will think long and hard before you start playing with fire."

"The last thing I want to do is cause trouble with your friends, Sarah."

Sarah felt like she meant it. But then Ella checked her face in the mirror. And then her teeth. Another dead giveaway.

10

"WAKE UP, SLEEPY HEAD," Carrie sang. Sarah pulled the comforter over her head, trying to get her mom to stop tousling her hair. It was only eight in the morning, and Carrie knew they'd gone to a party. While she probably didn't think they'd been getting high and doing shots, it seemed a little naive for her to expect them to pop up and engage like they'd spent all night doing each other's hair. Sarah moaned and turned toward the window.

"Come on girls," Carrie insisted as she ripped off the comforter. Sarah glanced at Ella lying on the floor. Ella stared back with one giant eye peeking over a tightly gripped chenille blanket. Sarah clumsily swung her legs over the side of the bed and steadied herself as she stood up.

"We're coming. Just give us a sec." She rubbed her forehead.

Carrie and Linda were sitting in their far-too-cheery-for-a-hangover—or for a Linda, for that matter—kitchen, sipping coffee out of matching yellow mugs. They were obviously in the middle of a serious conversation that stopped when the girls walked in. Sarah grabbed a floppy piece of bacon and hopped up onto the island, hoping this awkward situation wasn't going to require much participation from her.

"Good morning, ladies," Carrie said with an overly enthusiastic smile. "Why don't you come join us?" She patted the white vinyl seat cushion of the chair next to hers. "Sarah, can you grab the orange juice?"

Linda caught Sarah's eye briefly before she resumed staring at her plate, using her fork to play with the few remaining slivers of pancakes. She'd eaten three large pancakes, as evidenced by the tiniest scrap of their outer edges stacked three high. Sarah smiled to herself as she thought what a great investigative reporter she'd make someday. The fact that Linda's appetite had been unaffected by the *situation* told her all she needed to know. Everything about to come out of her mouth would be a lie. She poured two glasses of orange juice and took a seat next to Carrie. Ella grabbed a glass and reluctantly pulled up a chair next to her.

"So, Linda and I have had a very productive talk this morning, which goes a long way toward explaining what went on last night. I'm sure everyone will feel a lot better after you hear what she has to say. Linda, do you want to tell the girls what you told me this morning?"

Linda took her time as she looked up with post-sobbing eyes. "Ella, Sarah, I want to apologize for my behavior last night. Sarah, I don't know how much Ella has filled you in, but things have been extremely difficult lately. The reason we're moving back is because

Alan lost his job and has been out of work for a long time."

"I told her, Mom. How about you just get to the part where you're sorry, it won't happen again, blah blah blah." Ella picked up a pancake, looked at both sides of it, and put it back on her plate.

"Ella, how can you be so *cold?*" Linda slumped in her chair.

"When you've heard the excuse as many times as I have, that's what happens."

"Oh, and I suppose you told her *all about* the strain on our marriage, not to mention our finances. I'm *so sorry* I've had such a hard time *coping.* I suppose you know *all about* how hard it is to keep a family going under that kind of pressure, when you're all of *seventeen.*"

Linda dropped her fork. It clanked loudly against her plate, which seemed to startle her. She took a deep breath and folded her prematurely aged hands in her lap. "Unlike my *daughter,* my *doctor* could see the toll it was taking on me. And he *insisted* I try some anti-anxiety medicine. Valium. I'm starting to think that Valium and wine aren't a good mix, though, because I assume Ella told you it's happened a handful of times lately. But I promise, with the help of our good Lord, I will fix this," she said tearfully.

Ella rolled her eyes. Carrie immediately came to Linda's defense.

"Ella, you'll see as you get older that life can be *stressful.* Providing the *basics* for a family is *hard enough,* and that's just *one small part* of *parenting.*" Carrie was doing this angsty overly dramatic word emphasis paired with some weird head-bobbing thing that made Sarah want to pull her hair out. "Mothers feel responsible for everyone else's happiness, which means she's feeling *your* pain on top of her own. So, when a family is in crisis, the *mom* hurts more than *anyone*. And who's taking care of *the mom?*" Carried paused and then used both hands to point to Linda, presenting it as some magical bombshell that was going to just *fix this whole thing*. But Ella wasn't having any of it. She stood up and tossed her napkin on her plate.

"Then why even have kids if it's so stressful? All I hear about is how hard her life is. Mom, if money's that tight, why don't *you* get a job?" And then she ran up the stairs. As if on cue, Linda placed both hands over her eyes and began sobbing again.

"She's just *impossible*." Linda laid her head down on the table. Carrie caressed her hair.

"It's okay, Linda. A lot of this is just teenage stuff. Sarah and I have our moments too."

Sarah lurched her neck forward, her mouth hanging in disbelief as she stared at Carrie. Carrie avoided her gaze, which was no surprise, considering they'd never had anything remotely close to those kinds of moments. Ever. What the hell was wrong with her?

"I'm gonna check on *Ella*," she said loudly, trying unsuccessfully to get Carrie to look at her. She then put together two plates of pancakes and bacon and brought them to her room, where she found Ella sitting in her bird's nest chair, staring at absolutely nothing.

"Here." She handed her a plate.

"I'm not hungry."

"All that stress and you don't eat either? No wonder you're so skinny." She set it on the dresser.

"You know everything she said is a load of crap, right?"

"One hundred percent."

"The Valium thing? I've heard it a hundred times. The problem is, not only can she not quit drinking, but now she can't quit the Valium either. I told her I thought it was making her crazy, and she slapped me across the face." Ella put her hand to her cheek, as if the sting was still fresh.

"Oh my god. Has she gotten any help?"

"Oh, she's asked for it. From the good Lord, of course."

"Doesn't she know that God helps those who help themselves?"

"That's a good one. I'm gonna use that next time," she said, laughing. "Can you hand me a pancake?"

Ella went on to devour everything on her plate, while sharing more details about what had happened to her family over the last five years. How her mom controlled even the most minute aspects of her life, like not letting her choose her own clothes and not letting her use tampons, claiming it's immoral because it's "this close to having sex."

"Okay, Mom. Like I'm going to get pregnant from a tampon. So I keep them hidden in my room. I have to sneak out to throw away tampon wrappers. How sad is that?"

"That is like . . . child abuse! What does your dad say about everything?"

"You mean the *worthless piece of trash*? The *pathetic joke of a human*? He's a good man. He's just so depressed. He literally can't handle anything right now."

"Well, why don't you get a job and buy your own clothes?" Sarah felt a primal urge to help Ella. She hated Linda. Everything about her.

"I do work. She takes eighty percent of my paycheck, because it's my *obligation to contribute to the household expenses*. But still . . . she *picks them*, Sarah. The only thing I can buy for myself after her cut is pot. I work at a grocery store so I can buy pot. Pathetic, right?" She set her empty plate on the floor. "At least I can get high and forget all about my bad clothes." She eyed her purse. "Is it too early?"

Sarah ignored that and immediately jumped into problem-solving mode. "Why don't you get a job at a restaurant? You could wait tables and totally skim off of your tips. She'd never know."

"*Sarah!*" Ella lit up. "That is a *great* idea."

"And there are some great thrift shops in Chicago with really cool things for like nothing. We go thrift shopping all the time. We could easily put together a wardrobe for you."

"You are a *genius*." Ella threw her arms around her from behind. "Thank you, Sarah. These last twelve hours have made me hopeful for the first time in a very long time."

"It will all work out, Ella. I promise," she said.

Sarah took the word *promise* very seriously. And she didn't know what it was, but something made her regret that promise the second it came out of her mouth.

11

IT WAS ONE O'CLOCK when Sarah's mom woke her for the second time. Ella and Linda had left shortly after their very *un*productive conversation to pack their life for the big do-over. Sarah went right back to bed for some much-needed hangover healing, until Carrie insisted she go with her to their favorite coffee shop, Brew. By the time they got there, the combination of bacon and sleep had worked their magic, and Sarah was good as new.

Brew's front door was slightly warped and always required a shoulder push. But the door wasn't actually heavy, which caused it to go flying every time anyone opened it, which could be a source of great entertainment on a day with nothing better to do. Sometimes the girls would go there specifically to see if they could catch *a good one*, which was defined as some sort of spastic display, usually a middle-aged woman from another town who didn't know any better. And there were a lot of them, as Brew was well known for its charm. "Exposed brick walls, mismatched flea market tables, and baked goods so delightful that smell alone is worth the trip" is the way the local magazines described it. It was adorable and homey, and it invited deep conversations, especially the mother-daughter kind.

Carrie ordered at the counter while Sarah melted into her favorite plush lavender chair. Carrie returned with two mugs and a cinnamon scone and set them on the white crackled table. "I got you a cappuccino—perk you up a little bit. How late were you out last night?"

Sarah went to take a sip, but purposely stopped to admire the leafy design the barista had created in the foam. "I always feel bad ruining their artwork so soon. How do they make these?"

"Don't think I don't notice you're trying to change the subject."

"All right, all right. Close to two," she confessed.

"Sarah, please don't do that. I don't want to have to start worrying about you not keeping your word."

"I know, Mom. I'm sorry. It won't happen again."

"Thank you. So how was it being out with Ella? She must have been pretty upset."

"Actually, no. She had a *great* time."

"Really?" Carrie tore open a raw sugar package and poured just half of it in her cup. It's the small things that make a difference in keeping your figure, she'd always say. Sarah liked that she took care of herself. That she highlighted her dirty blond hair—a color they shared, that she cared enough to put on makeup, that her outfit mattered. They could be mistaken for sisters. The oldest and youngest in a large Irish family, but still. It seemed like it would be hard to relate to the mom-jean wearers who'd let themselves go.

"I guess when you have that kind of stress for that long, you learn to put it away somehow." Carrie shrugged. "Did she fit in with the girls okay?"

"Yes, actually, they really hit it off."

"You know, girls can be so catty when someone new is brought into the mix. I'm sure they were so welcoming to her because of their respect for you," Carrie said with a misguided pride in her eyes.

"Oh, I'm sure that was it." Sarah laughed into her napkin. "I'm a little worried, though."

"Why? Did something happen?"

"No . . . not yet, anyway. You know how Dalia is obsessed with Shawn?"

"Oh, yes. Shawn Matlyn. I can't blame her." Carrie took off her glasses and suggestively put one arm in her mouth.

"Mom, stop. That's just gross."

"Hey, I can look."

"Great. My mom the pedophile."

"What, he's not eighteen yet?"

"Seriously Mom?"

"Okay, I'll stop." Carrie laughed. "Back to Dalia."

"Well, I'd forgotten that Shawn and Ella used to have a thing. Actually, they were each other's first kiss."

"When was this?"

"Grade school, middle school. They'd make out at church camp."

Carrie looked over her glasses and leaned forward on her

elbows. It suddenly dawned on Sarah that Carrie never knew why she'd liked camp so much. She felt unreasonably guilty.

"Wait a minute. Is that what went on at camp? Some big Catholic make-out fest?" Carrie probed.

"You just figured that out? Dick Johnson. He was my make-out partner. I wonder whatever happened to him." Sarah stared off as she tried to picture the full-grown version of her first crush.

"I'm not thinking anything good. Dick Johnson? What kind of horrible parent names their child *that?*"

"I know. But the girls loved him—he was super cute. I'm sure I wasn't the only one he was making out with," she said, breaking her scone into small chunks and shoving one into her mouth.

"How did I not figure out that's why you wanted to go to camp? All those years. I tried to do the right thing by exposing you to religion, and you were being corrupted instead?" For a second, Carrie looked at her as if she were a stranger. Like if Carrie hadn't figured this out, what else didn't she know about her daughter.

"Oh Mother, it wasn't all for naught. I learned a few things there."

"Well, that's good."

"So did Dick Johnson." Sarah smiled and stuck out her tongue.

"Great," Carrie sighed.

"Can we get back to Ella please?"

"Continue, please. I think I know where this is going." Carrie grimaced.

"Yep. So, Shawn showed up as we were leaving last night, and Ella almost peed in her pants, she was so excited."

"Oh boy." She sipped her latte, without taking her eyes off Sarah.

"And the worst part is, I think Shawn felt the same way! I couldn't *believe* the way he was looking at her. I mean come on. They were *kids.*" She set her mug down harder than she intended. She still couldn't believe it.

"She is gorgeous, you have to admit."

"She is. But what happens when Dalia finds out? I told Ella she has to steer clear of him."

"Sarah, you can't do that. Dalia does not own him. If something happens between them, she's just going to have to deal with it. This is not your problem."

"Mom, this is Dalia we're talking about. She will *make* it my problem." Sarah used her spoon to collect the chocolate shavings at the bottom of the mug and dripped them into her mouth.

"Dalia will get over Shawn if she has to. And it's good for Ella to have something to be excited about."

"I know. But Dalia could use a win too these days." Sarah broke the last chunk of her scone in two and offered Carrie a piece. "I'm not sure she could handle it if the only thing she's excited about gets taken away from her—*especially* by a friend of mine."

"You know, for as hard as it is being a parent, it's not much easier being a teenager. I don't miss that drama at all."

"Speaking of drama, I'm not sure you should be buying what Linda's selling. From what Ella says, she's been an absolute nightmare," Sarah said. She scanned her mom's face for any indication that she could see Linda for the farce that she was—nothing.

"I think you need to take what Ella's told you with a grain of salt," Carrie responded. "You didn't see Linda this morning. She's had a very hard time these past few years. And you shouldn't judge another person until you've walked a mile in their shoes. Didn't they teach you at camp?"

"I must have missed that part. I was probably behind the boathouse with Dick Johnson."

"I want my money back."

12

THE SUN WAS STILL HIGH in the sky later that day when Sarah pulled into Stacey's driveway. It was another perfect pool day, but she'd been told that the hangover situation at Stacey's made her dark basement the only option. An empty Miller Lite can was sitting on top of a bush. She picked it up and let herself in the house. It was shockingly quiet, considering what had gone on just hours earlier, and remarkably clean. Aside from the lone beer can, the only evidence of the party was the open windows and the smell of bleach. After much searching, Sarah found the girls in Stacey's unreasonably large, Parisian-themed bedroom. The four of them were sprawled across her ultra-king-sized canopy bed, which she had long ago outgrown. Maturity wise, that is. Size wise, it could never be outgrown by anyone. Stacey had wanted to get rid of it, but the girls wouldn't let her. Despite being almost adults, they still loved that they could all fit on it and close the curtains to the world around them.

"There you are. What's up *bitches?*" Sarah imitated Dalia. "Nice cleanup job."

"It actually worked out that Craig was here. All of the fun, and none of the work." Stacey shrugged. She was wearing her favorite DKNY T-shirt. For some reason, she always wore it when she was hungover. "Other than the phone situation, I think it's all good."

"Phone situation?" Sarah didn't feel like arguing over who was going to move over to make room for her, so she plopped down on a furry black bean bag and grabbed a pillow that said *Bonjour!*

"Someone stole the kitchen phone, so Jenny and I bought a new one this morning."

"It's *so weird*," Jenny said. "It looks *exactly* like the old one, but the ring is *completely different!* Do you think your parents will notice?"

"I guess you'll find out next week," Tori said. She rolled onto her back and swept the brunette bangs, which she'd been trying to grow out, off of her face. "I'm dying." She sighed dramatically.

"This is what we get for doing shots," Dalia cried out irritably. "Tori, do you mind not taking up the *entire bed?*" She grabbed the slack in Tori's pink velour sweatpants and moved her leg over. Tori must have really been suffering because she didn't even bother to yell at Dalia.

"I feel fine. I hardly drank," Sarah said, looking at the pile of them in their sorry state. "I think I'll quit drinking and become a stoner."

"Sure you will. Where were you all night?" Tori asked.

"Playing pool."

"With Jake?" She started to get up and then lay back down. "I think I might get sick."

"Don't you puke in my bed!" Stacey threw a pillow at her. "I bet the cold bathroom tile would feel good on your face, Tori. Go lie down in there."

"It started with Jake, but then every guy, of course, had to try to beat me. And then he had to go, so I didn't even get to see him alone. He did say we should meet up at Metallica, though."

"*That's great, Sarah!*" Jenny popped up. Sarah loved that Jenny was always happy for her friends, regardless of what was going on with her.

"Well, it's progress," Stacey said. "Someone else made progress too last night." She grinned and nodded in Jenny's direction.

"Rob kissed me, Sarah." Jenny placed her hand on her heart and put on what the girls referred to as her *ever since I was a little girl* face.

"Good for you, Jenny!"

"Getting high was a really bad idea." Tori put the heels of her hands over her eyes. "Speaking of, where's Ella? I really liked her."

"She flew home to pack," Sarah responded.

"Well, let me know when she gets back because we need her," Dalia said. She got out from underneath Stacey's duvet. She still had on last night's clothes.

"Have you guys even gotten out of bed today?" Sarah asked.

"Those two haven't." Stacey pointed to Tori and Dalia. "You guys seriously need showers. And you're washing my sheets!"

"*Fine!*" Dalia got up and grabbed two ginger ales from Stacey's mini fridge. "So, Ella told me she's a gymnast. And with her dance training, and her size, she'd be a perfect flyer. We need to fill Kim Roland's spot."

Dalia was captain of their cheerleading squad and took it very seriously. Almost as seriously as she took Shawn. She always kept her eye out for new talent, handpicking the squad long before tryouts, which rendered the *actual* tryouts meaningless.

"That's a great idea," Stacey said.

"Sounds good to me," Tori agreed. "Anything to keep Jessica Carroll off the squad."

"So, what do you think, Sarah? Would she be interested?" Dalia asked.

"I don't know. I would like to not have to deal with Jessica if we don't have to, but we'll see."

Listening to Dalia talk about Ella becoming a constant fixture in their lives made Sarah uneasy. She wanted to change the subject and knew just how to do it. "Hey, someone go pick up muffins at Brew."

"Not it!" they all yelled.

They played Not It all the time. Tori had never lost, not even once. Sarah thought she might get her today, given her state. But once again, it was Jenny.

"Why do I *always lose*?" she whined. "It's *so unfair*. We should take turns."

"Rules are rules, Jenny." Stacey pointed to the red Fendi purse on her desk. "Just take my purse. I'll even buy, if it makes you feel better."

"It doesn't!" Jenny flared her nostrils like a frustrated five-year-old as she grabbed Stacey's purse and stomped out the door.

Tori and Dalia used the pause to shower, and the girls reconvened in the kitchen. Suddenly ravenous, they raided Stacey's pantry. Tori went right for the Gatorade. Sarah laid out Oreos and Cheetos. Dalia got the Entenmann's doughnuts and a box of Froot Loops.

Stacey was sprawled across two kitchen stools eating mini Slim Jims. Sarah, Tori, and Dalia stood at the counter, stuffing their faces, when Sarah noticed something odd. She made a tiny pointing motion toward Stacey. The girls watched as she peeled open a Slim Jim, took it out of the wrapper, gave it some sort of evil look, and then chewed it like she was trying to murder it.

"What the hell are you doing?" Dalia asked.

"It's part of my therapy. They're like mini *penises*, and they're called Slim *Jims*, like Jim's got a small *penis* . . ." She didn't even look for acknowledgment that anyone understood what she was doing and just went on chomping away.

Sarah tried to follow her logic. The only part she understood was that Stacey was referring to her ex-long-term boyfriend Jim, who'd crushed her heart six months earlier. Everyone, including their parents, had been sure they were going to get married, despite Jim leaving for college a year before Stacey graduated. "No amount of distance could keep *them* apart," Jim's mom had said. Stacey felt the same and, in fact, was so sure about their future that she convinced Jim to follow his lifelong dream to go to Boston College, even though Jim was leaning toward Northwestern just to stay close to her. "I don't want him to resent me for it later," she'd said. It was a fateful mistake, and she was very far from over it.

Stacey swallowed hard and continued. "It was the first thing that made me laugh after we broke up, so I bought some. Turns out they're not only therapeutic, they're delicious."

She peeled open another one and started the whole process over again.

"What other weird secrets do you have that we don't know about?" Tori asked.

"Just that one."

"Okay, then. Dalia, I saw Shawn come in as I was leaving last night. "Did you see him?" Sarah asked.

"She saw him," Stacey said. She and Tori looked at each other and laughed.

"She gave him a blowie." Tori smirked.

"*Dalia*, why do you do that? You don't want that to be all you guys are about."

"Look, assholes." She had a handful of Froot Loops but still managed to raise her middle finger. "Just because you guys don't get how things work doesn't mean I don't know what I'm doing. So, check this out. I read in my mom's magazine that if you make a guy cum, then it creates a connection between you. And you create this instinct thing, where he thinks of you and it makes him think about how good you made him feel, and then he comes back for more. It's like that dog thing. The Russian one or some shit."

"The *Russian dog*? Is that like a kinky sex position or something?" Stacey asked.

"Is that the one where you do it doggy style while you're drinking vodka?" Sarah laughed. "And call each other Russian names like Olga and—"

"Pavlov!" Tori shouted.

"Oh, ha! Pavlov!" Sarah high-fived her.

"Yeah. That guy. So, that's what I'm doing."

"So, that's your plan? You keep giving him blow jobs, and he'll keep coming around?"

"Yes, Sarah, it's *working*." Dalia rolled her eyes.

"So how many dates has he taken you on?" Tori shined a spotlight on what none of them had ever dared.

Sarah figured it was the impatience of Tori's wicked hangover that made her come right out and say it. So far, their subtle hints had gotten them nowhere.

"*Tori*, you *know* that's next. He's gonna *have* to date me, if he wants my *virginity*, which of course he *does*. I'm not sure what you guys don't get about that."

For as many times as she'd laid it out, it still made so little sense that no one could even venture to try to argue with her. So, they'd shake their heads behind her back and change the subject. But hearing the word "virginity" conjured up a memory from Sarah's past that she thoughtlessly shared with the room.

"I wonder if he's saving himself for marriage. Ella and I used to go to church camp with him every summer, and they talked about that *all the time*. I should ask him about that," she said, and then quickly tried to shove that comment back in her mouth with a handful of Cheez-Its.

"Yeah right. Like that exists anymore." Dalia dismissed the thought. But Tori didn't.

"Hold up," she said. "Did you say *church camp*? You're joking, right? When was this?"

"Oh god, years ago. Childhood. Where is Jenny with those muffins?"

"Wait a sec. I thought Ella didn't really know him," Dalia said, in a way that was expectedly suspicious, which put Sarah on edge.

She wasn't exactly sure what Ella had told her when she was off playing pool, so the less she said now, the better.

"She barely did. It was *ages* ago."

"Well, did he remember her?"

Her sluggish brain wasn't prepared to come up with answers to questions that could have consequences in the future. The whole thing was so stupid. They were kids, for fuck's sake. And it shouldn't mean anything. But it did mean something because Ella was excited about him. And worse, he was excited about her. She should have told them about the first kiss thing right then and there, but she didn't feel like dealing with the dozens of questions that would inevitably follow if she did disclose that tidbit, so she lied. Her dad's disapproving voice popped in her head once again.

"I think so? I mean, I don't know if he actually remembered *her*, or just the *name* and was just being *nice* . . . you know how he is. All Mr. Polite all the time. And I was still pretty stoned so . . ."

Just when Sarah thought she couldn't manage any more questions, Jenny walked into the kitchen.

"Muffins, anyone?"

13

"OH, THANK GOD. I so needed that." Tori crumpled the surprisingly loud muffin wrapper into a ball.

"You mean thank *Jenny*." Jenny batted her cornflower eyes.

"You don't get thanked when you lose Not It. It's your obligation," Stacey pointed out.

"You guys are such bitches," Dalia said. "Thank you, *Jenny*." She blew her a kiss.

"You're welcome, *Dalia*." Jenny blew one back.

Sarah took notice of the bright-eyed exchange between Dalia and Jenny and looked to Tori for confirmation. Tori didn't respond to Sarah's glance. She was too busy opening one decorative cabinet after another, searching for the garbage can. It didn't matter, though. Sarah didn't need Tori to affirm once again that, like Tori and Sarah's special bond, Dalia and Jenny had apparently developed one of their own. Though cloudy on details about the whens and hows of its origin, Dalia seemed to have grabbed onto the fact that, despite being one of *those people,* Jenny was vulnerable. And maybe in her mind that put them on equal footing, because lately, protecting Jenny seemed to make Dalia feel valuable. And Jenny ate it up.

The plan was to lay low at Stacey's. But Dalia was angling to get the guys in the mix, making the case that they shouldn't let the fact that Stacey's parents were out of town go to waste. She'd even worn a tight black T-shirt with a wide red arrow pointing down to her cutoff shorts. Tori gave her all sorts of shit for it, saying, *first of all it's just gross,* and then asking why she would wear something like that when they'd already agreed *days ago* that this would be a girls' night. Dalia said she wore it *just in case.* Tori doubled down and told her it's *disgusting either way,* and she really should just *throw it in the garbage.* And that's when Stacey intervened with an executive decision. "You guys, it is *girls'* night. *Just* us. Go downstairs, and I'll be right there. Sarah, can you help me?"

Sarah put together a pitcher of Stoli lemonade and a tray full of tumblers, while Stacey grabbed some snacks and a hefty stack of magazines. They went downstairs, where they found the girls sprawled out in their favorite corners of Stacey's giant leather sectional.

"So, what'd we miss?" Sarah asked as she handed out beverages.

"We were just talking about Ella," Dalia said. "She told me all about her mom last night. What's up with that paycheck bullshit? I was just saying she should work at Gatto's and hide her tips. I could get her a job, if she wants."

Sarah hesitated for a moment, considering whether she should talk Dalia out of it and then decided against it. Maybe if Ella got a good dose of Dalia's nicer side, she would leave the Shawn thing alone. "Thank you, Dalia." She smiled appreciatively. "That would be really nice of you."

"So, what are we doing tonight?" Jenny asked between handfuls of potato chips.

Stacey held up the June editions of their favorite magazines and then sat on the carpet. She fanned them out in front of her and tossed the *Glamour* to Dalia.

"*Seriously?*" Dalia protested as she pushed it off the couch and onto the floor. "I can't believe how *lame* you guys are being! Aren't you getting tired of this nun bullshit, Stacey? We should call *the guys* over. How are you ever going to get over Jim if you won't even look at another guy?"

Despite the promise of nightly phone calls, a few weeks into Boston College, the flood of calls turned into a creek, and then a trickle, and then a drip. Stacey *knew* something was wrong, but the girls assured her it was fine.

Though, when Jim came home for Christmas, it was not fine. Stacey tried to kiss him, but he said he had a virus, which went on for an entire, agonizing week. Until Christmas Day, when he finally came clean. The virus was named Gemma. They'd met the first day of class and had "gotten serious" just before Thanksgiving. Whatever that meant. It was safe to assume getting serious meant fucking, which was a problem because even though Sarah assured Stacey that *Germa*, as they named her, would work her way out of his system, she would still be a permanent stain on their relationship. Stain notwithstanding, they were wrong. There

99

wasn't even a transition period. Jim stopped calling and didn't even come home for the summer. He told his friends that he was *summering* at Germa's parents' house in Martha's Vineyard, and that was the end of that. Only a complete tool would use the word *summering,* so they knew she'd lost him forever.

"Why should I date someone our *senior year* just to date someone?" Stacey asked. "And I really doubt you guys will get serious with your guys. Sarah, are you going to marry Jake? Is Dalia going to marry Shawn? Even if you do actually date them at some point, what are the odds that you'll marry them? Think about it."

Even though Tori seemed to be the most mature of the group, it was mostly because of her practicality. She prided herself in her ability to handle any situation, whether it required a logical assessment or a tool in her well-stocked purse. But Stacey was the one who was truly wise beyond her years. Yet, she was fun, and nice, and beautiful. Jim was a *fool* to have let her go.

"Probably not very good," Sarah agreed as she sat next to Dalia on the couch. Jenny passed her the bowl of potato chips. Sarah looked at it and put it down. "We need some real food."

"So, what's the point? You're just setting yourself up for a breakup in the future. I'm saving myself the trouble," Stacey reasoned as she got up on her knees and reached for the side table drawer. She pulled out a handful of takeout options and began to flip through them. "But you guys can go on all you want, fantasizing about your guys. And I won't bug you about it, even if I think it's unrealistic."

"What's *unrealistic* about me and Shawn getting married?" Dalia sat up quickly.

"It's nothing personal, Dalia, but odds are you and Shawn won't get married. But you can go after him all you want, and I will

be there with you one hundred percent. How about Mr. Fong's?"
She held up the soy sauce-stained menu.

"Why do you *say* that?" Dalia grabbed it from her and threw
it on the floor.

"Dalia. This has nothing to do with *you*. It's just what usually
happens to relationships at our age, because lots of things *change*.
And you can't control that. And you definitely can't stop someone
from falling in love with someone else," she said, making a pouty
face, sniffing back fake tears.

"Bullshit." Dalia waved her speech away. "You just want
to think that because it makes you feel better. You have as much
control as you *take*. I've never told you this before because I didn't
want you to feel bad. But if I were you, I would have *never* told
Jim to go to Boston."

"*Dalia!*" Sarah kicked her in the thigh.

"No, that's fair," Stacey acknowledged. "She's probably
right."

"I told you I've been reading my mom's magazines lately—
there's this article, 'How to Get and Keep Your Man,'" Dalia
continued. "And there are four steps. One, make yourself
gorgeous. Two, find out what kind of woman he wants and
become *that*. Three, find out his needs and fulfill them. And four,
get rid of the competition. That's why I would have kept Jim close.
You nailed one, two, and three, Stacey. Without competition, you
would have won."

"I wish I'd heard that last year. Too late now, I guess . . ." Stacey
folded her arms and then rested her cheek on her open palm. As
she somberly stared at the floor in front of her, something seemed
to catch her eye. "Dalia, look at this," she said as she picked up a

magazine. "You should do this quiz. 'How Long Will Your Love Last?'" Stacey held up the cover and then flipped to the page.

"Nope, not doing it," Dalia shook her head.

"Come on, it's fun." Stacey reached for Tori's purse and helped herself to a pen. "Okay, one. He takes you to a party and introduces you to people you've never met. Does he A. Introduce you as his girlfriend? B. Introduce you using your first name? Or C. Not introduce you at all?"

"*La la la la la,* I don't *hear* you." Dalia cupped her hands over her ears.

"What do you guys think? B or C?" Everyone knew better than to answer, so Stacey just shrugged and circled the page. "Okay, two. You've just had sex. Afterward, does he A. Spoon with you? B. Go to sleep on the *other* side of the bed? Or C. Tell you he wants to spend the night but has to get up early? Hmmm . . . change sex to blow job and bed to car, and I think we're going to have to go with . . ." Stacey circled the page again. "Okay, three . . ."

Dalia sprang up like an unhinged Jack in the Box. She grabbed the magazine and the pen from Stacey and wrote TOTAL BULLSHIT and let it fall to the floor.

"*Dalia!*" Stacey was visibly taken aback with her aggression. While Dalia was famous for her moods, she'd never been like *this* before.

"What are you trying to say? That magazine is so stupid! And guess what, Stacey, you'd be all A, A, A when you were with Jim, like *Oh, look at us with our fifty points,* and sorry, but look how that turned out. None of that means anything once some competition comes around," Dalia shouted.

"Dalia, *what* is your problem?" Sarah stood up.

"Oh my god. Okay, *here's* an idea." Tori, who'd appeared to be tuning this out, tossed aside her *Marie Claire*, rose from the couch, spread her arms wide, and raised her voice to just shy of a yell. "How about we just focus on *us* this year? *Guys* will come and go, but *this* is what's important. Have you guys even thought about the fact that it's our last year together *ever*? Are we even going to stay in touch when we don't have school bringing us together every day?"

"Of course we are!" Sarah said, shocked she'd even suggest such a thing.

"Will we?" Tori asked. "It's easy to say that now, but like Stacey said, things change. And I was thinking the other day that we should make a promise *now* to meet up someday in the future—pick the date, place, everything—just in case we drift apart. And then I had an idea. What do you say we do a time capsule?" Tori said, nodding excitedly.

"Oh yeah! We can put souvenirs and letters to our future selves in it," Stacey said.

"Exactly," Tori went on. "But I think we should focus on goals for ourselves. And when we meet up in the future, we can see if we achieved them. So, how about we spend *our* night focusing on *us*?"

"I love this idea, but I need time to think about them," Sarah said.

"Let's just start with a few big ones now, and we can add to them—like fun ones or even some secret ones—all the way up until, say, Homecoming. And we can bury it the morning of the dance or something." She reached in her purse, pulled out a mini spiral notebook and some pens, and handed out the supplies.

Stacey spread out the magazines for them to write on. The girls sat in a circle and began to ponder their futures. Sarah noticed that Jenny seemed to struggle, while everyone else's goals flowed effortlessly from their pens. After ten minutes of scribbling, it was time to share.

"I don't want to read mine," Jenny said. "I couldn't think of any good ones."

"Don't worry, Jenny," Sarah reassured her. "Let's have a no-judgment rule. We can just read them and then put them away. We don't have to talk about them."

"Good idea. I'll go first," Tori volunteered.

Tori and Sarah's goals were predictably aligned. Journalism school at Syracuse, marriage and kids, and settling down in a big city. Tori specifically said New York. And she included a Prada backpack she'd been saving for, while Sarah included traveling to each continent. Jenny's first goal was to keep her nice hair. She also wanted to be Rob's girlfriend, to graduate, and to get married someday. Stacey's involved doing charity work, marrying well, and a house in the Hamptons. And then it was Dalia's turn.

"Okay, one, go to Homecoming with Shawn. Two, lose my virginity to Shawn *on* Homecoming. Three, win the state cheer-leading competition. And four, marry Shawn." She folded her paper and tossed it in the middle, on top of the rest.

Sarah was just about to violate her own no-judgment rule and opened her mouth to comment on the disturbing concentration of Dalia's goals on one man, but Stacey subtly shook her head, so she switched the topic to logistics. "So, where should we meet and when?"

"Well, twenty years from Homecoming is October 28, 2015. We should probably meet in a high rise—somewhere we're sure will still be there," Tori said. "Top of the Empire State Building? World Trade Center?"

"How about the 95th floor of the John Hancock?" Sarah suggested. "It's where my dad proposed to my mom. They still go there for dinner every year on their anniversary."

"That's a great idea!" Stacey said. "I've been there—to the restaurant part. There's a cool-looking bar above it too. It's really nice."

"Okay, then it's settled!" Tori clapped her hands together proudly. "October 28, 2015, on the 95th floor of the Hancock at, let's say, one o'clock? I'm sure we'll need all day. And I'll hold on to these until we buy the capsule."

As Sarah watched Tori collect the papers, she smiled and thought about how many times they'd done exactly this. The five of them lying around Stacey's basement. As she looked at each of the girls, she laughed at how different they were—and then at how the same they were. And then marveled at the fact that, despite the spats and annoying traits, they all loved each other. Would their futures turn out like they'd hoped? She was dying to find out. But she knew there was nowhere she'd rather be right now than with her friends, without a care in the world. Life was good.

14

SARAH PICKED UP the Victoria's Secret catalog sitting on the coffee table and started fanning herself with it.

"This is *total crap*. You didn't even *ask* me. It's only ten a.m., and it's already a hundred degrees. And with the heat index? I don't think it's safe to be outside." She wilted into the cool leather chair and reached for the remote.

"Don't you dare," Carrie warned.

Ella arrived for good on a hot and humid Saturday. And Sarah was pissed that her mom had volunteered them to help with the move. Physical labor in scorching heat aside, she was missing a pool day at Jenny's. "A *pool* is where you're supposed to be on a day like this. Moving someone is the exact opposite of *that*."

"They need our *support*, Sarah," Carrie retorted.

Sarah watched her stomp around the kitchen and begin rinsing the coffee pot. This was not their usual friendly exchange, and Carrie's pursed lips and angled brows made Sarah realize she'd pushed her too far.

"Okay, okay. I just wish you would have checked with me first." She pulled her shirt away from her skin and blew down it.

Jason Blake plundered down the stairs, his middle-aged body attached to his child-like face. "We need to be home in time for the Agassi match. I've been looking forward to it all week." He put on his Cubs hat and grabbed his keys from the hook. "Ready?"

Kevin, who had been hiding behind a half-eaten banana, looked up at his dad, horrified as if he'd just set Freddie Krueger free from dreamland.

"*What is with you people?*" Carrie turned from the sink to face them. "Doesn't anyone feel like they need to sacrifice anything, *ever*? Does anyone realize how *lucky* we are?"

She set the coffee carafe down so hard there was an audible crack. "Great. Now I have to buy a new one." She picked it up, inspected it, put it back down, and slapped both hands on the counter as she took a breath so deep she might be able to use it to talk forever. "You know what? *These* are the kinds of problems *we* deal with. Cracked coffee pots. *This* is your hard life."

"And I don't even drink coffee," Jason said for some odd reason. Apparently, he didn't know whose side he was supposed to be on.

"We don't deal with *any* of the problems that *lots of* other people do. And you kids get to do pretty much what you want, whenever you want. I ask for just *one day* for you guys to think of other people, and I get nothing but . . . *bitching*. Things are gonna change around here. And that goes for you too." Carrie pointed at her husband, who looked like he'd just been given detention for something he didn't do. He waited until she turned away and mouthed "menopause" and then smiled and nodded as if this had nothing to do with him.

Sarah didn't have nearly the grounds to complain that Kevin and her dad did. Carrie roped them in, too, and they had *no* vested interest in Ella's family. But she managed to whip everyone into shape with her not-so-gentle speech, and they headed to the new apartment. And true to her mantra of letting things go, her mood lifted on the ride over.

The complex was nice enough. It had a pool and tennis courts, and some clubhouse-looking thing. Further down the road, there was a small pond that had just one picnic table underneath some large weeping willows. And then she saw it. The crown jewel. A tiny, secluded liquor store. Sarah started to see potential and felt like they might be able to get some use out of this place. While Dalia's apartment complex was sad and scary, this one looked like it could be fun. The girls spent a large portion of their free time trying to find places where they could drink unnoticed. A secluded picnic table, hidden by trees, with a no-name liquor store where she was pretty sure their fake IDs would fly just ten yards away? It could be perfect!

"There it is. Building K," Carrie said. "Oh, and there are the Connors." She rolled down her window. "*Hi guys!* Jason, just park here."

"*Hi everyone!* Thanks for coming," Linda said as the Blakes got out of the car.

Sarah was horrified that Linda was wearing pale pink spandex, but thankful she wore a black T-shirt that was long enough to cover what she imagined was an enormous camel toe. And then she was mad that she had to be thankful for something like *that*. She slammed the car door shut and tried to erase the distressing mental image. Instead, it was punctuated by Linda's voice.

"You're just in time. We could really use a hand with these boxes. Alan's cardiologist started him on blood thinners. With all his health issues, he's not supposed to lift anything heavy. Alan, you remember Jason, right?"

"Sure, I do." He extended his hand. "Although, I'm not sure we've ever had the chance to have a beer together." Alan was dressed in golf attire, but he didn't look like much of a golfer. More like a bowler. An amateur bowler who'd picked it up later in life just to get away from his wife. Sarah chuckled at the thought.

"I'm not sure we have." Jason shook his hand. "I'm thinking today's the day, though. Nothing better than a cold beer on a hot day. So, are you a tennis fan?"

"Alan, do you really think a beer is a good idea?" Linda interrupted. "Jason, I don't know if Carrie mentioned that Alan recently had a heart attack. It was minor, thank the Lord, but they just started him on this . . . what's it called, honey? Warfarin. To thin his blood. I'm not sure mixing medication and alcohol is a good idea."

"Oh right." Alan vigorously scratched his right ass cheek. He used to be a classy guy, but he didn't seem like he gave a shit about anything these days. "It's only a good idea when *you* do it, *honey*."

His contemptuous glare was palpable, which didn't seem to bother Linda at all. Sarah wondered how a person could be so oblivious to the fact that everyone hated her. She thought back to the psych class she and Tori took together. *Narcissist,* she nodded to herself.

"The doctor said we have to make sure Alan doesn't get injured, and to be especially careful of head injuries. That thin blood is good for the heart, but not so good if you get hit in the head, apparently." Linda handed Jason a box. "Here you go, sir. A heavy one for the *healthy* man. Got to appreciate it while you've got it," she said. "I know Alan sure didn't."

"*Sorry*," Carrie mouthed in Jason's direction.

"I'm sorry too," Alan said with a friendly smile.

The apartment was bigger than Sarah had expected. It was a nice two-story unit with three bedrooms and an office, and brand-new appliances. And the furniture was nice enough, beige and boxy, but it didn't look cheap. Sarah was glad that money didn't seem to be too much of a problem.

But that still didn't mean anything for Ella's wardrobe, she concluded, as she hung up one sad outfit after another. The girls started in Ella's room that, once they got past the clothes, turned out to be way more fun than Sarah had anticipated. They laughed at old camp pictures, flipped through yearbooks, and read notes folded into tiny triangles that they'd passed to each other in grade school. When they finished, they took a break to get drinks. But when they got downstairs, Ella caught her dad with an open beer.

"*Dad*," she called him out.

"This?" He took a sip of his Michelob. "Honey, your mother's just trying to control—I mean, the doctor never said I couldn't have a beer. He's just worried about me falling down and hitting my head, so I promise that I'll stop before there's any chance of that happening." He smiled as he fed cable wires through the entertainment center to Jason's waiting hands.

"Beer isn't *bad*, girls, it's just *fun water*," Jason joked.

"Oh, okay. I'm gonna use that one, Dad." Sarah laughed.

Sarah and Ella took their lemonades upstairs and started on Ella's parents' bedding, which Sarah found completely disturbing. And annoying. "Where is the other corner on the long side of this? God, I hate these things. I swear, someday I will reinvent the fitted sheet. Hey! I'm going to put that in the time capsule!"

"What time capsule?" Ella asked.

Sarah told her all about their plans. Ella loved the idea and seemed to be hinting to be a part of it. Sarah felt that uneasiness again. An encroached-upon feeling. Yet they'd been having so much fun together. She wished she could keep Ella in a little box, away from the rest of her life, but she knew that wasn't possible. She started to accept that she had no choice but to let her in, regardless of her reservations. So, when Ella started asking specifically about their goals, she answered more candidly than Dalia would have appreciated.

"Wow. Now I get why you were so worried," Ella responded exactly as Sarah had hoped she would. "So, did anything happen with them at the party?"

"They hooked up, like they always do."

"Fooled around or sex?" Ella asked as she fluffed out the flat sheet.

"No sex. She's dead serious about it happening on Homecoming. I don't know why that part is so important to her. She doesn't want it to happen at a party or in a car somewhere. It's like those girls who dream about their wedding day their whole lives. She wants it to be something out of a movie, I guess." Sarah rolled her eyes. "It's weird. It's so weird we can hardly talk to her about it. But every other part of her life is super shitty, so we just go with it."

"Well, I hope it works out for her," Ella said. "So, where are you keeping the time capsule?"

"We're going to keep it in that old toy chest in my bedroom until we bury it on Homecoming day."

"And where's that going to be?"

"We haven't decided yet, but we *do* know where we're going to open it. Here, toss me that pillow." Sarah shimmied a white, sateen case over a king-sized pillow. "We're meeting at the 95th floor restaurant in the Hancock Building, October 28, 2015."

"That's so cool! I want to do a time capsule." Ella stopped hinting and came right out and said it.

Sarah didn't know how to respond because there was no way Ella could be part of their thing, at least at this point. She had no choice but to change the subject.

"Hey, you didn't mention your dad had a heart attack. That is *so scary.*"

"I know. I don't like to talk about it. Supposedly, if he cuts down his stress and takes his medication, he'll be okay. Although, that brain bleed stuff scares me. Just the words *brain bleed.*" Ella winced as she put her fingers to her forehead. "I wish I'd never heard them."

"Now you sound like me. Don't worry. Lots of people take blood thinners. My grandpa did."

"How's he doing?"

"Well, he's dead. But, other than that . . ." She laughed. "Sorry. He died from old age, if it makes you feel better. He did always have these weird bruises, though. Nice that your dad has the heart attack, and your mom gets the Valium."

"Right? That's so messed up."

Sarah placed the last dusty blue decorative pillow on the bed and smoothed out the duvet. "Okay!" she said, admiring their work. "I think we've put in enough hours for one day. Now you are going to get your bathing suit, and I'm going to *tell* Linda that we're meeting the girls at Jenny's. And get this—I'm going to make her let us take her car. It's the least she can do after I made her damn bed."

"Sarah Blake, I think I love you."

15

JENNY'S QUIET POOL DAY had somehow turned into a scene out of *90210*, though less Rodeo Drive and more mullet. Sarah took a visual inventory. Dave Taylor was running alongside the pool with Tori in his arms and threw her in the water. The splash broke Jenny and Rob out of their second make-out session ever. And just beyond Jenny and Rob, Sarah saw Jake, just chillin' with some friends. *"Oh my god, what is he doing here?"* she said, beaming.

On the other side of the pool, Stacey was lying on a lounge chair, having her own private dance party using only her fingers. And Dalia, sporting the tiniest white bikini she could legally get away with, was prancing with purpose toward her lounge chair, carrying two plastic cups with limes gracing the edges. Sarah recognized these as Jenny's mom's famous margaritas and wasn't surprised when she saw Mrs. Baker behind the outdoor bar. A crowd of teenagers surrounded her like eager pigeons as she filled their cups.

Sarah followed Dalia with her eyes and watched her give the lounge chair a subtle lap dance as she seated herself next to Shawn's face. She handed him a margarita, but he shook his head and set it on the concrete next to him. Sarah scanned the pool one more time. Jake didn't look like he was leaving anytime soon, so she decided to lay low with Dalia and Shawn, and she sent Ella to the pool house to change.

"It is scorching out here." Sarah set down her beach bag. "Wow, there's a lot of people here."

"Hey! You made it. And *Jake's* here! Take this. You have some serious catching up to do." Dalia handed her Shawn's drink. "He's being boring today."

"I love you." Sarah pulled an ice cube out of the cup and ran it across her forehead. Sticky margarita juice dripped down her face and onto her chest, leaving a salty residue. She patted Dalia's thigh to move over and sat next to her.

"So how was the move? I can't believe your mom made you help them move in. Why can't they move themselves?" Dalia asked.

"Who did you move? Ella?" Shawn asked. He raised the back of his lounge chair and started looking around. Dalia squinted her eyes at Shawn—and then at Sarah.

"Is she here?" He wiped sweat off his forehead with the corner of Dalia's towel.

"Mmm hmmm," Sarah mumbled as she gulped her margarita. She motioned with one finger for them to hang on, trying to figure out what to say next. "Hey, I'm surprised you remember her."

"*What are you talking about?* How many summers were we at camp together?"

"I don't know. It just feels like forever ago. I hardly remember it at all." She leaned back on her hands. Playing dumb seemed like a good move.

"Those were some good times. Everything was just fun back then. And easy. You know, it's weird. I really miss it."

"Miss what? Camp?"

"Camp, the way things were. I miss the times. Think about it," he said, taking off his Oakleys. "We had nothing to worry about back then. No homework, no job, no ACTs or college to think about, no pressure at all."

"No freedom, no driving, and I don't seem to recall *any* margaritas," Sarah said, taking another sip.

"That's exactly what I'm talking about. We didn't need margaritas to have fun back then. Not that I don't like margaritas, but what changed? I don't know why I've been thinking about this so much lately. Maybe it's because it's our senior year. But I keep wondering when bowling stopped being fun without sneaking in drinks. When did everyone decide they need to get high just to watch a movie?"

"When did Ping-Pong become beer pong?" Sarah smiled at Shawn.

"*Yeah!*" He laughed. "Can you imagine any of these guys going to a park now or just playing a board game? We never do those things anymore because someone decided they're not fun. But why aren't they?"

"I don't know." Sarah shrugged as she considered his question. "Maybe we got bored with those things, and beers and drugs make them fun again."

"I never got bored with them. But you're probably right that everyone else did," he lamented.

He was in one of his *pensive moods*, as Sarah called them, a phrase she'd stolen from Carrie. "Why so pensive," her mom often said when Sarah found herself gripped with worry about some random thing that would probably never happen. Shawn wasn't a worrier, but he wasn't the lightest guy in the room. He liked to have fun, but he was a thinker. And to Sarah, that set him apart from most of the guys they knew. Even when Dalia laid out all the reasons she liked him so much, she never mentioned what was his single best quality in Sarah's mind. And that was a big difference between them. It was hard to understand why Dalia was so sure he was *the one*.

"Well, this conversation got serious," Dalia said. "You two need to get going on those drinks." She tried to give Shawn her cup, which he pushed away.

"I told you I'm taking it easy today." He was visibly annoyed. But not for long. Ella walked up with a big smile on her face.

"What are you guys talking about?"

"Oh, Shawn was just whining that nothing's fun anymore without alcohol," Dalia said.

"That's so funny that you say that. I think about that *all the time*. When did it all change?" Ella asked. "When you're a kid, you play some games, you go swimming, you roast marshmallows, and that's like . . ."

"*A great day*," Ella and Shawn said at the same time and immediately started laughing. Neurons visibly fired between them. And the look, the one exchanged only a handful of times in life when there's an instant connection with someone, did not go unnoticed by Sarah. Or Dalia.

"But now it's like, we have to get drunk to have fun doing anything. I mean, I'm as guilty as anyone, but it doesn't make a lot of sense," Ella said.

"Well, maybe your childhoods were fun, but mine wasn't," Dalia said. "The day I got my driver's license—*that's* the day *my* fun started. And I wouldn't trade margaritas by the pool for *anything*."

"I'm just saying, it would be nice to do some things that don't constantly revolve around alcohol. I wish we could go back to where the fun was the thing itself, and not how banged up we were when we did it," Shawn said.

"I did see a fire pit in my apartment complex, so any time you guys want to roast some marshmallows, let me know," Ella volunteered.

"I like roasting marshmallows," Dalia said, raising her hand.

Though Dalia was doing a pretty good job of hiding it, Sarah could tell that Shawn and Ella's connection was blipping furiously on her radar. And Sarah knew Dalia would take control of the situation. But what she came up with was a *complete* surprise.

"Hey Ella, how about we throw you a little welcome back party at your apartment. It'll be like camp. We can have a cookout, and we can bring the marshmallows from work. Gatto's makes that marshmallow pie dessert. George will let us take a couple of bags, right Shawn?" She nodded in his direction. "And I can teach you all about apartment living."

"Or we could just *buy* them," Shawn added, being unnecessarily rude to her.

Out of the corner of her eye, Sarah saw Ella glance at her, as if she wanted Sarah to know she'd picked up on Shawn's rudeness. Or wanted to make sure Sarah did. Sarah refused to engage.

"I bet we could roast marshmallows right here if we had a magnifying glass," Sarah said. "*Hey,* I think Jenny's dad has one of those giant magnifying glasses. He's got that big leather book of maps on the table in the library, and I think there's one sitting on top of it. I'm going to get it and see if they have any marshmallows. Shawn, come with me?" She needed a second alone with him, even if she didn't love the idea of leaving Dalia and Ella alone together.

16

DALIA PATTED the lounge chair next to her.

"Sit here," she instructed. It was time to figure out exactly who she was dealing with. "So, Ella . . . what's your last name?"

"Connor. Ella Connor."

"Ella Connor. Dalia Jacobs. Let's get to know each other. I know you're a gymnast and a dancer. I know you *really* like to smoke pot, and I know you have a crazy mother." Dalia raised her margarita to Ella's empty hand. "Oh, you don't have a drink. Just take Sarah's. Sounds like your family sitch is about as fun as mine."

"It's a blast." Ella laid out her orange-and-pink Arizona beach towel. "Can I use that?" she asked, pointing to Dalia's suntan oil.

"Are you insane? You've got a good base tan going, but you are not ready for this. I'm sure Sarah has something to protect your skin. She always lectures me about skin cancer. I swear, sometimes I think she's like thirty years old," Dalia said.

"She's always been like that. Sarah the Protector." Ella laughed. "Shawn and I nicknamed her that when we were like ten years old. It sounds like a really lame superhero name."

"Sarah, the really lame superhero. Sounds about right. So, you and Shawn called her that?" Dalia turned on her side to face Ella. She let her sunglasses slide down her nose to get an unfiltered look at her in the light of day.

"Yep. You should have seen her at camp. She was always warning us about things. Like poison ivy, or bees, or cuts getting infected. If anyone had the tiniest scrape, she'd pull out the Bactine and chase us with it. And she had the biggest first aid kit you've ever seen."

"Doesn't surprise me. That girl worries about everything."

Ella held up the sunscreen she retrieved from Sarah's bag. "SPF 50. Figures." She began rubbing it on her face. "Shawn and I would straight up ditch her when she got too annoying."

"Huh. So, the three of you. Good friends?"

"The best! Shawn's family and my family went to the same church growing up. That was when my family was normal. And we went to camp together every summer. Sarah didn't start coming until later on, though. But she was there for all the best years."

"The best years?" Dalia couldn't imagine what could possibly be so great about church camp.

"Yeah, like when you're more adventurous. Staying out past curfew, making out behind the boathouse . . ."

Dalia was slightly disturbed that Ella had previously omitted details about her past with Shawn. And she didn't at all like whatever that *great day* bullshit was. But she didn't quite know what to make of it. She needed more.

"Sneaking out at church camp? You little rebel. Here, let me get your back."

"Thanks." Ella turned around, and Dalia began slathering lotion on her.

"So, these boys you used to make out with?"

"Oh, there was just one," Ella said. "Just Shawn."

Dalia stopped slathering, leaving a thick white glob on Ella's shoulder.

"You and Shawn?"

"Yep. Actually, he was my first kiss. And I was his," Ella said, looking over her shoulder. "It was only at camp, though. We'd get back to school and it was like it never happened."

"Typical guy," Dalia responded, not sure where to go from here. Though she figured she should finish with the sunscreen.

"It was like Danny and Sandy in *Grease*."

"And now? You must be pretty happy to see him." She closed the sunscreen and handed it back to Ella.

"Definitely," Ella said as she turned to face her.

Dalia mulled that one over for a bit and then decided she'd better set some ground rules.

"Well, just so you know, Shawn and I are more than just a fling, so—"

"Oh god, Dalia, I know that. It was ages ago. Like I said, he's still a kid to me. I wouldn't have told you all that if I was *interested* in him. *Ew*! I mean, ew as far as I'm concerned."

"Good. Then we can be friends. You started to worry me because I have *big* plans for us, and *no one* is going to mess those up," she said. "Did Sarah tell you about Homecoming? I have it all worked out."

"What's your big plan?" Ella asked.

"My big plan is that we're going to get a hotel room the night of Homecoming. In the city. Not some bullshit suburb thing. And it'll be on a high floor with a kickass view, and we're gonna drink champagne, and we're gonna have sex. It will be both of our first times, and it's gonna be *amazing*." She exhaled slowly as she traced her collarbone with her finger.

"*Really*. That is some plan. So, he's asked you already?"

"No, but he will. It would be a total dick move for him to ask someone else, after all the times we've been together. And every girl at school knows better than to even *think* about going with him."

"And Homecoming is what. Four months away?"

"Yep."

"Well, that sounds great. Good luck!" Ella said.

"*Good luck?* What's *that* supposed to mean?" Dalia snapped.

"It doesn't mean anything. I don't know. It's just something you say, like break a leg. Or, break a hymen in this case." Ella laughed.

"That's just weird. Whatever. It's going to be perfect." Dalia laid her chair back and closed her eyes.

"I hope you're right. I don't know . . ."

"You don't know *what*?" Dalia's eyes popped open.

"Sex the first time is *totally* overrated. I mean, I didn't think it hurt like some people say, but it's over in like two seconds. And the guy is all happy and that was amazing, and you're like *that's it?!*" she said as she reached for her drink. "I just hope you're not making too much of it. The losing your virginity part. I wouldn't want you to be disappointed after all that planning."

"It won't be like that with Shawn. I know it. And I don't even care if I like it. If he's all oh my god, that was amazing, that's all I need."

"Well good. He'll for sure be like that."

Dalia had seen and heard enough to know she needed to keep a close eye on Ella. And she wasn't happy at all that Sarah seemed to be hiding things from her. But she'd clearly established her position to Ella. And that was all she could do . . . for now.

17

SHAWN AND SARAH WENT IN through the solarium
and made their way to the library. The tall, painted white shelves
were stocked with books, which didn't make much sense. No one
in Jenny's family seemed like they'd read much of anything. Yet
somehow, they were drowning in money. Word on the street was
that a trust fund was involved—Stacey had even asked Jenny about
it one day. But when Jenny responded with a "what's that?" it was
permanently relegated to unsolved mystery status.

"Hey, so Ella . . ." Sarah pulled Shawn into the room and shut
the double glass doors behind them.

"*Yeah* . . . it's *great* to *see* her." He smiled, the telltale dimple
rising to the occasion.

"So, what's the deal? Are you interested in her?" She didn't
know why she bothered asking, when she could have just skipped
to the lecture part.

"I don't know, I guess. She's really hot."

"We're all hot, Shawn. It's a hundred ten degrees outside."

"Haha, you're funny. You have to admit, she's gorgeous. She was pretty before, but *wow!*" The word practically exploded from his mouth.

"But what about Dalia?"

"What *about* Dalia?"

"Um, *you and Dalia? Duh.*"

"Sarah, you know that's just for fun. She's hot and all, but she can be tough to be around sometimes."

"Then why are you wasting your time with her? Or, more importantly, *her* time?" she asked, suddenly offended on behalf of every girl who'd ever been used.

"Did you miss the part about her being hot?" he said casually.

Sarah locked eyes with him and crossed her arms.

"Don't do that." He turned away from her and began aimlessly searching the library. "I'm pretty sure she's having fun because she keeps coming back for more."

She keeps coming back? Dalia's Pavlovian dog theory popped into Sarah's mind. Never in a million years would Dalia have suspected that all this time, *she* was the dog.

"Shawn, don't make me lecture you." She wagged her finger at his back.

"Uh oh, is that Sarah the Protector I hear?" He cupped one hand behind his ear. "God, I haven't called you that in years."

"And you'd better not start now. It's *right there!*" She pointed sharply to the magnifying glass, which was right where she'd said it would be. Shawn picked it up off the book of maps and inspected it.

"Should we even be doing this?" Closing one eye, he held the magnifying glass to the other and looked at her.

"It's for looking at things close to you, dummy." She laughed at his enormous eye staring at her. "It's fine. But dicking around with two girls is *not* fine, so *don't do it*. Let's go raid the pantry."

Sarah walked ahead of him in a bit of a huff. When they reached the kitchen, they saw Jenny's mom cutting up limes at the kitchen counter. Shawn quickly tucked the magnifying glass under his shirt.

"Hi Mrs. Baker. Do you mind if we get some snacks?" Sarah asked.

"Help yourselves." She swayed as she motioned toward the pantry.

"Here we go." Sarah grabbed a jumbo pack of Stay-Puft marshmallows. And right behind it was a box of graham crackers and full-sized Hershey's bars. They put everything on a tray and brought the bounty back to the pool. Sarah passed Jake along the way and playfully pinched his butt as she walked by. She turned around smiling and pointed at Shawn.

"Nice," Shawn said.

"S'mores on the Lido deck in five minutes." She held up the bag of marshmallows.

They walked up to the girls and into an unexpected conversation.

"So, Shawn," Dalia raised one eyebrow at him. "What's this about you making out with Ella at camp and then acting like nothing happened at school? Who do you think you are, Danny Zuko or something?"

"Jeez, remind me not to leave you two alone again. I can't believe you're talking about that." He rubbed his eyes. "I was kind of a jerk, wasn't I?" he said to Ella.

"You think?" Ella smiled. "I thought maybe I was the jerk."

"No, I was definitely the jerk. You were the sweet one." He sat next to her on her lounge chair. Sarah watched in horror as his thigh leaned into hers. "Make it up to you?" He took a graham cracker, split it into two pieces, and put one on a paper plate. "Chocolate?"

He held his hand out to Sarah. She unwrapped the Hershey bar and handed him two squares, which he placed on the cracker. "Marshmallow?"

As Sarah placed the marshmallow on top of the chocolate pieces, her eyes were focused on the two thighs that should not have been touching. Why the hell wasn't Ella pulling hers away?

Shawn picked up the magnifying glass and inspected the angle of the sun before directing the sunlight through the glass. The marshmallow sizzled, turning a golden brown. Everyone watched as it changed shape. By that time, Jake and a few other guys had joined in to observe the scientific experiment unfolding. When the marshmallow started oozing over the edge, Shawn placed the other half of the graham cracker on top and handed it to Ella. Everyone began to cheer. That is, everyone except for Dalia.

18

THROUGH HER CLOSED EYES, Sarah could sense Jake's eyes were open as he was kissing her for what seemed like an eternity. Or no time at all. She had no idea how much time had passed, but she knew she never wanted it to end. Sarah opened one eye to find him staring at her and pulled away.

"What are you looking at? You're not supposed to open your eyes when you're kissing."

"But one eye is okay, winky?" He stared at her, laughing.

"Why are you opening your eyes at all?"

"Because I wanted to see you. And then I noticed *that* . . ."

He motioned with his chin to the sky behind her, so she turned around. She shivered as he put his arms around her waist from behind, his hands dangling just beneath her bikini line. Above Jenny's house was the most beautiful sunset she'd ever seen. A fireworks display of oranges and pinks surrounded by a dusky purple. The sight was as breathtaking as the exhilaration bubbling through her, having finally reached this moment with Jake. This perfect moment that was everything she'd hoped for and more.

"It was a sunset just like this that made me want to start painting. I was seven or eight. We were at my cabin in Wisconsin, and I couldn't believe how cool it was, so I asked my mom to take a picture of it and buy me some paint. I haven't seen one as nice since then until now."

"Yeah? It is pretty. But it could be just the company."

"Could be." He kissed her cheek lightly and then grabbed her hand. "We've only got a few minutes. Let's sit down and watch it set."

Sarah let him lead her to a grassy area. He pulled her onto his lap. She was so happy to be with him, she didn't even mind the thick, sticky grass blades poking her bare legs.

"It's so beautiful." She gazed up, pressing her back into his chest. "So how did the painting turn out?"

"Not bad, actually. It's still hanging at my house. My mom framed it with the actual picture in the corner. You should come see it sometime." He squeezed her knee.

"I'd love to." *Finally!*

But her happy moment was interrupted by a very unhappy Dalia. "*There you are.* Sarah, we need to talk. Sorry Jake." She held her hand out to help Sarah up.

Sarah looked back at Jake and reluctantly grabbed it. While she was being dragged across the lawn, she tried to create a perfect mental record of every moment that led up to this one. It started when she made a s'more. She took a bite, which she hadn't noticed left a sticky string of marshmallow hanging from her lip. And that's when Jake asked if it was good. She said, "So good." Then he asked if he could try it, and when she said sure, he kissed her, and then said, "You're right. It *is* so good." In front of everyone, which was a very good sign. Their kiss invited lots of attention, so as soon as they could, they snuck off to the gazebo where they'd been making out and talking ever since. Until Dalia came along.

Dalia led her into the pool house, past cubbies filled with rolled towels. Dalia sat on the long wooden bench that separated two sets of full-size wooden lockers while Sarah took the opportunity to change out of her bathing suit.

"What the fuck, Sarah? You said Ella and Shawn didn't really know each other. Really? Their families go to the same church? He was her camp boyfriend and her first kiss?"

"No one ever said they didn't know each other. I said I didn't know if he'd remembered her, and I stand by that." She quickly reached for her shorts.

"Going to camp every summer with the two of them? It's hard to believe you didn't remember they used to *make out* all the time."

"It was *years* ago! And there were a lot more people at camp than just those two. Besides, I was way more interested in Dick Johnson than I was in Shawn or Ella."

"Dick Johnson?" Dalia laughed, thankfully breaking the tension.

"I know. He was really cute, though. But the kissing thing? I honestly didn't remember it at first. Looking back, it hardly seemed like a big deal."

"Well, she better not get any ideas, I swear to god. She will be very sorry if she goes after him." Dalia puffed her chest out like a street thug prepping for a fight.

"Dalia, I think you're overreacting. They were *children*. Think of someone you had a crush on in middle school and tell me his new girlfriend should feel threatened by you. Seriously, you're acting crazy, and you should stop. Here. Put this in the hamper." Sarah tossed her the towel.

"Overreacting? I saw the way he looked at her, all that *great day* stuff, and the whole marshmallow thing. And their thighs were *touching*, Sarah!"

"I don't know *what* you're talking about," Sarah lied. "But *I'm* pretty sure your mom's magazine would tell you that there's nothing hot about a jealous chick. So, if you're worried, I suggest you keep that to yourself and just do what the magazine said. What was that second step? Figure out the kind of woman he wants? Maybe start *listening* to him. Maybe not call him *boring* if he doesn't feel like drinking. Maybe come up with some non-drinking things to do. Maybe just try to be a little, I don't know, sweeter," she counseled her, trying to be delicate, yet firm. It suddenly dawned on her that this might work. She could be Switzerland and may the best girl win.

"Sweeter." Dalia raised one knee up onto the bench and rested her chin on it. "Yeah, I don't think so. That's just not me."

"Then maybe Shawn isn't the guy for you. Because you heard all that talk about not wanting to party all the time, and you saw how he reacted when you told him he needs a drink. If you like what that article has to say, maybe you should *try* it. And if you want to find out the kind of woman he wants, you need to *listen* to him."

"I know you guys are like *best friends*, but maybe you don't know him like I do. That choir boy thing he was doing today, it's all bullshit. He likes to get a little freaky," she said, ignoring Sarah's suggestion completely.

"So what? Liking to get freaky does not mean it's not important for someone to be sweet to him. Speaking of freaky, has he even tried to have sex with you?"

"Well, no, but that's because *I* haven't—"

Sarah interrupted. "The more I think about it, the more sure I am that there's a reason for that, and it may not be because you've been withholding it. How many guys that good-looking are virgins their senior year?"

"Okay, okay, I'll think about it. Sorry, Sarah."

That shut her up. Sarah could see the wheels turning in her mind, like suddenly her whole plan was turned on its ear. She'd had *becoming the woman he wants* as a goal "in progress." But maybe she was starting to understand that she hadn't been doing a very good job of it.

They left the pool house and each other on good enough terms, and Sarah walked back to the grassy area where she'd been manhandled away from Jake. She was disappointed but not surprised that he was gone, as she'd doubted he'd be sitting there by himself in the dark. But she was really upset once it was confirmed that he'd left the party altogether. Across the pool, she found Tori sitting by herself.

"There you are." Tori eagerly motioned for Sarah to join her on a lounge chair. It was quite a different scene from when she and Jake had first disappeared. The pool, once overflowing with people, now stood empty, casting a peaceful turquoise hue onto the surrounding landscape, the dance music replaced by the song of crickets.

"I have a *message* for you," Tori said, her eyes percolating. "I talked to Jake, and he wanted me to tell you that he had to leave and to say bye."

"*Really?* Tell me everything. *Verbatim*, please." Sarah squeezed her palms together and rested them against her mouth.

"Okay. So he said, and I quote, 'I have to get some guys home, so can you tell Sarah bye for me?'"

"That's not verbatim. Start from the beginning."

"Okay. From the top. And one and two." She snapped her fingers like they were about to start a dance routine. A tipsy grin spread across her face. Sarah gently palmed her fist.

"Sorry," she said, laughing. "Okay. So, he came up to me and said Tori and I said what's up Jake and he said can you do me a favor and I said sure. And that's when he said I have to get some guys home, so can you tell Sarah bye for me. And I said sure. And then he started to walk away. And then he turned around and said do you think she'd mind if you gave me her phone number and I thought about it and then I said I don't feel comfortable doing that and then he left."

"Are you serious?" Sarah's huge grin deflated, as if someone had let the air out of it.

"Hmmmm . . . wait. No. That's *not* what I said. I *said* let me get a pen, which I did. And then I wrote down your number, and then I gave it to him."

"Really?" Sarah squealed. "Thank you, Tori." She threw her arms around her, planting her face in Tori's sweaty tequila hair. Tipsy Tori was usually just an exaggeration of her normal self, so it wasn't surprising that she went on to give herself props.

"Thank me for what?"

"For giving him my number."

"And . . ."

"Oh my god. And for always having a pen."

"You owe me, you know. Who else would have had a pen and paper in their *beach bag*?"

"Just you, oh queen o' preparedness." Sarah bowed to her. "Oh my god! Do you know what this means?"

"That you're lucky to have me."

"Well, that, and that this might be for real! *Finally!* It took, what. Nine whole months of flirting?" Sarah looked up to the sky counting.

"Well, I hope you used a condom, because in another nine months you might be celebrating *something else*." Tori used both hands to demonstrate a pregnancy bump.

"We did not have sex. But I'm pretty sure we're going to. He's like the perfect second guy to have sex with. Get the first time over with, with someone you don't care about that much, then you know more what you're doing for someone you really like. Why isn't that a thing?"

"Should be." Tori fully reclined her lounge chair. "Maybe Dave will be my number two. Wow. Lay your chair back, Sarah. You have got to see these stars."

Sarah joined her at her vantage point, and they took in the starry sky silently for a moment.

"Hey Tori. Guess what?"

"What?"

"I think I have a boyfriend."

"You're welcome."

19

"**WHAT IS THAT NOISE?**" Jake mumbled into Sarah's mouth.

"Mmmmm . . . acorns, maybe."

Jake's lips moved down to her neck, and the tapping noise got louder. "Can't be acorns. It's June."

"What are you, a botanist . . . or what's that . . . tree person . . . an arborist?" she said breathily. She was lying on the slightly reclined car seat, eyes closed, fingers tracing the length of Jake's back as his lips brushed against her earlobe. It was two thirty in the morning. They'd just gotten back from a midnight showing of a Led Zeppelin rockumentary and were sitting in Sarah's driveway, listening to the soundtrack, among other things.

"Shhh," he whispered into her neck. At the third, more aggressive round of tapping, Sarah's eyes popped open. She gasped as she saw a shadowy figure hovering outside the steamy car window. She broke away from Jake and wiped away a bit of fog, just big enough to reveal the identity of the shadowy figure: her father. Somewhere between terrified and relieved, and rapidly approaching mortified, she righted her shirt situation. But before getting out of the car, she used her finger to draw a big smiley face on the fogged glass. And once she saw him smile back, she opened the door.

"Hi, Mr. Blake." Jake leaned apologetically toward the passenger door.

"Bye Jake." Jason Blake opened his hand and snapped it shut just once.

"Bye Jake!" Sarah grinned the grinniest grin in the history of grinning, which she couldn't contain even as she faced her dad.

"So . . . good night?" he whispered. He put his arm around Sarah more firmly than usual and scooted her into the dimly lit kitchen. The house was so quiet that the hum of the refrigerator seemed intrusively loud.

"Dad, it was *uh-mazing*."

"Uh oh." He peered into her eyes. "You've got it bad for that kid."

"Well, *yeah*, that too. But I was talking about the movie. You should have come."

"Well, *that* would have been awkward . . . especially that part at the end." His round face contorted into horrified amusement.

"*Dad!*" Sarah laughed so hard she snorted. "I meant instead of Jake! I would have loved to see it with you. But you were all 'It's at midnight and Sunday, and I have to work,' so when Jake called—"

"Lesson learned." He put his hand on her shoulder. "So, you know I have to give you a little bit of talking to, right?"

"Yes, Dad."

Strung across the refrigerator was a thin, magnetic wire displaying family pictures secured with colorful clothespins. Parrots on their shoulders in Hawaii, tubing in Wisconsin Dells, horseback riding in the Grand Canyon. Sarah's dad unclipped his favorite, the two of them holding ice cream cones on their front porch. He set it on the counter and touched Sarah's five- year-old chin with his thumb.

"You see this little girl with that big smile? I want you to love her like I do." His eyes reddened around the edges. "You'll never understand how much that is until you have a daughter of your own, but please treat her well, Sarah, she deserves it."

"Thanks, Dad." She wrapped her arms around him. His three a.m. shadow prickled her cheek.

"I know this is just how life goes, but I wish ice cream still made you this happy."

"Ice cream *does* make me that happy, Dad. Want some?" She opened the freezer and pulled out a pint of Chunky Monkey. He looked at the 2:47 displayed on the microwave and sighed.

"What the hell." He quietly grabbed two spoons and they ate right out of the carton, just like they did when Sarah was a child. But the very adult talking-to continued. While he didn't seem upset with her, Sarah sensed something different in him. Something about him seeing her in the car with Jake seemed to instantly change him. Change them. The mature conversation juxtaposed against their childhood ritual felt like a transformative moment. A bridge being crossed from past to future, from childhood to adulthood. They were on that bridge together, suddenly aware that they were much closer to the end than to the beginning.

"So, just be careful," he said. "And selective, and you know, self-respect and all that. And I know I'm like a broken record with this, but I have to know that you will come to us if there's *ever* a problem, no matter how uncomfortable it might be, because—"

"Small problems become big problems when you try to hide them. I will Dad, I promise." Unexpected tears welled up in her eyes, and she had to diffuse them. "And you don't have to worry because I've listened to *everything* you've told me. You know, like I should give away *all* the milk cuz then I'll get free cows or something, and how I should put all my eggs in one basket . . . and something about fish. Oh! There's only one fish in the sea. So when I find it, I should hold on tight no matter what, because, well, there's only one. Yes Dad, I've listened to *every word.*"

"Glad you've been paying attention." He laughed. "There is something that's making me feel like I swallowed a goldfish, though." He paused. "It's the tattoos." His voice was pained with hypocrisy, because he had two. His frat letters on his ankle, and another he wouldn't talk about. Sarah opened her mouth to point it out. "I know, and I know it's a small thing, but he's not even old enough, and it just seems a little *shortsighted.*"

"Well, Father, I think I can make you feel better about that. He works at his cousin's tattoo parlor, and you kinda have to have a tat or two to work there, so let's call it a uniform. And his cousin did them, so he wasn't like *breakin' the law.* And he wants to open his own shop one day." She clinked his spoon away as he went for the last chocolate chunk. "He talks about his future more than any other guy I know. He's like Forrest Gump's shrimp boat buddy."

"Bubba? Really." His eyebrows looked to be wrestling with two opposing perceptions of the kid that had his daughter's attention—

Sarah offered him the last spoonful of ice cream hugging the edge of the carton. And with that, the late hour finally caught up to him.

"Okay, that's it for me." He started up the stairs.

"One more thing, Dad. Don't you tell me you should never judge a book by its cover?"

"No! You got it *all wrong*. You should *always* judge a book by its cover. Goodnight, Sarah."

"Goodnight, Dad."

20

"JAKE'S COMING TODAY, RIGHT?"

Hearing how excited Jenny was for her reminded Sarah how much she loved Jenny. But at the same time, Jenny was taking up time she didn't have.

"Yep!" she replied quickly. Still wrapped in a towel, Sarah cradled the phone tightly between her shoulder and ear. The cord, stretched to maximum capacity as it barely reached her mirror, made putting on mascara very risky. At any moment, the phone could snap back and cause a makeup disaster. She had to hang up ASAP.

"So, that means he's your boyfriend?" Jenny's pitch rose with each question, along with Sarah's impatience.

"I think so!"

"*Sarah*, aren't you *so excited?*"

"Yep!"

"Oh my god. Okay, Dalia said to tell you we'll be there in ten minutes, and to tell you to tell Ella that we'll meet at that picnic place in twenty minutes."

"Okay, bye Jenny." Sarah looked at her watch. She didn't have to call Ella. They'd already told her what time to meet and were right on schedule—assuming Sarah could choose an outfit in time.

This was a very big day. No human or magazine could argue that seven phone calls plus three dates in a week, *plus* two meet the parents didn't equal official couple status. It probably also meant that today's outfit called for a little more focus on undergarments. Sarah had bought a black-and-purple lace bra set at Victoria's Secret six months earlier that she'd been saving for the right moment. And it felt like that moment had finally arrived.

The cool breeze came through her window, knocking over a framed picture of the girls. The fickle Midwest weather apparently didn't care that it was June, as it ushered out the scorching heat and replaced it with a crisp sixty-five degrees. So, the highlight of her outfit would have to be hidden under layers: a Soundgarden T-shirt, a flannel, and jeans. It would be a nice, unexpected surprise for Jake, if he got that far, she decided as she slipped on her Vans.

It was also a big day for Dalia, as it marked the official debut of her sweeter side. The big reveal, she'd only shared with Sarah, was to take place at the welcome back cookout she'd offered to host at Ella's apartment complex. She needed some time to practice, she'd said. To figure out *how*, exactly, to be nicer. Sarah pictured her reading *Ladies' Home Journal* or *Good Housekeeping*, as she doubted her mom's life manuals would offer anything useful. She couldn't wait to see what Dalia had come up with.

"We've arrived!" Dalia announced, one hand pointing high in the air, the other lugging one side of a densely packed cooler through the grass leading to the picnic table at Ella's. They still had thirty minutes before the guys would get there, and though Ella was the guest of honor, Dalia was the host. So, she'd chosen the guest list and the start time. Curiously, though, when they arrived at the table, Ella wasn't alone.

"And looks like so has everyone else," Dalia said, looking at the guys sitting around Ella. The empty beer bottles on the table provided an unsettling timestamp. The question was, did someone get the start time wrong or did Ella arrange this pre-party without them. She better not have—Ella had already committed one foul with the thigh-touching incident. A pre-arranged pre-party, without regard to Sarah's or Dalia's feelings, would be a flagrant second.

Ella was seated between Shawn and Dave, and across from Rob and Mike. She turned her eyes toward the girls, but not her head, as she was in the middle of delivering the punchline of a story. "So, I turned on the light, and it was a *scorpion . . . in my bed!*"

"That is *crazy*," Dave said.

"Right? I was scared to death when I first moved there, but you get used to it. The snakes, though . . . *never.*" She shuddered as she swung her legs over the bench.

"Hi guys." Her ponytail bounced around as she hugged each of the girls. "Welcome to the luxurious International Village Apartments. Oh my god. Did you notice all those dumb signs with all the beautiful people smiling?" She lowered her voice. "International Village. It's not just living, it's a *lifestyle*. What the heck does that mean? A picnic table, a fire pit, and a liquor store. That's all it has. It's more like—" she put her beer bottle to her mouth and used it as a microphone "—International Village. Lifestyles of the Rich and Famous, minus the rich, the famous, and the fun."

It wasn't even funny, but the guys all laughed heartily, which Sarah found straight up annoying. The whole situation felt just a little too fast, considering Sarah had invested years in these relationships. Dalia didn't react and instead went right into host mode, bringing Shawn on as co-host.

"Shawn, what are we thinking? How about we put this in the shade?"

Shawn had just opened a beer but dutifully got up and helped.

"What the heck did you put in here?" He grunted as he picked up the cooler.

"Pretty much everything we need for a *great day*." Dalia couldn't see his face, but Sarah could. And his curled lip told her he didn't care for the reference.

Sarah had just opened her first beer when a familiar smell crept in. A pair of strong hands began to massage her shoulders. "Need anything?" Jake asked.

"*Hi!* Yes. For you to never, ever stop what you're doing right now." She let her head and shoulders slump forward and melted into his fingers. "And you can tell us what you think of *these*." She pointed to their new fake IDs that she'd laid out to show everyone. Dalia had gotten them from a cook at Gatto's. Sarah thought they were perfect and planned to use them at the liquor store. But Jake was not impressed.

"I don't know if you want to risk it, babe. It's kind of shoddy." He held hers in front of him, inspecting it front and back with his artist's eye. "Look. It's crooked in the laminate. And there's a shadow in the corner," he pointed out. "And they spelled *Indiana* wrong."

"Really?" Sarah grabbed it out of his hand.

"No." He laughed. "But I wouldn't try it if I were you. You've got college to think about, and I don't think you would do well in jail."

"Yeah, orange is definitely not my color. But I could totally rock one of those black-and-white striped prison outfits."

"You would never survive prison," Dalia said as she tried to light the coals, the brisk breeze defeating each strike of the match.

"Dalia, for once I agree with you one hundred percent," Tori nodded. "Here, I've got that." She took a fireplace lighter out of her purse.

"Why not? I can be tough," Sarah argued. Everyone, including Jenny, laughed at that one. But no one argued when Dalia said the same.

"I could handle jail, if I had to."

"This is something you've thought about?" Stacey asked.

"When you have a dad who's been in jail, you think about these things," she said as she laid out hot dogs, ketchup, and French onion dip. "You know, when I was little, when my parents were still together, my mom told me my dad had to go away for a while. And she told me the truth, that he was in jail because he took something that didn't belong to him, which I found out later was a car . . ."

Dalia went on to share a very personal story—one she hadn't ever shared about a time she attempted to steal a stuffed elephant from a department store. Somehow, at the age of four, she'd figured out that stealing meant jail, and jail was where her daddy was. So if she wanted to see her daddy, she had to find a way to get to jail. The whole thing ended in tears, though, when, despite Dalia's cries of "Take me to jail to see my daddy," the cashier told her they couldn't take her to jail. Maybe Dalia thought it was funny. Or maybe this *sharing* was somehow part of her plan to be sweeter.

The guys, including Shawn, didn't seem to know what to make of it—there was a lot of squirming and not a lot of eye contact—and the story threatened to change the general vibe of the afternoon. Dalia seemed to immediately regret telling it, as evidenced by her own squirming and lack of eye contact. Eventually, Jenny broke the awkward silence.

"Oh my god, Dalia, that's like the saddest story ever." She placed both hands firmly on her face, leaving red marks on her cheeks.

"Yeah, my mom was so embarrassed she made me stand with my nose in the corner when we got home. She laughs about it now, though." She tugged at the pink stone charm on her necklace. "So yeah. Shawn, you want to help grill the hot dogs?"

21

DALIA ACTED AS IF she and Shawn were the hosting couple, gently telling him what to do, and brushing her hand low across his back as she scooted by him. She used the term *we* every chance she got. *I think we should turn those over,* as he poked the hot dogs around the grill. *Do you think we should add more coals? We should see if anyone needs anything,* each *we* coupled with a hand on his shoulder or touch of his forearm. He looked like a middle-age husband appeasing his wife as he took her suggestions, though it was obvious to everyone he thought he should be sitting around with the rest of the guys.

Sarah wasn't sure *any* of Dalia's behavior met the criteria for sweet, from Shawn's perspective anyway, but she wasn't going to interfere. So, she turned on her "Summer Fun" mixtape, because it was a "Sweet Home Alabama" kind of day—sitting outside and drinking beers. Until the beers ran out and they were forced to decide whether to try out their IDs.

"I know they're not perfect, but I think they'll work," Sarah said upon returning from a brief recon mission at the store. "It's just one guy there. Some young Indian guy. With a very big nose."

"Oh my god, he has like the biggest nose you've ever *seen*." Dalia mocked him, forming a big triangle over her nose with her hand, but then awkwardly tried to pull it back. "I feel so bad for him."

"I doubt he knows what an Indiana driver's license even looks like," Sarah said. "And I've got all my information memorized."

"If you say so," Tori handed her a crisp ten. "I'll take a four pack of Zima."

"And a twelve of Miller Lite," Mike said. "And a six pack of Corona." Rob stood up. "And whatever Jenny wants." He handed Sarah a twenty, a grinning Jenny behind him.

"Hold on, you guys. I can't carry everything."

"I'm coming," Dalia said. "Jenny, come with us, I have an idea. And sorry guys, but we're not taking orders—we're just getting beers."

The girls cut through the wooded area and followed the narrow dirt path that led to the liquor store. A thorny bush grabbed Sarah's calf, leaving little burrs stuck to her jeans. She ran to the parking lot and propped her leg up on a fire hydrant. "You guys, wait. I have to look for ticks."

"Sarah, those aren't ticks, they're *burrs*. And you're wearing *jeans*!"

"One of them might be!" She inspected her leg, removing them as quickly as she could confirm they weren't ticks. But not quick enough for Dalia.

"Oh my god, can you hurry?" Dalia picked off a burr. Sarah smacked her hand away. She knew Dalia didn't want to leave Shawn and Ella alone for long, but her tick situation was much more important. To her, anyway.

"Stop it! I have to look at each one. So, what is your plan?"

"Jake's right. There's no way these IDs are going to work. So, we're gonna ask to use the bathroom." She folded her tiny T-shirt into a tinier half shirt.

"And then what?"

"I've got it, Sarah. You just stay here *picking your ticks*, but in no more than ten minutes, come to the store and wait for us outside."

Sarah didn't understand how the plan would work, or she never would have gone along with it. But the plan, as she knew it, was that Dalia and Jenny would walk in first and ask to use the bathroom, and all Sarah had to do was wait for them to come out. Then she would go in, look around for ten minutes, buy plastic cups and ice, and meet them back at the table. Which she did. And somehow, by the time she got back to the table, Dalia and Jenny had two cases of beer.

"These beers are warm!" Dave spit out the first sip.

"Yeah, sorry, their refrigerator was broken. But we have ice," Dalia said as Sarah walked up. Sarah looked down at the bags she was holding, confused as to what she'd just participated in.

"So, the IDs worked?" Jake asked.

"They didn't even ask for them. Sarah just flirted with the guy. She might have taken it a little too far, but hey. It worked."

"Really," Jake said. "What did you say to him?" He shifted uncomfortably, almost imperceptibly. Just the tiniest shoulder twitch, but Sarah caught it.

"Nothing, I—" She started to defend herself, but Dalia interrupted.

"Don't worry, Jake. He just *kind of* got the idea that we would hang out with him and his friends later. So, if he comes *over* here, we are *outta* here. He'll be looking for a date."

Sarah looked at Dalia, while she sensed Jake looking at her. He didn't say anything, but she could tell he thought it was shitty to lead the poor guy on, even in the pursuit of beers. So, Sarah got him alone the second she could. "Can we take a walk?"

It was dusky and chilly now, and Jake's demeanor was making it worse. He wasn't being a jerk, but there wasn't a lot of warmth as they sat down on a bench just between the picnic area and the parking lot.

"What happened to summer?" Sarah shivered and curled up in the stiff crook of his arm.

"So, what's up?" he asked.

"Jake, none of that happened."

"Good." His chilly attitude warmed immediately. He pulled her close and kissed her temple. "It didn't sound like something you'd do. So, how'd you really get the beers?"

"*I don't know.* All I did was buy ice and cups. I wasn't even in the store the same time they were," she said, exasperated. "Dalia and Jenny went in first, and Dalia said they were going to ask to use the bathroom. And she told me to wait till she came out, and to go in after they did, look around for ten minutes, and then buy cups and ice. And that's what I did."

"So, they stole it." Jake concluded, quite sure of himself. He gently pulled Sarah's knees toward him to face her.

"What? Stop it." She leaned away from him. "Jenny would

never do that. And I really don't think Dalia would either. And they weren't even in the store that long, and they didn't have anything when they came out, and—"

"And somehow showed up with two *warm* cases of beer, and you with cups and ice. Refrigerator broken? How did she know you'd need cups and ice before she went in? Think about it."

She thought for a second . . . and thought he was wrong. Probably.

"Dalia wouldn't do that. You heard the story about her dad. She's never told us that, because that's embarrassing to her, and I know that she wants to make sure her life is nothing like the life she's grown up with."

"Yeah, but it's also *normal* to her, Sarah. Maybe you need to be careful around those two."

"Not Jenny. She never does anything wrong. She *does* do whatever Dalia tells her, but that's because she trusts her, but that's another situation. Okay, smarty guy, how did they do it?"

"Think about it."

"What do *you* think? They grabbed them out of the back when they went to the bathroom? But how would they get them out, hmmm? I told you, they didn't have anything when they came out."

"You're getting there, but you could never be a detective."

"Or a criminal, apparently."

"Yeah, no way. So, Dalia and Jenny ask to use the bathroom, and they ask you to wait till they come outside."

"Yeah . . ."

"And while they're back there, what do they do?"

"According to you, they steal the beer."

"Sarah . . ." He chuckled, shaking his head.

"*I don't know!* But I'm guessing not use the bathroom?"

"Ding ding ding, they did not use the bathroom. They *pretended* to use the bathroom while they propped open the door in the back so they could go in *through* the back when you distracted him when you bought the ice."

"Oh my god, I'm so stupid." She put her hand over her mouth. "That's exactly what they did."

"Hey, I think she's got it! Don't feel bad." He tucked a runaway hair behind her ear. "You were just too close to it to see it. The more messed up part is how she told everyone you made that guy think you liked him just to get something from him. What if I believed her?"

The sincerity in his eyes made Sarah feel safe. Like he really liked her and wanted their relationship to be built on good things. It also made her feel like it wasn't safe to be as close to Dalia as she was, as the answer to his question wasn't a good one.

"She'd just say what's his problem, it was a good thing, because at least we got beers." She sighed, covering her face with her hands.

Putting it together, Sarah knew what Dalia had been thinking. They couldn't run out of beers, or the night would end. And Dalia couldn't take credit for the flirting herself because that would look bad to Shawn, so she blamed it on Sarah. And if Jake was upset, he'd be overreacting. It wasn't unusual for Dalia to do those kinds of things. Though they were usually harmless, Sarah always called her out on them. And when she was called out, Dalia would try to be better. Or she would be there for the girls in some amazing way. Or Sarah would end up feeling sorry for her for something. The pattern had been going on long enough, though, that the shitty things were dismissed as *that's just Dalia*. It wasn't fun hearing an outside perspective, as she knew she should be more upset than she was. But she didn't want to think about that right now.

"Well, I'll tell you what's disturbing to me is that you figured it out so fast. What does that say about you? You've obviously got the mind of a criminal."

"Yeah, but I use it for good." He put both hands behind Sarah's head and kissed her. "Now let's go drink some *hot* beers."

"Haha, you're so punny."

The bonfire was glowing from a distance as they walked back to the group. The gathering had moved to the ground, and couples had paired off. Tori was laughing at something Dave had just whispered to her. Sarah elbowed Jake in the arm and pointed at the two pairs of entwined shoes, attached to Jenny and Rob, sticking out from underneath a blanket. Shawn and Mike were sitting next to each other, beers in hand, staring at the fire. And then there was Stacey, with a blanket all to herself.

"I feel like someone should be playing a guitar or something." Sarah motioned for Jake to join the guys and sat down next to Stacey.

"No. Mike and Dave were singing earlier. Be happy you missed it," she said. "Where'd you two run off to?"

"Jake was upset that Dalia said I was flirting with that guy just to get beers, so I had to explain what happened," she whispered. "And now he thinks Dalia *stole* them." Sarah had to run the theory by someone else before she accepted it.

"Of course she stole them. Refrigerator broken? Come on. Does she think we're stupid?" She pulled her cardigan closed around her neck and crossed her arms.

While Sarah was feeling stupid next to Stacey, Dalia and Ella returned with sticks for marshmallow roasting.

"So, Ella, have you thought about a job yet? We can get you one at Gatto's if you want. You'd have to start as a hostess, but you could work up to waiting tables from there. That's where the good money is. Right Shawn?"

Shawn looked up from his conversation with Mike.

"Uh . . . yeah. You definitely want to be waiting tables."

"Would you really? Thank you!" Ella popped a marshmallow in her mouth.

"For sure," Dalia said. "Stop in when you can, and we'll introduce you to George. Oh, and ladies, there is that cheerleading matter we need to talk about. I don't know if Sarah told you, but the flyer on our squad is moving, and we need someone to fill her spot."

"Oh my god, yes!" Ella clapped excitedly.

"Good. Then it's settled. We need someone your size, especially for what I have planned for the state competition. Plan on coming to the gym next week to practice with us."

"That sounds so fun!" Ella said. "And thank you for this—my apartment-living tutorial," she said, smiling broadly.

"No problem. We take care of each other, Ella." Dalia placed a marshmallow on her stick, and then one on Ella's. "Okay everyone, roasting time." Dalia took Ella by the arm and sat with her next to the fire.

"Let's have a marshmallow toast. To new friends." She tapped her marshmallow against Ella's.

"And old," Shawn said as he scooted next to Ella.

The three of them put their marshmallows in the fire together. Sarah felt a sense of dread as she watched a single flame engulf all three. But a *more* dreadful situation quickly grabbed her attention. "Uh oh. Look!" She pointed to the path in the direction of the liquor store. Four Indian men were headed in their direction. "Shit. Someone grab our stuff. We'll meet you by the cars. Jenny, let's go!" Dalia shouted. "Sarah, you need to go. Now," Jake insisted. "Meet me in the parking lot."

Sarah, Dalia, and Jenny ran to the cars, leaving the rest to deal with the liquor store fallout. After several nerve-wracking minutes, Sarah saw Jake emerge from the clearing. She ran over to him and threw her arms around his neck. "So?" she whispered in his ear.

He told her it was anticlimactic—the men looked around, and when they didn't see the girls, they left without saying a word. And while everyone else thought they were looking for a date, Stacey and Jake knew the truth—that they figured out Dalia had stolen from them. Sarah and Jake shared a warm kiss goodnight. And as she made her way back to the girls' cars, she pondered Jake's words. Maybe he was right. Maybe she shouldn't spend so much time with Dalia. But that would not be so easy.

22

WHILE DALIA WAS PANICKING over the thought of getting arrested, she went into full-on frenzy mode when she realized two things. One, she prematurely ended a night she'd expected to spend with Shawn. And two, she just created the exact situation she'd been trying to avoid. Shawn and Ella alone together, especially at the *end* of the night.

As the rest of the girls showed up at the cars, she caught a glimpse of Shawn and Ella off in the distance. They were walking slowly out of the clearing, transforming into silhouettes as they headed in the direction of Ella's apartment. The caustic feeling in her stomach was in charge now, and she knew what she had to do. She had to get the girls to leave and pretend she was stranded there. If they left without her, she could tell Shawn she needed a ride home.

"You sure?" Stacey asked. "We can go get food and come back if you want more time."

"Yes, I'm sure. Now *go!*" Dalia whispered loudly, practically shutting the car door on Jenny's foot.

"Good luck," Tori called out as she pulled away.

Once Dalia was alone, she was completely disturbed by what she saw. She ducked behind a tree to assess the situation. Shawn and Ella, while not touching, were definitely violating each other's personal space. They were both leaning on his car, laughing and smiling. The good news was that they were facing outward. The bad news was that their shoulders were about an inch away from touching. Shawn had his arms folded while Ella told a lively story, complete with lots of hand gestures. Shawn laughed; Ella looked up at him and smiled. Wishful thinking told her there was a possibility that it was just a friendly conversation—after all, they weren't kissing. But she knew better. She watched for a few minutes when it dawned on her that the longer it went on, the stronger the possibility they might kiss, and then there'd be a real problem. She had no choice but to intervene immediately.

As disturbed and upset as she was, she found the competition very motivating. And now she was more determined than ever, ready to outsmart Ella at every turn, if that's what it came to. Waiting until she knew they couldn't see her, she slinked out from behind the trees.

"Hey! Where did everybody go?" she asked, feigning surprise that they were all gone.

"Everyone left," Ella said. "I thought you went with them."

"I ran back to get my sunglasses and now I can't find them.

We had two cars. They probably both thought I was going with the other one. Oh well. Shawn, can you give me a ride?"

"Um. I guess." He looked at Ella. "Sure."

Dalia and Shawn pulled out of the complex and turned down Elm Street, passing through the quaint streets of their tiny downtown. Past the coffee shop, the knitting shop, the ice cream place. Passing all the places she'd passed a thousand times, but never with Shawn. Somehow just being next to him, intoxicated by him and the smell of his new Saab, made her feel like she was seeing things for the first time. Everything was more beautiful, more vibrant, more inviting. Somehow being with Shawn made even the hardware store seem warm and cozy, like she could just cuddle up in it. He was *irresistible*. And she wanted more.

"Well, that was fun," she said.

"Yes it was. Those poor dudes. You guys ruined their night. That was *harsh*."

"Whatever. I'm sure at some point in their lives they did something to deserve it."

"And if they didn't? Isn't that bad karma?"

"Bad *karma*? I'm not worried about *karma*. The universe completely owes me after the shit it's laid on me."

"Whatever makes you feel better," he said as he flipped through radio stations. "It was nice of you to set that up for Ella, so maybe you're even for today." He chuckled.

"*Yeah!*" She laughed. "I feel bad for her. It sounds like her family is really messed up right now. And I just wanted to help," she said as she dug around in her purse. She pulled out her lip gloss and opened the lighted mirror. "That's why I told her to come to the restaurant and talk to George about a job."

"That's cool," Shawn said as they approached a red light. "You girls . . ."

Dalia turned from the mirror to see Shawn smiling and shaking his head at her.

"*What* you girls?"

"Always so worried about what you look like. Don't you know that guys don't care if your lipstick is perfect, or if you're wearing it at all? We don't care about those things."

"Yes you do."

"No we don't. We don't even *notice* it."

"Uh, not true, Shawn. You just think that because you only see us after we've already put in the effort. Trust me, you wouldn't be interested in us at all if you saw us with no makeup on. We *have* to wear it."

"That's what *you* think," he said. "You know what I think? I think you girls do it to yourselves. *You* are the ones putting pressure on each other—and *that* turns into pressure on yourselves."

"You think you're pretty smart, huh," she said, putting her purse by her feet. "Well I, for one, am *not* competing with other girls."

"Sure you aren't," he said dismissively as the light turned green.

"Wait! I have proof! Okay. Girls are boy crazy from like the day they're born. You sit there and do all your disgusting boy things, and we're still crazy about you. But you *boys* don't even look at us *girls* until we start wearing makeup. So there. I win." She clapped once and put her hands up in victory.

"You don't win anything, Dalia! You *girls* start wearing makeup literally the day you get your boobs. And *that's* the day we start paying attention. I rest my case."

"Wow. So, we've been wrong this whole time?" she asked as they laughed together.

Dalia, so loving this conversation, hoped that Shawn wasn't heading directly to her apartment. But it appeared that he was. They'd left the downtown area and were back in strip mallville, about a half mile from her apartment, when she started to panic, frantic to buy more time with him to show off her sweeter side. Progress was clearly being made, and she didn't want to interrupt the momentum. On an impulse, she asked him to pull into an empty parking lot, the site of a former gas station. It wasn't ideal, but she was out of options at this point.

"For what?" he asked.

"Do you mind? I just want to stay out for a few more minutes before I go back to my sad little apartment. Can we just sit and talk for a bit?"

"Fine. But not for long," Shawn said and then pulled in. He parked next to the boarded-up store and turned off the car. "So, what's up?" he asked tersely.

Dalia wasn't sure how to respond. He'd obviously hesitated before pulling in, and he sounded annoyed that she'd even asked. As the day's progress seemed to be vanishing from her grasp, she thought about how to hold onto it. *Be sweet,* she told herself. *Listen to him.*

"So, tell me more about this camp thing," she said.

"Camp? Why?"

"I don't know, years of Bible Camp? I just never thought of you as *that* religious of a guy. I knew you went to church, but—"

"Well, it's not really something I talk about. It's personal. I guess I don't talk about it because people might not understand. And I don't want to be, you know, misunderstood. It's better I keep it to myself."

"Right," she said. "Well, it sounds to me that by *not* talking about it, you're sort of being misunderstood, right?"

"I never thought about it that way. Maybe . . ."

"Do you know I've never once been inside a church?"

"Really? Not even for a wedding or something?"

"Nope. So, this can be your good deed. Please teach me?" she asked sincerely. "Tell me what you like about it."

"Okay . . . well, for one, it makes me feel safe. I don't worry too much about anything because I know it's in God's hands. Have you ever heard anyone say let go and let God? Whenever I'm upset or feel like something is out of my control, I say that to myself, and I feel better."

"Really? Must be nice." She stared out the windshield into the midnight sky. "Whenever I tell my mom I feel bad, she says *the world is a shitty place* or *get used to it.*" She was surprised when a tear fell from her eye. Shawn used his thumb to catch it.

"Dalia, that's a terrible way to live."

"Ooh, I'm sorry." She sniffed. "I have no idea where that came from."

"You don't have to be sorry. That's got to be hard for you."

"It's fine." Dalia leaned on his shoulder and breathed his soothing scent. "So, what else do you like about it?"

"Well, I have great friends there. They're different from the guys you see me with. Mike and those guys are great and all, but sometimes I get tired of the competitiveness. And the dumb gags and having to be *on* all the time. It gets old. I have a lot more in common with the guys at church. Things that are important to me that those guys would never understand."

"Like?"

"I shouldn't tell you this stuff," he muttered under his breath, as if he hadn't meant to say it out loud—which meant it had to be important.

"Well, now you have to," she said with a fervent curiosity.

But the second her curiosity was satisfied, she wished she'd never asked. Wished she could go back to a minute earlier when this *situation* didn't exist! Her body tensed against him as she tried to wrap her mind around what she'd just heard. Abstinence pledge? Was that a thing? He couldn't possibly be serious, could he? After an excruciatingly awkward pause, she pulled away from him and leaned her back against the door.

"You're kidding me, right? So, you're waiting until you're married?"

"Well, that's the plan, but it is *way* harder than I thought it would be."

That made her feel a *little* better—obviously he was having a hard time resisting *her*, so it wasn't hopeless. But it would require way more effort than she'd anticipated. She clenched her toes, trying to quietly ground herself as he went on.

"I want to at least hold out for the girl I know I'll marry someday."

"So, if you're engaged it's fine?"

"Not exactly. I'm saying it has to be someone I would want to marry, if the circumstances called for it. And that would only happen when we both decide each other is *the one*." He stared at her blankly, making it impossible to get a read on what it meant for her—which was extremely irritating.

"But blow jobs are fine? So, you're just like a *taker*, that means." She reverted right back to the snarky Dalia she was trying so hard to suppress.

"A *taker*? I'm not a . . . see, this is why I don't talk about it. You know what, never mind," he said. The keys jingled as he turned the ignition.

"Wait." Dalia tried to rein it in when she realized this could be a make-or-break moment for them. It had to be a *make*. "I'm not judging you. I'm just trying to understand. Can you at least tell me why?"

"Well, okay. But just so you'll understand." He let out a groany sigh. "I was taught that sex is a magical gift that God has given us. This *gift,* though, can cause a lot of problems—but those problems only happen outside of marriage. *In* marriage, those problems don't exist. And the cool part is, if you wait for the person you'll spend the rest of your life with, then you two, and only you two, will have shared this magical gift together."

Dalia hung on his every word.

"You may think it's weird, but it's how I was raised, and it makes perfect sense to me."

"No. *That* doesn't sound weird at *all*." She leaned close to him. Her breath bathed his neck as she spoke. "It actually sounds kind of sexy, when you put it that way."

"Right?"

"My only thing is, don't you want to *try* the merchandise before you buy it?" she asked as she slid her fingertips along his thigh.

"There are other ways to try the merchandise," he said, laughing. "But like I said, it's more about not marrying someone for the wrong reason—*and* wanting the two of us to have only been with each other. I couldn't be with someone who has been with someone else."

He smiled and nodded, seemingly to himself, almost proudly, like this made him a good person or something. Better than her, maybe. Which made Dalia think this would be a good time for *her* to do a little sharing.

"Well, Shawn, you're not the only one who's waiting."

"What are you *talking* about?" He laughed almost snobbishly.

"You think I'm gonna give this up to just anyone?" She sat back and hoisted up her chest.

"You're saying you've never had sex."

"Never."

"Now *you're* the one who's got to be kidding *me*," he said with a self-satisfied grin on his face. She knew this should piss her off. But somehow, it steeled her resolve.

"*Hey!*" She jabbed him on the shoulder.

"Well, you seem like you know what you're doing. I just assumed—"

"I'm going to take that as a compliment, but you assumed *wrong*. I know I'm worth waiting for. Besides, my mom got knocked up with me when she was seventeen, and she's been paying for it ever since. Raising me on her own, guy after guy in her life, and the only one she ever loved is my dad, who completely blew her off, because of me."

"Where is he now?" he asked flatly, as if it was more of an obligation to ask than actual interest. And then he checked his watch, which she didn't like *at all*. But she wasn't about to let it deter her.

"Who knows? He comes around every couple of years when he needs money and then he leaves and breaks her heart again. And then she's *my* problem. And I've always thought—well, and she always *says*—that if she'd just never gotten pregnant, they'd still be together. I guess they were really happy until I came along."

"See, that's what I'm talking about. Maybe they *were* meant to be together but then you—"

He stopped and hung his head for a moment.

Dalia knew he'd come close to saying something terrible. About her. Her entire existence. *But then you came along and ruined everything* is how that sentence was gonna go. She could tell he felt bad for even thinking it, which obviously meant he cared about her. And she was pretty sure she could get him to make it up to her. She stared out the windshield, blinking several times, and then sniffed as she ever so slightly turned down the corners of her mouth. And just as she'd hoped, he pulled her in for a hug. She folded into him.

"I'm sorry," he said as he held her.

There he was . . . the protective Shawn. The one she couldn't get enough of.

"It's fine. I know what you were going to say, and you're right," she said as she lingered in his warmth. "You know, it's hard to believe that we were brought up completely opposite, but we both made the same decision. It's pretty amazing if you ask me."

As she slid her hand down his chest, she felt his heart jumping. *Instinct* entered her mind, and now it seemed easy. All she ever had to do to make him want her was to get him alone. Draping one leg over his, she began to unzip. But he stopped her with a firm *no*. Disappointment swelled inside her—until he said, "Hang on."

Shawn guided her to the passenger seat and then moved over to her side. Sliding the seat into its fully reclined position, he stared into her eyes as he pressed his chest against hers.

"My turn," he said.

It was the first time Shawn returned the favor, his mouth bringing her to places she didn't know existed. She stared at the top of his head and anchored herself, gripping his shoulders while her bare foot pressed against the frigid windshield. She couldn't believe what was happening, couldn't imagine sex could be better than this. It was so incredible that, just for a second, she didn't care if she ever had sex with him. But then she remembered that in Shawn's world, sex meant commitment. And she had to have it. The whole thing.

After an immeasurable amount of time, Dalia returned the favor. And with the click of the ignition, it was over. Shawn continued the drive to her apartment.

"Still think I'm a taker?"

Dalia looked over at him and smirked. "So where does a nice Catholic boy learn to do *that?*"

"Camp." He glanced back at her. "During the day they teach you the rules. But at night, you learn how to get around all those rules."

"Shut up! That does not seem like something a guy can just tell you how to do."

"Who said it was a guy?" He laughed nervously. "There were ladies there too."

"*Ladies?* How exactly old is a *lady?* Twenty? Twenty-five? *Thirty?*"

Shawn responded with only a smile as he pulled up to her apartment. "Goodnight, Dalia."

As she lay in bed, she reveled in the turn of events. She had been so close to leaving the party with the girls. And who knows what would have happened with him and Ella if she hadn't stayed behind. But none of that mattered now.

She relived the events in her head. The conversation, the *magic*. Now everything made sense. She was *sure* the reason they'd never actually dated was because he'd thought she was damaged goods. And now she was sure she had nothing to worry about, as she felt more connected to him than ever. Now that he knew, everything would start moving in the right direction. But she knew she had some work to do.

Let go and let God? I don't think so.

23

"LET'S TAKE A BREAK, you guys." Sarah grabbed her water bottle off the freshly shellacked gym floor. Summer had barely started, yet here they were, already back in the school gym preparing for fall cheerleading tryouts. Even though Dalia claimed she'd gotten permission to be there, it felt wrong. Uncomfortably quiet. The typical droves of students had been replaced by one questionable janitor rolling around a squeaky mop bucket. Torn carpet fragments littered the hallway and only half of the lights were lit, which made Sarah think Dalia hadn't gotten permission at all. Normally, she wouldn't have questioned it or even cared, though now that Jake had put these things on her radar, she couldn't not notice them.

"Ella, you are really good. You don't cheer?" Dalia asked as she toweled the back of her neck.

"Not since grade school. Gymnastics is my sport," Ella said, tying her T-shirt into a front knot.

"Well, let's see what you've got." Dalia motioned to the open floor. Ella walked to one corner of the gym. She took off like a bullet, effortlessly catapulting into a round-off back handspring, finishing with a perfect full twist. She stuck the landing and raised her hands high. Her form was perfect. Her grace was inspiring. The girls stood up and applauded.

"Wow, Ella, that was incredible," Tori said.

"She was in the Junior Olympic Program when we were like ten, right Ella?" Sarah asked. She had been so impressed by that, proud to even know her.

"Yeah, I did it for a while, but it wasn't for me. Those girls' whole lives are gymnastics." She shrugged off the accomplishment.

"Well, I am excited. You're going to be our secret weapon at state this year. You're not scared of any high-flying stunts, are you? Our other flyer was good, but she would get nervous, so I was never able to really push it with her."

"That's my specialty." Ella held her head high.

"This is going to work out *perfectly*." Dalia turned to the rest of the group. "You guys, we are going to win state this year, so I'm expecting a lot out of you. Period. And I need everyone to decide how committed you are because if you're not willing to put in the work for us to bring home that state trophy, I'll find someone else who is."

"Oh god, here we go," Tori whispered.

"I heard that," Dalia shot back.

"Okay, yeah, we're committed. Not to change the subject, Dalia, but what happened after the party? Did your little plan work?" Tori asked.

"Party? Are you talking about Ella's? When you guys *left me* when I went back to get my sunglasses?" Dalia subtly glanced toward Ella.

"Oh." Tori paused.

No one knew anything about the possible situation brewing with Ella at this point. If anything, they had quite the opposite impression, considering the amount of praise and inclusion Dalia had been dishing out. So naturally, Tori wouldn't have filtered their normal conversation. But she obviously figured out she'd said something she shouldn't have because she very quickly came up with the perfect response.

"We left you? I thought you went home with Stacey."

"*What?* I thought you went home with Tori," Stacey said.

Sarah saw the tiny thumbs-up by Dalia's thigh. Her signal to Stacey and Tori that their improvisation had hit the mark.

"So how did you get home?" Stacey asked.

"Shawn. And you guys are lucky. Thanks to your leaving me, I had the most incredible night *of my life*." She tipped her head backward, closed her eyes, and held her hands out to her sides as if a light from above was shining upon her.

"Are you gonna tell us what happened?" Jenny asked.

"I'll tell you that it was perfect. Amazing. *Beyond* amazing."

"Start talking . . ." Tori insisted.

Dalia's overly dramatic lead-in included her refusal to say a word until everyone was sitting in a circle around her. But while she usually insisted on giving a play-by-play, she was oddly light on the details of her latest tryst. There was a long conversation where Shawn told her things he'd never told *anyone*. And there were buzz words she'd never used before, like *connection* and *bonding*. She even used the word *intimate*.

Sarah was excited for Dalia. And proud of herself! The whole thing sounded like her good advice was paying off because apparently Shawn didn't want the night to end. Dalia described how he went up to her apartment. And after talking for an even longer time, he started kissing her. But just when Dalia was getting to the good part of her story, she ended abruptly with a "Sorry, bitches, that's all you get. But there was *a lot* more." She coyly raised and lowered her eyebrows.

"Come on," Stacey said.

"Nope. It's our secret."

"So, you guys are for real dating now?" Jenny clasped her hands together.

"After what we did, you could say that."

"Did you have *sex* with him?" Sarah asked, pretty sure the answer was no. But she couldn't imagine what Dalia could be so excited about.

"Maybe, maybe not. Let's just say that what we did was better than sex. But I can't say any more than that." She turned around and kicked her foot up behind her.

"So, have you seen him since?" Stacey asked.

"No, he took a few days off. Some camp thing with his brother and then some other thing. He'll be back tomorrow, though. Hey, and Ella's starting at Gatto's tomorrow. You guys should come have dinner," she said, as she pulled papers out of her binder.

Ella was noticeably quiet, which Sarah half expected. But the fact that she seemed to be deliberately avoiding eye contact with any of them seemed weird, especially considering they'd had such a good first practice. Sarah and Ella had plans to go to Brew afterward. She would check in with her then. In the meantime, she was not settling for no details. Sarah walked over to her gym bag, rifled through it a bit, and then called out to Dalia.

"Can you come help me for a sec?"

"One sec. So, there's everything we covered today and what you need to know for next practice." Dalia handed printouts to the rest of the girls and then brought one to Sarah.

"What do you need?"

"I need you to tell me what happened, asshole," Sarah demanded.

Dalia grabbed her hand and squeezed it hard. "You can't tell anyone."

"*Never.*"

"So, we had the big talk. And we started fooling around, and Sarah, he wouldn't even let me give him a blow job. I started to get upset, but then he said . . . get *this.*" She put both hands on Sarah's shoulders. "He said 'my turn.' And then, oh my god."

"Oh my god *what?*"

"He went down on me." Dalia's face turned as red as Sarah had ever seen a face turn. She tried to hide it with splayed fingers and let out a high-pitched squeak. Sarah had never seen her so happy.

"I don't *believe* it. I can't believe you *let him!*"

"I can't believe it either, but *oh my god!* See, I told you he gets a little freaky."

"So how *was* it?"

"Better than anything you could imagine. Like I said, best night *of my life.*"

"I need to be clear here. You let him perform . . . hey Tori.

What is that fancy word for oral sex on a chick?" she shouted toward the girls. Of course, she knew what the word was, but this was huge, and the girls had to know immediately.

"Cunnil . . . why are you asking?" Tori said and then looked at Dalia. "*Oh my god, really?!*"

"Shhhh!" Dalia put her hand over Sarah's mouth.

"You didn't kiss him afterward, did you?" Sarah asked.

"No . . . well not right away. He had a mint first."

"And you think a mint got rid of . . . I can't even. Forget it. I don't want to hear anymore," Sarah said, as disgusted as she was fascinated. "See, I knew things would work out. He just had to see that part of you that we all love. The part that's not such a—"

"Bitch?"

"Well, I was gonna say hardass, but okay, if you like that better."

"Can I get serious for a minute?" Dalia's face softened into the person who drew out Sarah's empathy, regardless of what was going on at the time.

"What's up?"

"I just wanted to say thanks for everything. You're always straight with me, and you give me such good advice. And you never desert me, even when I'm being a crazy bitch."

"Well, I want you to have good things in life. But Dalia, don't you *ever* use me like you did at the liquor store again. It could have really messed things up with Jake, so listen. I *really* like him. And if you cause *any* trouble for us, we will *not be friends* anymore. Do you understand?" Usually, Sarah's warnings to Dalia were along the lines of *I'll be so pissed if you do this thing.* She'd never threatened to end their friendship before, and she hoped Dalia would realize how very serious she was this time.

The creepy janitor wheeled his bucket toward them.

"Let's walk and talk." Dalia grabbed Sarah by the arm and steered her toward the exit. "I know. That was shitty. It just came out, and I feel really bad about that. And I know I've been a shitty little asshole lately. This whole Trudy thing—it's been a lot. And I'm sorry, Sarah. I won't do that again."

And just like that, she made it impossible for Sarah to stay mad at her.

But when Sarah relaxed into her favorite chair at Brew, she found out she had another asshole to deal with. They were supposed to be celebrating Ella's first cheerleading practice, but no sooner had she sucked down the first creamy sip of her frozen mocha, Ella dropped a bomb on her. It happened right after Sarah had lavished her with praise for her performance, which made it that much worse.

"I didn't want to tell you this," Ella started, setting down her tea. She refused to look at Sarah and instead focused on the tea bag bobbing up and down in her cup as she tugged on its string. "But Shawn kissed me the day of the cookout. When you guys went to the liquor store."

"*What?! Ella!* Oh my god. Please tell me you're not serious. Not now. Not after the best night of her life. And you'd for shit sure better tell me you didn't kiss him back."

"I can't do that," she said, matter-of-factly, no emotion at all. She should have led with *I'm sorry* or *I feel terrible*. But no. After a long pause, she added, "And it gets worse. I'm sure after what I tell you, you'll never want to speak to me again."

Great. "What did you do?!" Sarah realized she was still holding Ella's hand from when she was talking about how fun it was going to be to have her on the squad. She yanked it away as if she'd suddenly noticed Ella was covered with warts.

"Well, Greg was going to camp, too, so Shawn and I drove them up together," she said, eyes still on her tea. Ella picked up the mug and blew into it, holding it in front of her face. Hiding behind it.

Sarah looked around to make sure no one they knew was in the coffee shop. She lowered her voice and spoke in the loudest, firmest whisper she could.

"Ella, what are you saying? Did something happen during your drive?"

"It was more than just a drive. Sarah, I am so sorry. I know I made you a promise, but I couldn't help it."

"Ella Connor, you tell me everything that happened right this minute."

It wasn't her fault, she tried to explain. Her mom ran into Shawn's mom, and they figured out that the boys were both going to camp the same day, and Shawn's mom offered to drive Greg, and when Shawn found out, he called her to tell her they needed more counselors and asked if she wanted to help, and it was three days of work, and she needed the money. Sarah moved her hand in small impatient circles, urging her to get on with the excuses and get to the part that really mattered.

"I mean, you can probably guess what happened. It was just like old times." *Now* she looked Sarah in the eye, as if it being like old times, like when there was no Dalia, somehow made it okay.

"Including the make out part, I assume? Any more than that?"

"Just a little. Second base, I guess."

"Ella, you promised. *Solemnly promised*, as I recall. And I'm guessing that little pre-party at your apartment wasn't an accident?"

"He just showed up! But, I'd be lying if I said I wasn't happy about it. Sarah, please try to understand. You have no idea how horrible things have been. And this is the first time I've felt excited about anything since, well, probably since the *last* time he kissed me. Pathetic, I know."

Sarah was about to give her a high horsey *everyone has problems* and *that's not an excuse* speech, but she could tell Ella was trying not to cry, which got to her for just a second.

"Shawn Matlyn. What is it about him? I know he's good-looking, although it's hard for *me* to look at him that way. Personality wise, I love him. But the whole jock thing . . ."

"I know, not your thing."

"Yes, thank god."

Ella went on to list all the things she liked about him. How he listens, how he cares about people, how he's just a really good guy. The whole thing was a disturbingly, practically verbatim list of all the reasons Dalia liked him too. Sarah felt like she was in a parallel universe, sitting at a table where someone had just swapped out Dalia for Ella, which led her to point out the obvious.

"Ella, how interested could he be if he's leading both you and Dalia on?"

"We talked about her." She sat back in her chair, her posture more relaxed now that they were having an actual conversation about it.

"And?"

"And he's not into her. It's just physical with them."

"And that makes it okay? For him to screw around with Dalia, yet what? You're the one he really wants? How would you ever know?"

"I mean, it's obviously too soon to know for sure, but we do have this really great connection."

Connection. There it was again. Shawn was getting a little too busy *connecting* with people, Sarah thought. And then a disturbing image entered her mind, one that she thought she would share with Ella. "You do realize that he kissed you, and then that very same night, he *went down on* Dalia, and then he kissed you again like what. A day later? You better hope he keeps up with his oral hygiene, because basically, you just—"

"*Stop it!* Going down like . . ." Her eyes narrowed. "He did that?"

"Yep. You didn't hear us talking about it? And what, all that time you spent *connecting*, he failed to mention that? I'd be *very careful* with him if I were you. I mean do what you want, but when it all blows up in your face, I'm gonna tell you I told you so."

"Okay, Sarah. I get it. But like I said, I don't know why she gets to claim him. They're not even dating."

"Well, she thinks they are, now more than ever! But forget about me. How could you do that to *her*? She's been *so nice* to you."

"I'm sorry. I know. I feel terrible about it because she has been great. But it's not like I asked her to do any of those things. I don't even *know* her. And Shawn isn't ever going to date her, so I'm not taking anything from her, am I? How do you take something from someone that was never theirs to begin with?" Ella let the question hang, but it stayed hanging because Sarah didn't have a good answer. "It's not like I'm not thinking about her. It's just a shitty, shitty situation."

"Whatever. Suit yourself. But I don't want to hear any more about this from you. Ever. Not one word. And I'm going to pretend I never heard about it in the first place. Did you see how excited she was? If you care at all about the position you've put me in, you will never speak to me about Shawn again."

"Okay, I won't. I promise."

"Coming from you, that doesn't mean much."

They didn't say a word to each other as Sarah drove Ella home. She stared forward, not even acknowledging Ella as she got out of the car. She was so upset that she screamed and banged on the steering wheel as she drove away. Here she welcomes Ella into their group, and Ella turns everything upside down. She should have trusted her gut from the beginning.

Usually when Sarah was this mad, it was because of something Dalia had done. But this time, she was aching for her. Aching for how excited she was. Does she tell her and break her heart or pretend she doesn't know? But then she thought about Ella. Was it really fair to be pissed at her? Is she supposed to keep her distance because of some loyalty to someone she barely knows? And then she wondered why it is that in every love triangle, the girls always get pissed at the other girl, while the guy gets off scot-free. She realized that for as pissed as she was at Ella, Ella wasn't *necessarily* the bad guy here. Ultimately, the responsibility for this mess fell squarely on Shawn. Sarah had no choice but to go to the source of all this trouble.

She tore out of the parking lot and headed to Shawn's. She skipped the doorbell and just marched right into his house, where she found him sitting in his family room. He was watching basketball, just sitting there with a half-eaten ham sandwich and a can of Fanta. His bare feet were kicked up on the coffee table, like he didn't have a care in the world. And this incensed her even more.

"What *the fuck* do you think you're doing?"

"Sarah . . . what are you . . . ?"

"*Don't you what me!*"

"Oh . . . okay."

She watched the realization creep onto his face. Somehow, like a big stupid asshole, he must have thought Ella wouldn't tell her.

"I'm sorry! I couldn't help it! We were having this talk. And it got all serious, and then things just . . . happened."

"The sad thing is, based on *that* description, I don't have a *clue* which one of them you're talking about."

"It does sound like it could be either of them." He sighed. "I'm talking about Dalia."

"So, things happened, and you *couldn't* stop them. Sure. On the same day you kissed Ella?"

"Well, I was actually *trying* to do the right thing and draw some lines with her, Sarah, because I thought about what you said. But it ended up backfiring, and then I felt bad for her. And I know." He put his palm forward. "It was *not* cool." He took his feet off the table and rested his elbows on his knees.

"Great. And what about Ella?"

"What *about* Ella? We're in high school, Sarah. Give me a break."

"Shawn, you don't understand. Dalia is not stable. And you know what? Neither is Ella! You're fucking with two *very vulnerable girls*! Are you interested in Dalia at all?"

"It's not that easy." He offered her a seat next to him. She reluctantly accepted.

"I'm obviously attracted to her. Very attracted to her. She brings something out in me that I don't really understand. But personality-wise, she's not my type. At all."

"And Ella is?"

"One hundred percent. She's warm and funny. And she's *nice*! We had a really great time together at camp," he said with a childlike sincerity in his eyes that, under any other circumstance, Sarah would have been gushing over how sweet the whole thing was. "And it felt good, like what I was talking about at Jenny's. Fun and simple. Like how things used to be. Like I *want* them to be, Sarah." He tilted his head and looked at her, as if waiting for a signal that what he said made some sense. She refused to give him one.

"How about this? It's like Dalia is a party, and Ella is . . . breakfast. A good one," Shawn added.

"*Breakfast?* I'd take the party any day!"

"Okay, it's like a party is fun. And sometimes, it's really fun. But even if it was the best party of all time, it's still a party. Eventually it's too much, and you want to go home. But breakfast, you wake up and you want it, and you're happy you had it, and the next day you wake up and you want it again."

Sarah scoffed at his analogy, even though it was spot on.

"I know you know what I mean. Look. I don't owe anyone anything. But I know what you're saying. And I don't want to hurt anyone, so I have not promised *anything* to *anyone*. Like I said, we are in high school. And I really don't think you should be yelling at me."

As much as she hated to admit it, he was kind of right.

"Well, I get that, and I'm sorry for barging in here. But, whatever you're doing, I am stuck right in the middle of it. And you're potentially hurting a lot of people. So, as your friend, I'm asking that you are honest with both of them. I know you're a good guy, and I *know* that's important to you. So, I'm pretty sure you can understand where I'm coming from. Just do the right thing, Shawn." She stared at him for a moment and then walked out.

Sarah got in her car, more confused than ever. First, she was *sure* that Ella was the bad guy. And then she was *sure* that Shawn was the bad guy. But maybe there was no bad guy. Maybe none of them really could help themselves. Maybe no one owed anyone anything. And maybe it was like Ella said. Just a shitty, shitty situation.

24

"TABLE FOR FOUR, PLEASE." Jenny's hand was low by her waist, waving to Ella who was behind the host stand.

Gatto's catered to all tastes and budgets, so on any given night, you could find anyone from entire kids' soccer teams to business executives enjoying brick oven-fired pizzas and homemade cannoli. Tonight was one of those nights when everyone decided to come at once, which was probably not the best night to start hostess training. Barbara, the brutish, salt-and-pepper-haired woman training Ella, waited for her to respond.

"What, are you gonna just sit there and stare at them?" she barked in her pack-a-day smoker's voice.

"Hi ladies, how many?" Ella finally responded.

"They want to sit with Dalia. Just take them to table two." Barbara pointed with her doughy arm as she handed Ella the menus.

"What about our crayons, Barbara?" Stacey asked.

Barbara sighed and handed Stacey a small tin bucket of crayons. "No dirty pictures this time!"

"Right this way," Ella said.

Sarah was quietly avoiding her while she processed the events of late. She still didn't know if she should cut Ella some slack, but she wasn't about to be rude to her in front of everyone, so she hung back, taking in the May-December romances among the bar crowd.

"How's it going so far?" Tori asked Ella.

"It's okay. First days are always awkward. And did you smell that? Barbara *reeks* of Love's Baby Soft. I feel like I'm gonna puke."

"Oh, it's her signature scent. It's a wonder she's still single." Stacey laughed, fanning her nose.

Before they could even sit down, Dalia came over with a breadbasket and took their drink order. She was radiating joy. *Best night of my life* practically tattooed on her forehead. Sarah could hardly face her.

"Drinks? Sarah, iced tea, Jenny, water, Tori, Coke, Stacey?"

"I think I'll go with a Pellegrino today. With a twist of lemon," she said.

"P with a T-L," Dalia said, writing on her notepad. "Right back." She shoved the pen in the pouch of her black apron and hurried toward the bar, stopping to chat with Shawn. She grabbed his arm, leaned in close, and pointed in their direction. He gave her a quick nod and headed over.

"Well, look who's here. So, what are *you* girls up to tonight?" He flashed his Rob Lowe smile. The one that makes everyone immediately like him. "Sarah? You good?"

"I'm fine." Sarah reached for the breadbasket. "We need some butter."

"Ooookay," Shawn said. "I'll get right on that."

"Why are you being pissy with Shawn?" Tori asked the moment he left.

"I don't want to talk about it." She slammed her menu shut and put it on the table.

"What is it?" Stacey asked.

"You guys, I wasn't going to say anything, but—"

"Just say it," Tori said casually as she picked the crust off her bread.

"Okay, but if I tell you, you're going to have to keep a secret from Dalia, and I'm not sure you want to carry *that* burden around with you."

"*Dammit, Sarah.* This is supposed to be a drama-free summer." Tori groaned as she tossed the fluffy center of her bread on the table. "*Fine.* Just tell us!" She closed her eyes, bracing for impact. But just then, Dalia showed up with a trayful of drinks. And everyone got quiet.

"Jeez, you guys. Who died? And why is Tori closing her eyes?"

Jenny promptly went back to her coloring. In red crayon, she'd drawn a very swirly "Rob and Jenny." While she worked on replacing the vowels with little hearts, she decided to try to break the silence. "She was just trying to . . ." But then she trailed off, making it obvious that they'd been talking about Dalia. And then Tori, another supremely bad liar, left no doubt.

"I was just trying to remember who sang that song, you know that 'Give It Away' song."

"*Chili Peppers!* What, are you high? How do you not know that?"

"We just couldn't come up with it," Sarah said.

"All of you. *All four of you* couldn't come up with the band that sings one of our *favorite* songs? Nice try, *bitches*. I'll tell you what. *I'm* going to deliver an order, and then *I'm* going to come back here, and *you're* going to tell me what you were *really* talking about," she said and then quickly stomped off.

"What is going on, Sarah?" Tori asked with urgency.

Suddenly, an idea came to her. She didn't have to tell them everything. They didn't have to hate Ella. Not yet, anyway. The jury was still out in Sarah's mind, although Ella being the promise-breaker made it hard to defend her. But they did have to know that whatever happened after the party meant a lot more to Dalia than it did to Shawn.

"Okay, but there is a third party involved in this situation, and you can't hold it against said third party. It wasn't her fault. Deal?"

"Yes, fine, go," Stacey said.

"Well, you know that perfect night he had with you know who?" She used one hand to hide the fact that she was pointing at Dalia with the other. "Well, that *very same day* he tried to kiss Ella." Sarah let it sink in. "The *same day!*"

"That *motherfucker!*" Stacey shouted as she locked her eyes on Shawn from across the room. He was just going about his business, smiling while he took an elderly couple's order, having no idea that Sarah had just shredded him in the girls' eyes.

"Oh my god, oh my god." Jenny started to hyperventilate. "What did Ella *do?*"

"Well, you guys don't know this, but they were each other's

first kiss, so I was a little worried. But she told Shawn she wasn't interested, thank god," she lied. She wasn't sure where she was going with this, but it felt the most *okay,* for the time being.

"First kiss? Are you kidding me? Thank god is right, she turned him down. Can you imagine? It would be a *total shit show.*" Tori turned around to get a glimpse of Ella.

"Don't look at her!" Sarah's stomach folded on top of itself. She hated lying to them. She couldn't believe she was doing it, even as it was coming out of her mouth.

"Well, *now* what?" Tori asked borderline despairingly. "We can't let her go on thinking the other night meant what she thinks it did, can we?"

"See? Aren't you sorry you made me tell you?" Sarah saw Dalia approaching and signaled to the girls this conversation was on hiatus.

"Here you are, *bitches.* And one of you is going to tell me what's going on before you leave here, so you'd better get your story straight." She set down their salads and marched off.

"So, we all have to agree on some lie here? Not cool, Shawn, *not cool!*" Stacey said in his direction.

Sarah twisted with uneasiness again. But it began to morph into something more sinister. As she imagined Dalia's reaction to the Ella news, it started to feel like a *premonition.*

"Or we tell her the truth and break her heart," she said. "I confronted him. He feels bad about it, but he told me he would never date her. She should probably know that."

"He'll *never* date her? She needs to know," Stacey said. "But maybe not lay all of it on her at once. Maybe we just tell her the kiss part. Does everyone agree?"

"Yes," they collectively moaned.

Sarah lost a not-so-lively version of Not It, so she went to find Dalia who was refilling a pitcher of Sprite. She tugged on her apron and told her they needed to talk to her after work.

"After work? No. Now," Dalia insisted.

Dalia led the girls out the front door of Gatto's. They stepped into the steamy night and gathered around Stacey's car. "I have about three minutes before George fires my ass. Now what is it?"

"Shawn hit on Ella the day of the cookout," Sarah said as short and truthful as possible. Somehow, she couldn't get out the word *kiss*, so she watered it down the best she could. But Dalia didn't respond at all like Sarah had assumed. Instead, she just nodded, slowly and deliberately.

"I know."

"*What?* What do you mean you know?" Sarah asked.

"Well, I didn't *actually* know, but I'm not surprised. When I stayed back to get a ride home, I could see him flirting. And I thought something might have happened when we were getting beers."

"And you're not upset?" Tori asked.

"*Of course I'm upset!*" She swatted a mosquito away from her face. "But tell me. What did Ella do?"

"She *totally* blew him off!" Sarah said.

"Okay good. I figured she would. After all I've done for her . . ."

"Dalia, I can't believe you're not *freaking out*," Stacey said.

"I was, but then I thought about some things Sarah said to me. I don't know if the rest of you noticed, but I've been trying to be nicer lately . . ."

Sarah chuckled as she noticed the *aha* on Tori's face, like suddenly a lot of things made sense.

"... and then I reread that article in my mom's magazine, and I got it together."

"'How to Get and Keep Your Man'?" Stacey laughed.

"You laugh now, but you'll see. So I read that, and then I read some other ones, and now I know what I was doing wrong. Sarah's right. He wants someone to be *sweet* to him. So, I have to do *that*. I have to *listen* to him, I have to be *patient*, and I have to stay *confident*. This changes nothing," she said. "I will not lose Shawn to that little midget, that is for sure." She looked at her watch.

"She's not your cute little dolly anymore?" Tori snickered.

"Not anymore. So, don't get any ideas that she's going to be hanging around us all the time. But it doesn't matter. I'm telling you, something amazing happened between us, so I'm not worried about anything that happened before that night. And I'm being really nice to Ella, so that's my backup plan. She'd be *crazy* to fuck with me after everything I've done for her. But if she were to become a problem? I'd get rid of her. Get rid of the competition."

"Pffft . . . and how exactly would you do *that*?" Tori scoffed.

"I have some ideas. Actually, I have a lot of ideas. I have to go, but it's really easy, if you think about it. The easiest thing would be to, you know, hurt her reputation. Like turn her into something gross. What happens to that girl at every high school who has to go to the emergency room cuz she got a hot dog stuck in her? No one hangs out with that chick again."

"It's really mean . . . but it would totally work." Jenny shrugged.

"What's *mean* is if she thinks she can come here and fuck with my life. And I don't think she will. But I have a hundred other ideas just in case. If Ella Connor wants to fuck with me? She's gonna wish she could go back to whatever desert she crawled out of."

"Wait," Tori said. "Why did you get her a job with you guys if you knew all this?"

"At first, I was trying to be *nice*. But then I figured I better keep an eye on her. And I do the scheduling, which basically means I have total control over both of their social lives. But like I said, we *totally* connected that night, so I'm really not worried at all. Whatever he thought during the day, that all changed that night." She checked her watch again. "I have to get back."

"Oh my god, you guys," Sarah said once Dalia was out of earshot. "Did you ever think for a second she wouldn't have a total nuclear meltdown?"

"Hey, isn't that Shawn's car?" Stacey pointed to the white Saab facing hers. "*It is.* Cover me." She pulled a bobby pin out of her hair, hurried over to the passenger side and crouched to the ground. "This one's for you, Jim," she yelled into the night. She twisted off the cap on his tire and used the bobby pin to let out the air. "There. All better."

25

SARAH WAS GREETED by the barking of Jake's dog, which saved her the trouble of ringing his doorbell. He never mentioned a dog, but she wished he had. She didn't like dogs, and they didn't like her.

"Sadie, it's okay girl," Jake held the wriggling German Shepherd by her collar as he opened the door. "She's not usually like this."

"It's me. Dogs don't like me."

"She will. She's just not used to you. Stay here. I'll lock her up."

"Well, you can't do *that*. Then she'll never like me. She'll be like, oh, here comes that chick that gets me locked up all the time. And then it will be all awkward and uncomfortable, and she'll talk bad about me to your family, and it'll be this whole thing." Sarah awkwardly patted Sadie's head as she scooted by her.

"What are you *talking* about?" He laughed. He always laughed at her weird jokes. That had to be a good sign.

"She's fine. But just so you two don't start off on the wrong foot, we'll get some drinks, and I'll leave her in the kitchen while we go downstairs."

Other than the dog, his house was exactly what Sarah had pictured. Nothing fancy, but warm and homey. From the scented dried flower arrangements, to family pictures, to the positive sayings on plaques, it exuded kindness in a way that reminded her of her own. There was a mom in this house who loved her family, and Sarah couldn't wait to meet her.

After securing Sadie in the kitchen with a child safety gate, Jake opened the hollow door to the basement. He pulled the string from the light hanging above the stairs and illuminated the cream shag carpeting that tickled her toes. He led her around the pool table. "There it is." He pointed to the back of the room and sat down on a beige-and-brown plaid couch.

There were posters, books, and boxes everywhere. Sarah took a second to visually sift through the organized chaos to figure out what he was talking about. And then she saw it.

"Ah . . . the artistic debut?" She stood back with her hand on her chin and admired Jake's first painting. The one of the sunset he'd painted when he was eight years old. It was hanging on the wood paneled wall, and just like he'd said, the actual photograph of the sunset that inspired it was tucked in the upper right corner. It was amazing.

"Jake, that is *so good*! You could easily get a million for it."

"Oh, at least. That's why it's hanging in my basement," he said, laughing from his seat on the couch. His arms were spread along the top of it, a nonverbal invitation for her to join him. But a sky-blue recliner caught her attention, and she had to try it out. She plopped down and pulled the lever, expecting just the footrest to come popping out. Instead, it made a clunking noise, and the whole thing reclined, almost spilling her onto the floor, which Jake found hilarious. Once she steadied herself, she folded her hands on her chest and studied the pattern of the drop ceiling.

"I suppose for now, that's where it should be. Until you're dead, anyway. That's when you make the real money. Well, your family will." She tsked. "Such a shame you won't be around to enjoy it." The recliner squeaked as she bravely rocked it back and forth.

"Well, *that's* a dark thought for a Wednesday afternoon." In two distinct motions, he turned toward her and leaned away from her.

"Is it?" She laughed. "That's nothing. I've got dark thoughts for every day of the week."

"Really?"

"*Yeah!* I haven't told anyone this, but I actually have a thing I call dark thoughts of the day."

"Come on."

"I'm serious. Give me a day, I'll give you a dark thought."

"You are serious, aren't you? Okay, Sunday."

"Sunday. Okay. Lots of people believe in God only because the alternative, that life is random and meaningless, is too horrifying for them to think about."

"And they have these thoughts on Sundays?"

"Sunday is the day for God thoughts, *obviously*." She rolled her eyes. "There's also one about waking up and regretting what you did Saturday night. Okay, next?"

"Damn, that's dark. Okay, Friday. You can't have dark thoughts about Fridays."

"Fridays? Pffft . . . Fridays you have all these people who are going about their week, like 'just got to get to Friday.' And then they get to Friday, and they're like this isn't any better than the rest of the week. But the next week they do it again. So, they just wish their whole lives away."

"What the hell, Sarah, you are one freaky chick. Maybe Sadie's right about you." He smirked.

"I tried to warn you." She uprighted herself and reached for the warm lemonade he'd made her from a powder in the kitchen. The powder was all clumpy and had probably expired three years ago, but it was the closest thing they had to iced tea. And it came from Jake, which somehow made the part of her that worried about food poisoning not care.

"Whatever you do, don't get me started on Wednesdays."

"Wednesdays?" He walked over to her, took the glass out of her hand, and set it on the table. He took her chin in his hand and tilted it up toward him. "Well, I don't know if you noticed, but today's Wednesday. Whatever dark thoughts you have about Wednesdays, I'm thinking we can do something to change them." He took his thumb and wiped away a bit of yellow No. 5 powder from her lip.

"What did you have in mind?"

She knew exactly what he had in mind the moment he mentioned he had the house to himself all day. The purple bra set whose unveiling had been thwarted by Dalia's thievery was about to have its big day out.

"You're gonna have to come upstairs to find out."

"Upstairs like . . . in your kitchen?"

"Mmmmm, a *little* further upstairs." He pinched his thumb and forefinger together.

"Oh, like *all the way* upstairs?"

"It has something to do with *all the way.*"

"So, you're luring me to your bedroom with the promise of changing my dark Wednesday thoughts? That is some hookup line."

"Is it working?" He ran his hand along the inside of her thigh up to the cuff of her shorts and back down to her knee.

"It is definitely working." Her thigh quivered. She felt like it might not be able to support the rest of her. Sarah took his hand and let him lead her upstairs, right past Sadie's judgy stare.

Jake led her down the upstairs hall and opened his bedroom door. There was no mistaking the smell of wet leaves, plus a hint of dirty puppy, topped off with a bit of sweat and a dash of cologne. This was a guy's bedroom. Not to mention the fact that the entire thing was blue. Gray-blue walls, midnight blue bedding, and a plaid pattern uniting the two colors, decorating the sheets and pillows.

"Get over here," he called from his bed as she stopped to look at his Metallica poster.

The house was perfectly still except for Sadie's nails clicking against the linoleum kitchen floor. While she and Sadie had their issues, she was slightly comforted that Sadie would give some warning if someone came home unexpectedly. The thought of Jake's parents catching them was making it hard to relax. And the quiet was starting to get to her, as she sat next to him on his bed.

"Can we put on some music?" she asked.

Jake looked into her eyes for a moment, before reaching across her and putting on a Nirvana CD. As the grungy strings of "Lithium" played, he started kissing her. His tongue was cold, and his mouth tasted like the Coke he'd just sipped. Sarah closed her eyes for a moment . . . she didn't want to feel new to this. And though she'd never read any of them or even knew what they were, she pretended she was a seasoned reader of Dalia's mom's magazines and made the first move. Pulling his T-shirt out from his jeans with one hand, she reached underneath it with the other, sliding her fingertips up and down his back as he stared down at her.

He turned her on her side and reached under her shirt. Putting her arms in the air, she gave him permission to take it off.

"Look at you," he said, pleased with the purple bra. Funny thing about the bra. Its only job was to get itself tossed aside as quickly as possible. *Which it did very successfully*, she thought, as she saw it staring at her from the floor like she owed it one.

Sarah had sex with Jake for the first time that afternoon. It was slow and sweet and nothing like her first time. As she curled up in the crook of his arm, she understood why it might someday be a big deal. She laid her head on his chest as he held her.

"So, what do you think of Wednesdays now?" he asked.

"You mean hump day?" She laughed and added, "They're looking up!"

"Oh my god. How do you come up with these things?"

"They just happen."

"And the dark thoughts? What's up with those? Is that like your alter ego or something?"

"No, it's just me. They're more like observations that just happen to be dark. I shouldn't have told you about those." She turned away from him and buried her face in his comforter.

"Why not? Everyone has their things, Sarah. I want to know *your* things." He reached over her shoulder and turned her back toward him. They lay in his bed, their faces two inches apart. Sarah was tempted to make another weird joke in that moment. But something made her trust the guy behind those crystal blue eyes, so she let him in.

"I don't know. I feel like there are a lot of sad people. And I notice them every day. But most of the dark thoughts are more like terrible worries. About everything and everyone. All the time. My friends know I'm a worrier—they always tease me about it. But really, it's bigger than that. I'm just a scared person. I was born scared. And *totally* superstitious."

"You? What are you scared of? You always say your life is so good."

"*That's the point!* Why doesn't anyone get that?" She sat up. "Pretty much everyone I know has had bad things happen to them, except me. Dalia always points that out."

"Well, I wouldn't listen to Dalia. There are lots of people who've never had anything bad happen to them. I never have."

"Don't say that!" She covered his mouth with her hand. He put his tongue on her palm and laughed when she pulled it away. "Here come the dark thoughts. Now I have to worry about you."

"Sarah," he said mid-laugh. "It's not good to think like that. What good does being scared all the time do?"

"You can prevent bad things from happening, if you know you should be looking out for them. But if you're not looking for them . . ."

He pulled her back down and buried his face in her neck. "You can't stop bad things from happening. All being scared does is make you miss the good stuff. Like right now. Are you scared right now?"

"Please don't ask me that." She couldn't tell him that in that very moment, she got scared she'd fall in love with him and get her heart broken someday.

"You know what you need? You need to come to our summer house in Wisconsin. You can't worry about anything when you're there. It's impossible."

"What makes you so sure?"

"It's totally chill. We just play around all day. Drink some beers, smoke some pot, throw Frisbees—it's on a lake. So, you can go swimming, fishing, whatever. I think you'd love it."

"That sounds really nice." She wrapped her arms around him and squeezed him tight.

"Every year I take a group of guys up for the night. We've been going since we were kids. But there's so much room up there, I've always wanted to have a big party."

"I like big parties."

"Really? You?" He kissed her forehead and smiled. "So how about you bring all your friends, and I'll tell Matlyn and those guys. But everyone would have to bring tents and food and stuff. And make sure you tell everyone it's nothing fancy. We can use the house for the bathroom and to put some stuff in the fridge, but make sure they know they'll be camping."

"I have just one question. Will you protect me from the wild animals?" She stared at him as she pictured a bear sniffing around their tent. "See, I already found something to worry about."

"Sarah, no worrying allowed."

"But will you protect me?"

"Yes, babe. I will protect you."

At that moment, in Jake's arms, Sarah wasn't worried about a thing.

26

ELLA SPRITZED GIORGIO perfume in the air and waved her wrists under the mist, and with that, she was ready. She hoped she could sneak out without having to talk to her mom, but Linda was standing at the kitchen sink.

"So, you're going ice skating?"

"Yes, Mom. How many times are you going to ask?" Ella grabbed her fair-condition, camel-brown Coach bag. She wished she didn't have to buy used, but it didn't matter too much. She'd never been great at taking care of things, so even if she'd bought new, it wouldn't be long before it looked used anyway.

"You know, if it was anyone other than Shawn, you wouldn't be going." Linda wrung out a dish rag and laid it between the sink bowls. "Christian family, money . . ." She spotted the bag strung across Ella. "Come *here*. Where did you get that?"

"Dalia loaned it to me."

"Look at those scuff marks. You'd think she'd take better care of an expensive bag like that. Kids are so spoiled these days."

"Whatever, Mom. I'll see you later."

Ella walked out, closing the door on frustration behind her and opening the door to elation in front of her. *It's amazing how something as simple as a door can divide one life from another*, she thought, as she stepped into the suffocating humidity. It was way too hot for jeans. And carrying a big sweatshirt around wasn't helping. She got into Shawn's car and tossed the sweatshirt in the backseat.

"We're ice skating again?" Shawn laughed.

"Just drive please, before she changes her mind."

This was the fourth time Ella had used the ice-skating excuse. While they usually had youth group activities as an excuse to sneak off together, if there wasn't something in the church calendar, she had to make something up. The first time, Shawn did take her skating. But when her mom subsequently said no to the movies, because *we all know what teenagers do at the movies*, and no to the beach because *we all know what boys want when they see girls in bathing suits*, Ella tried ice skating again, and her mom said yes. So, Ella kept returning to that well. Apparently, Linda was hard-pressed to find a problem with something that required neck-to-toe clothing and little kids everywhere.

Shawn and Ella saw each other frequently these days, though it was mostly at places their relationship needed to be kept a secret—work and church. While she was grateful to have rejoined her childhood church and hoped it would settle Linda down, the last thing she needed was for the youth group gossip train to start something that Linda might get wind of. One wrong rumor and Linda would put an end to them.

As Shawn reached for her hand, she thought about how much she hated that secrecy. She wanted to share her happiness with the *world*. With *Sarah*. If Sarah just spent some time with them, she would see that this wasn't just some childhood crush. Maybe she'd cut her some slack and they could be friends again. Ella had tried, and so had Sarah. But they couldn't get past the "what have you been up to" questions when what she'd been up to was the forbidden topic. And the couple of cheerleading outings Ella had gone on were totally awkward, considering all anyone ever talked about were guys and clothes. So, it seemed best to wait Sarah out, hoping she'd get past it someday. It started to gnaw at her, but then she looked at Shawn. At how adorable he looked in his backward baseball hat. And the happiness she felt trumped everything else. He was more than enough for now, she told herself as they pulled in his driveway.

A light rain patted his family room window as they lay together on his denim sectional. Ella was relaxed and wished they could do this all day. But Shawn seemed nervous, the way he kept glancing back and forth between her and the window. The onset of rain meant his family could come home at any moment, as one crack of lightning would mean the end of his brother's soccer tournament. He got up again and raised the blinds.

"I think we've got time," he said. "And I should be able to hear them pull in the driveway, but let's put in a movie. *Back to the Future* okay?" he asked, reaching for a VHS tape.

"You know it is." She smiled at him. They'd talked at least a hundred times about how it was their favorite movie.

He started the movie and sat back down. Ella watched him

staring at her as she lay on her back. They didn't even make it through the opening scene before he started kissing her.

It had only been six weeks since Shawn had reentered her life, but the pace of it all made it feel much longer. They'd even talked about having sex. Or how it sucked that they couldn't, which evolved into *shouldn't*. Shawn had brought it up enough times that she could tell he was feeling her out. Like he was having second thoughts about the abstinence pledge they'd made years ago and hoped she felt the same. She did. Ella was straight-up eager to have sex with him, but she wasn't going to tell *him* that. At least not yet. There were still some things nagging at her, things preventing her from trusting him. And once again, her body reminded her that she just wasn't there yet: a queasy sensation came over her as his hand flattened against her stomach. His fingertips inched inside the waist of her jeans. That was when she grabbed his wrist.

"Wait," she said firmly.

"I'm sorry." He dropped his head and exhaled.

"What's going on with you and Dalia?" She sat up and pulled down her top to cover her exposed midriff. He groaned as he turned on his back and laid his head in her lap.

"Ella, I told you. Nothing. It's completely over." He stared up at her.

"I know you say that, but I still don't understand why you're taking her out." She rested her hands on him, one on his head, one on his chest. She took a cleansing breath, trying to adjust to the new mood she'd ushered into the room.

"I get that it's weird, but if you knew how I felt about you, you'd know you have nothing to worry about."

Ella tried to contain the smile that, left unchecked, would

reveal exactly how happy these words made her. She wanted to hear more. But she wasn't ready for *that* conversation, the one that might make her vulnerable to him, so it was better to leave it alone for now. The Dalia situation, however, could not be left alone.

"So, what *exactly* are you doing?" she asked.

"Well, after talking to Sarah, I knew I had to say something to officially end things with her—I couldn't just blow her off. So, I tried to let her down easy." He stopped. He let way too much time pass before he elaborated.

"*And?*" she asked impatiently.

"And . . . now she's scaring me."

"*Scaring you?* What do you mean she's *scaring* you?" Ella grabbed Shawn's hand and interlaced her fingers with his.

"Well, the night you started at Gatto's, the night I told her we should cool things off . . . someone let the air out of my tire."

"And you think it was her. Are you sure you're not just flattering yourself? How do you know it wasn't just flat?" She squinted one eye as she stared down at him.

"Because the cap was lying right next to it!" he said, laughing. "The tire is fine. It had to be her."

"But what would be the point of that?"

"To let me know she's pissed? To scare me into being with her? I don't know. *You're* the girl."

"*Ha!*" Ella laughed out loud. "I'm the girl. So, you think that I know what a *possible* girl was thinking *if* a girl let the air out of your tire?"

"Well, *I* don't know."

"So what, you think we have all these girl meetings where we talk about these things?"

"Yeah, all guys think that. Are you denying it?" He looked at her suspiciously.

"No, we do. It's the third Wednesday after the full moon. We meet at the nearest tampon store and talk about all the *evil tricks* we can play on guys. In fact, we talked about letting air out of tires *just last meeting*. Had to be her." Ella picked up a corduroy pillow and hit him over the head with it. "What is wrong with you?"

"I'm sorry."

"Just finish the story."

"So, she was acting weird when we were talking. Like we were dating or something. Ella, I swear, I have never told her we were dating."

"Hmmm . . . well, you've never *said* you're dating. But she *thinks* you're dating because of what you did the night of my party. We took a vote at the last tampon meeting. All the girls agreed. *That* means you're dating," she said, pointing directly at his face.

"I'm so stupid." He stared at the ceiling as he rubbed his Adam's apple.

"Shawn, we've all done stupid things. But you better tell me if anything's happened since we got back from camp."

"Nothing has happened, I swear to God." He made the cross sign over his heart.

"Okay, so what gives?"

"Promise not to laugh?"

"No."

"Fine. I tried to break it off with her by telling her that . . ." he said and then exhaled sheepishly, "that we have to take a step back because I'm *too* attracted to her, and I'm afraid if I'm with her that way again, that I won't be able to *not* have sex with her, which will ruin my promise to wait until marriage."

"Remind me to never believe a word you say." Ella turned his face away from hers and then wiped her hand on the couch as if removing germs. She wanted to do more than that—she wanted to shove him off the couch and step on his head as she stormed out the door. How could she *ever* feel okay about them with Dalia thinking Shawn can't *control himself* around her? *Seriously?*

"I know. I'm a jerk. So, I told her we'd started fooling around before we got to know each other, and we should fix that by spending some time dating before we do anything again."

"Shawn. *Are you serious?!* How does that not mean you're together?!"

"I'm getting there. This is the part that you can't laugh at."

"*What.*" Ella folded her arms tightly across her chest. She was right back to middle school. To that crushing disappointment those couple of weeks before she moved, when she'd said hi to him in the halls, and he'd pretended he hardly knew her.

"My plan is that if the dates are boring, she'll lose interest in me."

"*Boring?*"

"Yep." He smiled proudly. "They are literally the worst dates I can think of, right down to the conversation. And get this. I keep Good & Plentys in my pocket and eat them the entire time because I know she can't stand the smell of black licorice."

"You are either the dumbest person I've ever met or a total genius. *How can you do that?*"

"Trick her or sit through the awkward stuff?"

"*Both.*"

"Believe me, it sucks. Do you know how hard it is for *me* to be *boring?*" He pointed at himself with both thumbs.

"You? I think you'd be great at it."

"Aren't you funny. Well, I couldn't think of any other way to end it with her without hurting her feelings."

"Okay, truth. Are you still attracted to her?" Ella stared pointedly into his eyes, hoping they'd reveal if he was being honest with her.

"Ella," his expression flattened, "what do you want me to say? I'd be lying if I said I don't think she's attractive. Pretty much anyone would be."

Even though Ella appreciated his honesty, she still felt a jolt of jealousy hearing him say it.

"But *you* are who I want," he went on. "And I've never been with her unless we've been drinking. Can we just get through the summer doing this? I promise, she'll be so bored and disgusted with me that by the beginning of the school year, she'll wonder what she ever saw in me."

"Did you know she thinks she's going to lose her virginity to you on Homecoming night? She's got *big plans*," Ella air quoted. "She even told *me* about them."

"*What?!* Who said we're going to Homecoming together? Do you see why I have to do it this way? I feel sorry for her. If I'd known how messed up she is, I would have never touched her to begin with."

"So, you're really doing this just to not hurt her?" Ella appreciated what a good guy he was. She also thought she should be a better girl. But that's not so easy when you're in love.

"Yes. I don't want to date her, but I do care about her feelings.

And the only idea I could come up with is to still be her friend, but to make sure she's not attracted to me anymore. That way everyone comes out of this okay." He reached up and caressed her cheek with his thumb.

"Okay. I understand. I don't want her to be hurt either. It's actually pretty sweet that you're worried about her." But there was one thing nagging at Ella, especially because he said they'd only hooked up when they'd been drinking.

"So, you think you'll be fine with her at Jake's cabin?"

"Jake's? That's just guys."

"Nope. The girls were talking about it at practice this week. They're all going, and all *your* friends are going, right?"

"Yes," he said with a sigh. "Well, I guess I shouldn't go if she's going to be there."

"You can't miss it if all your friends are going." She held her breath, hoping he'd commit to not going. She knew she had to tread carefully, as telling him he *couldn't* go might be riskier than allowing the two of them to be at an alcohol-influenced over-nighter together.

"I don't want to miss it, but I will if it bothers you."

"No. I want you to go," she lied.

Middle school Shawn was a jerk. And while she knew that was a lifetime ago, she still had trouble trusting him. But everything he said felt genuine. "You really don't like being the bad guy, do you?" She put her hand flat against his heart.

"No. I don't. And I really wish I'd been nicer to you."

Hearing *mature* Shawn's perspective made Ella feel like maybe *she* should have been nicer and respected Sarah and Dalia more than she had. She also knew that nothing Dalia could do would

ever make Shawn fall in love with her. But the two of them drinking together at an all-night party could mean that everything
Shawn said today wouldn't matter. And she couldn't risk that.

27

THE ORNAMENTAL TREES and exotic flowers at the Botanic Gardens weren't doing anything to spruce up Dalia's mood. She was bored, frustrated, borderline depressed. And Sarah's mood was the polar opposite, which made it that much worse.

"How *perfect* is this day?" Sarah lifted her nose and inhaled as they meandered through sweet-scented gardenias. Usually Dalia loved this smell, but today it was making her nauseous.

"It's okay, I guess." She half shrugged.

Today was the Gardens' Annual Art Fair, which had become a tradition for just the two of them. It fell the weekend before the Fourth of July when what seemed like the entire high school went to their summer houses. Sarah and Dalia always made a day out of it, treasure hunting for handmade jewelry. Though this year, Dalia wasn't into it.

Her head was a toxic stew of thoughts. Rancid thoughts, not much different from the *who knows how old* condiments in her refrigerator. And she'd needed to talk to Sarah about it, but the few nights she'd had off work, Sarah had already made plans with Jake. So much for the *make every day count* summer.

"What's going on? You okay?" Sarah put her arm around Dalia as they strolled through the English Walled Garden.

Dalia loved the English garden. It was a real live version of her favorite book, *The Secret Garden.* She'd had many childhood fantasies about a life better than her own. Though by anyone else's definition, they weren't fantasies. Mostly, they were dreams of a life where her most basic needs were met. A refrigerator filled with actual food, a home where she felt safe, *one* decent parent. Which is why she'd instantly connected with the unwanted child in the only book she owned, the child who'd found happiness in a garden just like this. She usually felt a sort of magic when she was here. But even the fluffy pink roses couldn't snap her out of today's funk.

"I'm fine. I don't know." Dalia sat down on a Victorian-style metal bench and slumped against the back of it. She noticed a chip in her Vamp polished thumb and started picking at it.

"I'm just bored. And I feel like I haven't seen anyone in ages. This summer's been a complete waste of time."

"A complete waste of time? Come on. We've had fun. And we've seen each other at practice. But my mom made me take that nanny job, and you're working almost every night."

Dalia had been especially busy lately. And she didn't expect everyone to drop everything to spend time with her on her schedule, but it was total crap that everyone else could just do whatever they wanted and didn't have to worry about things like supporting themselves.

"I don't have a choice. Trudy's making it pretty clear that after this year, I'm on my own."

"She said that?"

Dalia saw Sarah's stomach contract. While the rest of the girls would nod and tell her how sorry they were when she complained about her very real problems, Sarah was the only one who visibly cared about her.

"No, but she's pretty much moved in with the Italian now. She comes home to get her clothes and then leaves. She did leave fifty bucks on the table for groceries the other day." Dalia snarled and tossed imaginary money onto an imaginary table.

"Dalia, I know things are hard at home. But I also know you'll figure it out. You work harder than anyone I know. And as far as this summer's going, it's not like you've missed much. I've been mostly hanging out with Jake."

"Well, lucky you," she sneered.

"Come on," Sarah said. "So you missed a couple of pool things. And that night at Mike's house, which wasn't a big deal. And Josh's party. That one was fun, but that's really it. And we have a lot of summer left, so . . . how have things been with Shawn?"

"See. You don't even know what's going on. I haven't seen you in—"

"Twelve days, and that's including days we did see each other at practice. I counted because I knew you'd bring it up today." Sarah popped an Altoid in her mouth and offered one to Dalia, who declined. Who cared if she had a mint if no one was close enough to notice.

211

"He's been taking me on *dates*." She peered through her sunglasses to judge Sarah's reaction.

"*Dates? Oh my god!* How did *that* happen?"

"The night you guys were at Gatto's, after you left, I told him I knew about Ella."

"You *did?*"

"Of course I did. I can't let him think I'm *stupid*. But I was totally cool. I did all the things I was supposed to do. I told him that I understood how it happened, like obviously he was missing his childhood and all that bullshit. And I said—you would have been proud of me—I said it's no fun being rejected like that. And he said he was sorry. And I told him I can get past it and that it doesn't have to change anything with us. And then we started making out in the parking lot, and then he said he wanted to take me out."

"Dalia." Sarah looked at her the way Tori does when she's about to tell her she's crazy. But before any words came out of Sarah's mouth, she seemed to choose a different path.

"That's *amazing!* So, details? Where has he taken you? How's it been?"

This was the part where Dalia needed Sarah's opinion, because she wasn't sure what to make of the whole thing. Well, not necessarily her *honest* opinion. What she needed was for Sarah's opinion to be that everything *was* amazing so Dalia's doubts about the whole thing would just disappear. But Sarah's high-pitched tone and exaggerated enthusiasm probably meant her honest opinion wouldn't do anything to quash her qualms.

"We went to dinner, Fuddruckers, we saw a movie, *Congo*, and it's been just okay."

"Fuddruckers—that's the place where you stand in line the whole time, right? And isn't *Congo* that monkey movie that got the really bad re—?" Sarah stopped. A crease formed between her eyebrows as she drew her chin to her chest. It obviously seemed weird to her too. But then Sarah put that crease away and tried to pretend it had never been there in the first place.

"Well, that's *great*, Dalia! *Wow!* So, it's just Trudy bothering you?"

"*It's everything!* It's like I did what you said, and we had that night together, so it worked! I was *so nice* at Ella's. To *everyone!*" She shook her head at the pointlessness of all that niceness. The whole thing seemed like a gigantic waste of energy. "And then he tells me he wants to take me out on dates, which I was like *finally!* But then he said he wants to take it slow and get to know each other better. So now we're doing *that,* I guess." She looked up and saw a screechy mob of Girl Scouts walking toward them. "Let's go. I can't handle them right now."

They left the English Garden for the quiet of the Lake Garden and sat on a bench under a large weeping willow.

"So, you're dating now. What's wrong with that?" Sarah asked.

"I don't know, but *something*. It's like backward. I feel like I was making more progress with blow jobs."

A family of three ducks swam toward them. Sarah pulled out a Ziploc bag of crackers and handed some to Dalia. Dalia crunched one in her hand and tossed it to the baby, but the mother duck beat the baby to it. "*Asshole!*" she yelled at the mother duck and kicked dirt in its direction.

"Maybe you're just not used to someone being nice to you, Dalia."

She'd actually thought about that. Maybe it *was* that. But what if it wasn't?

"Whatever it is, it's taking a long time."

"Since when is a couple of weeks a long time? Didn't we talk about being patient and staying confident?"

"I know. But it's like, I'm thinking about what he needs and all that bullshit, and he seems to like it, but it's only *kind of* working. It might have been better if it didn't work at all. Then we could go back to the way it was."

Dalia felt trapped. Stuck in personality purgatory. For as much work as she'd put into being sweeter, it was a lot harder than she'd thought. And if it wasn't delivering immediate results, she didn't want to keep up the effort. But it did deliver something, so she didn't want to give up on it quite yet.

"Blow jobs at parties? Is that really what you want?" Sarah said for the hundredth time.

"We're not just *blow jobs at parties*, Sarah, so stop saying that."

"I'm sorry, Dalia, but it's okay to take things slow. It's called *dating*. Maybe you've just been seeing a bad example from your mom."

"Maybe." She tossed the last of the crackers. "Let's see if the turquoise lady is here."

Sarah and Dalia headed to the artists' booths, touching handmade totes, sniffing fragrant candles, and holding necklaces to their chests as they talked their way through this latest development.

"Look at Jake and me. We've been flirting for ten months, and we *just* had sex."

While Sarah seemed to think this should make Dalia feel

better, it felt like an icepick to her sternum. Dalia turned away from the mirror where she'd been checking out a pair of dangly earrings and forced a smile. "That's good, Sarah. I'm happy for you." She set the earrings on the table and kept on walking.

Weaving through old ladies in wheelchairs and young moms pushing strollers, they made their way to the turquoise lady, a former flower child with gray hair down to her waist. It was impossible to tell how old she was. She either looked great for sixty or terrible for fifty. But she'd been at Woodstock, and they'd always liked her stories. Sarah gave her a friendly hello, while Dalia ignored her completely.

"I just don't know what else I'm supposed to do," Dalia said as she tried on a silver ring looped around a large turquoise stone.

"Dalia, just stick with your plan and have some faith that things will all work out. *Either way*. Hey! Look at *this!*" Sarah picked up a silver bracelet with "Faith" etched in cursive on it. Two turquoise beads separated the word from the band. "I will buy this for you, and every time you're doubting yourself, just look at your wrist!"

"That bracelet's good luck, girls," the turquoise lady said. "I wore one just like it when I—"

"Wait! Let me see that." Dalia grabbed the bracelet out of Sarah's hand and laid it out across her wrist. "That's *it!*" She smacked her forehead, as the angst she'd been feeling began to dissipate. She rolled her neck as a smile of relief spread across her face. "How did I not see it sooner?"

"What's it?" Sarah asked.

"*Faith! Church!* I'm going to start going to church!"

"You are not."

"Yes I am! That's what's missing!" In an instant, Dalia felt alive again. It all made perfect sense.

"Dalia, did you forget the fact that you think church is ridiculous?" Sarah asked.

"Just hear me out. There's no way he doesn't want to fuck me."

Sarah looked mortified, like she wanted to drag Dalia away. It wasn't the first time. But the turquoise lady didn't seem to mind at all. She smiled at Dalia, as if the exact same words had come out of her mouth in another life.

"And we have all these talks and shit now, so what's missing? I've been driving myself *crazy* trying to figure it out, and now I know! He wants a *church person.*" Dalia drew an imaginary halo around her head. "What's the name of that church he goes to?"

"Dalia, this is a terrible idea."

"This is a *sign*, Sarah," she said as she put a twenty on the table. "What have I got to lose?"

"Your dignity? Your self-respect?"

"You think I've ever had those? I am one hundred percent sure that *this* is what's missing for us. Figure out the kind of woman he wants and become *that*. It's *right* out of the article! I'd be an *idiot* not to do it."

"Well, you'd better not touch the holy water. It might burn you," Sarah said. Sarah and the turquoise lady laughed together.

"Sarah, *you* were the one who told me if I wanted to be with him that I had to *not* be myself."

"That's *not* what I said *at all*. I just said to tone down the things you know he doesn't like."

"Riiiight. So, doesn't it make sense to add something that I know he does like?"

Sarah's silence meant that Dalia had made her point.

"Fine. But you can't go with Shawn, because he goes with his family. So, if you're going to become a *church person*, you'd better find another church. If he sees you there, he'll think you're stalking him."

"No he won't. I'll just tell him that he makes it sound really nice, so I wanted to see what it was like, but that I didn't want to bother him. It's like *all* he's been talking about lately. And I can say like . . . I'm missing something in my life. Some bullshit like that."

"Okay, well I guess you have to do what's right for you. But don't do it just to get close to Shawn. Maybe try to get something out of it for yourself too."

"I am, *Sarah*." Dalia gave her a hard roll of her eyes. "I'm getting Shawn out of it. Do people still go on Sundays? And what do they even wear? Oh my god, sorry, Sarah. I have to bail. I need to go clothes shopping!"

28

ON A DAY TAILOR-MADE for camping, the girls pulled up to Dalia's apartment. Sarah hit the buzzer about a hundred times. She was dying to get to Jake's cabin.

"Really, bitches?" Dalia snapped over the intercom. "I'm almost ready. But, come up. I need help carrying all this stuff."

The girls crowded into the combination kitchen-living room, taking up most of the available space. Sarah looked around and realized they'd never all been in Dalia's apartment at once. It was small for a two bedroom. Disturbingly small, considering Trudy had no shame when it came to bringing strange men home. Sarah couldn't help but imagine Dalia hiding under her bedspread with a pillow over her head, trying to muffle the sex noises that surely pierced through the paper-thin walls. At least the apartment didn't seem so gross without Trudy sprawled on the couch.

"What is all this?" Stacey asked, surveying the menagerie of food and various containers strewn about the apartment.

"Well, Stacey, this is a watermelon," Dalia said. "And I used a melon baller to make melon balls, which are soaking in Skyy Vodka that I took from . . . never mind." She stopped. Another incident now on Sarah's radar, thanks to Jake. How had she not picked up on them before? She still wasn't sure if they should bother her, but Jake seemed to have planted a warning system in her mind. And it was sounding the alarms a little more frequently these days.

"And in those bags, we have chips and buns. All the delicate stuff, so we need to keep those on top." Dalia tapped her forehead as she went over her to-do list. "The brownies. What do you think? Should we cut them up and put them in foil? I don't know if I should bring the whole glass pan. I should have used a metal pan."

The girls looked at each other slack-jawed as Dalia went on to give them their orders. "Jenny, you and Tori grab that cooler. I have burgers and hot dogs and some homemade dips—a layered taco dip and guacamole. Did you know that if you put the avocado seed in with the guac, it won't turn all brown and nasty?"

"Wow, Dalia, when did you get so good at this?" Jenny asked.

"So *domestic*," Tori added.

"I don't know. I kind of liked hosting Ella's party, and *Glamour* had a whole thing on summer picnic ideas, so—"

"You don't have to pretend, Dalia." Sarah turned to the girls. "She's trying to impress Shawn. Speaking of, how's life as a *church person*? Have you gone yet?" Sarah steered her eyes toward Tori, giving her the signal to run with this one.

"Who and what is a *church person?*" Tori asked, eyes big as full moons.

Dalia gave Sarah a dirty look as she handed her a spatula, the Faith bracelet slipping down her thin wrist. "Cut the brownies," she said through gritted teeth.

"Come on. It's not like they weren't going to find out." Sarah smiled as she began to divide the mass of brownies into small squares. She shoved one in her mouth when Dalia wasn't looking.

"Fine. I went twice."

"And?" Sarah asked.

"And nothing. I didn't see him."

"You better not be stalking Shawn at church, Dalia. God doesn't like that," Stacey chimed in from the black pleather couch where she was wrist-deep into a bag of Fritos. The girls all laughed, which Dalia didn't seem to like at all.

"Put those back!" she barked. "Listen, bitches, I'm not stalking him. I'm just trying to improve myself."

"Bullshit," Tori said. Sarah motioned for her to go easy.

"Okay, because Sarah can't keep her mouth shut, I guess I'm going to have to explain it to you guys. It makes *perfect sense* for me to go to church."

"Why are you going to church?" Jenny asked.

"Remember how I told you guys we had that totally deep conversation *that night?*" She looked at each of them as she emphasized *that night*, as if somehow they might not know which night she was talking about. Of course, they knew. She must have said "that night" about a thousand times since *that night*.

"The cunnilingus night?" Tori asked. Stacey and Sarah laughed. Jenny laughed, too, but she didn't seem to know why.

"What does that mean again?" she asked.

"I'll tell you later, Jenny. But yes, *that* night. Anyway, he totally opened up to me about how important his religion is to him. I'm not supposed to *tell* you, but since you're being *bitches,* I have to."

"How important are we talking?" Tori asked.

"I don't know, like *all the way* important. But I'm not going to get into all that."

"*I told you,*" Sarah said. "Didn't I tell you? He doesn't really advertise it, but he's super into it."

"Just let me finish. So, I figured it out," she said as she tore off a large piece of aluminum foil. "Ever since that night, he's been talking about church, like nonstop. And, at first, I'm like what the fuck? I'm gonna hang myself if I have to listen to another church story. But *then* I figured out that that's his way of inviting me without pressuring me."

"*Inviting you?*" Stacey's face contorted like she'd just done a shot of Jack.

"Yes, Stacey, I'm *supposed* to go. The whole thing is a test."

"*A test?*" Tori glanced at Stacey and then back at Dalia.

"Okay, let me spell it out for you. If you wanted me to try something, what would you do?"

"I'd say *hey Dalia, try this,*" Tori said quickly.

"*No, Tori.* That's not what I mean. Let me finish," she said. "I mean, every time we were together, would you not talk about it at all, would you talk about how awful it is, or would you talk about how great it is?"

"Is this a *Cosmo* quiz?" Tori laughed.

"C! C!" Stacey raised her hand excitedly.

"Exactly. So, it's obvious."

"*What's* obvious?" Stacey asked.

"*Oh my god.* It's *obvious* that he's *trying* to get me to go to church!"

"Then why wouldn't he just *ask* you?" Tori asked.

"Two reasons. One, it's a family thing, and two, he doesn't want to pressure me. It's totally a test. I told Sarah that I can't believe it took me so long to figure out that he wants a *church person*. It's *right* out of the magazine. Figure out the woman he wants and become that. That's what I've been doing wrong! The only thing missing between us is this church thing. He obviously wants that, and it explains why that thing happened with Ella. It's the *only thing* she has over me, so now I'm doing *that*." She shook her head. "Is that clear enough for you?"

Stacey was speechless. Tori was not.

"So, let me get this straight," Tori said. "You're just going to go to church and hope he sees you there? Are you going to tell him you're going or just wait for him to see you?"

"So, I *am* going, and *when* he sees me, which I know he's *hoping* to, I'm going to tell him how he made it sound really nice, so I decided to check it out. And I'll just say he opened my eyes or some bullshit like that. There's a word I was going to use. What was it? He says it all the time. Oh! *Impact.* I'll say it really made an *impact* on me. He must jerk off to that word or something. He gets a total hard on about it."

Sarah made sure she spoke before Tori had a chance to start her tit-for-tat argument with Dalia. "So, how's it been?"

"It's *awful*. I don't know how people sit through that shit. And there's like three sessions on Sundays. I keep going to the wrong one, I guess. He doesn't always go at the same time."

"You mean *masses*," Sarah said. "They have them on Saturdays too. And a couple of days during the week."

"You've *got* to be kidding me," she moaned.

"Dalia, if you and Shawn ever get serious, you know you'll be going to church every weekend, right?" Sarah pointed out. She glanced at the wall behind her and noticed that a picture of Dalia's mom and presumably the Italian had replaced the previously framed picture of ten-year-old Dalia with her mom. She wanted to smash it with a hammer.

"Just while we're dating. Once we're married, I won't have to go anymore."

"You're seriously insane, Dalia," Stacey said.

"Actually Stacey, I'm perfectly sane. I know exactly what I'm doing. You'll all see," she said confidently. "And I'll tell you why. It's going to be a compromise. He's gonna teach me why I should be more like him, and I'm going to teach him why it's okay to be more like me. Right now, I see why he's all *we shouldn't party so much, we should have like this pure fun*—it's a total guilt trip. And he was raised that way, so he doesn't know any better. So my job will be to show him that he can be both. He can be this church guy, but he can also party and have fun and have sex, *without guilt.* He needs to see that having fun doesn't make him a bad person. And the first lesson is gonna start at four o'clock today." She grinned like the Cheshire Cat. Tori and Stacey looked at Sarah as if she should have talked her out of this long before it made its way to them.

"So, what do you think of my new top?" Dalia showed off her black wrap top that tied on the side. "Watch this," she said. With one pull of the string, the top came flying open, revealing a sheer, black lace bra that displayed her nips for all to see.

"Jesus, Dalia." Stacey covered her eyes. "Put those things away."

"*Irresistible,*" she said, beaming as she wrapped herself back up.

"Dalia?" Jenny said. "I know you're like in love with him, but maybe you could find someone who's more . . . like you, maybe. You're so much more fun than all that church stuff."

No one said a word. If Jenny, who never judged or even questioned anyone, had something to say about it, maybe Dalia would listen. Or maybe not.

"Jenny, he's my only chance at a normal life. You guys are all leaving next year. And if things don't work with Shawn, I'll be stuck in my bullshit life forever."

"Okay." Jenny shrugged.

"Thank you, Jenny." Dalia blew her a kiss. "All right, let's do this!"

Sarah resisted the urge to point out that Shawn would be going off to college too. But Dalia was right about one thing. In a handful of months, she'd be on her own. All alone, while the rest of them faced their futures with starry-eyed optimism.

As she tucked Dalia's perfect brownies into plastic baggies, she felt that ache for her again. For everything she didn't have. For her futile pursuit of someone who didn't want her. And as she snapped plastic lids onto containers of homemade dips, she thought about Ella. Why couldn't she have respected Sarah's wishes and kept her distance? Why did Ella have to put her in this position where Sarah couldn't possibly get close to her without betraying Dalia?

Why couldn't she have just been cool about the whole thing? Ella should be going to Jake's *with* them and finding her *own* guy to get excited about. Instead, she'd come along and bulldozed Dalia's dreams. Sarah had felt bad about having to cut Ella off, but she really had no choice. And as she nervously watched the excitement radiating from Dalia, she felt a lot less bad about Ella.

It took two trips to lug the food to the car. Between that, the clothes, and the camping gear, they could hardly fit themselves. After a rock-paper-scissors session determined who got shotgun, windows open versus air conditioning, and who got to choose the music, they turned on Alanis Morissette and hit the road for what was to be the night of all nights.

29

"IT'S LIKE GOD'S COUNTRY up here," Sarah said, taking in the simple splendor of the nature engulfing the open road. There was something about the way the Wisconsin sun illuminated the trees and cornfields that always felt spiritual to her.

"God's country?" Jenny asked.

"I don't know. I should probably come up with a better phrase, considering we've maxed out our God talk limit for one day. But that's always what pops in my head when I'm in Wisconsin. That and cheese."

"How many cheese stores does one state have to have?" Tori said.

"I don't think they even sell cheese in those stores. I think the signs are a warning that you're entering the land of cheese, as in cheesiness. Like, careful now, things are gonna get weird. Anything outside of Lake Geneva and Milwaukee? Hillbilly city," Stacey said. "See, look!" She pointed to a billboard that said, "Don't bury that pet, call Ted's Taxidermy. The words overlaid a picture of a rugged man holding a shotgun over his shoulder, while his free arm embraced a glassy-eyed golden retriever. "That's *so creepy*."

"Did you see that strip club a ways back? Cruisin' Chubbies?" Tori chuckled.

"All right, be nice. I don't disagree, but this is my *boyfriend* we're talking about, who was kind enough to invite, quoting my good friend Dalia, all you *bitches* to his house for the night, and you accepted, so I don't want to hear any complaining," Sarah warned.

"I won't complain," Dalia said. "What time is it?"

"Twelve thirty. And we should probably take it a little easy on the day drinking. We've got a long day ahead of us, and we don't want a repeat of Lollapalooza, *Tori*."

It was almost a year to the day that Tori had decided it was a good idea to start drinking on the train on the way *to* Lollapalooza. Big mistake. She was throwing up by the third band, forcing the girls to take turns babysitting her the rest of the day. She didn't even remember seeing Beastie Boys, which was straight-up tragic.

"I know, no shots before sunset," Tori said.

"Look at that!" Stacey pointed as the Jeep crunched down the gravel driveway. There was a sign that said "Hillbilly Hilton" with an arrow pointing ahead to a rickety wooden cabin. "Was I right? Or was I right?"

"You were right." Sarah sighed.

There was no way that Jenny or Stacey had ever experienced anything like this before. The cabin looked almost uninhabitable from a distance. But as they got closer, Sarah realized it was made to look that way as part of its charm.

"Tent first, you guys," Sarah said as they began to unpack. She did a brief recon mission and didn't see Jake, so they lugged their things to a suitable spot as close to the house as possible and set up camp.

As they put up the tent, Sarah surveyed their surroundings. There was a picnic table right next to a wasp nest, a swing hanging from a dead branch that looked like it could come down at any moment, and a trampoline without a safety net. Jake didn't know what the hell he was talking about when he said she couldn't worry about anything here. She'd been there five minutes and had already identified several serious safety hazards.

"Okay," she said once they'd finished. "Before anyone goes anywhere, here's the bug spray. Put it on now, and don't go in the woods without pants on."

"But topless is okay, right?" Stacey teased.

"Ya know what, go in the woods topless if you like. But I don't care how good an idea it seems at the time or who dares you, no one is going on that trampoline." She handed the spray to Jenny. "Is everyone up to date on their tetanus shots? If you're not, *do not* take your shoes off. Or swing on the swing, or walk on the dock, and probably don't sit at that picnic table either. Oh, and there are wasps over there so . . ."

All at once, the girls' bored-with-Sarah's-lecture faces erupted into smiles. Sarah looked over her shoulder and saw that Jake had sneaked up behind her.

"Sarah," he said, grabbing her shoulders. "I told you, no worrying allowed here."

"Me? I'm not *worried*. I'm just making sure that no one gets tetanus. Or breaks their neck, or gets crushed by a branch, or gets Lyme disease. It's *preventive*, Jake. I'm taking steps *now*, so I don't *have* to worry *later*. There's a difference, ya know."

"Don't bother, Jake," Tori said. "We know better than to try to change her. You just gotta go with it."

"Look around you." He nodded to the people around them. A group of guys tossed a football to their right. To their left, three couples sat in lawn chairs, chillin' and drinking beers. Down by the lake, a couple of guys cast fishing rods, while a group of girls worked on their tans. "Does anyone look worried to you?"

"No. But they should be," she said, jealous of everyone's ability to ignore the potential land mines all around them.

"Babe, everyone's having a great time, and there's nothing to worry about. I've got you." He hugged her from behind. "Tonight's about you and me."

"And those fifty other people."

"Yeah, them too." He leaned in and kissed her cheek. "What's up guys, was the ride okay?"

"Yeah, but Dalia tried to fit the entire grocery store in the car. My back's killing me," Stacey said.

"I got something that can help with that, if you want." He pinched his fingers together and inhaled a fake joint.

"I want! But not yet. Thanks Jake," Stacey said as she grabbed her bathing suit out of her bag.

"Dalia, you having a good time?" he asked.

"I will be." She tightened the string that was barely keeping her top closed. "And thanks, Jake. I am *so excited* for tonight," she said, pausing before she added, "Hey, can I talk to you later?"

Jake looked at Sarah, seemingly for approval, which she signaled with a nod.

"About that thing at Ella's. No biggie, just when you get a sec," Dalia added.

"I gotcha." He conveyed with his eyes and a nod that he knew what she was talking about, and that it was okay. "It's cool, Dalia."

"Thanks, Jake." She smiled graciously. Jake had a way about him, a natural body language that made the people around him comfortable. Sarah smiled to herself as she watched him work his calming magic on Dalia.

Jenny was bent over digging through her bag, when suddenly she started jumping up and down, shrieking. "Where is that coming from?" She wiped off the back of her thighs and looked around. Rob poked his head out from behind a neighboring tent and revealed a fluorescent green squirt gun.

"Come on, we're going swimming."

"Okay, Rob," she said, grinning. "Are you guys coming?"

"I'm not getting my hair wet," Dalia said. "I'll put out some snacks, and then I'll come stick my feet in."

"Is Shawn here already?" Sarah asked, surprised to see his friends this early. Dalia couldn't stop talking about all the things that were going to happen at four o'clock.

"No, he had something to do. He'll be here at four," Dalia said.

"You coming, Sarah?" Jenny asked.

"I'll meet you in a little bit. I want to say hi to Jake's parents first." She turned to him. "Can we?"

"My cousin offered to come up to keep an eye on things instead. But she has a camper, so we get the house all to ourselves."

He put his hands around her waist. "Wanna go check out the bedroom?" he asked playfully.

The cabin door creaked as it opened but quieted the rest of the world when it closed behind them. All at once, the silence and the smell of incense transported Sarah into another universe. Their own little oasis amidst the flurry of activity outside. The cabin was inviting and kitschy, as if two hippies got together and brought every meaningful trinket they'd ever collected and lovingly displayed them. Sarah was in awe.

"Wow . . . what is this?" she asked about a looping wooden sculpture on the coffee table.

"Isn't that cool? It's a unity sculpture from Kenya. They got it on their honeymoon."

"That's *so* cool. And so is *this*," she said as she beelined toward a bamboo basket chair hanging from the ceiling. Planting her feet on the terra cotta tile, she swung back and forth, absorbing the pure magic of the colorful surroundings. Every trinket had a purpose or a story. She could have spent all day poking around, but Jake seemed to have other things in mind. He grabbed her by the hand and led her from the chair to the laddered loft entrance. "It's either up there or we pull out the sofa bed," he said, dragging his finger along her hip.

Up there did not disappoint. Sarah didn't know if it was the ambiance or the practice paying off, but she felt like she and Jake had reached another level. She started to wonder how many levels there might be, how good two people could make each other feel as she gazed at the dream catcher and the Buddha statue, each decorating a corner of the room.

"So, what do you think?" Jake asked, cradling her arm as they lay side by side.

"I think I'm in love."

As his eyes met hers, she realized her blunder. "Oh my god, *with this cabin!*" She buried her face in the pillow.

"Yeah?" He laughed. "Well, I think I'm in love with *this cabin* too." He pulled her closer.

Sarah collapsed into a state of bliss as she lay on his chest, listening to his heartbeat.

"Hey, Jake?"

"What's up?"

"Nothing. I just wanted to say that I'm happy."

"I'm happy too, babe."

She turned on her back and stared at the Turkish lamps hanging from the ceiling. "I know I worry about everything, and I know you think I shouldn't. But today's a perfect example of why I do. Not the safety stuff. The dark thoughts stuff. The people being sad ones."

"What do you mean?"

"So, Dalia's doing all this stuff to try to impress Shawn. Like trying to be all domestic, going to church . . . she's basically trying to make herself into someone he wants. And *we* don't have to do any of that stuff. I'm just me, and I'm pretty sure you're just you, and we're all good," she said.

"That's because they're not right for each other. If they were, she wouldn't have to try so hard."

"*That's* what I'm trying to figure out. Should she change? I mean some of it might actually make her a better person. But it's just not *her*."

"That's tough. I don't know if there's a good answer to that. But if one person is doing all the changing, it's probably not gonna work."

"Yeah, you're probably right." She sighed. "I know you're not the biggest fan of hers, but it's like the entire universe has been against her from the start. I'm pretty sure her mom tried to trap her dad. And he's a total jerk. He only comes around when he's in trouble, and then he leaves again. And her mom has taken it out on Dalia her whole life."

"Jeez. That's rough. Look, if you want my opinion, I say you just be a good friend, but don't get too caught up in it."

"Yeah, you're right. So, I know you guys didn't start off on the best foot, but I hope you can keep an open mind about her. She's not a bad person."

"Okay, I'll make you a deal. I'll keep an open mind about Dalia if you keep an open mind about Sadie."

"Sadie? No."

"Sarah . . ."

"*Fine!*"

"Okay, you can start right now by taking her for a walk with me."

Sadie didn't look like she was willing to give Sarah a chance as she awkwardly untied her leash from the front porch. She took a deep breath and let Sadie lead, sniffing her way down to the dock, where the girls were laying out.

"What the hell? What are *you* doing with a dog?" Tori asked. Sarah wouldn't even go to Tori's unless she locked up her dog.

"Don't ask," she said as Sadie wrapped her leash around Sarah's legs. "You see what she's trying to do here, Jake?"

"You've *got* to *try* these," Dalia said, pointing at the bowl of vodka watermelon balls. "The watermelon is *so sweet.*"

"Aren't those the vodka ones?" Sarah asked.

"Yeah, they didn't really soak up much of the vodka. You can hardly taste it." The bowl was half empty, and Dalia was half in the bag.

"Dalia, do you even know how strong those are? I thought you weren't going to drink yet."

"I'm not *drinking, Sarah.* Those are like *nothing,*" she said as she sat up on her towel. She seemed surprised when she had to steady herself. If she'd just been lying there the whole time, she probably hadn't noticed how drunk she'd gotten. She grabbed Tori's wrist to look at her watch. "T minus fifteen to Shawn, *bitches!*" she said unreasonably loudly. Tori took back possession of her wrist and then moved the watermelon out of Dalia's reach.

"You trying to get me back for Lollapalooza? What's going on?"

"*What.* I'm *fine!*" Dalia sneered with belligerence.

She was not fine. But Sarah hoped she'd get fine before Shawn saw her.

"All right, we're taking Sadie for a walk," she said as she sprayed Jake, herself, and Sadie with a protective layer of DEET. "We'll start the coals around five, so bring the food up by five thirty. Have fun guys!"

Sarah looked at Sadie. Sadie looked back at her with her big doggie eyes and let Sarah lead her to the woods. And it was actually kind of nice.

30

"THESE ARE READY," Sarah said to Jake as she poked the sooty coals. In the distance, she saw Jenny hurrying toward her, arms flailing, face frozen. Immediately, Sarah assumed one of her many safety hazard scenarios had played out. "What happened, Jenny?"

"It's Dalia. She's really drunk, and she's starting to freak out because Shawn isn't here yet."

"I'll be right back, Jake." Sarah looked at her watch. Five fifteen. He wasn't crazy late yet, but if you've been waiting all day for something, or all summer, or your whole life, it probably felt crazy late to Dalia.

"I'm worried about her, Sarah, she's so upset."

"It'll be okay," Sarah said. But she suspected it might not be. They passed Mike, who was bent over, digging through a cooler.

"Have you seen Shawn yet?"

"Nah, he said he'd be here at five or six."

"Move over." Sarah nudged him aside with her hip and helped herself to two of his Red Bulls.

"Hey, those are mine!" he shouted after them.

"Thank you!" She waved as they ran off. "Okay, that's good. She should calm down once she knows he's just running late. But we have to sober her up."

This would prove to be quite a challenge. Sarah found Dalia sitting on her beach towel, head between her knees.

"Dalia . . ."

Dalia looked up at Sarah, her lash-thickening mascara now salty black streams running down her cheeks. Sarah cracked open a Red Bull. "Drink this."

"What the *fuck*, Sarah? I go through *all this* trouble, and he's not even gonna show? He doesn't care about me *at all.*"

"Sure he does."

Sarah's stomach churned with guilt as she put her hand under Dalia's chin. She should have told the truth about Ella from the start. The confident goddess who'd been prancing around earlier was unrecognizable. Two crusty circles of dirt covered her knees, the tie holding her shirt shut wasn't doing its job, and the humidity wasn't doing her hair *any* favors.

"She threw up in the woods," Stacey said.

"The woods?" Sarah began checking her for ticks. "Now, you've *got* to listen to me. I just talked to Mike, and *he* said Shawn wouldn't be here until five or six."

"*Really?*" Dalia sniffed. "He told me four *just yesterday.* What the *fuck?*" She began to survey the damage. She tried to brush the vomit stain off her shirt. "*Fucking Ella.* Everything's been *so fucked up* since she moved here. You should see the way he looks at her, *Sarah.* I make sure they don't work together anymore because I *can't take* watching it. I think there's something going on between them. Is there something you're not telling me?"

"You see her more than I do, Dalia." That wasn't a lie, but Sarah hoped she wouldn't press her. While she hadn't talked to Ella at all about Shawn, it was probably time to fill the girls in on what she did know. But not tonight.

"He looks at her like he's *in love* with her. Like all fucking *googly-eyed.*"

"Like you right now?" Sarah teased.

"How bad is it?" Dalia wiped under her eye and saw black sludge on her fingers. She sloppily wiped her fingers on her shirt and then wiped under her eye again, like she was trying to determine if her fingers or her face was the source of the sludge.

"It's bad, but it's not hopeless. Now listen to me. You have to drink these, get cleaned up, eat some food, and pull yourself together." Sarah looked at her watch. Five thirty. "Jenny, can you get Dalia's makeup bag? And some toothpaste? And this shirt has to go. Go into my bag and grab a shirt."

"*Fucking watermelon balls!*" Dalia picked one up and threw it in the lake. "I haven't had *one sip* of alcohol. And you know what's worse? I didn't even get that idea from *Glamour.* I got it from *Family Fucking Circle* magazine!"

"*Family Circle?* Dalia . . ." Tori's jaw dropped as if, of all the day's events, this was the most troubling.

"I was too embarrassed to admit I was reading it. How can

they put that recipe in there without warning you it's like doing fucking *shots*?! Fucking bullshit *family* magazine."

"Okay, we don't have time for all that now. But you gotta try to stop slurring. And crying." Sarah grabbed a crumpled napkin and wiped Dalia's nose.

Jenny returned, breathless, trying not to drop the armful of supplies. "Here's everything."

The four of them immediately went to work restoring Dalia to her previous self. Surrounding her, they took off her vomit-covered shirt and replaced it with Sarah's Oasis T-shirt. Jenny used makeup wipes to wash the dirt off her knees. Stacey got to work on her makeup, while Tori turned her hair into what looked like a purposeful sloppy bun. They made good progress, but it was the equivalent of fixing a leaky pipe with bubble gum.

"This is how hillbillies get ready on their wedding day." Stacey laughed, which prompted a small smile from Dalia.

"Okay. Red Bull, check. Dalia restored to former goddess . . ."

"Check!" Jenny said.

"Okay, let's go eat," Tori said. She and Sarah got on each side of Dalia and helped her walk.

"Are you sure we shouldn't just put her to bed?" Tori whispered as they maneuvered her into a seated position at the picnic table. "This isn't like one of us having to keep an eye on her. We're gonna be all *Weekend at Bernie's* all night."

"Let's give the Red Bull and some food a chance to kick in and see," Sarah responded.

"I hope it's okay I got your food," Jake shouted over as he flipped sizzling burgers. "She okay?"

"You are the best and not even close," she said as she walked over to him. "We performed a miracle on the outside, but she needs food like *right now.*"

Jake scooped a hot dog into a bun and handed it to her. "That enough for ya?"

"Thanks babe." Sarah turned around and delivered the hot dog to Dalia.

She really wished Jake had handed her a burger because the hot dog seemed to trigger a memory of a plan Dalia had tucked away, just in case. Dalia stared at it for a moment. Then she picked the hot dog out of the bun and began jiggling it, before turning it into a vertical position. Her eyes got smaller as the corners of her mouth sloped into a disturbing smile. With the upright hot dog on display in one hand, she reached across the table with the other to take Dave's freshly opened Coors bottle. She set it down too hard in front of her. Foam came pouring over the sides.

"You could've just *asked* for one."

"Sorry, Dave." She raised the bottle. Beer ran down her arm and onto Sarah's shirt. "Who wants to play *I Never?*"

"I'll go," Sarah said as she plucked the beer out of Dalia's hand. "I *never* think this game is a good idea."

"I *wasn't* gonna *drink* it, *Sarah.* Pffft." Dalia shooed her away. "I don't even need it to play. Okay, I'll go first. Ready everyone?" she slurred. "Okay. Ready, okay!" She laughed, trying to put her hands on her hips and clap like they do in cheerleading. She fell to the side and the hot dog dropped to the ground. "Whatever. I don't need that either. Okay. *I never* stuck a hot dog up my vagina and had to go to the hospital to get it removed."

The background chatter ground to a halt as the scene began to unfold.

"What?" Jake started laughing. "Where did you come up with that?"

"Come on, no one? *Oh right. Oops!* Silly me. *Ella's* not here," she snickered. "She'd be drinking *for sure.*"

"*Dalia*, you stop that right now," Sarah ordered.

"*What, Sarah?* I just think it's a funny *story.*"

"What story?" Rob asked. She had all the guys' attention now.

"Well, our little Ella, you know, the *new girl?* Well, she shoved a *hot dog* in her *vagina* to see what it was like to have *sex.*"

"No way!" Mitch Ingalls exploded with laughter.

"Wait, wait. It gets *worse*," she slobbered. "*Get this.* A piece of it broke off and got *stuck* up there, and she had to go *to the hospital* to get it out."

"That didn't happen," Jake said. "How did she even get it in there? It's too soft."

She pointed her finger at Jake. "She *froze* it first."

"Oh my god!" Mike said. "That's so twisted."

"Not true, Mike, none of it's true," Tori said.

"Whatever, *Tori.* So, wait. Just *listen* to me because there's *more.* So I said it was *frozen*, right? So then, it got *warm*, and then a chunk *broke off.*" She said, nodding. "And it was in there for like *a week*, cuz she was too scared to *tell anyone.* But then, it started to *smell.* And it was *so gnarly* up there like, well I'm not *sure* this part is true, but I heard something about *maggots.* But it was *so gnarly* up there that she *had* to tell her parents."

She was so detailed and disgusting that even if no one believed her, the mental image starring Ella was sure to leave a wretched taste in anyone's mouth.

"Okay, Dalia, that's enough," Stacey said.

"But I'm not *finished*, *Stacey*. So, her family is a bunch of religious *freaks*. And one of the *workers* at the hospital went to their *church* and told *everyone* about it. They couldn't show their *faces* there, her parents were *so* embarrassed. And so that's why they moved back here. Okay *Stacey*, I'm done now."

"That is *so nasty!*" Rob said.

"*Oh wait!* I'm *not* done. One more thing. So, if any of you *guys* are thinking about *getting* with her," she said, pointing at each one of them, "you probably, you're gonna, you might just, you should just . . . *not*. And if you *do*, and you get some nasty *cow* disease or like *rat part* disease, don't say I didn't warn you. Okay, for real I'm done," she said with a smirky smile.

The guys were howling. Sarah had to yell "guys" about a dozen times to get their attention.

"All of you look at me." She stood next to Dalia, put her hands on the table, and leaned in. "None of that is true. And I don't want to hear it repeated. *And if I do,* I'm coming after *each* one of you. Snip, snip." Sarah cut each of their balls off with imaginary scissors. Regardless of Dalia's feelings about Ella, or her own feelings, for that matter, this was out of bounds. No one should be the victim of a lie they don't get to defend themselves against.

"*Whatever.* Sarah's just trying to be a good friend. *Sarah,* you're such a good friend. *So loyal.*" Dalia kissed her elbow. Sarah wiped it off.

"I'm going to get you a *hamburger*, Dalia. Now let's see if you can behave yourself."

Just then, a beautiful, blond, tattoo-covered girl poked her corn row braids out of the cabin. Jake's cousin Nina, who Sarah had been dying to meet, delivered the final blow to Dalia's evening.

"Hey Jake, some guy named Shawn left a message on the machine . . . something about he had to go into work, and he's sorry he can't make it."

"*What?*" Dalia stood up fast from the picnic table and scraped the front of her leg. Holding her thigh, she inhaled through her teeth and swung her leg to the other side of the bench, almost falling in the process. "He didn't have to *work* tonight. That's a fucking *lie! What the fuck!* Oh my god." Her eyes went dark. "That *little, tiny, fucking, evil, little, short, little, fucking, cunty cunt!*" she shouted. She stumbled over to the cooler and tried to open it.

"Cunty cunt?" Nina tilted her head. "I like that. But what's she got against short people?" She pointed with a craned arm. "Jake, I think this one needs a nap."

"Okay, Dalia," Sarah said, shutting the cooler. Dalia shoved her hand out of the way. Stacey swooped in and sat on the cooler.

"Dalia, you are done. It's time to lie down," Stacey said.

"*You* guys don't get to tell *me* what to *do*." She grabbed the cooler handle with Stacey sitting on top of it.

"I got her. Come on." Jake picked up Dalia and threw her over his shoulder, which was a feat, considering they were the same height, and she was pounding on his back like a hundred-pound toddler. There was no way he'd get her all the way to the tent, so he reluctantly settled on the cabin. "You girls wanna get the door?"

It took all five of them to hold her limbs, just so they could get her inside. Sarah laid out a towel in case she got sick. And Tori repaid her Lollapalooza debt by staying with Dalia until she fell asleep.

31

DALIA WOKE UP IN DARKNESS, an unfamiliar pillow scratching her face, an unbearable thirst coating her tongue. She rolled over and unstuck the hair from her lips. Where was she, and why was she wearing Sarah's T-shirt? She placed her thumb and forefinger on her eyebrows to stem the searing pain in her head. Then the memories started trickling in. Just glimpses at first. Then bigger ones. A vicious heartbeat erupted in her chest. Burning humiliation ulcerated her stomach as the Polaroid of the evening began to develop. Oh god. What did she do? Someone was carrying her . . . she screamed to be put down. And she was hitting them . . . but why were they carrying her away?

She found the bathroom sink and frantically cupped water from the faucet into her mouth. The taste of vomit resurfaced, and with it, more memories. Did Shawn see what happened? *Shawn.* That part she remembered crystal clear. He never came.

She slowly ventured into her reflection in the mirror and studied her makeup-smudged face. *How did I let this happen,* she wondered, as she went over the events in her mind. The weight of her foolishness began to suffocate her, the gargantuan disappointment of what should have been was swallowing her whole. She raced to the kitchen and found a clock on the stove. Eight forty-five. It was so early to everyone else, their night filled with promise. But her night was over. There was laughter outside. They were laughing at her for whatever she'd done, she was sure. There was no way she could face them. She had to get out of there.

Her purse. It was probably still in the tent. Not that it would do her any good. It's not like she could call a taxi to drive her home from Wisconsin. She felt utterly helpless, desperate . . . until she saw Sarah's purse. Reaching inside, she wrapped her fingers around a set of keys. Humiliation trumped any and all reason as she tiptoed across the yard, started Sarah's dad's car, and drove off into the night.

She drove aimlessly at first. In the distance, she saw a Mobil gas station and pulled behind it where no one could see her. Her head pounded. She was paralyzed, as the crushing silence inside the car was equally as intolerable as the deafening sound of crickets outside the car. But she needed coffee.

Dalia put Sarah's dad's sunglasses on to cover the mess on her face. Even from behind the sunglasses, the neon store lights were blinding as she made her way to the coffee carafes. The burnt, bitter smell of hours-old coffee made her nauseous as she poured it into a Styrofoam cup. She reached into the refrigerator and grabbed a Red Bull. At the counter, she grabbed a pack of NoDoz, ripped open the package, and washed down four pills. She should have made sure Sarah had some money before she did that, she thought, as the sparsely toothed clerk asked if she had a long drive ahead of her.

"Sure. Yeah," she said. "Where's I-90 from here?"

"A mile north." He peered into her eyes. "You'd better be careful with all that. Makes you real edgy."

She handed him Sarah's money without saying a word. Sitting in the car, she downed the Red Bull before working on the sludgy coffee that had cooled to a drinkable temperature. As her head began to clear, she felt herself seething with anger—at Shawn, at Ella, at herself. She'd planned everything so carefully. How had Ella managed to get Shawn to skip Jake's? Her relentless thinking, her need for clarity, or even finality, left her no choice but to go to the restaurant to confront her. How could Ella do this to her after all she'd done for her?

She drove and drove, trying hard to stay in the lines. She opened the windows when she felt her head bobbing and turned the music up as loud as it could go as her eyes darted back and forth between the road and the speedometer. By some miracle, two hours later, she pulled across the street from Gatto's.

It was closing time. On a Saturday, Ella would be totaling her receipts for the night. It wouldn't be long now. Dalia wasn't exactly sure what her plan was. Would she confront her at Gatto's? Tell her what a conniving little bitch she was? How *ungrateful* she was? She didn't want to do that in front of George. It would be better to follow her. To catch her at Shawn's, or wherever they were meeting. Yes, it would be much better to confront the two of them together. *Fuck her* for being a conniving cunt and *fuck Shawn* for stringing her along.

Twenty minutes later, she saw the front door of Gatto's pop open. Two busboys came out. Then Barbara. Two other waiters soon followed. With each movement of the door, Dalia caught her breath. No Ella yet. The door popped open again—this time it was Shawn, all by himself. Shawn always walked the girls to their cars late at night, so if he wasn't walking Ella out, Ella wasn't there. Where was Ella? What was happening? Why did Shawn work tonight and not Ella? Even hungover, she had the wherewithal to be certain that somehow Ella was behind this.

He pulled out onto Main Street. She let one car go in front of her before she pulled out after him. Fully expecting him to make the next right toward Ella's, she was surprised when he didn't and instead went straight home. He pulled into his driveway and entered through the front door. *Ella must be coming to him*, she thought as she waited across the street from Shawn's cul-de-sac. The last she remembered, it was midnight. The next thing she knew, birds were chirping.

For the second time in a day, Dalia awoke having no idea where she was. But this time, she very quickly recognized Shawn's house. And the fact that it was six thirty in the morning. And the fact that she'd *stolen* Sarah's car. Sarah's *dad's* car. If she thought she felt desperate last night, it was *nothing* compared to the utter despair and self-hatred she felt now.

Once again, the urge to flee took over. She had to get back to Wisconsin before anyone noticed she'd left. What was she thinking? Of course they knew she'd left. They were probably sure she was dead. Unless they noticed she'd taken the car, in which case, they might still think she was dead. But if she wasn't, they'd never speak to her again.

Dalia started back on the road and was about to get on the highway when she noticed the red E illuminated on the gas gauge. "Fuck!" she yelled, hitting the steering wheel as she realized she'd have to stop. She repeated last night's stop at another Mobil, orange juice and a stale doughnut replacing the Red Bull and coffee.

Her detour had the unfortunate, unintended consequence of taking her right past St. Joseph's church, where the sign advertised a seven o'clock mass. It was six fifty. The parking lot was busy. Try as she might, she couldn't resist pulling in. She wouldn't go inside. She would just sit in the parking lot and take a peek. At this point, another ten minutes wasn't going to make much of a difference. Or so she thought. She could hardly catch her breath when she saw Ella and Shawn, all smiles, talking at the entrance. Rage overcame her as she slammed the car door shut and marched over to confront them.

"So how did you do it, *Ella?*"

"*Dalia.*" Ella looked up at her. "What are you *doing* here?"

"What are *you* doing here?" Dalia put her finger against Ella's chest.

"This is my *church.*"

"How *convenient.* So, Shawn, how did she talk you into not going to Jake's?"

"*Not here, Dalia.*" He grabbed her firmly by the arm and led her to his car. She didn't care who she was embarrassing, as she went on to lambast the two of them in the church parking lot, calling them liars and disgusting, telling Shawn what a slut Ella is, that they deserve each other. Maybe it was the NoDoz and the

Red Bull or the hangover or the humiliation. Or maybe she'd just had enough of her life, and any stimulation or closure or *something* was better than the constant barrage of every day of nothing special, of not being loved by anyone, ever.

"Dalia, I was *sick*." Ella stepped backward. Shawn stepped forward, extending his arm in front of Ella.

"*Sure* you were, *Ella*," Dalia said.

"I have *strep*. I couldn't *work*."

Dalia couldn't determine if the look on Ella's face was guilt or fear.

Shawn got between them. "So, George called me and told me Ella was sick as I was walking out the door and asked if I could come in. What was I supposed to do?"

"Well, you sure don't *look* sick," Dalia scoffed.

"I went to the doctor Friday afternoon. He said I wouldn't be contagious after twenty-four hours, but when I called George Saturday, he said to stay home. I can show you my prescription if you want. And *yes*, I'm feeling *better*, thank you, so my mom made me go to church this morning, and I ran into Shawn just now." Ella shook her head. "And my family is inside. Would you like me to prove it to you?"

Dalia stared into Ella's blinking eyes. A wave of regret took hold of her, as she knew she'd ruined everything now. She couldn't take their stares of contempt, and worse, their pity. "I'm sorry," she said. Tears began flooding her face as she ran off, frantically looking for her car. Rushing up and down the lanes, not finding her car anywhere, she could feel Shawn and Ella's eyes on her. She came to a sudden stop, her heart sinking when she remembered it wasn't her own car she was looking for—it was Sarah's dad's.

Dalia took layers off the tires as she screeched out of the church parking lot, narrowly missing a mother pushing a stroller. The adrenaline rush shocked her into the understanding that she needed to get control of herself, especially if there was any hope of recovering from this. The question of whether there *was* any hope would have to wait. "Focus!" she yelled out loud.

She adjusted the rearview mirror and caught a glimpse of her reflection in the process. The tattered mess staring back at her split the wound even wider. Had she looked in the mirror before she left the gas station, she wouldn't have even considered pulling into the church. Maybe. And she for sure wouldn't have gotten out of the car. Probably. She snapped up the mirror so not even a strand of her hair was visible and then reached across and slammed the passenger side mirror shut. She saw Sarah's white scrunchy on the gear shifter. Wiping it across her eyes, she used the moisture of her tears to wash away what she could of the remaining makeup. She looked at the mascara-stained scrunchy and threw it out the window as she pulled onto the highway.

Would this feeling ever leave? This reality squeezing her? This feeling that seemed to be taking up permanent residence inside her? She didn't want to feel this way for even a moment longer. She *couldn't* feel this way a moment longer. As trees and telephone poles whizzed by her at eighty miles per hour, she cursed the flat Illinois landscape—she wasn't sure a hard yank of the steering wheel would be enough to put an end to this feeling. What if it just paralyzed her? That might be the only thing worse than what she was dealing with right now. *Unless Shawn felt sorry for you and married you.* The thought, accompanied by a video of Shawn pushing her in a wheelchair, her looking back at him, the two of them smiling at each other as she places her hand on his, came out of nowhere. The fact that it even entered her mind appalled her, making her recoil . . . from herself. "Stop it!" she shouted to whatever demented part of her brain was responsible for such a horrifying thought. The part that, for just a moment, she recognized as a separate entity from herself. An unwelcome part, a small but powerful voice that seemed to be in charge these days. A part that was determined to have Shawn at any cost.

The grisly thought snapped her to attention. She hadn't noticed that the temperature in the car had become unbearably hot. She frantically cranked open the window; the breeze quickly cooled the sweat droplets on her chest. It felt exquisitely good. Finally, a sensation other than torment. It slowed the racing in her head to a tolerable level and loosened the vice grip of the day's events, opening up space for her to endeavor into the why. Why Shawn . . . what was it about him? She was seventeen. She was stunning. Of course, there had to be more than just one guy in the world who could make her feel this way. But then she thought about her mom. Trudy had fallen permanently in love at the exact same age. She was living proof that there might not be, even if you *are* beautiful.

She thought about the first time Shawn flirted with her at Joey Bennett's house and how empowered she felt as he followed her around all night before finally kissing her. And the rush she felt that day he came into Gatto's and asked her for an application because, of course, it was to get close to her. She thought of the comfort she felt all those late nights he insisted on walking her to her car. And the sheer delight she felt every time she heard someone use "Dalia and Shawn" in a sentence. Because even though they

PAULA RIEHLE

weren't technically boyfriend and girlfriend, they were recognized as two things that go together. Like matching socks. Where there is one, you expect to find the other. She thought about the pride she felt just being in the passenger seat of his car, and how just sitting next to him electrified everything else in the world. And how dull the world was when she wasn't with him.

And that didn't even include the hookups, she told herself as she went through the twelve times they'd touched each other, each filed away with stunning recollective accuracy, as she'd relived them over and over in her head to the point that they'd gelled. This wasn't just some teenage crush. If it was, she would only think about the hookups. This was *connection*. This was *real*. And none of those things even included *that night*. That night began to replay in her head like a 4D movie, complete with scent and touch. How he listened to her, shared with her, confided in her, wiped a tear from her eye, comforted her. His smell, his taste, his mouth on her. The *thrill* of it all. Just the thought of it triggered dopamine to spill once again. No way were they not meant to be together. The question was how to fix this. What did she have to work with? She had her friends.

And she had to fix that before she could even begin to think about fixing anything else, she decided as she pulled into the gravel drive of Jake's summer house.

32

"OH MY GOD, DALIA, are you kidding me?" Sarah screamed, as Dalia flopped out of the car and sat on the ground.

"Where the fuck did you go?! I was just about to call my parents to come get us! Do you have any idea how frantic we've been? We thought you were dead! We called the hospitals, the police station, your house about a thousand . . ."

Dalia gave no indication she could even comprehend what Sarah was saying. Her glazed eyes stared blankly at the patches of grass spread throughout hardened dirt. She sat quietly, unresponsive for a moment. She began pulling at the blades of grass and letting them fall from her fingers. And then her chin began to tremble. And then the sobbing began.

Dalia was a proud "not a cryer," making the scene before them that much more dramatic. In fact, Sarah would've bet the last time she *did* cry was the day of the elephant theft when she was four years old, given the ferocity of today's tears. They were flowing as if a lifetime of frustration had bubbled up, breaching her capacity to contain it. An emotional magma finally breaking through her hardened outer layer. The unexpectedness of it shut Sarah's lecture down mid-sentence. As Tori moved in to comfort her, Sarah asked Jake to go help Jenny and Stacey finish collecting their things.

"Dalia, just tell us what happened." Tori sat next to her, cradling her head against her cheek.

"I don't know," she said, weeping. "I woke up, and I didn't know where I was." Dalia pulled her hair back into a ponytail and held it there. "And then I remembered what a complete asshole I made of myself, and there was no way I could face anyone." She finally looked up.

Her face was puffy, masking her usual gauntness. Her cheeks were just-pinched pink. She looked raw, natural, and pretty. *Vulnerable.* Shawn might have liked this look, Sarah thought.

". . . and then I saw Sarah's purse, and the next thing I knew, I was in the car."

"Dalia," Tori toed the line between scolding and empathizing. "I feel like I can skip the lecture about how dangerous what you did was, but you scared us to death! Why didn't you come talk to us?" she asked.

"I . . . I don't know," she stammered. "I was just so embarrassed, I couldn't face anyone."

"Embarrassed? *Why?*" Sarah asked. She knelt down and put her hand on Dalia's shoulder. "You didn't do anything that all of us haven't done in one way or another, when we've had too much to drink."

"So, you guys don't hate me?"

"Hate you? If we were gonna hate you, we would have plenty of better reasons to than this." Tori turned her palms to the sky.

"*Totally.*" Sarah jumped in. "Remember when you switched our Bon Jovi tickets when I wasn't looking so you and Jenny got the tenth-row seats, and we got stuck with your lawn seats?"

"Oh, oh," Tori snapped her fingers. "How about the time you left us at that middle-of-nowhere party just so Jenny could follow Steve Michaels?"

"I can't believe we hitchhiked home," Sarah said. "We're lucky we're not chained up in some creepy guy's basement."

"Okay you guys, I get it." Dalia pushed her palm forward for them to stop. "I am very sorry about last night. And I'm sorry about all the other stuff too. Well, not Bon Jovi. Jenny loves them way more than you guys do. I did it for her."

"But *we* stood in line all night for the tickets, and it was *freezing*!" Tori reminded her. "*And* you told Jenny *you* got them for her."

"Well, I did get them for her, didn't I?" A slight gleam unveiled itself in her eye, which made Sarah feel better that she was feeling better.

"Tori," Sarah said, scratching her chin. "Have you ever noticed how a lot of the really asshole stuff is all for Jenny?"

"Interesting observation, Sarah. Why is that?"

"Even more interesting is the fact that Jenny never asks for these things. She has no idea they're ever even happening," Sarah said.

Dalia contracted every muscle in her face and lurched her head backward. "How do you guys not see that she *needs* me? Or *us?* You three are always all good. Like, *oh, look at us and our perfect lives.* And you look at Jenny like she's all good because she has money." She brushed pieces of dried grass off her leg. "But you know what? That's *all* she has. Take away the money, and her life's not much better than mine."

"She has a point," Sarah said, feeling bad that they'd never given Jenny's family situation the attention it deserved. Jenny was just so easy. She didn't walk around wearing her troubles like Dalia did.

"Well, we need to be better about that. And, for the record, if we were going to hate each other for dumb drunk things, we'd never be friends. So, don't go changing the rules now," Tori said.

"What would we laugh about if we didn't do all the stupid stuff?" Sarah said. "And Dalia, it may feel bad now, but one day we're going to laugh about this too. Together." Sarah opened her eyes as wide as humanly possible and stared right at her until she knew Dalia knew they were okay. That she was okay.

"So, where did you go? Did you pull down the street and hide or something?" Tori asked.

A breeze rustled the towering trees as the question stayed unanswered. They'd figured she left because she was embarrassed. That she'd gotten a room or something, just to get away and process everything. Truth be told, Sarah hadn't worried too much until about an hour before she showed up, as Dalia Houdini-ing when she was upset about something wasn't out of character. But there was a shame in her eye that made Sarah ask a question she was afraid to hear the answer to.

"You didn't drive home, did you?"

Dalia's shoulders went limp. She stared at her flip-flops. "Is it okay if we don't talk about that yet?"

Sarah didn't know how much longer she should, or could, ignore the alarm bells at this point. As she and Tori exchanged knowing glances, she knew that whatever had happened, they'd indulged Dalia's fantasy for far too long. But she'd wait to talk to Tori alone before she made any decisions as to how to handle it. "Whatever you need," Sarah said. "We're just glad you're okay."

Jake and the girls came back, each limb strung with duffle bags and coolers. As the girls loaded the car, Sarah told Jake she was okay, and told him again how much she loved *his cabin*. A horsefly aggressively stalked her ear, interrupting their kiss, which was her cue to leave. A good girlfriend would have stayed behind to clean up the empty beer cans and food wrappers. But today she had to be a good friend, she reminded herself, as they drove down the gravel drive and back to civilization.

33

FIVE BEST FRIENDS hit the road once again, though looking slightly less glamorous than they had twenty-four hours earlier. Sarah was dying to get breakfast, but Stacey reminded her they didn't need hash browns and cinnamon rolls so close to cheerleading season. She'd actually said *she* didn't need them, but it was a reminder, nonetheless. So, she jumped on the highway, and the girls passed around warm Coke and the last of the Fritos as they recapped the night's events.

Stacey had popped her cherry, Sarah joked. She and Jack Reynolds had hooked up, which was a miracle. And because Stacey had gone so long without hooking up, Sarah declared that she'd revirginized herself. The laughs continued as Jenny and Tori spilled the details about their nights, both having had sex with their second people. Jenny kept calling them the *juicy* details and didn't seem to get why everyone thought *that* was so funny, which made the whole thing even funnier. It was a night to be celebrated. It was sad that Dalia couldn't celebrate with them.

Sarah let Dalia be quiet for as long as she needed. At some point, the Wisconsin sun seemed to hang back, distancing itself as the lovely state of Illinois greeted them with wispy gray clouds that thickened the further south they went. Just a raindrop or two splashed the windshield, then the sky opened up. And so did Dalia. Shortly after crossing back into the land of strip malls, her story came pouring out.

"You guys, there's something wrong with me."

It was as if somehow the change in weather did it, like the dreariness of the rain coaxed her along and said, "It's time."

"Dalia, you're fine," Stacey said. "You're safe. That's all that matters now."

"No. You were right when you said I was insane, Stacey. I am. I ruined everything."

"I was joking, Dalia. Whatever happened can't be that bad."

Stacey was wrong. It was that bad. It was *worse*. And Sarah knew Dalia wasn't equipped to handle what she'd done, each part of her story more appalling than the last. Sarah didn't know the ending, but she didn't want to know. She wanted it to just *stop*. It could have stopped at so many points! Like when Dalia woke up at Jake's. Or when Ella wasn't at Gatto's. Or when Shawn went to his house, alone. Or when she was at the gas station. Sarah wished she could've grabbed Dalia by the throat and told her to just get on the damn highway. It was *awful*.

After debating the implications of her actions, they all came to the same conclusion. That her only choice was to apologize.

She should tell Shawn and Ella the truth, that she'd eaten a bunch of vodka-soaked melon balls that she had no idea could even get someone drunk.

"I mean, if that's not an excuse, I don't know *what* is," Tori said. "Would any of us believe that you could get that drunk from *fruit?*"

"And maybe say someone slipped something in your drink?" Stacey suggested.

"*That's so smart, Stacey,*" Jenny said, clearly relieved they might have come up with something that let Dalia off the hook. "With all his cousin's friends there, that could totally happen."

At this, Dalia opened her arms and looked at the girls, epiphany-eyed. "Maybe it *did* happen," she said. "You know what? I bet that is *exactly* what happened. There's no *way* it was just the watermelon. God, I feel *so much better.*" She clapped her hands together and rubbed them back and forth, as if eager to move past this. "You need to tell Jake, Sarah. That is *so* not cool."

Sarah gripped the steering wheel tightly, trying to discharge her irritation with Dalia's comment onto something other than her.

"So, I'll tell Shawn *that*, and I'll tell him what a *nightmare* Trudy's been." She nodded to herself.

"Shawn will forgive you, Dalia," Jenny said. "He's a good guy."

"Yeah, a little too good," Dalia said. "So, I might as well tell you guys everything. I mean, fuck it," she said with a shrug. "Sarah was right. He *is* saving himself for marriage, well for the person he plans on marrying. And he said we had to take a break from hookups, because he's *too* attracted to me, and he's afraid he'll give in. Isn't that *crazy?* He says *he* can't control himself around *me*." She pointed at her face with both hands. "He said he wants us to go back and get to know each other better without the sex stuff distracting us. To do it right . . . to make sure I'm *the one*."

As Sarah would later discuss with Tori and Stacey, it was a move right out of the Total Pussy Playbook on how to get rid of someone and not have to feel bad. But Dalia seemed to not recognize this at all, as she gave the play by play, once again, of the events of *that night*.

". . . and since then, we've been *dating*. I could actually call him my boyfriend if I wanted, which I just haven't because, you know, we want to keep that between us. *That's* what made me crazy last night. Well, whatever someone put in my *drink* made me crazy. *That's* just what I was upset about," she said indignantly, making it clear she now felt very little responsibility for her behavior. "Because it was the first night that we were going to just hang out like we used to. And I tried so hard to make it perfect. And then Ella gets strep, and I get drugged. How *fucked up* is that? I mean, in the moment, I was sure something was going on with them, but that just seems *crazy* now." She sat up straight-backed and then inched forward, as if willing the car to get her home faster.

Something seemed crazy. But the crazy Sarah saw couldn't be reasoned with, so they drove in silence until the mounting discomfort begged for a distraction. She turned on the radio. They didn't say another word about it.

Sarah came in through the garage, leaving her things in the car, and went right to her room. She called Ella immediately, hoping Ella would say it wasn't a big deal. She didn't.

"She's crazy, Sarah. I don't know how you can even be friends with her. And Shawn is completely freaked out. I mean, I'm sick, and she starts screaming at us at church. At *church*, Sarah! And do you know that she's been messing with our work schedules so that Shawn and I hardly ever work together anymore? We've been keeping track."

Without coming right out and saying it, she made it very clear she and Shawn were now a "we." But Sarah still didn't want to be put in a position where she had to lie to Dalia, so she didn't say anything. Instead, she said that Ella doesn't know Dalia, and it's too bad she probably never will.

". . . and I get that it was weird, but you *have* to give her a break, Ella. If you care at all about *anyone* else's feelings, you *won't* talk about it. To *anyone*. She's really fragile right now. I gotta go. I guess I'll see you at practice."

"I won't tell anyone. And I'm sorry for causing this mess."

"I don't want to hear it," Sarah said and then hung up without saying goodbye. She went into the bathroom and turned on the shower, letting it run until her face disappeared from the steam-covered mirror. The water was uncomfortably hot. She didn't care enough to change it, as she struggled to make sense of what was happening to Dalia. Was Dalia going crazy? Or was this just normal in-love behavior and her trying to save face in a momentary lapse of reason? Sarah didn't know. And she didn't know how to help either way. But she knew for damn sure that if Dalia had any kind of parent at all, this wouldn't be happening.

"Sarah," her mom said as she knocked on the door, "make sure you clean out the car when you get out. And then I want to hear all about your night."

"Out in a sec!" Sarah suddenly felt desperate to see her mom.

She hadn't spent much time with her at all lately and hadn't realized how much she missed her until she thought about Dalia. She
hurried out of the shower, put on a robe, twisted her hair up into
a towel, and ran down the stairs. Today they were going to have
a coffee date, she decided. Her plans were dashed, though, when
she saw Linda sipping tea at the counter.

"Oh. Hi, Mrs. Connor."

"*Hi*, Sarah. Your mom was just telling me your boyfriend has
a summer house? Aren't you lucky?"

"Yeah, we just set up tents in their yard. It was so fun, though.
It's too bad Ella was sick." Sarah's stomach growled loudly, and
she remembered she hadn't eaten yet. She grabbed an apple from
the fruit bowl and took a bigger bite than she could manage.

"Sick? No." Linda took off her glasses and started cleaning
them on her shirt. "You know I would never let Ella go sleep at
some strange boy's house."

"She doesn't have strep?" Sarah asked, trying to maneuver
around the chunk of apple in her mouth without spitting it all
over the place.

"Gosh, no." Linda laughed. "Is that what she told you? She
probably didn't want the girls to know how *overprotective* I am.
You teenage girls sure are funny."

She popped her glasses on her face and smiled so condescend-
ingly, it made Sarah want to scribble all over her face with a
Sharpie. She aggressively threw her apple into the garbage and
left to unload the car.

*Well, well, well. Pretending to be sick with such a detailed
story? Ruining your boyfriend's night with his friends just to keep
him away from a girl? Who's the crazy one now?*

34

AT THE ENTRANCE TO Washington High School, a group of giggling girls made themselves at home on the steps. *A little too at home*, Sarah felt—the way they were sprawled out, taking up as much space as possible, forcing others to step between them. They were decked out in Class of '00 spirit wear. Apparently, no one told them you don't just plop yourselves down wherever you feel like it and advertise that you're freshmen on your first day of practice.

Their red-and-white pompoms were brand new—pristine and flat, not yet scrunched into the giant puff balls they would become. The rest of their afternoon would surely be spent at one of their houses, talking about how excited they are for high school while they scrunch the plastic strands. A pang of jealousy tried to distract Sarah from the more painful fear of change. She hated that these girls were about to embark on the greatest four years of their lives while she and her friends' high school years were coming to a close.

"The freshmen look *so young*," she said as they walked through the newly crimson-carpeted hall. She stopped abruptly and pointed to the floor. "What the hell is *this*? It's not even the right shade of red!" The old carpet had been replaced with new, just like they were about to be.

"Yes it is," Stacey said. "The old carpet was just dirty."

"Dirty with our memories," Sarah pouted. "Three years of our history just . . . poof." She magician-flicked her fingers.

"I can't believe it's our first *official* practice of our *senior* year," Tori said.

"Do you think Dalia will be okay today?" Jenny asked.

"Dalia is way better when she's cheering. Plus, she has us for moral support," Tori said. "We should just act like nothing happened and keep it light."

Dalia hadn't seen Shawn or Ella since *that day. That night* and *that day,* the two new phrases the girls had added to their vocabulary this summer, unless they wanted to count *church person.* And Jake and Sarah would probably add, "*I love this cabin,*" if they got more serious. But they hadn't added any fun phrases like they usually did. The summer had been kind of weird for Sarah. At one end of the spectrum there was Jake, who was amazing, and at the other end Dalia, who was not. The dichotomy was a little exhausting, having to temper her excitement about Jake while tending to Dalia's needs. So, Sarah was ready for summer to end, ready for the structure that the school year would bring. But she wasn't ready for high school to end.

Per Sarah's advice, Dalia had called out of work for a few days, a much-needed recovery period. More importantly, it allowed her to avoid seeing Ella until the girls were all with her, rather than having some big thing go down at Gatto's. She didn't spend her time off alone, though. They smothered Dalia with their company. Mani/pedis, haircuts, shopping, all the beauty rituals they hadn't done enough of over the summer. Whatever would go down with Ella today, at least Dalia would be looking good when it did.

Keep it light, Sarah thought as she walked into the gym. Dalia was sitting on the edge of the bleachers, writing notes in a binder. Sarah sneaked up behind her and put her mouth right up to her ear. "What's up, you sexy bitch?"

"Jesus, Sarah, you scared the crap out of me." Dalia jumped up and flung her pen at Sarah. She nodded over to Ella, who was at the opposite end of the bleachers, swapping her flip-flops for Keds. Dalia grabbed Sarah's arm and raised her voice. "Did you get my message about that party next weekend? It's gonna be *amazing.* College guys. I'll tell you all about it after practice. Okay, everyone, we're gonna get started," she shouted to the girls. The gymnasium went silent as Dalia took the floor.

"I'd like to start by introducing the fabulous Coach Liz, who, if you're new to the squad, I'm sure you've at least crossed her path in the tardy office." Dalia and Coach Liz exchanged fake smiles as the squad responded with an equally fake chuckle.

Coach Liz was hardly fabulous. She was very nice, and if she grew out her mouse-colored bob and put on some makeup, she could be cute. A former varsity cheerleader herself, now a sad divorcee who handed out tardies to high schoolers.

"Thank you, Dalia. First, I'd like to welcome the new girls, Kayla Evans, Emily Jensen, and Ella Connor." The squad golf-clapped. "You should all have your binders. On the left you will find several forms—I will need all of them filled out no later than Friday. There is also information about this year's state contest. I think this group has a real chance, so . . . let's *do this.*" She awkwardly raised her fist. "And Dalia will take it from here."

"Hi everyone. As most of you know, I'm Dalia Jacobs." She clasped her hands together, pacing back and forth in her shiny white Keds, short black shorts, and her She-Vikings T-shirt. "A little bit about me. This is my fourth year of being captain of our squad, which most of you know already. To the new girls, I'd like to welcome you to our little family." Dalia led the clapping. "I don't want to waste our practice time with a lot of talking, so I'll keep this short. Yes, cheering at games and pep rallies is important, school spirit and all that crap. But what matters more than anything is winning state this year. I want to see that trophy in the case. And anyone who knows me knows that once I set a goal for myself," she said and then paused, "I don't quit until I achieve it. So, you need to ask yourself every day whether you are helping or hurting our chances. Whether you're *giving to* the squad or *taking from* the squad, from your *family.* Let me help you there. *No one* likes a taker."

The comment was awkwardly disguised as part of a motivational speech, but anyone in the know would recognize she was talking to Ella. She continued to pace around, making eye contact with each of the girls. "So now that we're clear on what this year is about, let's have some fun. Jenny will be leading you through warmups. And Ella, come with me. Sarah," she said, wiggling her finger, "you too."

Dalia scooted them over to the supply closet door. "Ella, really quick. I am so sorry for what happened the other day. Honestly, I barely remember it. But I *do* know what happened to me. And I don't know how much Sarah told you, but there were all these freako hillbillies at the party, and one of the toothless wonders put something in my drink. Right Sarah?"

"Yeah . . . I hadn't told her," Sarah said, not confirming or denying her claim.

"It was *crazy*! One minute I'm laying out, and the next minute I'm a total freak at your church. And I don't have a *clue* what happened in between. Like some crazy time warp." She snapped her fingers. "Took me days to get back to myself. 'Roofies,' the doctor said. He said I'm lucky I didn't die. And I'm thinking, thank god I *did* drive back, because I would've *totally* been raped if I'd stayed, and maybe even killed. So, worth the embarrassment—you know, if you're choosing between two bags of shit, better the one that didn't kill you, right? Oh well, it's a good lesson for all of us. Okay. Practice time." Without giving Ella a chance to respond, Dalia shooed them to join warmups. "And Ella, I want you to show the rest of the girls what you can do on the floor at the end of practice."

Drill after drill, they ran through formations. Dalia ducked in and out of the routines, making adjustments to everyone's form like a boot camp yoga instructor, while Coach Liz sat with her nose in a book. Two hours and two routines later, Dalia led everyone to the bleachers.

"Okay, ladies. Before we go, I'd like Ella to show off her excellent gymnastic skills. This kind of talent is exactly what this squad needs to get us that state trophy. All yours, Ella." Dalia sat next to Sarah.

Ella squeaked across the gym floor. She positioned herself under the basketball net, raised her hands, and took off into the most incredible tumbling routine that took her across the entire length of the gym. Then she turned around and did it again, each flip and twist perfectly executed. Cheers erupted from the squad as Ella flew through the air. Watching her perform gymnastics always brought Sarah back to their childhood. They'd taken gymnastics together, but once it got dangerous, Sarah got scared and quit. It never rattled Ella, though. She was amazing. Sarah hated that she hated her right now.

Sarah looked at Dalia, watching her take the whole thing in. There were only two things that excited Dalia in life. Shawn and cheerleading. Her eyes were alive for the first time in a long time. Sarah could practically see ideas for new routines and dreams of that state trophy dancing in her head. It must have been quite the mental wrestling match, though, that the person responsible for destroying one of her dreams was the same one helping her achieve the other.

"Well, at least she's good for something," Sarah said. "She's so talented."

"Yeah. Fearless. The way she's okay going that high without a mat, there's *so* much more we can do. *She's* gonna make the difference." Dalia sat back, nodding her head. But then, out of nowhere, she flinched. Suddenly. As if someone had flicked water on her face. Yet nothing outwardly visible caused the flinch.

"You okay?"

"I'm fine." She folded her arms tightly across her chest. "I just thought of something."

Whatever was going on in her mind, she seemed to be protecting it.

"What's going on?" Sarah asked.

"It's nothing. Just something for a routine. I'm not even sure it would work."

"Well, you wanna run it by me?"

"It's just an idea. I have to see where we could fit it in. We might not even need it."

"How about we ask the girls before we leave today? Might help you work on it later," Sarah suggested, encouraging any thought process that had to do with something other than Shawn.

"*Jesus, Sarah.* Just let it go," she snapped.

Sarah didn't know what she'd done. But her patience with Dalia was wearing thin. So she got up and left.

35

ELLA FUMBLED WITH THE KEY to her apartment, twisting it until her fingers turned red as it stubbornly refused to turn. As Shawn reached to help, she swatted his hand away.

"I *got* it," she snipped.

"Sorry, El," he said, holding his hands up. He had a big stupid grin on his face that was annoying her. She wanted him to just stop smiling.

Her irritable mood confused her, as she'd been excited about this for weeks. But now that the moment was upon them, it felt awkward, pressured.

The bolt finally clicked, and she pushed open the door. The apartment was quiet, except for the ticking of the grandfather clock in their entryway. It was barely audible, but Ella always noticed it when she was feeling impatient.

Her family had gone to visit her grandma in Indianapolis for the night. They'd tried to make her go, but she'd convinced them she had to work, inventing a slightly too elaborate story about someone having a big anniversary party at Gatto's. They have it every year, everyone has to work it, the tips are supposed to be huge, she'd said. The truth was she'd never had to work at all tonight and now would likely have to give her mom extra money this week because of the supposed big tips she'd promised. Shawn called in sick for the occasion, which he never did. But they'd agreed they shouldn't let the opportunity pass them by.

"Do you want something?" She opened the refrigerator.

"A drink would be good. Whatever you're having is fine. I like this place," he said as he toured the living room for the first time. He flipped through books on shelves, inspected trinkets, and looked at framed family pictures. The family photos were all the same, only their ages and choice of background differentiated them. "What's up with all the Sears Portrait Studio pictures? Don't you have any from the Grand Canyon or anything?"

"Nope. We never went."

"Come on. You're telling me you lived in Arizona for five years and never went to the Grand Canyon?"

"That's right. My parents started fighting about five seconds after we moved. It would have been zero fun, and quite possibly dangerous, being stuck in a hotel room with them, or in a car for more than ten minutes. My mom is way too crazy."

Ella laid out two coasters on the coffee table and set down glasses of lemonade. "Speaking of crazy, did you and Dalia have the *big talk* yet?"

"If you wanna call it that, but yeah. Last night. She caught me walking out of the restaurant." Shawn joined Ella on the couch. "She apologized. I just listened to the story, same thing she told you. Some guy put something in her drink, she had no idea what she was doing, it doesn't matter. I'm just glad it's over."

"So, you guys are fine now?"

"Fine? I don't know. It just happened. I avoided her for what . . . two weeks? But I told her I wasn't mad, if that's what you mean." He picked up an unscented candle and sniffed it. "She did ask if we could still be friends."

"What did you say?"

"I said sure. What was I going to say?"

"No, that's fine. And the dates?"

"Those are over. We didn't talk about it, but she knows. She actually seemed okay about everything. Kind of normal."

"Well, that's good."

Shawn took a sip of his drink and put it down. Ella put her glass to her lips. Shawn put his hand on her thigh. He looked at her like he couldn't wait another minute.

She wasn't a virgin, but she wasn't going to tell *him* that. It had happened in another state, in another life. So it didn't count, she decided. And really, it wasn't any of his business. Yes, she knew all about his big plan, his *commitment*, to only have sex with the person who he was willing to be with forever. He never came right out and said it, but she knew he wouldn't be with her if she'd already *shared herself* with someone else.

He never asked about Dalia's "slut" comment, though he did ask if she'd ever done it before. She didn't like to lie, but it was a skill she'd developed living under Linda's thumb, a survival mechanism rooted in being forced to lie about even the most basic things. She didn't want this habit to spill over into the rest of her life, but sometimes it just happened. That was some of the pressure she was feeling. The pressure of the lie. Would he be able to tell he wasn't the first? *Of course not.* He didn't know what it was like to be with anyone, so he'd have nothing to judge it against. She would have to remember to pretend it hurt a little bit. And not to take him to any high school reunions in Tucson.

She sipped her lemonade while he slid his fingertips up and down her thigh, inching closer to the cuff of her shorts. Her head was full of thoughts as she tried to reason away the anxiety preventing her from enjoying this moment.

Sometimes it turned her off, the way he would get all starry-eyed when he talked about them being each other's "onlys." The way he fawned over her like she was some delicate thing. She was hardly delicate, and it bothered her that he might think of her that way. And it wasn't always easy being around such a *do the right thing* guy. Volunteering, youth group, helping the elderly. She was totally on board in the beginning, when her attraction to him was the motivating factor. But sometimes, she didn't want to do the right thing. Didn't want to change Mrs. Ellis's light bulbs, didn't want to play *board games* on a Saturday night. And yes, they'd had drinks together a few times. But he could never just let loose, which was the entire point of having drinks. Worse, he didn't want her to let loose either, the way he always seemed to be keeping track of how much she was drinking, asking if she was *sure* she needed another. It took all the fun out. And she wouldn't dare tell him she gets high. He'd probably report her to the authorities, it being *the right thing* to do and all.

Maybe the ambivalence creeping in was because he was pretty much the only one she ever hung out with these days. Sarah was obviously still upset with her, and though the rest of the girls were nice to her, they weren't going to reach out to her if Sarah wasn't. And she hadn't made any other friends. Or maybe it was none of those things, and she and Shawn were just bumping up against that three-month mark that wears the shiny finish off of new relationships.

Regardless of any doubts she was having, he was all she had. And having been exiled from the girls, she wanted to make it work, she thought, as she ever so slightly opened her legs, allowing just enough space for his fingers to slide up her shorts. He pulled her underwear aside.

Even from the awkward angle, he managed to find the spot. The spot she'd discovered herself at age eleven, the age her mom started the dreaded masturbation lectures . . . to her brother, not her. Ironically, if her mom hadn't mentioned it, she might have never found it. One summer she'd asked Laura, the nerdy sixteen-year-old camp counselor, what masturbation was, referring to it as *that thing that boys do.* Laura thought that was hilarious. Ella immediately regretted asking, until Laura told her exactly what it was . . . and how to do it.

She lay back on the couch, raising her hips against Shawn's thumb. He pressed it against her firmly, as if responding to a request. He got to work unbuttoning her shorts with his other hand and slid them down as she lifted herself up. Still using his thumb, he used his other hand to slide his fingers inside of her. Somehow, Shawn knew exactly what he was doing. This was like a drug. No wonder Dalia couldn't let him go.

Her thoughts began to pixelate, losing form and function as he kissed her stomach, both hands still furiously busy below. She couldn't even tell where his hands were anymore, as the sensation they were creating reached far beyond anything he was touching. And then it happened. She grabbed his arm hard. She didn't know it could be like this.

"Upstairs," she whispered once she'd recovered enough to speak. Shawn smiled, moving her hair out of her closed eyes. He quickly reached into his gym bag and put something in his pocket.

Ella reached for his hand and led him up the stairs to her bed. It was dark. She pulled off her bedspread, spilling decorative pillows everywhere. She heard his belt unbuckle. It clinked as his jeans hit the floor. A tearing noise, a package ripped open. He was facing away from her. She took off her shirt and bra and rolled onto her back. He joined her, lying on his side, and continued where he'd left off. It didn't take long to get her there again. Her head lurched backward, her body trembled and then went still.

"You like that, huh." He smiled, kissing her neck.

She used her hand to answer him, pulling his hips closer to hers.

"You sure?"

She raised one knee and stared into his eyes. "I'm sure."

He rolled on top of her. She let her other leg fall to the side. He felt around awkwardly for a bit, trying to gently open her. He propped himself up and began to slowly work his way in.

"This okay?" he asked. Ella nodded. He asked again, and again, and again.

She didn't want to do this part, this pretending. This delicate flower virgin act. She wrapped her leg around him and forced him deep inside of her, pretending to wince just a little in the process. He asked again. She covered his mouth.

They rocked together, slowly. Then faster. It was nice. Not as nice as his fingers, though. He'd been so aggressive with his fingers. Now, he seemed like he was trying not to hurt her. She grabbed him with both hands, pushing him deeper inside, as she pressed her hips hard against his. She managed to get a rhythm going. His breath was hot on her neck. He was almost there. One more deep thrust. He made a grunting noise as his face fell into her neck.

And then she felt a snap. Their eyes popped open, Shawn's moment interrupted. She gasped as the reality of what just happened hit her. The condom broke.

36

THE CHERRY RED MARKER ran dry long before Sarah put the final touches on Shawn's football poster. She wet her fingers and tried to spread the dried marker from his first name to his last name, but all that did was cover it with pink fingerprints.

"Oh well, Shawn, that's what you get for being a dick," she said.

"Sarah, a little help please?" her mom called out from the garage. Sarah looked over to see Carrie's foot nudging the door as she tried not to drop two overstuffed grocery bags. She jumped up and caught one just as it began to topple over.

"You could've taken two trips, Mom. It's like an extra ten feet." Sarah laughed.

"Well, it was ten feet more than I wanted to walk. Okay, I hope I didn't forget anything. I got Doritos, a veggie tray, stuff to make brownies, and some strawberries. I don't know how good they are, so I got some grapes too."

"Thanks, Mom. What about the toilet paper?"

"Here comes the toilet paper," Sarah's dad sang to the tune of "Here Comes the Bride." She couldn't even see his face behind the jumbo packs of Charmin, stacked four high. "I got you the good stuff. How many houses you plan on hittin' tonight?"

Every year, the night before the Crosstown Classic football game, the cheerleaders made signs with each player's picture, stuck them in their yards, and then TP'd their houses. The concept of TPing someone's house that you like seemed weird. What's the point of leaving them a giant mess to clean up? Sarah had always argued they should be TPing their southside rivals. But she never got anywhere because it was a tradition.

Carrie held up the poster board. "You trying to punish Shawn or something?" She smiled at the sloppy artwork.

"Yep. I'm trying to express to everyone who sees it just how little he means to me. And look. I even signed my name, just so he knows who couldn't be bothered to do a decent job on his poster."

"Oh, that'll show him." Carrie glanced at Sarah and laughed.

Shawn was on Sarah's shit list. He never checked in with her about Dalia. Never even returned her phone calls, which was total shit because *she* never did anything to him. Sarah guessed he was just done with her, done with the drama. And maybe didn't want her to yell at him. Their friendship just another casualty of Ella's return. "I hope she's worth it," she said to his giant face.

"So, how's Dalia been?"

"A little better. School's been a good distraction . . . and cheerleading."

After *that day*, Sarah made it a point to spend more time with her mom. Over coffee and lunch dates, she filled Carrie in on everything that had been going on, basically catching her up on all the things she would have told her had she not been spending all her time with everyone but her. It felt good to get it all out there. They stood together at the island, Sarah prepping the brownie batter while Carrie smeared Crisco onto a metal pan.

"I had lunch with Linda today."

"Ew. What did *she* have to say?"

"Well, you were right about Ella and Shawn. Sounds like they're quite the item."

Sarah cracked an egg too hard, sending shell fragments into the glass bowl.

"She sucks so much," she said as she used her finger to fish them out. "I think deep down Dalia knows, but she's still gonna freak. This is *not* how senior year is supposed to start."

"What is this? Some sort of love triangle?" Her dad popped his head around the corner. Making fun of high school gossip was his guilty pleasure.

"It's not funny, Dad."

"*I know.* I never liked that *Dalia.*"

"Ella, Dad. You're supposed to not like Ella in this one."

"Oh, sorry, I never liked that *Ella.*" He made a snotty teenage girl face and flung his wrist. "What'd she do?"

"Stole Shawn away from Dalia."

"*Ooooh* . . . she needs to pay for that." His eyes lit up. "What should we do? Put hot peppers in her pizza?"

"Dad . . ."

"Hair remover in her shampoo bottle?"

"Dad . . ."

"Laxatives in her chocolate milk?" he said, getting more excited with each suggestion.

"*Dad!*" Sarah laughed. "Did you ever actually do any of these things?"

"Maybe." He looked at Sarah and smiled. "Sarah, you know you're gonna look back at all the drama and laugh someday, right? So why not laugh now?" He patted her head.

"Yeah, I told Dalia the same thing . . . *oh my god*, do you know what this *means?*"

"That we get to do some pranks?"

"No, it means I'm turning into *my father.*" Her jaw dropped.

"Just think, Sar. Someday, you get to have one of *these.*" He smiled proudly as he rubbed his big, round belly.

Just as Sarah placed the brownies on the stove to cool, the girls started to arrive, the decibels per girl ratio rising with each new arrival. It was astonishing how loud a group of girls could be, the way they automatically started competing to be heard. There was so much noise that she hadn't even noticed Ella wasn't there yet. Until she heard Linda's shrill voice rise above the rest.

"I hope you don't mind, Carrie, but I haven't gotten to meet *any* of the *girls* I hear so much about," she said as she walked into the kitchen, a visibly mortified Ella in tow. Linda set down a plastic tray of sprinkle-covered cookies and made herself at home. "*Hi girls*, I'm Mrs. Connor, Ella's mom. And you're . . ." She stared at everyone, blinking an unacceptable number of times. After a painfully long pause, Tori extended her hand and introduced herself. And one by one, the rest of the girls called out their names.

"Well, it is *so nice* to meet you all." Linda nodded her puffy face.

The state of Linda's face led Sarah to conclude that she'd replaced her alcohol habit with French fries and doughnuts. As she watched her cheeks flap around while her mouth spit out nonsense, her mind started drifting. She found herself imagining Linda going through the drive-thru at McDonald's and ordering fries, and then immediately going to Dunkin' Donuts, where she actually has to get out of the car to go in and pick her doughnuts. And then Sarah decides Linda's mad that she didn't go to Dunkin' Donuts first, because now her fries are going to get cold, so she sits in the car and debates whether to eat the fries first. But the fries are a little too hot, and she doesn't want to wait for her doughnuts, so she decides to take the fries *into* Dunkin' Donuts with her. She got to the part where Linda's ordering a Bavarian cream *while* she's eating the fries, when Linda said something that actually got her attention.

"You girls sure must be excited about Homecoming. I know Ella is."

"Really?" Stacey took a step back as if she'd just noticed a blistering rash on Linda's lip. "So, who are you going with, Ella?"

"You mean she didn't *tell you*? My, times sure have changed. Back in our day, the *first* thing we did was tell our girlfriends if a boy asked us to a dance, right Carrie?"

Carrie was as deer in the headlights as anyone.

"Well, Ella, do you want to tell them or should I?"

"Shawn asked me to go with him," Ella said, looking at her hands resting on the counter. Linda smiled smugly for the both of them.

Sarah wasn't exactly surprised, but it still made her catch her breath when she heard it. They had done a really good job of keeping their relationship a secret, so it was a complete shock to the rest of the girls. They'd all thought Dalia's suspicions were in her head.

Dalia, on the other hand, seemed to be fully prepared for this possibility, as if she'd rehearsed for it a thousand times.

"Aw, that's so cute. I wish I could go, but Tom says Homecoming is for kids." She dipped a carrot stick in ranch dressing. "What is the word he used? *Juvenile.* That's it. We'll be going to the city that night. To a hotel. He wouldn't be caught *dead* there."

Suddenly, the only sound in the room was Dalia crunching away on her carrot. Sarah saw Tori on the verge of asking who the fuck Tom was, when she thought better of it and shut her mouth. Ella, however, needed to know immediately.

"*Tom?* Who's *that?*" she asked excitedly.

"You don't know about *Tom?* He's my *boyfriend.* We've been dating like what," she said, counting on her fingers, "six weeks now? He goes to Northwestern. We met at a party, and we've been together like nonstop ever since. He's at my apartment *all* the time. We basically never get out of bed."

"Well, Dalia, that's just lovely," Carrie said. "Who's ready for pizza?"

"That's so *great, Dalia!* I can't wait to *meet* him!" Ella gushed joy and relief, as if the thorn that had prevented her from being close to the girls had been removed. Her gushing continued unabated over slices of pizza, and in the car, and at each house as rolls of toilet paper sailed over tree branches, and even when they TP'd Shawn's house. She wouldn't stop talking about how *perfect* this all was.

She asked *all about* Tom . . . what he's like, what he's studying, where he's from, what kind of party it was. Remarkably, Dalia had answers for *all* of her questions. Then she asked Sarah all about Jake, and on it went with Tori and Dave, and Jenny and Rob, even telling everyone she wanted all the *dirty details*, as if they'd actually share them with her. Then she moved on to Stacey, asking how she was doing with the whole Jim thing, trying to cram three missed months of friendship with five girls into three hours. She acted as if she could just pick up right where things should have been, with no consequences for lying or betraying Sarah's friendship. Like she thought she could come out of this with both Shawn *and* the girls' friendship.

By the seventh house, Stacey said she'd had enough. "Sarah, I want to go. Let's tell the other girls to finish without us."

"Good idea," she said.

Sarah assumed Ella would get a ride from one of the other girls, but she didn't. She hopped right into Stacey's car and kept hanging around even after they got back to Sarah's house. Sarah sat in the kitchen with Ella and Carrie, hoping to recruit her mom to facilitate Ella's departure. But, apparently, Ella decided she should catch up with Carrie, too, while she was at it, chatting over fistfuls of caramel corn.

The rest of the girls had gone up to Sarah's room to work on the time capsule, while Sarah was trying to get rid of Ella. She didn't take any hints, though. In fact, after Ella took way too long in the bathroom, Sarah found her sitting on the floor of her bedroom, with everyone else, like she belonged there. Sarah thought back to when she appreciated how easily Ella could insert herself into their conversations. But now she recognized her as a hanger-on-er, worming her way into someone else's life.

"So that's the time capsule? That is *so cool* that you guys are doing that! Did you decide where you're going to bury it yet?" Ella said to a hostile audience.

Maybe she'd forgotten that Dalia's time capsule goals had everything to do with Shawn, and Homecoming for that matter. Or maybe she thought that Tom meant Dalia was over him. But Sarah had never been so disgusted with another human in her life. She looked at the girls, whose scowls showed they felt the same way. Tori decided to take charge of the situation and grabbed the time capsule protectively.

"Ella, sorry but this is our thing. Honestly, you shouldn't be here."

"*Please leave*," Jenny said, her eyes red and misty. Though Dalia could hide her disappointment, Jenny could not.

"Oh, okay." Ella's eyes sank to the floor.

"You guys, stop being bitches," Dalia said. "She can stay."

"No, I'll go. You guys don't want me here. I get it." And she left.

"*Finally*. I thought she'd *never* leave," Stacey said. "Dalia, oh my god! Are you okay?"

Dalia plopped down limply into Sarah's bird's nest chair.

"Fuck it. I am not going to let that little midget get to me."

"I think it's pretty incredible you handled it the way you did," Tori said.

"Don't make it weird. Let's just finish the time capsule."

"Okay," Jenny said. "Is there anything you want to take out of it?"

"*Fuck* no. This changes *nothing.*"

"Good," Stacey said. "*Fuck her.*" And then Stacey's brow furrowed as she seemed to try to process Dalia's words. But no one dared ask how *that* was gonna work.

"Okay, then." Tori opened the cylinder and poured its contents onto the carpet. Stacey handed out the individual baggies that housed each of the previous contributions. The room was filled with the rustling of paper and crunching of plastic baggies. Jenny suddenly had lots to contribute, scratching furiously away with her pen. She'd been quiet all night, visibly affected by the big news. She glanced over at Dalia and wrote and wrote and wrote. Everyone shielded their notes for privacy, as these were their *secret* goals that wouldn't be revealed even amongst themselves for twenty years. Tori passed around the time capsule, and they each tucked them away. When it got to Sarah, she snapped it shut and put it back in her toy chest.

"I guess that's it! We'll bury it right after the Homecoming game, behind my shed. Someone just remind me to dig it up if my parents ever decide to move," she said.

"Your parents aren't going anywhere," Tori said.

"I know, but just in case. Okay you guys, that's it for me. I need to crash."

Sarah lay in bed that night, staring at the ceiling, wondering what the next twenty years would bring. Would they still be friends? Absolutely. Would she ever forgive Ella? Her broken promise? Her lies? Doubtful. And then she wondered what the hell Dalia meant by "This changes nothing." Trying to figure that out ushered her into a deep, long sleep.

37

THE SECOND HER CAR DOOR separated her from the rest of the world, Dalia came undone. It was more than just Shawn and Ella upsetting her tonight. The Homecoming thing wasn't a total surprise, as the more she'd thought about it, the more sure she was that Ella had lied about being sick, which she'd only have done if something was going on between them. Dalia had even taken steps to prepare for the possibility. Planning her response and the invention of Tom, among other things. That wasn't so much what was eating away at her tonight.

Being at *Sarah's* was what had gotten to her. Usually, she loved going there. Loved being out of her apartment, living a normal life. Sometimes when she was at Sarah's, she secretly pretended it was *her* house, *her* family. But tonight, she found herself jealous of Sarah. She watched Sarah's mom serving food, watched her dad telling funny stories, each warm moment chipping away at her, a brutal reminder of everything she didn't have.

What was this joke of a life she'd been born into? Jenny, at least, understood how she felt, her dad constantly gone while her mom curled up with a bottle of vodka every night. But Jenny's mom was at least in the house, and she was nice. And Jenny didn't have to worry about things like rent money.

Dalia complained mostly about her mom, but it wasn't just her mom, it was *everything*. Why did she get a mother who stopped wanting anything to do with her and a father who *never* wanted anything to do with her? And even if he didn't want anything to do with her, why did he have to be a drug-addicted criminal who comes around, fucks everything up, and then leaves again? Why couldn't he just be off with his new family and wear a suit to work and send her checks?

Why did her mom have to bring strange men home? Why did she have to hear them having sex and then sit through awkward bowls of cereal? Why did her mom have to be a bartender at a shitty hole in the wall? Why couldn't she have gotten a day job, at least when Dalia was little, instead of leaving her to fend for herself?

And why did she have to live in this nasty subsidized-housing apartment in the middle of a nice suburb, where everyone else had perfect houses and perfect families and safe cars, where the townspeople for sure didn't want this place there, and she didn't blame them. But all the towns had to have low-income housing, so lucky her. She got to go to a good school. It would be so much better if she were living in the inner city where everyone had these problems. *But then you'd never know how to get out.* Her way out was Shawn. And Ella was ruining everything.

She pulled into her apartment complex. Her bullshit car sputtered to a stop. She yanked up the emergency brake and looked at her surroundings. Bullshit cars everywhere. She rested her arms and forehead on the steering wheel. *See, this is where you belong. Why would Shawn ever be interested in you? You're white trash,* her harsh inner critic said.

"Shut up!" she screamed. Opening her eyes wide, she fanned them with her hands, halting her tears just as they were about to spill onto her face. She slammed the car door shut and walked quickly toward her building.

Three guys were sitting around a car. As she got closer, she recognized them—her neighbor Rocco and his friends. They were in their twenties, definitely drug dealers, and always harassing her. She tried to avoid them, but there was no getting around it. Usually, she could handle herself, but tonight she wasn't in the mood for what she knew was coming. Walking with her head down, she hoped they'd leave her alone.

"Hey honey, how 'bout you come over here and suck my dick?" Rocco said. He moved his fist back and forth by his mouth and stuck his tongue into his cheek.

Dalia looked over to see them laughing. It wasn't the first time he'd said it. He'd said it pretty much every time she'd crossed his path for the last two years. She usually responded with a "you wish" and didn't give it another thought. But tonight, she'd had enough. She stopped dead in her tracks and stared at him with steely eyes.

"You want me to suck your dick, Rocco?"

"Yeah, honey. And I wanna see those sweet titties."

She marched over to them and pulled up her shirt. "You like these? You want me to suck your dick? Fine. Pull your pants down."

Rocco and his friends just looked at her and laughed.

"Yeah, big talker? What are you waiting for? Now's your chance."

She reached in her purse and felt around for the little pink spray bottle Shawn had given her for protection. One night when he walked her to her car, she told him that she regularly got harassed walking around her apartment complex at night, that *that's* where she needed someone to walk with her. She was hoping he'd offer to follow her home. He didn't. But he did come into work one day and said he had a surprise for her. She got way more excited than she should have, considering it turned out to be pepper spray. But she was happy that he was at least thinking about her. If anyone else would have given it to her, it would be sitting in a drawer somewhere. Because it was Shawn, she carried it with her everywhere she went.

Rocco's friends began to egg him on.

"What are you waiting for, Rocco." One of them gave him a shove toward her.

"Get on your knees, honey," the other one shouted.

Rocco spread his legs and thrust his hips toward her. Dalia walked toward him. Rocco looked over his shoulder at his friends, then back at Dalia. He unzipped his jeans and pulled them down.

Dalia inched closer to him and bent down. "Ya know what? I think *Rocco's* the one who should get on *his* knees," she said to his friends. Then she lifted the pepper spray out of her purse and sprayed it all over his naked self. Rocco screamed and fell to the ground. "You bitch," he yelled as his friends bent over with laughter.

As Rocco writhed in pain on the cement, she turned around slowly and walked to her apartment. She didn't care if they came after her. She had so much anger in her, she could probably take all three of them. And if she couldn't, so what? Take her away from this life? Have at it. She wouldn't even bother fighting back.

Suddenly, she felt empowered. A vibrant energy gushed through her like a geyser. She'd just brought a terrible man to his knees. But more empowering was the realization that when you have nothing to lose, you can do *anything*. And here she was, with nothing to lose.

She opened her apartment door and walked into her bedroom, right up to the full-length mirror. She studied herself. It didn't matter what flaws were underneath. Those could be fixed. But from the outside, she wouldn't change a thing, she thought, as she ran her fingers through her hair. She pulled up her shirt to check out her tight abs and posed like a Victoria's Secret model. Yes, Ella was pretty, but she was stunning.

She grabbed her mom's magazine from under the bed and read the article again. Step one, make yourself gorgeous. Step two, find out the woman he wants and become that. Step three, figure out his needs and fulfill them. She was doing that. She just hadn't been able to show Shawn because Ella was in the way. It was time for step four.

Get rid of the competition.

38

EVERY SO OFTEN, Dalia would surprise the girls with a factoid they'd never heard before, which no one would believe because they'd assume if it was true, at least one of the four of them would have heard it already. And then she'd be forced to prove herself.

The source of the factoid in question was the claim that the pink stone charm on her favorite necklace was actually sea glass she'd collected from Lake Michigan on a rare childhood outing with both her mom and dad. Tori had concluded it wasn't an *actual* memory, but a story her mom had made up, which is why today they drove an hour to the Indiana Dunes. To verify Dalia's claim that Lake Michigan has sea glass.

"How have none of you guys been here before?" Dalia asked as they hiked up the sand path.

For Stacey and Jenny, that answer was easy. They didn't go anywhere that didn't require a plane ticket. Tori and Sarah did a lot more local traveling, and as Sarah took in the magnificent scenery, she asked herself the same question.

Lake Michigan was glistening as blue as the Caribbean. Sarah thought it must be the angle of the September sun, but a sign said that sediment being kicked up by changes of the season was responsible for the majestic hue. Another factoid no one would have believed if Dalia had told them.

"Now, about that sea glass," Sarah said to Dalia.

"Nope. First we roll down the hills."

"I'm not rolling down anything," Stacey said, looking at the coral pink polish on her freshly manicured nails. "I am here only to observe. And drink some beers."

"You weren't supposed to bring those! This is a kickass work-out. And when we're done, we get sea glass."

"How do we get sea glass from a lake?" Jenny asked.

"You can get it anywhere there's moving water. It's just old beer bottles and crap," Dalia explained.

"There's no way that's true," Tori argued.

"Yes it is. That's why there's so much brown and green. Everyone throwing their Budweisers and Heinekens in the lake. I told you. The waves and sand smooth the edges, and that's where you get sea glass. And that's why this one is so rare," Dalia said, playing with her necklace. "When's the last time you drank beer out of a pink bottle?"

Something seemed to have changed in Dalia since the night she'd received the news about Homecoming. Something unexpected. She seemed better, more confident, as if the news finally answered the question of will it or won't it happen, and now she could move on. She seemed almost enthusiastic about life these days, and Sarah was beyond happy to have her back.

"Can you believe how nice this day is?" Dalia asked as they reached the top of a large hill.

"I know. I love this time of year," Sarah said. "Only in September do you get days like this. And this place is *amazing*." In front of her were giant sand hills with tufts of greenery peeking out. At the bottom, a large stretch of flat beach, and beyond it, the Great Lake.

"I told you. Okay. Now, start jogging down the hill and see if you can do it without falling. And guess what. You can't. So, you're gonna start rolling, and you're just gonna go with it."

"Not it," Sarah said.

"Fine. Come on, Jenny. Follow me."

"Brown sea glass anyone?" Stacey handed Tori and Sarah bottles of Miller Lite. They stood at the top of the hill and watched Jenny and Dalia run, then fall, then roll . . . and then laugh like they were ten years old again. It did look fun. Sarah was tempted, like reverse peer pressure, to put down her beer and try something wholesome.

"Hold this." She handed Tori her unopened beer. "I'm going in."

She took too fast a running start, fell immediately, and rolled down the entire hill. It was so fun, so freeing, she didn't care that every crevice of her body was being blasted with sand. Once she regained her equilibrium enough to stand up, she used the inside of her shirt to wipe sand from her eyes and saw Stacey and Tori tumbling toward her. When they reached the bottom, they all laughed together, blown away by how fun it was.

The sensation brought up memories of Sarah and Ella when they were little. How they spent hours on end spinning in circles until they fell down. How they would lie on the ground and laugh and then get up and do it again. How had she forgotten how fun that was? It made her wonder what other childhood pleasures she'd forgotten about. And it made her think Shawn might be on to something. And it made her miss him. If they ever worked things out, she would be sure to bring him here.

They hiked up and rolled down those hills for hours. With every step, the earth gave way beneath their bare feet, the effort just to stay standing was an unbelievable workout. And the rolling down, the reward. Eventually, their burning thighs couldn't carry them up the hill anymore, and they moved to the water's edge.

Sarah waded into the cool water and sat, her overworked thighs grateful for the relief. As waves rolled in, she cupped water in her hands and de-sanded what she could. She put her hands behind her and let the sun shine on her face, taking in what was likely one of the last warm days of the year. And then she began her search for sea glass. She scooped a handful of sand and started poking through it, letting the water draw back the small grains. On her fourth attempt, there was a stunning, sapphire blue piece of sea glass resting on her palm.

"You guys! Look!" She held it out. The girls, who so far had come up empty-handed, promptly stepped up their search and one by one began to find treasures of their own. They cheered like little girls each time they found another piece. After an hour of sifting through wet sand, they had several pieces in various colors and shapes. Sitting in a circle, they piled the glass pieces in the middle.

And just as Dalia had said, the colored ones were mostly brown and green. So Sarah held on tight to her sapphire blue treasure.

"We are *so* making jewelry out of these," she said. "And we all owe Dalia an apology for ever doubting her. I'm sorry, Dalia."

"Well, I will let you guys make it up to me." She smiled. "There's something I need your help with."

"What do you need?" Jenny asked.

"Okay. Well, I don't think I need to give you a refresher on what's gone on with Shawn. But I've thought a lot about it, and I decided there's no way I'm going to let Shawn and Ella go to Homecoming together."

"What do you mean you're not going to *let* them?" Tori whipped her head toward her.

"Just hear me out. Ella stole something from me, and I want it back, so I'm going to take it back. *I* am going to Homecoming with Shawn, and Ella is not. And I figured out how to make that happen, but I can't do it by myself."

"What are you *talking* about?" Stacey asked.

"So, on the day of the Homecoming pep rally, you guys just sort of . . . not catch her when we do the Tick Tock move."

"*What?*" Tori's voice tightened. She put her hand on her forehead and stared straight at Dalia.

"You heard me. If she gets injured, she won't be able to go. And I obviously can't do it. I'm not near her in any of the stunts, so I need your help to make it happen."

"Wait. Let me get this straight," Tori continued. "You want us to *drop* her so she gets *injured*, so she can't go to Homecoming with Shawn. And then somehow he's going to take you instead?"

"Yes."

"This *plan* makes no *sense*," Tori said with an aggressive shrug.

"What do you mean?"

"What do I *mean*? There's so much wrong with it, Dalia, that I don't even know where to start."

Sarah was relieved that Tori had taken the lead in this conversation. The suggestion was so shocking, it required the kind of beat-down only Tori could deliver. Stacey and Jenny seemed to feel the same way, as they just sat back and let it happen.

"Like?"

"I can't believe I'm even going to have this discussion with you, and this shouldn't even be my first question for fear of actually encouraging you, but out of curiosity, how do you propose we do this?"

"Well, near the end, when you guys are holding Ella all the way up, she does a vertical split and then she switches legs. All you have to do is when she does the switch, you just loosen your clasp. Just a little, so she doesn't have a solid landing. I'm not talking like straight up *drop* her," she said, rolling her eyes. "Just don't give her a solid landing. So that she stumbles at the end. Think bruised hip, not broken leg. Next?"

"Oh my god." Tori's knuckles turned white as she clenched her fists. "Okay, I will humor you for about a second because my curiosity won't let me not. So, Ella bruises her hip, and she can't go to the dance. Why is he going to take you instead? Why wouldn't he just stay home with Ella?"

"Because it's his senior year and his last Homecoming, and he'll definitely be Homecoming King. He's not going to want to miss it. And I've been really nice to both of them ever since that day. We're totally cool now, and we'll be like the only two in the group without dates. I'll pretend to feel bad about it, and I'll offer to go as friends."

"Okay," Tori said, shaking her head. "And why is Ella going to let him take you? You don't think she'll have a problem with that?"

"*No.* She *won't*, Tori. Because, as far as *she* knows, I have no interest in him anymore. And again, I've been super, super nice to that little backstabber. Yes, I know it didn't stop her from saying yes in the first place, but I've been so cool with it that I'm sure she thinks I'm over him. I have Tom, now, *remember?*"

"Really."

"*Yes!* I've been dating Tom as far as she knows. You should hear some of the shit I tell her at work." Dalia seemed to get quite the little kick out of herself as she stepped away from the seriousness of the conversation. "She thinks we have this *totally kinky* sex life. She *eats it up.* I mean, some of the things she believes? It's been so fun just coming up with weird shit to tell her." She smiled proudly.

Sarah suddenly realized why Dalia's enthusiasm for life had seemed to return. She'd never given up on Shawn; she'd been having all sorts of fun setting this plan in motion.

"Oh my god. Okay, and why aren't you going to Homecoming with this *Tom?*"

"Because he's in college! And I told you guys at Sarah's that he won't go to a high school dance. Tori, please try to follow along. It's not that hard."

"Tom, or more like *no* Tom, you don't think Ella's going to have a problem with that? She's not *stupid*, Dalia. No one's ever even seen your imaginary Tom, so they probably don't believe he exists."

"Well," she said, stopping for a second. "Maybe I'll have to do something about that part. But if she doesn't let him go, she really is a bottom of the barrel bitch for ruining Shawn's last Homecoming."

"I'm not so sure *that's* true, but okay," Tori said, glancing up in the air as if searching for how to bulletproof her next point and then giving up. "And I'm guessing I already know the answer to this, but don't you feel bad at all about hurting her?"

"*No*, Tori, I *don't!* I'm just talking about a bruise or a sprain or something minor. Injuries happen all the time in cheerleading. It's no big deal. And if you want to talk about who hurt who—"

"But it's *wrong*, Dalia," Tori cut her off.

"It's *not* wrong. *She* is what's wrong. *She* did the hurting here. Do you think a bruised hip even compares to how she's hurt me? I want you to think about that. *You* tell me what's worse. A sprained ankle or a betrayal! She's a straight-up *thief*. Everything was *great* before she came along. She ruined *everything*. Her injury will heal. But what she's done to me . . . tell me, Tori, what's worse?"

"Am I supposed to answer that?"

"No. Whatever. Just stop with all your moral, better-than-everyone bullshit, which is *hilarious* because some people would say you're a murderer."

"*Dalia,*" Stacey said. "Did you really just say that?"

Dalia was obviously referring to Tori's abortion last year. It was one of those moments that made everyone grateful for her, the way she took charge and made Tori feel okay with her decision. And she'd made them promise to *never* speak of it again. Yet, here she was, using it when it suited her. It was a dick move.

"I'm just talking about a minor injury." She ignored Stacey and shut Tori right up. "She's a lying bitch. She faked that whole sickness thing. I'm *sure* of it. '*Oh, want to see my prescription?*'" she said, imitating Ella. "I'm *so stupid!* I should have said yes and called her bluff right then and there, and then Shawn would have seen what a psychopath *she* is. *Not* me. *She* ruined that night for me. That was *the* night. *My* night to be alone with Shawn, and she straight up stole it from me."

Dalia was practically hyperventilating at this point. It seemed best to just let the moment run its course, like waiting out a child's tantrum, hoping they just go to sleep.

"Shawn and I had a plan—to take a step back and actually *date* each other. She *robbed* me of that, Tori, don't you get it? And on top of that, she made me get all crazy that day and look like a complete jackass. I *never* act like that. And. *And* she made me think I was losing *my mind*. She is like *the devil*. If Shawn had gone to Wisconsin, like we'd planned, we wouldn't be in this situation. I'm sure of it. I just needed *one* night with him to get us back on track, so I'm just taking that night back. Taking back what is rightfully mine. It's *that* simple. After this, we'll be even. And if I have my one night with Shawn, and when that night is over, if he still wants her? She can have him." She stood up. "Let's just go."

Tori quickly stood up with her, as Sarah, Stacey, and Jenny stood frozen in their tracks. "Come *on*," Tori shouted.

The conversation continued as they made the brutal trek back up the hill, Sarah now twice as sore as she'd been just an hour ago.

"If you hate her so much, why even have her on the squad?" Tori went on, holding her flip-flops as she maneuvered barefoot around the grassy patches.

"Jesus, Tori, have you not been paying attention? What are my two goals? Homecoming with Shawn and winning state. Sorry bitches, but without her, state's not happening."

"So, you're going to injure your star cheerer so you can steal her Homecoming date. You're right, Dalia, it makes perfect sense."

"State isn't til *April, Tori,*" she said, completely exasperated at this point. "What college do you plan on going to? Do they know you can't figure out simple logic?"

Sarah couldn't stay quiet any longer. "Dalia, I *can't even believe* what is coming out of your mouth. And you *seriously* expect us to believe that if we help you with this, and Shawn still wants to be with Ella, that you'd be willing to let it go?" she asked, trying to push through the pain in her thighs as they continued to climb.

"Completely. One hundred percent over it, cross my heart, hope to die, I will never talk about him again, I swear on all of your lives."

"Great," Stacey muttered. Sarah was usually the superstitious one, but Stacey hated the swear on anyone's life phrase, especially given that Dalia said it backward. "Aren't you supposed to swear on your own life, Dalia? You might as well have just stuck us with a bunch of voodoo pins. You totally just cursed us."

"*My* life. *Whatever.* Stop being so dramatic. I'm just saying that I really mean it. I *promise* that if you help me with this, I will surrender to Ella. She can have him, and I won't bother them . . . *or you guys* . . . at all anymore. You can *all* be rid of me."

Tori shrieked as she tripped on a knotted branch sticking out through the sand. Reflexively, Dalia caught her. Tori stared at her sheepishly.

"Good thing I've always had your back, Tori, huh? But see? Injuries happen all the time."

"Maybe you should take her hiking then." Tori walked away from her.

Suddenly Jenny screamed from up ahead. *"Get it away, get it away!"* Dalia darted ahead to see what was wrong. *"Relax.* It's *just* a dead bird." Dalia kicked it into the bushes with her bare toes.

Something about the callousness in Dalia's voice, or the way she kicked the bird, made Sarah shiver. It felt foreboding. And she didn't know what that meant. But she hoped she'd never find out.

39

SARAH'S MOM THOUGHT she might want to do some-
thing special for her birthday this year, it being her eighteenth and
all. To Carrie, it was a milestone to be celebrated. Sarah could
vote, get her own credit card, and join the Army if she wanted.

But Sarah wasn't thrilled about the expiration of the protec-
tions being a minor offered. She could be criminally charged as
an adult, if circumstances called for it. Her parents could just kick
her out, if they felt like it. And she certainly wasn't ready to give
up home-cooked meals or her bills being paid. It seemed more like
something she should pretend wasn't happening than something
to be celebrated. So, when Carrie asked what she wanted to do,
she said the same thing she did every year. Apple picking. But this
time, she wanted to bring Tori.

"Hey, are you sure this is all you want to do for your birthday? I feel bad," Tori said as they plodded along. The muddied path was smattered with sunbaked, half-eaten apples. Sarah took in the sweet aroma.

"Absolutely! This is my *happy place.*" She smiled the biggest, dumbest smile she could at Tori because they hated that phrase.

There was something about the orchard that affected Sarah deeply. The spectacular fall breezes, the beauty, the simplicity. It elicited a joy so profound that the bees didn't even bother her. It felt safe. The way she wished all of life could be, especially lately.

"I know you guys want to throw me a party, but I really just need a break from all the drama."

Homecoming was rapidly approaching, as was the end of apple-picking season. Though her birthday was still a few weeks away, all the good apples would be gone by then. So, they always celebrated early.

"I hear ya," Tori said. "Well, let me know if you change your mind." She yanked a Golden Delicious off the tree, taking the bud with it.

"Twist, Tori," Sarah said, demonstrating as the apple guide had done about a hundred times. "You just killed next year's apple."

"Sorry, *bud,*" Tori said to the apple and then laughed at herself. "Get it, bud, like buddy, like apple bud, or is it a blossom . . . never mind. So has Dalia talked any more about her *evil plan?*" She took a big bite. "Wow. Why don't they taste like this in the grocery store?"

"I don't know. Farm fresh? Isn't that a thing?"

"Makes sense. So, evil plan?"

"No. You did a pretty good job of shutting her down."

"Yeah, no thanks to you guys."

"There's no way she's serious, I mean, come on. She's come up with some crazy shit before, but this . . ." Sarah took a deep breath and shook her head. "Have you talked to her?"

"No way. Not after that murderer comment. I always knew she'd throw that in my face someday."

"Just ignore her. She's really going through a tough time. I'm sure she didn't mean it."

Tori stopped and rested her bag of apples like a baby on her hip. "She's *always* going through a tough time, Sarah. I'm sick of it."

"I am too. But she legit has a bad life, Tori. Think about it. We don't know what that's like. And I feel like there's enough good there that we can manage the bad. Dalia needs us," she reasoned. "You know, I saw Jake after we got home that night . . ."

"Did you tell him?"

"That's the thing. I was going to, and then I'm like she does this shit *all the time*. She comes up with these crazy ideas, and we straighten her out, and then it's like she never said anything."

"True."

"Here." Sarah moved a branch over and pointed to a cluster of three perfect Red Delicious apples. "Grab those. Anyway, if I'd told him, he'd never want to be around her. And maybe not even me, and maybe rightfully so, because yes, I recognize what a complete fucking loon she comes off as sometimes. So, I decided not to. Because, you know, once it's out there, anyone who doesn't know her . . ." She sighed. "He'd never understand how I could be friends with her."

"For sure. Look, I'm guessing she didn't mean it. But there's a *line*, Sarah, and she keeps crossing it. I'll be there for her, but I am done listening to her bullshit. Like no more conversations about anything weird. And she'd better do some serious ass-kissing if she wants me to forgive her."

"That's fair." Sarah looped her arm in Tori's and led her to the row of Granny Smith trees. "Now, don't eat these ones. They're sour. For making pie."

"Got it."

"I'm hoping after Homecoming, after she's officially failed, she'll move on."

"Doubt it." Tori took a bite of a Granny Smith, spit it out, and threw it on the ground like it was the apple's fault.

"I told you. Well, the good news is, Shawn's going away to school in ten months, and so are we, so it won't be our problem anymore. I say we just pretend it never happened."

"Easier said than done."

"Tori, what she said to you was shitty. Really shitty. But she was like lashing out. And you'd feel pretty bad, too, if you had no real parents and the love of your life dicked you around like that."

"Fine. I'll try." She put one finger in the air. "But if she says *one* more word about this dropping thing, I'm telling Ella. And Coach Liz. And maybe even the principal. She'll get suspended. And maybe even expelled. You can pass *that* on for me."

"I totally agree. If I think for a second she's serious, I'll be right there with you."

"Saaaarraaah," Carrie called from a distance. "Come meet us for doughnuts when you guys are finished, and then we'll head to the tree."

"The tree?" Tori asked, looking around at the hundreds of trees surrounding them.

"You know, the giant evergreen, the one in our Christmas card picture every single year? Which I'm guessing you don't even look at?"

"Oh, right." She smiled. "*That* tree."

Sarah's mom shared her fondness for the apple orchard and insisted they take the same family picture every year. After stuffing their apple bags to maximum capacity, it was time for the main attraction.

"Tori, it is doughnut time."

Sarah opened the wooden screen door to the land of small-town pleasures, floor-to-ceiling shelves of every sweet treat you could think of. Apple doughnuts, homemade fudge, caramel apples, saltwater taffy, cocoa mixes, and gallons of fresh cider. When their cart couldn't hold another thing, they wheeled their way back to where her family was seated at their usual table in the country cafe.

"Is that your idea of low carb?" Carrie motioned with her chin and laughed.

"I'm going to eat it all tonight and then back on the wagon tomorrow," Sarah said as she sat in a wooden rocking chair.

"So, how's Dalia's new boyfriend. Tom is it?"

It was no surprise to Sarah that Carrie went right into gossip-seeking mode. She generally did when she got the chance to sit down with one of the girls.

"Oh, he's just *great*." Tori laughed.

"Mom, I thought you knew she just made him up to save face in front of Ella."

"I figured. So, they're not spending all day in bed together?"

"*Carrie!*" Sarah's dad covered his ears.

"*Not* spending the day in bed together, Dad. I told you, she's not like that. And Kevin, you'd better keep your mouth shut." Sarah wagged her sticky finger at him.

"Well, that was quite some acting there. I know you girls are close to her, but anyone who can lie on the spot like that, so convincingly, you need to be a little careful of."

"I agree, Carrie." Tori took the opportunity to say her piece. "She's out of her mind with this Shawn thing. Did Sarah tell you about her *evil plan* to . . ."

Sarah kicked her hard under the table. Hadn't they just discussed what would happen if this got out?

"*Ow!*" Tori crossed her leg up over her knee and began massaging her shin. Sarah's dad had just opened his mouth to start on his second doughnut but put it down. Sarah knew exactly what was coming as he fixed his eyes on her.

"Sarah, what do I always say about kicking people under tables?"

"That you shouldn't do it?"

"That's right. Kicking people under tables means someone is hiding something they shouldn't be. So, out with it."

"It's nothing."

"If something's going on, you need to tell us," he insisted.

"Just *stop.*" She put her hand up in protest of his firm tone. "I tell you everything. If there was something worth telling, I would."

Tori's guilty eyes told them otherwise. Sarah widened her eyes at her to stop.

"That's a lot like kicking, Sar." He gave her a long look.

"Trust is still a thing in this family, right?" She gave him enough time to answer. He didn't, so she changed the subject. So, Homecoming. Dad, can we take your car?"

The change of subject worked, and the rest of the conversation focused on Homecoming, college, and the future. After four doughnuts and a hot chocolate, Sarah had had her fill of sugar and suggested they go take their picture.

"Let's do it. And this year we have our own *photographer*." Carrie put her arm around Tori. "We usually have to bother some stranger, so let's take our time and do it right this year. Tori, is that okay with you?"

"Sure thing, Carrie."

Tori grabbed the Nikon and put the strap around her neck. They made their way out the back of the store and walked to their very favorite evergreen decorated with gold and silver balls that glinted in the sun. They stood in their standard pose—boys on the left, girls on the right. Despite doing only one pose, Carrie made Tori go through an entire roll of film to make sure they got it right.

Aside from the small conversational hiccup, the birthday outing was exactly what Sarah had wanted it to be, full of good weather, good food, and lots of love. It was so nice that Sarah promised her mom she'd come home from college every year to keep up the tradition.

One week later, Sarah watched her mom beam at the once-elusive, perfect family picture they were finally able to capture. Carrie proudly hung the framed eight by ten in their study, alongside all the other years' orchard pictures.

If anyone had told them that would be the last family orchard picture they ever took, none of them would have believed it. And they most certainly would not have believed the why.

40

"ELLA, WHAT'S GOING ON with you today? Where's your showmanship?" Dalia looked up from her conversation with Jenny on the locker room bench. The Homecoming pep rally was days away, and Ella's performance was lackluster at best, nothing like her usual dazzling display. Dalia had coaxed the girls into a double practice, insisting that their last Homecoming pep rally performance ever should be *friggin' perfect*. Though her real motive was to see if her plan was feasible, considering Jenny was the only one who'd agreed to participate. It wasn't looking good. But she'd thought long and hard about it and come up with some additional measures. A way to covertly persuade the girls to help her, whether they wanted to or not. It was a long shot, but it was worth the risk. She felt a little bad about having to recruit Jake. But really, it was Sarah's fault that she needed him at all, so she didn't feel *that* bad.

"I'm sorry, Dalia. I'm just not feeling great," Ella said, spreading her fingers wide across her stomach. "I've got the routine down. I promise. Do you mind if I skip the second practice? I just need to lie down for a bit before work tonight."

Dalia leaned away from her. "What's wrong with you? You better not be contagious."

Dalia felt dizzy as she feared things might unravel once again. There was no room in her plan for a wrench like illness, she realized as she stared at Ella's annoyingly pretty face.

"I'm not contagious. I just really need to use . . . the bathroom . . . alone . . . at my house. I ate something bad. It like . . . won't stop."

"Oh my god, *TMI, Ella*! Well, we can't have you shitting all over everyone's heads. Go. Get out of here."

"I'm sorry," she said. The color drained from Ella's face. Dalia shrunk back as she saw tiny sweat droplets forming on her lip.

"*Now!*" she yelled.

Ella hurried off. Dalia heard the locker room door click open and waited for it to shut in its predictable rhythm. She had a few things to discuss with Jenny now that she was sure they were alone, but the door hadn't given her the all-clear yet. "What the fuck's she doing?" She started to get up—she wouldn't put it past Ella to try to listen in on their conversation. But the subsequent heavy slam saved her the trouble of checking it out, so she sat back down and got right to it.

She got some logistical business squared away—who would ride with who, flowers, dresses—but just as Dalia was about to do the deep dive, she found herself looking up at fiery-faced Tori.

"Dalia, what the hell are *you* picking up a dress for?"

"Oh, so *now* you're gonna speak to me? When you decide you have something to *yell* at me about?"

"You haven't even said you're sorry. And yes, I'm going to yell at you if I think there's even a chance you're still considering doing anything to Ella. Did we not make it clear enough that no one is participating in your *evil plan?*"

"Oh, you made it clear."

Dalia tried to mask her shock that Tori had overheard them. She didn't know how much she'd heard. Though quickly reviewing her conversation with Jenny in her head, she was pretty sure it was fine. But she knew the situation called for an apology, if for no other reason than to get Tori to back off.

"Tori. I'm *sorry*. I shouldn't have said that stuff. Any of it. I was just freaking out about everything, but I didn't mean it. So, relax. Yes, we were talking about a dress. I'm going with Jenny to help her choose between *her* two dresses. Obviously, I'll be staying home Saturday, *alone*, while you guys are all having fun without me, at our last Homecoming. But it's still fun to look at dresses." Dalia sulked, and Tori's icy attitude began to melt.

"You know, you still could have gotten a date if you hadn't gone all in on the Tom thing. You could probably *still* get one. Just say you guys got in a fight or something."

"It's too late. Anyway, Nick Davis is the only guy without a date. And I mean, come on. Can you say desperate? Whatever. Do you want to come shopping with us?" Dalia added for credibility purposes, praying she'd turn her down.

"No. But I need you to promise me . . . you're not planning *anything*, right?"

"Tori, I *promise*! That was *so dumb*. I can't believe it even crossed my mind. I know I've been a fucking handful the last few months, but you know I could never do anything like *that.*"

"Do I?" Tori stood with her feet planted firmly on the ground, both hands on her waist.

"*Yes.* Plus, if you can believe it, I will admit that you guys might be right. About Shawn maybe not being the right guy for me. Church every weekend? I could never handle it." Dalia moved her gym bag out of the way and patted the bench for Tori to sit with them. Tori declined.

"Okay. Well, that's good," she said. She pulled out her wallet. "I'm going to Taco Bell. Do you guys want anything?"

"Meximelt, please." Jenny raised her hand.

"You actually lost Not It? That's the first time ever! No. I'm okay. Are *we* okay?"

"If you really are done with this, we'll get there. I'll be back in twenty."

Dalia held one finger to her lips to shush Jenny while she once again waited for the door's signal. And once again it took longer than usual, but Dalia was too flustered by their close call with Tori to worry about it.

Jenny's eyebrows pinched together in confusion. "Wait. Are we doing it or not?"

"Tori's not, but Sarah and Stacey are. Just ignore her. I don't know why she's got such a bug up her ass about it. But *don't* talk to them about it. Everyone knows what they're supposed to do."

"And they're for sure okay with it?"

"They're *totally* okay with it. But I don't want *anyone* to talk about it cuz if anyone finds out, it won't work. We shouldn't even be talking about it now."

"And you think it will work with just the three of us?"

"For sure. There's no way Tori can do it on her own."

"But, Dalia, I'm a little worried. What if she gets . . . hurt hurt?"

"Jenny." Dalia grabbed her hand. "Listen to me. There's *no way* she can get *hurt* hurt. You guys are dropping her a few feet. It's *nothing*. And you are the *greatest* friend in the world for helping me."

"Well, you always help me, so . . ." Jenny smiled. Until her face was paralyzed by the appearance of another slinker.

"What are you guys talking about?" Ella asked.

"Ella, what are you doing here?! I thought you went home!" Dalia jumped up like someone put an ice cube down her shirt.

"I forgot my gym bag. So, tell me what you were talking about."

"What we're *talking about?*" Dalia shifted in her shoes and gripped her own elbow.

"If you must know, because it's just *so interesting*, I have to go pick up my dress tomorrow. For my night in the city with Tom, not that it's any of your business."

"Oh. Where is he taking you?"

"It's a surprise. But he feels bad I'm missing Homecoming, so at the last minute—he's *such* a guy. Like I even have time for this. He told me to buy a Homecoming dress. And he's going to wear the suit he wore at his senior year Homecoming. Isn't that hilarious? I can't decide if it's cute or weird."

"Oh. That's cool. Okay, I'll see you guys." Ella threw her gym bag over her shoulder. Dalia watched as she walked away. But when Ella reached the end of the lockers, she gymnastics pivoted right back to them. Jenny looked up at her like a girl in a horror movie when the thing just won't die.

"But what was the other thing you were talking about. Dropping someone? I for sure heard you say 'dropping her.'"

"*Dropping her?* What are you . . . we didn't . . ." Dalia's heart started to race, as a million questions and possible responses entered her mind. How did they not hear her come in? Had she heard them talking to Tori? Did they say her name?

"Oh. I know. Jesus, Ella, nosy much? Dropping her *off.* We were talking about dropping Sarah off after practice. Tori can't do it, so one of the three of us has to, which is totally out of the way. Like we all have stuff to do, but of course Tori's the one that *can't.* More like *won't.* You know how she gets."

"Oh." Ella squinted her eyes and used her middle finger to scratch her eyebrow. "But I could swear I heard you say something about someone getting hurt."

"*Hurt?* Like . . . feelings hurt, um . . . because no one wanted to drop Sarah off maybe? I don't remem . . ." Dalia paused and then snapped her fingers. "*Oh!* Getting *her,* Ella. Like getting her home. What's with the weird questions? Don't you have to go take some Pepto Bismol or something?"

"Yeah. Okay. I guess I'll see you at work."

Dalia's heart was still pounding as she watched Ella slump away. She had no idea if Ella bought her explanation. But after two close calls in five minutes, she knew she'd better step up her game.

41

IT'S NOT EASY WAITING TABLES while trying to make sense of your life, Ella figured out. But that was about all she figured out because nothing else made any sense anymore. Her relationship with Shawn didn't, her family didn't, the conversation in the locker room didn't. She went over and over it in her mind, and while Dalia's explanation kind of made sense, it kind of didn't. But neither did what Ella thought she heard. None of it mattered, though. It's not like she could talk to anyone about it. Or about anything else going on right now. From the deepest depths of her mind, she felt herself reaching, arms outstretched, praying someone would pull her out of this. Or just give her a hug and tell her it would be okay. As she stared down at her order pad, her head felt heavy, almost not worth the effort it took to hold it up, as she realized she'd never been more alone in her life.

"Excuse me, miss? Our ketchup?" a harried father of three reminded her.

"Oh, sorry. I'll be right back with that."

As she headed to the kitchen, her mind was overwhelmed with thoughts of people's reactions when they discovered her situation. Images of her father dropping dead on the spot. Her mother's rage and self-righteousness. The stares and whispers from her fellow students. And then Shawn. If there was any certainty about this situation at all, it would be Shawn's insistence that they *do the right thing* and get married. And then she pictured the two of them living at his parents' house, raising a baby, while everyone they knew went off to college. She wasn't anywhere near ready to commit to her ever after, and certainly not willing to define it with a teenage pregnancy, which is why she told Shawn they'd come out of the condom situation unscathed.

She grabbed a bottle of ketchup.

"*Ella,*" George bellowed at her. "Table six's food has been sitting there for five minutes."

"I'm sorry. I'm coming." She went to the serving station and tucked the ketchup under her arm, then picked up two plates and tried to balance them as she pinned the ketchup bottle against her side with her elbow.

"*Ella,*" Barbara called after her. "Don't hold the ketchup like *that.*"

"Sorry." Ella whipped around and lost her hold on the ketchup. As she tried to catch it, she lost her balance completely, sending plates of linguini crashing to the floor. Barbara rushed her disapproving face over to Ella and began to lecture her.

"Barbara, I've got it," Dalia said, stepping in front of her. "Leave that," she instructed Ella, who was reaching for the broken base of the ketchup bottle. "What's going on with you tonight?"

"Dalia, can you just not . . . I'm a total mess right now," Ella pleaded, presuming Dalia would say something to make her feel bad about herself. Surprisingly, she didn't.

"What, you think you're the only one who's dropped dishes before? It's no big deal."

Crouched over oily noodles and clam shells scattered across the tile, their eyes met. A look of concern crossed Dalia's face, a look that Ella was longing for from anyone she might be able to call a friend. Was Dalia trying to be her friend? So hungry for female connection, Ella recognized that Dalia's words felt disproportionately good. But she'd take it. It was the first time anyone besides Shawn had said anything supportive to her in ages.

The busboy arrived with the mop, and while George smoothed things over with table six, Dalia steered Ella toward the kitchen.

"We need two more linguini and clam sauce. Right away," Dalia shouted to the chef and then turned toward Ella.

"Hey, I wanted to ask you something. A favor."

"What do you need?" Ella would have done anything for Dalia at this moment.

"Sarah's being totally lame about her birthday. She says she doesn't want to do anything. The rest of the girls are all *we need to respect her wishes*, but I said fuck it, I'll throw her a surprise party myself."

"How can I help?" Ella gulped back tears.

"Well, George said we can use the private room on Sunday. The girls think they're coming in for one of George's food tastings."

"Okay . . ."

"And I need help setting everything up. On Thursday. I won't have time over the weekend, obviously."

"Dalia, Sarah hates me. And so does everyone else. I'm sure they won't want me to have anything to do with this."

"Don't make a bigger deal out of it than it is. You're not doing it for Sarah; you're doing it for me. You do kind of owe me, right?"

"I'm so sorry." She lost her grip on her tears. Dalia put her hand on Ella's shoulder.

"Listen, I'm over it. Because of you, I have Tom. So, I should be thanking you."

"Really?"

"No, you're just lucky it turned out the way it did. But what do I have to be mad about?"

"Dalia . . ."

"Let's just move on, okay? I want the rest of senior year to be all peace and love. We've got state to think about, and we're never going to win if we're all, you know, *drama*." She threw up jazz hands. "The party will be a good way for you to start working things out with everyone."

"Yeah." Ella lowered her chin. "This whole thing has made being on the squad really hard. And it's all my fault."

"No more of that. We'll throw a kickass party, and it has to be kickass, because Tom is coming. But it has to be like *mature*."

"*Tom's coming?*" Ella's chin popped back up. If Tom started hanging around the girls like one of the group, they'd definitely move on from the whole Shawn situation. And while they might never trust her, it would for sure offer her a chance at a fresh start.

"Yep. But you'd better keep your dick in your pants around him. I'll be watching you," Dalia pointed two fingers directly at her eyes.

"Oh my god, I would nev . . . that's *so great.*"

"So, you'll *for sure* be here Thursday?"

"Yes, of course," she said, and laughed through the tail end of her tears. She rubbed her nose and wiped her hand on her apron. "I hate to ask this, but I'm still not feeling well, and I forgot to pick up my dad's medicine today. Do you think you could cover my tables the rest of the night?"

Dalia sighed and handed her a napkin. "I give you my boyfriend, my friends, a job, a spot on the cheerleading squad . . ."

"A napkin . . ." Ella half laughed as she crumpled it and tossed it in the garbage.

"*And* a napkin. I deserve an award or something. Like a fucking peace prize. It's fine," she said and then smiled. "I'll tell George."

"Thank you, Dalia." Ella stood on her tiptoes and hugged her as hard as she could.

"Okay," Dalia pulled away. "That's enough of that. I gotta get back."

Ella cleaned herself up as best she could and rushed to the car. If she hurried, she could get to the pharmacy before it closed. She arrived just in time to stick her foot in the door as they were about to lock up.

"I'll just be one minute. I promise," she begged the annoyed teenager with the store keys in his hand. He looked at his watch and glared at her, making it clear she was interfering with his Saturday night plans, and then let her in.

"Hi, I have to pick up a prescription. For Alan Connor," Ella said to the silver-haired pharmacist. He flipped through the bin marked C and handed Ella her dad's medication. "Warfarin. This look right?"

"I think?" She took it out of his hand. "It's the blood-thinning one."

"That's the one." He handed her a pen and clipboard. "Sign here."

As the pharmacist rang her up, something on the printout caught her eye. A warning that read "Pregnancy Category X. Warfarin is contraindicated in pregnancy, as it may cause spontaneous abortion." *Spontaneous abortion? Is that like a real abortion? Because if it is, it could really come in handy about now.*

She bit her lip and started drumming her fingers on the counter. Dalia forgiving her and now *this*? She wondered if somehow there was the smallest chance that the stars were suddenly aligning in her favor. That maybe she could get her friends back. That perhaps this medication could fix her situation. That possibly she could go back to a life where Linda was her only problem. She laughed at how luxurious the prospect of Linda being her only problem felt. And with that little laugh came a lot of hope.

She hesitated before asking the question burning inside her, considering how she could phrase it as a curiosity and not bring any attention to herself. As the transaction came to a close, she felt pressured that the opportunity was about to pass her by. So, she said the first thing she could think of.

"So, you can't take this medicine if you're pregnant?"

The pharmacist looked over his glasses at her. "You really shouldn't take any medication when you're pregnant unless it's absolutely necessary, but this one can cause miscarriages, especially early on. Why do you ask?"

"Um," she mumbled, tapping her foot nervously, "I guess I've just never seen that before. Category X. Like wow. Sounds scary."

"It can be. Well, be sure to tell *Alan* that this is a serious medication that must be taken as prescribed." He looked at her curiously, like he was on to her. Which meant she'd better get out of there as quickly as possible.

"Will do." Ella grabbed the medication. "Thank you."

She hurried back to the car and inspected the label again. The heaviness that had sat with her since the day those two pink lines showed up started to lift just a bit, replaced by the slightest hint of optimism. Could this possibly work? It was definitely worth a try. But what about her dad? He needed the medication. Yet, for both of their sakes, so did she. She'd just have to tell her parents she lost it and pick up a replacement, she decided as she washed down two pills.

42

ELLA'S OPTIMISM BEGAN TO FADE when, five days later, she woke up and found herself right where she'd been—still pregnant, still nauseous, still alone in her life. Drowning in desolation, she couldn't get out of bed. Thoughts beyond the immediate hurled her into hopelessness. So, she vowed to face the day five minutes at a time. Willing herself through tiny incremental blocks, she prayed she'd one day find herself on the other side of this mess. *Five more minutes,* she repeated to herself, batting away dark thoughts as they nipped at her mind's edges. She made it through school. Pushed through her homework. Got ready for work. Survived the car ride with Linda.

She pulled open the door to Gatto's. *Five minutes at a time,* she reminded herself as she walked into the bustling restaurant. But Dalia derailed her five-minute discipline when she announced that her car had broken down and *Jake* would be taking her to get Sarah's decorations. Ella was looking forward to the break in her evening, but now she was distracted by thoughts of having to engage with someone who probably hated her. And two hours later, under the Harvest Moon, Jake made it clear that he didn't want to be with her either.

"I don't know how you talked me into this," he said to Dalia as the cool wind whistled around them. He paced for a bit and then sat on the bench next to Ella. "How's it goin'," he said and then looked away before she could answer.

"*Talked you into it?* You mean came up with a kickass idea that's gonna make your girlfriend wet herself every time she thinks about you? Jake. Sarah *loves* surprise parties. And her boyfriend throwing it for her?" Dalia held out one palm, like she was serving him the most obviously awesome thing ever.

"Yeah, but she doesn't like lies, and she thinks I'm out to dinner with my mom right now."

Dalia sat on the bench next to him. "Well, you kind of can't have surprise parties without lies, so that's *her* problem." She pulled a wad of cash from her apron and peeled off two twenties. "It's not like it's a *forever* lie. Even if she thinks you're hiding something from her . . . which she might, because she's really smart, and you don't seem like a very good liar. In the end, she'll just smack you on the shoulder and be like, oh my god, you *totally* got me." Dalia demonstrated, smacking him with the heel of her hand. "That's how surprise parties are *supposed* to work, Jake. So don't blow it, even if she thinks something's up. That's the fun! Now when you're finished, pull around to the back entrance. Ella, come buzz the door, and I'll take it from there."

"George is okay with you covering my tables?" Ella asked, hoping Dalia would just send Jake. "Why can't we just give him the list?"

"Ella, he's a *guy!* He can't pick the actual *colors.* But just leave the stuff in Jake's car so you can get back to your tables—and you have to watch my tables while I'm getting the stuff up to the party room. And don't leave, Jake! I'll be out as soon as I can to grab it. With both of you, it shouldn't take more than ten minutes to find everything. It's all in the same section." She handed Ella the money. "And I want change!"

"I don't know about this," Jake said as he glanced back and forth between Dalia and Ella. His nose was scrunched, like he smelled something terrible. Ella couldn't blame him. She wouldn't want to be with her either, after hearing what Sarah had to say about her.

"If your car's messed up, can't we just skip the decorations? The only thing I agreed to do was get her here on Sunday," Jake reminded her. "Honestly, I don't think I should—"

"*Oh my god.* Am I the only one on this planet who understands anything? A party needs *decorations*, Jake. And besides, *bringing her* here is not *throwing her* a party. That's called *going to* a party. You think I'm gonna be like, hey Jake, Sarah would totally dig it if you threw her a surprise party—and then I'm going to do all the work, and you're going to get all the credit when you wouldn't even help when my *car broke down?* We just need you to give Ella *a ride*, for fuck's sake, and to spend a *few minutes* helping her so she can get back to work. It's the least you can do. And *you're welcome*, by the way. Now go, you guys." Dalia marched off before he could even respond.

Ella opened the passenger door of Jake's Mustang. As she sat down, she noticed her swelling chest was stretching the buttons on her white work shirt, causing a gape. She tried to pinch the fabric closed, but it was no use. She rested her hand on her heart.

"So, what are we doing exactly?" Jake glanced at her and raised a brow in the direction of her hand. She looked down, as she always did when she was nervous. An open bag of Lay's potato chips was sticking out from under the seat. She nudged it with her Converse shoes.

"Nice kicks," Jake offered up a compliment.

But Ella didn't respond, now consumed with thoughts of her growing chest. She didn't know how long it would take for her dad's medicine to work, if it was going to work at all. But the fact that she'd gone up an entire cup size likely meant that it wasn't working. As did the fact that those potato chips sounded irresistibly good.

"Can I have these?" She unrolled the *who knows how long it had been sitting there* bag of potato chips and poured some into her mouth. Judging by their rubbery texture, it had been a while. But it didn't stop her from eating them. Jake looked at her sideways for just a second before pulling out of the parking lot.

"Okay." Ella tossed the empty bag and pulled out Dalia's list. "So we're supposed to go to the party store on Fifth Avenue. We need crepe paper, balloons, tape, candles, and a banner that says happy birthday. Oh, and it all has to be black, red, and silver. School colors, I guess." She shrugged and then reached for the breadsticks in her purse. She tried to covertly break off pieces and put them in her mouth when Jake wasn't looking. But the rustling of the paper wrapper got his attention.

"Do you always carry breadsticks with you? And eat stale potato chips?"

She glanced down at the four stuck-together sticks, now hardened by the autumn air.

"Sorry, I didn't get to eat earlier," she said. Now that she was caught, she went all in, breaking off chunks and shoving them into her mouth in one continuous motion until they were gone. She dabbed up the last crumb and breathed a sigh of relief as her nausea subsided.

"All better?"

"Yes. Thanks."

Jake pulled into a parking spot. He grabbed his wallet from the center console. Ella didn't even notice that they'd arrived.

"You ready there, Miss Spacy?"

"What did you say?"

"I said, are you ready there, *Miss Spacy*."

"Oh. I'm sorry, I've just got a lot on my mind right now."

"Everything okay?"

"It will be. I hope," she said as she faced him. And when she finally looked into his eyes, she saw something unexpected, something that looked like kindness. It calmed her, made her think that maybe he didn't hate her. Or maybe he just had an open mind. So now, instead of resisting this interaction, she decided to embrace it. Embrace the chance to show Jake she wasn't the terrible person the girls said she was. But she knew she wouldn't get anywhere while she was wallowing in misery, so she forced herself to swallow that misery. And then mustered up every bit of energy she could to summon the old, fun Ella. The girl she was before she ruined everything.

43

PULLING HER HAIR ASIDE to get a closer look in Stacey's mirror, Sarah winced as she dangled a fringy silver earring in front of her earlobe. Her most perfect of all Homecoming dresses was a super-fitted, strapless, black satin dress that, unfortunately, pinched every time she moved. Tori had tried to talk her out of it, pointing out right away that she'd be uncomfortable all night. But it looked too good for her to worry about something so trivial as moving around.

"Sarah," Tori said, laughing. "How are you going to dance in it if you can't move? It's not like you're one of those girls who's just going to stand off to the side. You *love* to dance, if you recall."

"Oh, I also can't breathe and walk at the same time, so . . ." She sighed, inching closer to giving up on the greatest dress of all time.

Homecoming was only two days away, and once again, Tori would be proven right. No dress is worth being uncomfortable all night, she'd said. Sarah had hoped it would loosen as she previewed it, making exaggerated movements in an effort to bend but not break it. It wasn't looking good.

"Well, what about these earrings?"

"Are you wearing your hair up or down?" Jenny asked.

"Up."

"I think they're too long."

"Down then. I love these."

Stacey dug through velvet boxes scattered around her bedroom floor. She had a jewelry collection that rivaled the Royal Family's. Though not as grand, it was close in quantity, so the girls helped themselves to it whenever they had a formal affair.

"Don't change your hair plans just because you like the earrings. Try this set."

Sarah opened a red box to reveal a gorgeous pave diamond choker and matching pair of earrings.

"Okay. This is perfect. *Ow!*" she cried out at the stitching digging into her sides. "Is there like a pin stuck in here or something?"

"Give me that." Tori held out her hand and then clasped the necklace around Sarah's neck. "This will go with your backup dress too."

"I can't do it, can I?"

"No. You can't," Tori said. "Let's just run to the mall now and exchange it. The other one is still on hold, right?"

"Yes. Can you at least take my picture in it before I take it off? I want to show Jake what he missed."

As Stacey dug through her closet for her camera, the phone rang.

"Dalia? Talk louder," Jenny shouted into the receiver. "I can't hear you. You need Sarah?"

Sarah shuffled over and grabbed the phone out of her hand. "What's up?"

"Sorry, I'm trying to whisper. Now listen. I'm going to tell you something, and you're not gonna like it. But don't go all crazy yet, because maybe there's an explanation."

"What is it?"

"Jake came to the restaurant."

"So? He's out to dinner with his mom." Sarah rolled her eyes at the girls and pointed at the phone.

"He wasn't with his mom."

"What are you *saying*, Dalia?" She began twirling her hair around her finger. Tori leaned in to listen.

"Just put it on speaker," Stacey said as she emerged from the closet with the camera.

Dalia's hollow voice filled the room.

"He came to see *Ella*."

"*Jesus Christ, Dalia.* Why are you doing this to me right before Homecoming? Seriously, it's not funny. What do you *want*?" Sarah asked, relieved that this was obviously some kind of prank. She didn't know what Dalia was trying to accomplish, but she could've come up with something more believable. Stacey held up the camera. Sarah smiled and posed in the only position she could. Standing straight up.

"I'm serious, you guys."

"*Ella?* Why would he go see *Ella?*" Sarah squeezed her

eyebrows together so hard, she thought they might stay that way forever.

"*I know!* It's weird. Ella said she had to run out for something. She was waiting in between the double doors, and she was acting super weird, like she was hiding something. She kept looking back over her shoulder, so of course I was like what the fuck is she up to. So, I ran out and saw her drive away in *Jake's car*."

"*What?* Dalia, are you high? That *can't* be true. Jake is for sure out to dinner with his *mom* tonight. There are a million black mustangs. There must be a mistake."

"EKJ 5850, right?"

"You saw his license plate?" Sarah's face dropped into her fingers.

"*Of course!* You think I'd call you if I wasn't sure? If you don't believe me . . . look, I'm not saying something's like *going on* between them. Like I said, there could be an explanation for it. But I know what I saw."

"Well, *what the fuck?*" Stacey looked to Sarah for an answer she didn't have.

"Dalia, are you like *you* sure or *me* sure?" Tori asked.

"What. You think I'm insane or something? *Don't answer that.*"

"But where did she say she was going?" Stacey asked.

"She didn't. But she did say she'd be back in a half hour."

"So, he just totally lied to me about what he's doing tonight? Why?" This couldn't be happening. Not with Jake. Sarah's head began to throb. The room started to go dark, as the world felt like it was caving in around her.

"I don't know. Maybe it's nothing. And you probably shouldn't ruin your last Homecoming over it, but I thought you should know."

"Well, *now what?* How could he do this right before *Homecoming and my birthday?*" She closed her eyes and tried to take a breath deeper than her dress would allow. A sinkhole rapidly formed in her stomach, swallowing her heart in the process.

"I don't know. Maybe just sit on it. Ask him what he did tonight and see what he says before you say anything. But I wouldn't go all crazy on him or anything."

"Wait. *You're* telling *me* not to go all crazy on him?"

"*Yes, Sarah.* I learned my lesson! Okay, you guys. I have to go."

Sarah pressed the receiver button and frantically dialed Jake's number. His mom answered. Now it wasn't just her dress making it hard to breathe. The phone dropped from her hand. Stacey grabbed it off the floor.

"Wrong number, sorry," she said and quickly hung up the phone.

"Okay, let's think about this," Tori said. "This is Jake we're talking about, and we all agree he's a good guy, right? Maybe it has something to do with Shawn, like Shawn asked him to do him a favor or something," Tori suggested. "You guys aren't fighting, right?"

"I don't think so, I mean he canceled our plans the other night, but that's because he ended up having to work, unless . . ." She suddenly flashed back to Wisconsin when Shawn canceled because *he* had to work. And *that* had Ella's dirty fingerprints *all over it.* Could something possibly be going on between them? She couldn't believe the thought even crossed her mind because she and Jake were good. In fact, they were *great.* But there wasn't even a single other possibility that made sense, so it was like a diagnosis of exclusion. Unless Dalia was wrong about what she saw.

"You know what? No. I totally trust him. It's seven o'clock. Maybe he already went to dinner with his mom. Or maybe he hasn't gone yet. And there's no reason to ruin Homecoming with some crazy jealous girlfriend accusation. I'm not going to stoop to that," she said. "Like, '*Oh, hi Jake, my crazy girlfriend followed you in the parking lot to check out your license plate to see if you were picking up my sworn enemy?*' And it came from Dalia of all people? You know what he'd say? He'd say that's exactly the reason not to hang out with her, and wherever she goes, there are problems, and like all the things he's said about her, and you know what? He'd be right. No way. Either there's a logical explanation for this that we haven't thought of, or Dalia's wrong."

"Sorry guys," Stacey said. "I get it. But remember when we had pretty much this exact conversation about Jim? Didn't we all agree Jim was a good guy? Never saw it coming. I hate to be this way, but if anything's going on, wouldn't you rather know now?" She pointed to her closet door.

Stacey still had a ten-by-thirteen picture of Jim's face that the girls had mounted on foam and turned into a dartboard. They'd thrown so many darts at it, his face looked like he'd been pecked to death by a rabid pigeon.

"You haven't taken that thing down yet?" Tori asked.

"Nope. It reminds me every day to never trust anyone, ever again."

"Very healthy, Stace," Tori said. "How about this? Ella is supposed to be back there in twenty minutes. Let's just run over there and take a look. And then you can decide what to do. Maybe it's not him at all, and Dalia made you crazy for nothing, which it wouldn't be the first time. Stacey, can we take your mom's car? So he won't recognize it?"

That sounded like a totally reasonable plan. It wasn't making a big thing about it and risking Homecoming being ruined. But if she *didn't* check it out, it would ruin Homecoming because she'd be thinking about it all night.

With the scales tipped ever so slightly in one direction, Sarah agreed to drive over to Gatto's, in her very perfect, very uncomfortable Homecoming dress, that ripped as soon as she sat in the car.

Fuck!

44

ELLA OPENED THE CAR DOOR and then shut it again.

"Wait." She dug elbow-deep in her bag and pulled out a cookie wrapped in a cloth napkin.

"Seriously, Mary Poppins? What else do you have in there? Ice cream?" Jake said.

"No ice cream, but I have beef jerky, Laffy Taffy, Twinkies . . . and a very appetizing banana, if any of this interests you." She dangled a mushy, brown banana in front of his face. "My stomach has been a little messed up lately."

"Maybe you should change your diet." Jake stared at her stomach.

"You think?" She held up the Twinkies. "Did you know these never go bad? I always keep Twinkies with me. In case there's a nuclear war. You can never be too prepared, as Sarah would say."

"I can see why you guys are friends. You're both a little strange."

"*Were* friends," Ella said, taking a big bite of the cookie. "I'm almost ready," she said with her mouth full, and then wrapped the cookie back up and put it away.

"I've got something that will fix your stomach if you want." Jake pulled out a one-hitter and a tightly rolled baggie from under his seat. Ella eagerly grabbed the baggie out of his hand and inhaled the friendly aroma. "It's so much harder to get here than in Tucson!"

"Not really, you just have to know the right people. You know how to use a one-hitter?" He handed her the pipe encased in a small wooden box engraved with a peace symbol.

"I have three of them. One has the Batman symbol on it. You know, the light he shines in the sky. I don't even like Batman, but it's cool."

"I can tell you don't like Batman. If you did, you'd know that *he* doesn't shine it. The *Commissioner* shines it to call *him*," he said, smiling. "You gonna be okay going back to work?"

"Well, the weed's not going to make me any dumber." She cringed at her Batman blunder, making a mental note not to say *that* again. Ella packed the paraphernalia like a seasoned professional.

"There's a lighter in the glove box," Jake said as he opened both windows.

With a flick of the cogged wheel and a deep breath, a sweet relief wrapped around her like an electric blanket on a winter day. It warmed them both, barriers turning to bridges as they entered the same mindset. Ella felt like herself for the first time in a long time, her problems now locked away in a distant part of her brain. For the time being, at least. And she felt like she may have found a new friend.

"We have to shop!" he reminded her.

"Oh *yeah*. I forgot why we were here. We don't have much time!"

"Ooooh . . . I love their Halloween stuff!" Ella said as they entered the store. Halloween was her favorite holiday. She loved the idea of being able to be someone else completely, if just for a few hours. An overly enthusiastic smile adorned her face as she wandered through the aisles of costume accessories, picking through wigs and feather boas. A motion-sensing skeleton shouted at them as they passed by. Ella jumped and screamed. Jake laughed like he'd never seen anything so funny.

"You need sunglasses just to walk through this place," he said, shading his eyes from the punishingly bright fluorescent lighting.

"We need sunglasses to hide our eyes." She noticed bloodshot spidering its way into the whites of Jake's eyes. Ella saw a pair of Blues Brothers sunglasses and a hat and put them on him. "There," she said, and then chose a Michael Jackson wig and aviator sunglasses for herself.

The two of them looked in the mirror and laughed so hard Ella's cheeks hurt. She couldn't remember the last time she had this much fun.

They checked off each item on their shopping list and reached the cash register in record time, the task at hand surprisingly unimpeded by the state they were in. "Candles." Jake ran off and came back with a one and an eight.

"See, that's why we needed you here. I would have forgotten the candles," Ella said.

"Are you guys buying the wigs too or are those yours?" the nose-ring clad checkout girl asked. They looked at each other and laughed yet again, eliciting a knowing look from the girl who all but asked if she could have some.

"Sorry, we'll put them back," Jake said.

"We got that done in only twelve minutes." Jake high-fived her as they sat back in the car.

"And we got to wear cool costumes."

"And we got to wear cool costumes," Jake repeated, nodding.

They looked at each other and cracked up again when they realized they were still wearing the sunglasses.

"I was wondering why it was so dark in here," Jake said.

"Me too! Did we pay for these?"

"I don't know." He slid them up on his head. "I won't tell if you won't."

"It'll be *our* secret." She raised her pinky to pinky swear. Jake didn't seem to know what that was, so Ella used it to scratch her chin instead. She liked that they had a secret, the makings of their own private joke someday.

"Wanna Laffy Taffy?" she asked as they pulled back onto Fifth Avenue.

"You got banana?"

She handed him the mushy banana she'd shown him earlier. He took it and threw it out the window. "You trying to kill me? Not *a* banana, banana Laffy Taffy!"

"Oooohhh . . . hahahaha! Lemme see." She fumbled through her bag. "Here we go. Okay. I'll open it and read the joke, and then you can eat it." It took the rest of the drive for Ella to peel the wrapper off the sticky candy.

"What's going on over there?" Jake asked.

"I don't want to rip the joke. I've almost got it."

They pulled back into Gatto's. Jake found a spot by the rear entrance and backed in while Ella was still fumbling with the candy wrapper.

"Give it to me." Jake took the candy and finished peeling off the label.

"Okay. These are so bad. How do you get a baby alien to sleep? Any guesses?"

"Nope."

"You *rocket*." He crumpled up the wrapper and threw it at her. "So bad. You know what they should put in Laffy Taffy? Dead baby jokes. Can you imagine, kids would open them up, and it would say what do you call a dead baby on a wall? Art. How do you get ten dead babies in a bucket? With a blender." He slapped his thigh and laughed so hard he seemed to stop breathing. "Can you see it? Parents give their kids Laffy Taffy, and they open them up and start screaming? They should do that on a prank show or something. That would be *so cool*."

Ella could sense he was looking at her, even though her hands were covering her face.

"Ella? You there?"

She didn't respond.

"Whoa ... what just happened? Are you crying? What is it?"

"The dead baby thing! I'm sorry. I'll go get Dalia." Ella reached for the door, her high suddenly vacillating between relief and a nuisance.

"Wait." He grabbed her arm. She couldn't look at him. "You just bugging out or something? I should have warned you. That stuff's pretty strong. And I shouldn't have told those jokes. That was weird. You're okay," he said. He reached over and tipped up her chin, turning her face toward his. "You're okay. You're okay."

She stared into his eyes.

"I'm not bugging out. Well, not weed bugging out. I'm ... pregnant." It was the first time the words came out of her mouth. It felt liberating. And then terrifying.

"Aw, come on. For sure? What did Shawn say?"

"I haven't told him—and you can't either. I know he'd try to make me keep it, and my parents would kill me. And I don't even want kids. Here, give me that." She motioned frantically for the one-hitter. She needed this terrified feeling to go away *right now*. Jake looked down at her stomach briefly before passing it to her.

"Ella, you have to tell him."

"I can't. Why burden him with it when there's no way I'm having it? My parents would kill me. And I don't care what my mom thinks, but my dad had a heart attack last year, and I know this would kill him. Please, Jake, no one can ever find out. I'm so sorry for laying all this on you. I'm going to go get Dalia."

Her temporary escape from life was over, her problems right back to front and center. And she'd ruined her chance to become friends with Jake. No way would he want anything to do with her now.

"Okay, I know you have to go, but just hold on a sec. I don't really know what to say, but if you need to talk, you can call me. And you can't go back to work looking all upset. Your makeup is like . . ." He took his thumb and wiped under her eye. "Okay, that's better. But I think we should read one more Laffy Taffy joke before you go in. To undo the bad ones. So, hold on." He quickly unwrapped the cherry-flavored piece she'd left in the cup holder. "Here it is. What did the egg say to the frying pan? You crack me up."

Ella managed a small smile and leaned over to give Jake a hug.

"Thank you. I know it didn't end very well, but I had fun tonight. You're a really good guy."

She got out of the car and headed toward the restaurant, but then walked back and tapped on his window. "I don't have your phone number." She pulled a pen from her apron. "Do you have anything to write on?"

"Here." He wrote his number on the receipt from the party store and handed it to her. She looked at it and folded it up.

"Thanks, Jake."

Halfway back to the restaurant, she turned around. She gave Jake a sweet smile and a friendly wave. Jake gave her an exaggeratedly happy smile and waved back. Ella turned back and pressed her hand with his phone number against her relieved heart. It felt *so good* to talk to someone. And despite her vibe foul, Jake seemed to like her. Which felt like a path back to Sarah. She smiled at the thought as she buzzed the back door to Gatto's.

45

"*WHAT THE FUCK! God! Look at her smiling and waving
at him like she's all fucking smitten and proud of herself. The look
on her face, it's almost like she knows we're watching her, like oh
my god, I just got Sarah's boyfriend to give me his phone number.
Fuck her!*" Sarah yelled as she watched Ella buzz the door. "Stacey,
let's get out of here before anyone sees us." She frantically palm-
blasted the back of her seat.

"You sure? It's your last chance to catch him in the lie!"

"*We don't know if he's lying yet! Just go. Please.*"

"Okay, hit the deck everyone." Stacey quickly shifted into
reverse.

The girls got out of there in a hurry and drove down Main
Street, which was annoyingly busy for that time of night. Sarah

cursed the cars blocking the road while trying to parallel park, shouting at them to get out of the way. She just wanted to get home.

She'd had a perfect view into Jake's car, able to see the two of them dead on, undetected, through Stacey's rearview mirror. As Ella and Jake laughed and cried and hugged and smoked pot, the girls went back and forth, speculating as to how they came to do whatever the hell it was that they were doing. The explanations ranged from Ella being upset with Shawn, to her buying pot from Jake, to her having somehow found Jake's wallet, returning it, and then hitting on him. They dissected the incomprehensible situation into every possible scenario, each of their conclusions obviously biased or wishful speculations colored by their own experiences.

Sarah held her breath when Jake put his hand on Ella's chin, sure they were going to kiss. But they didn't. And that was more confusing than anything. Tori concluded, quite sure of herself, that Ella wanted to buy pot, that it had just come up, and that Jake would tell her when he called her later. Stacey said for sure something was going on between them. Jenny went on about how sad it all was. But they all agreed that whatever it was, it was Ella's doing. Sarah had already thought she was the most disgusting human on the planet the night of the TP party, and here she was, leaving no doubt. It was hard to believe she'd ever been friends with her.

"I can't believe this is ruining my favorite moon too," Sarah said as she looked up at the Harvest Moon hovering over the worst night of her life.

"What about Homecoming?" Jenny asked.

"*I don't know!* What am I supposed to do? Tell him I was stalking him, accuse him of something, and ruin Homecoming? Our last Homecoming ever?"

"I don't want you to miss Homecoming," Jenny said. She looked at Sarah with her sad, doe eyes.

"You could take Dalia," Tori laughed. "Sorry, so not funny. I'm really sorry. Listen. He's supposed to call you later, so let's break this down into a plan. A decision tree."

"*A decision tree?*" Stacey pulled off the black skull cap and sunglasses she'd worn to disguise herself and tossed them on the floor. "That's the dumbest thing I've ever heard." Stacey was never rude like this. She seemed to be suffering from PTSD watching the whole thing unfold, as if it were Jim and Germa in the car, and *she* was the victim.

"Fine. Then just see how he is when he calls. I'm sure he'll just tell you," Tori said.

"And if he doesn't?"

"See, Stacey, *decision tree.*" Tori smiled.

"If he doesn't, you call him a fucking liar and break up with him!" Stacey hit the dashboard, as if any other response would be unthinkable.

"And miss Homecoming? No. That much I know. I'd rather go and fucking ignore him all night. It's our senior year. I'm not missing it."

"Okay, now we're getting somewhere," Tori said. "We don't want you to miss it either, so our goal for tonight should be to not ruin Homecoming. You only have to get through two more days to do that." Tori pulled out a pen and paper and started drawing boxes and arrows.

"Okay. He admits it. Good reason or bad reason? Good reason, Homecoming intact. Bad reason, you break up with him. Before or after Homecoming? Before, Homecoming ruined. After,

Homecoming intact. He breaks up with *you*, Homecoming ruined. But if you take Dalia, Homecoming intact," she said as she scribbled away.

"Please stop with that. And what if he lies?" Sarah asked.

"Sorry. Okay, if he lies . . . okay, we're back to the same thing. He lies. You confront him right away, Homecoming probably ruined. You wait two days, Homecoming intact. I think we have our answer. No matter what happens, you wait until *after* Homecoming to say anything. Everyone agree?" Tori folded up the decision-tree paper into an origami bird. She flitted it in the air and then placed it in Sarah's palm as Stacey pulled into her driveway.

"Good job, Tori. Your decision tree worked," Stacey said. "Now we just have to get through the pep rally."

"Oh god. How do I handle Ella?" Sarah unfolded the paper bird by its neck and reached for her pen.

"You don't need it. Just ignore her. Separate it like Dalia does. Put her in teammate status, get through the performance, and worry about the first plan." Tori clicked her pen shut and put it away.

"I hope I can. That might be harder than the Jake part."

"Call us after he calls," Jenny said.

"*If* he calls . . ." she said as she opened the car door. "Love you guys."

Sarah tiptoed into the house. Carrie was sitting at the kitchen table with her back to her. She sneaked right past her mom without saying a word, assigning some of the blame for this to her mom. She knew she shouldn't, but *Carrie* was the one who made Sarah take Ella out with her friends in the first place, despite her resistance. Carrie followed her up to her room.

"You're still wearing your dress?"

"Yeah, I hoped it would stretch, but it ripped."

"Oh, honey. Take it off. Let me see if I can fix it." She scanned the dress, trying to find the rip.

"It's too tight anyway. I have to buy another one."

"Everything else okay?"

"I don't want to talk about it."

Sarah wouldn't look at her. And this was the second time in a very short period that Sarah was keeping something from her. Sarah knew her mom would be concerned.

"You *sure*? I'm a really good listener," Carrie sang at her.

"Mom, please. I just had a weird night, and I need some time to think." Sarah aggressively leaned away from her, feeling violated by her questioning. Carrie was taken aback, visibly wrestling with whether to press her or not.

"Okay. I get it. But if you change your mind, I'm here. At *all* hours." She pulled Sarah in for a hug.

"Thanks, Mom." Sarah hugged her tightly, her instinctive need for comfort trumping any ill feelings she had toward her.

"Oh, and your cheerleading outfit is hanging in the laundry room. And Jake just called," she said as she closed her door.

What? I missed his call? Fuck!

She sure as shit wasn't going to call him. So much for the fucking decision tree. Sarah turned off the suddenly blinding lights in her room, buried her face in a pillow, and started to sob. The next thing she knew, the phone rang. Smearing the staticky hair off her face, she looked at the clock. Ten fifteen. How had she fallen asleep?

The brass handle of her bedroom door slowly turned and clicked.

"Sarah?" Carrie peeked in. "Were you sleeping?"

"I guess so." Her head pounded. Her mouth was sawdust dry.

"Jake's on the phone. Do you want me to take a message?"

"No. I've got it." She rubbed her forehead. Sarah cautiously picked up the receiver and waited for the click that signaled her mom had hung up. She swallowed hard, knowing that the next few minutes would determine her next few months.

"What's up?"

"Hey babe! How was your night? Did you pick all your jewelry?"

He was in an unforgivably good mood. She'd expected there'd be some detectable remorse in his voice. But there was none, which could only mean he's some sort of sociopath. How had she not seen it sooner?

"It was fine."

"You don't sound good. You sick or something?"

"Just tired. I fell asleep. So . . ." She hesitated for a moment and then got right to it. "How was dinner?"

"It was good."

"Really." Adrenaline took over. Fight or flight. It took everything she had not to fight. Sarah picked up the decision tree from her nightstand and unfolded it. Tori had written a big note at the bottom. *Love you. Remember, HOMECOMING INTACT!!*

"So, where'd you go?"

"We got . . . Chinese."

"*Chinese?* I didn't even know you *liked* Chinese food." *Breathe*, she told herself. *Homecoming intact, Homecoming intact, Homecoming intact.*

"Who doesn't like Chinese food?" he said, laughing.

"Well, I've never heard you talk about it so . . ."

"Okay. Well, Sarah," his tone became serious. "There's something I have to tell you."

Her heart splintered. She couldn't believe he was breaking up with her. She wouldn't even get to yell at him now because *he* was breaking up with *her*. He wouldn't be hers to yell at. He would have the right just to hang up the phone and never talk to her again, so she would get no satisfaction out of it at all.

"What is it?"

"I like Chinese food," he said and started laughing like he thought he was just the funniest thing ever, which he only did when he was smoking pot.

"Seriously, Jake? What, are you high right now?"

"Just a little. Sorry." He kept laughing.

"Who were you smoking with?"

"Who?" He paused, and then lied. "My brother had some friends over."

Silence.

"Sarah? You there?"

"I'm here." She tried to stay calm while collecting as many lies as possible, so she wouldn't puss out and not break up with him after Homecoming. She'd have to tell the girls right away so they could hold her to it. "So, you went to dinner with your mom, ran home, and got high with your brother *on a Thursday*, and now you're calling me?"

"I called you earlier, but you were still out. I wanted to hang out."

"With *me*?"

"*Yeah*, with you." He seemed to also find this hysterical, as Sarah found the whole thing infuriating. She couldn't make sense of anything, especially coming out of a dead sleep. She needed to get off the phone as soon as possible or she'd never be able to stick to the plan. Hopelessly confused, she was more desperate to talk to the girls than she was to finish anything with him.

"Jake, I have to go. We have the pep rally first thing in the morning, and I need to get some sleep."

"Okay, babe. So, I'll see you after the pep rally?"

"Yeah. Sure. See you then." She slammed the phone down.

"What the fuck is going on?" she screamed into her pillow. She immediately picked up the phone again and called Stacey.

"Stacey. Get everyone on party phone."

After a series of clicks, Stacey came back on the line. "No answer at Dalia's, but everyone else is on."

She told them what happened with Jake. They couldn't make sense of it either.

"The weird thing is, it's not like he wants to break up. I mean, he didn't *act* like he's cheating or anything."

"They never *act* like they're cheating, Sarah, that's how they get away with it," Stacey said.

"I know, but he didn't like, I don't know. It was like not a thing was different, except for this lie. He was *happy* to talk to me, and he *wanted* to see me. *What the fuck?!*"

"You know what, I'm more sure than ever that this is all Ella's doing, and we will get to the bottom of it *after* Homecoming," Tori said. "It's almost eleven, Sarah. There's nothing more we can do right now. Take some Benadryl if you can't sleep, and let it go for tonight."

"I agree," Stacey said. "At least Homecoming is *intact*, right?"

"Yeah, not with my ripped dress."

"God, I forgot about that," Stacey said. "We'll figure it out. Get some sleep, Sarah."

"Goodnight, you guys. I love you."

Sarah chased sleep unsuccessfully, images of confrontations with Ella projecting on her inner skull as she tossed and turned. The last she looked at the clock, it was three a.m. Her alarm went off at six. It was not going to be a good day.

46

ELLA SAT UP IN BED and rubbed the sleep out of her eyes. She swung her bare feet around, dangling them above the heat register, and looked out her bedroom window. A layer of frost coated the crisp, brown leaves. They looked delicate, like they'd shatter if you breathed on them the wrong way. They reminded her of herself these past few weeks.

But today she felt different. As the blowing air warmed her feet, thoughts of the past few days warmed her heart. Dalia was being so nice to her. She and Jake had had a *great* time. But more significant, she felt like *herself* again.

The deep reach she'd done to find the old fun Ella for just that small window of time seemed to reestablish her connection to the girl she once was, the girl she'd thought was gone forever. The girl so far away, she seemed more like an apparition, or a stranger.

Now she discovered that girl had never been *gone*; her access had just been restricted.

She imagined her problems as a blockage. A thick, scary, seemingly impenetrable hairy blob that she now realized just needed to be poked and jostled a bit, and off it would go. Not that all her problems had just disappeared with this development, but it was a start. *The start of a new start.* She laughed at the thought—how small but significant it was.

An old, forgotten sensation came over her. One she hadn't felt naturally since her first few weeks in Illinois when, for a brief period of time, life appeared to be offering her something special. She'd been sure she would never feel that way again, but here it was, genuine excitement for the Homecoming pep rally. It would be her first performance in front of the entire school. For sure she'd be recognized for her talent, maybe she'd even make friends out of it, she hoped as she reached for her cheerleading uniform. Today everything had to be perfect.

In the bathroom mirror, she stared at her reflection. Rather than her morning ritual of late, berating herself for the mess she'd made, she reminded herself of the decisions she'd made the night before. Positive ones that would right her path. First, she had to fix things with the girls, no matter what it took. Dalia's blessing and inclusion in the surprise party were inroads. So was her time with Jake. But there was a lot more that needed to be done.

She had to end things with Shawn. There was no choice, she decided. They were doomed anyway, as their relationship could never survive such an enormous secret. She'd wait until after Homecoming, though. Dalia had Tom now, so there was no sense in being cruel to Shawn. It's not like the two of *them* could magically go together, as if none of this had ever happened. Some things just couldn't be fixed.

Of course, her biggest stress was still hanging over her, but it felt more manageable now that she had a plan. It had been almost a week since she'd started taking her dad's medication. Still nothing. But she'd started tripling the dose—better to go at it hard for a short period of time. She had enough pills for five more days, and if it didn't work by that time, she'd have to borrow the money to get it taken care of. From who, she didn't know, but there was still time to figure that out. For now, she would focus on today.

In the shower, she lathered up her new rosewater body wash. She picked up her pink Bic razor and took her time shaving. Dalia had warned them not to cut their legs the day of a performance. "No one wants to see a nasty Band-Aid out there," she'd said. Ella noticed a dark purple bruise on her knee but couldn't recall where it came from. It was bad enough that she thought she should have remembered doing something to it. But it wasn't the first time she'd unknowingly banged herself up when she'd been smoking.

And then she noticed the red trickle down her leg. *Dammit.* She tried to find the source, the broken skin. But she didn't see or feel a cut. And then it hit her. She clasped her hands together and raised them in the air. "Thank you, God," she said out loud. She immediately wished she hadn't said that. God probably didn't like this at all, and the last thing she should be doing is drawing it to His attention. It certainly wasn't God letting her off the hook. It was her dad's pills. It actually worked; her pregnancy nightmare was over.

Ella quickly finished showering and took appropriate measures to contain the situation. She dried her hair and pulled it into a tight ponytail. After putting on her makeup, she stepped into her uniform and checked herself in the mirror. On her way out, she grabbed the letter she'd written to the girls from her nightstand drawer and tucked it in her bag. It had taken an hour for her to get it right. She smiled when she pictured them opening it.

Downstairs, her dad sat in his favorite brown leather recliner, sipping his coffee, watching the morning news.

"Hi, Daddy." She gave him a kiss on the cheek.

"Well, you're in a good mood. So, today's the big performance? How about I come and watch you?"

"Oh Dad, I'm sorry, parents don't come to the pep rally. But you can watch me at the game."

"I will be there. Ella, you should smile more often. Smiles look nice on you."

"Thanks, Dad." She gave him a big, long hug. As she buried her face in his neck, she decided that, as part of her new start, she would spend more time with him. After all, he was just as much a victim of Linda as she was. Maybe if she and her dad and her brother formed an alliance against Linda, they could extricate themselves from the poison in their life and form their own happy family. Now that she'd actually sat down and spent time taking inventory of her life, everything seemed to make sense. The path to happiness seemed easy. She wondered why she hadn't thought of it sooner.

"I have to run. I love you," she called out as she left.

Ella parked down the street from Sarah's house. She waited for the Blakes to pull out of the driveway and ran up to the door. Using the spare key under the mat that had been there for at least a decade, she walked right into the house and up to Sarah's bedroom. She opened the heavy top to the toy chest and dug through the blankets. Just as she'd hoped, the time capsule was still at the bottom. She slid open the top and placed her letter inside. She snapped the lid shut, slid it under the blankets, and closed the chest. *Was Sarah's bedroom door open or closed?* After checking her watch, she decided to leave it open just a crack. If she hurried, she wouldn't be too late. Sprinting to the car, she smiled to herself. It was going to be a great day.

47

"HI GUYS, SORRY I'M LATE." Ella bounced down the recreation hallway, her gym bag hanging over her shoulder, red and white pompoms in hand. She was in a good mood. Too good of a mood, an almost giddy mood that was splitting Sarah's every nerve.

"*You're late,* Ella," she barked so loud that the entire freshman squad turned and looked.

"I know, Sarah. That's why I said *sorry I'm late.* I had to make a quick stop before school." Ella's casual attitude was infuriating her, rapidly depleting her ability to control herself.

"Really. Where did you go?"

"Now *that* is a secret." Ella looked Sarah directly in the eye, pointed her tiny finger, and laughed. "But you'll find out . . . eventually."

Oh my god!

Dalia marched over.

"Ella, you can't be late, *especially* on such a big day. You should know better. And what's on your knee? Is that a bruise?" She bent down to get a closer look. "Jesus. Put some makeup on that! Hurry! And then warm up."

"It won't happen again. I promise." She looked down at her knee. "That's so weird. I don't even remember doing anything to it, and it's like growing. Sorry. I'll cover it up."

"You have a *huge bruise* on your knee, and you don't remember getting it? What, were you out partying last night?" Sarah wanted to hear *something* Ella had to say, *anything,* because the not knowing was killing her.

"What? *No!*" Ella stepped backward, breaking her stare. Sarah wasn't going to break it. Even if she wasn't going to say anything yet, she wanted Ella to know that she knew. That she knew she was trying to move in on Jake, and she wasn't getting away with it.

"I'm going to cover it, Sarah. Jeez. Sorry for getting a bruise." She crouched down and poked at it a few times. As she stood back up, she seemed unsteady on her feet. Dalia grabbed her by the arm. "Sorry," Ella said, putting her hand to her head. "Stood up too fast."

"Stacey has something to cover that up. Go tell her. Now." Dalia pointed at Stacey, who was sitting on the floor, touching up her lipstick. "And ignore Sarah. She's in a *fucking mood today that better not ruin her performance.*" Dalia's head snapped in Sarah's direction.

Ella walked toward Stacey. Dalia whispered in Sarah's ear.

"Now is *not* the time, so *stop it!* Promise me you won't start anything before the show. We've worked *so hard* on this."

Sarah forced her lips under her teeth to keep them closed, pressing them together until the pain of her teeth digging into them was too much.

"We go on in a few minutes. Just sit down, stretch, and take some deep breaths. And you'd *better* keep it together. For your *team*."

Sarah sat down and stared at the carpet, jaw clenched, hand in a fist that didn't want to let go. Her back tensed. She spread her legs and leaned into a forward stretch, letting her head hang. She took a deep breath and exhaled slowly. She came out of her stretch to see Jenny standing over her. Sarah looked at Jenny and shook her head, trying to hold back the tears that had begun to form. Jenny knelt down and put her hand on Sarah's shoulder.

"I only got three hours of sleep. I am out of my mind right now. I'm not sure I can go out there."

"It's gonna be okay, Sarah."

Coach Liz walked over and clapped loudly.

"Okay, ladies, it's time to line up. Is everyone excited?" She continued to clap.

Sarah looked at Jenny again. Gravity pulled on Sarah's face, making it impossible to smile. Her lips started to tremble. Jenny grabbed Sarah's hand and escorted her to her position behind Ella. They stepped to the edge of the gym floor. Principal Flynn's voice bellowed over the loudspeaker inside the gym.

"Let's give a big hand to the Washington High She-Vikings!"

The crowd cheered, ushering them into their last Homecoming pep rally ever. She should have been excited. *Or sad*, she thought as she watched the sea of red shirts clapping for them from the bleachers. But all she felt was anger and disappointment as she watched Ella's ponytail dance in front of her face. She should have been focusing on her performance, not wondering what the hell Ella was up to with her boyfriend. And Ella smelled like flowers, which was making her nauseous.

But the anger she felt was nothing compared to the absolute ire it boiled into a moment later. They walked toward Jake, sitting three rows up. He was clapping and smiling at Sarah when she noticed Ella raise her hand in front of her. The tips of her fingers peeked above her shoulder into the same flirty little wave she'd given him last night. He took his eyes off Sarah and waved back at her. At Ella. And Sarah lost it.

They lined up, facing the crowd, Ella two feet to her right. Sarah couldn't keep it in another second. Without turning her head, she unleashed some of the pressure building inside of her.

"Do you think I'm stupid?" she said only as loud as she needed to get Ella's attention.

"*What?*"

"I saw you back there."

"Back . . . Sarah, I don't know what—"

"I can't believe I was *ever* friends with you."

The moment the word "you" left her mouth, the music started. Thank god for muscle memory. She'd done the routine so many times, she didn't need to think about it. But everything felt surreal. As "This Is How We Do It" played over the loudspeaker, Sarah managed to put on a smile. She hoped it was believable enough on the outside that it masked what was happening on the inside. Because on the inside, the horror movie of Ella and Jake replayed in her mind in excruciating detail. The two of them, laughing in the car, his hands on her face, the way she leaned in to hug him, his bullshit lies. She needed to get away. Far away from Ella, from Jake, from her head. She needed this performance to be over.

It was time for the Ella show. The group of girls split down the middle and formed a lane for her to do her floor routine between them. While all eyes were on Ella, Sarah's were pinned to the gym floor. She didn't want to watch her, as that would be participating in celebrating her talent. She heard her hands and feet rhythmically hit the floor. She watched the crowd cheer as Ella stuck the landing on her second pass. Some of them even stood up. *They wouldn't be cheering if they knew what a horrible person she is,* she thought as they moved into their final positions.

Stacey, Tori, Jenny, and Sarah took their spots, forming a tight circle. They leaned down and clasped their hands together. Ella stepped into them. They lifted her shoulder high. Sarah could hardly get herself to touch her leg, counting the seconds until she could get away. They raised her again, as high as their arms would extend. Ella stood ten feet in the air. While the girls held her leg, she moved into a vertical split and held her raised ankle. The girls rotated her once around. The crowd cheered again. She came out of her vertical split and bent her knee. And then they tossed her up. Mid-air, she switched legs.

And that was the moment Sarah's life as she knew it ended.

Ella's leg buckled underneath her. Her other foot landed on Stacey's collarbone, as she tried to catch herself. Stacey screamed and fell to the ground. Ella came down fast. She managed to stay upright, trying to regain her balance as her forward momentum carried her. She put her hands out in front of her. And stumbled face-first into the giant speaker sitting on a cafeteria table.

Ella shrieked as the horrifying smack stopped her movement. The crowd gasped as she slumped over the speaker. But then she managed to stand up. Dazed, she put her hand to her face. And then the blood came pouring out of her nose. It ran down her forearm and dripped onto the floor. She pulled her hand away from her face and looked at it. She looked scared and confused, like she had no idea what had just happened. Her hand trembled. She stumbled backward and collapsed onto the ground. This time she didn't get back up.

The music faded into screams as everyone tried to collect themselves. Sarah fell to her knees and covered her eyes. *What just happened?* She prayed that what she'd just witnessed was happening in an alternate universe, and when she opened her eyes, everything would be back to normal. But when she found the strength to look, she understood that it wasn't, and in fact was getting worse. She looked over at Stacey holding her shoulder, her face twisting in pain as Tori crouched beside her. And then she looked at Ella. Ella was perfectly still, lying on her side in a pool of blood, even the bottoms of her Keds smeared with red.

Memories of their entire friendship flashed before Sarah's eyes. Their first ballet recital, holding hands in their pink tutus, playing hopscotch on the sidewalk, jumping rope in Ella's driveway, Sarah's first real campfire, the first time their moms let them go to the mall without them, all the firsts Sarah had shared with her up until that first day Ella came back, when Sarah found her in her bedroom with a towel on her head, looking up at her with those sad eyes.

"*Ella,*" she screamed as she crawled toward her, her knee scorching with every movement.

Principal Flynn and Coach Liz were kneeling over her. Shawn ran down and was promptly grabbed by a gym teacher.

"She's my girlfriend," he protested. It took two other teachers to drag him away.

Sarah got within five feet of her when she felt a pair of hands lift her up and drag her to the locker room where she collapsed with the realization that Ella might be seriously injured. And it was her fault.

48

SARAH AND ELLA WERE ON A BOAT. Adult versions of them, anyway. An old-fashioned sailboat, or a pirate ship. The sky was steel gray, the wind hissed, there was nothing visible on the horizon but black waves thundering around them. Each crash flooded the deck, tossing the boat to the verge of capsizing. Sarah struggled to stand up, frantically grabbing onto posts and rails to keep from being thrown over the side. Ella stood there calmly, somehow unaffected by the thrashing. She watched Sarah struggle and, after some time, spoke in a matter-of-fact tone. *I know what you did.*

Sarah popped up in bed and caught her breath. *Thank god, it was just a dream.* Her racing heart slowed. She fanned the sweat on her chest and stared at the gray peeking through the blinds. For a moment, she thought about how she was going to spend her day.

And then she saw her mom sleeping on the floor next to her bed. And the realization crept back in, as it had each of the past three mornings since the Connors took Ella off life support.

Carrie and Jason had been taking turns sleeping in her room, a suicide watch, no doubt. Sarah couldn't blame them. She'd hardly said a word to them since the day of *the accident,* as it would be called from here to eternity. It was no accident in her mind. Though she had no recollection of what *actually* happened in the moment, she knew how she *felt* in the moment. And she was sure that how she felt, how she couldn't stand the thought of being anywhere near Ella, or touching her, or even caring a thing at all about her, in the moment she was supposed to be responsible for her safety, caused her death. *Negligent homicide* she'd decided she'd be charged with once the police figured it out. And maybe today, that's exactly what they would conclude.

The police had wanted to talk to the girls immediately after it happened, but the school and their parents stepped in and shut that down, arguing they were too traumatized to answer any questions. Then they started showing up at their individual houses, assuring everyone it was just a formality. No one's parents would let them talk, but the witnesses interviewed before them had a few things to say. The freshman girls reported that Sarah had argued with Ella before the performance. And apparently, a handful of students noticed their heated conversation before the routine started. Tori heard that Janice Finkman said that Rose Anderson heard Sarah say, "I wish you were dead." The male gossip train had a different take. They'd concluded that this was a group effort. That the girls were jealous of Ella, the new girl, for being the center of attention, and an investigation was born. The parents collectively decided it would be best if the police talked to the girls all on the same day, in a comfortable environment, which was happening at the Blakes' house today. And just to be safe, Jason Blake asked Mr. Larson, a lawyer friend, to hang out and step in if necessary.

In the living room, Carrie set up a carafe of coffee. She laid out chocolate chip cookies and then added some cubed cheddar cheese, struggling with the appropriate menu for the occasion. After all, "Martha Stewart doesn't have a lot to say about what to serve at police interrogations." At the last minute, Sarah's dad decided to run to Dunkin' Donuts and grab a mixed dozen, "cuz, you know, they're police officers."

Before the police arrived, the parents, minus Dalia's mom, of course, sat down for a pre-interrogation discussion. Sarah sat at the top of the stairs, listening in as they tsked at the horror of it all and debated its implications for the girls' futures. Of course, none of them believed *their* daughter would commit such a heinous act, but they feared they would be permanently labeled, whispers of the town tarnishing their names forever.

Tori and Stacey arrived. They found Sarah at the top of the stairs and steered her into her bedroom, where they spread out on the carpet. They were both showered with full makeup on, as if it were any other day. Sarah was still in her three-day-old sweats, wondering if her appearance screamed grief or guilt. They hadn't spoken in person since the accident, and just as they were about to get into it, Dalia and Jenny walked in. Jenny sat down beside Sarah and hugged her knees. Dalia walked around the bedroom, shedding a restless energy.

"So much for Homecoming," Dalia said. She saw Sarah's dress hanging on the front of her closet door. "So, this is what you were going to wear? Cute! Too bad you didn't get to wear it." She pulled one side of the skirt up.

"Really. *That's* what you have to say about this?" Tori shot at her.

"What. I mean it's sad for her family and all, but of course it's a bummer about Homecoming. Not for me," she said, backpedaling. "I'm just saying . . . for *you* guys. For everyone. It just sucks that it was ruined."

"*Dalia*, are you kidding me? So, what did you—" Tori began her own interrogation but was cut off immediately.

"Don't you *dare* start reading into anything, Tori. And before you guys get your panties in a bunch, it's no surprise I wasn't a fan of hers. *Boohoo.*" She turned her knuckle back and forth under her eye. "The person who made me miserable is out of my life forever." She sniffed. "That's what's so annoying about dead people. They can be total assholes, but when they die, you're still supposed to feel bad."

Jenny looked up at her for the first time.

"Dalia, you don't feel bad?"

"Bad? About *what?*" Dalia asked, as if this was a completely foreign concept as it pertained to this moment. "It's *life.*" She plopped down on the bed. "See, this is the problem, you guys and all your pampered, fucking princess lives. Bad things happen *all the time.* You guys have just never had to deal with it. The shit my neighbors deal with? You have *no idea* what goes on *every day* in the rest of the world to perfectly good people who don't deserve it. But you never think about *those* people. *That's* why this is all so *tragic* to you. You spend one week talking to the people in my apartment complex, you'll see. This is nothing.

"*Nothing?* Okay, Dalia. I'm just gonna come right out and say it, because I find it hard to believe that you didn't have *something* to do with this. I mean, what are the odds, Dalia. Seriously."

"What are you talking about, Tori?" she asked calmly. "You guys were the ones catching her."

"Oh, I have my theories. Okay, Jenny. Did Dalia talk you into anything?" Tori asked.

Jenny, whose puffy eyes said more than she did, mumbled to the floor, "No."

"All of you, listen to me *right now*. It was an *accident*. Nothing else, and *no one* better say *anything* else," Dalia said. "Even if your bullshit theory were to be true, which it isn't, because that was never a thing, do you really think the rest of you couldn't have caught her? That's why the move uses four people. Something else went wrong. She just landed wrong or *something*. And I'm sorry, but people hit their heads all the time and don't fucking bleed like they were just shot in the face." She made quick, circular motions in front of her face with her flattened hand. "She did lose her balance in the hall before we went in, *remember Sarah?*"

The room sat silent. There was no way to respond to the callousness in front of them.

"Do you *honestly* think I wanted her *dead?* You *know* that's not what I wanted to happen. I'm *not* a terrible person." She grabbed some tissues and started to cry actual tears, though it wasn't clear which part of any of this she was sad about.

"Well, we know you're not sorry it happened," Stacey said.

"You're *right*, Stacey. It doesn't bother me *at all* that she's no longer here to bother me. But that doesn't mean I wanted her to die. Jenny," Dalia sat down and put her arms around her.

"Stay with me." Jenny's splotchy face had a bluish tint, as if she'd forgotten to breathe.

"It was an *accident*. No one did anything wrong," Dalia said. Jenny leaned into her and began to sob.

"And don't any of you for a second think about telling the police any crazy theories. Who knows?" She looked at Tori and Sarah. "They may decide to send you all to juvie. And you can kiss those fancy colleges goodbye."

"Jenny." Tori remained undeterred. "You have nothing to be afraid of if you just tell the truth. Did Dalia talk you into anything? Because if she did, you have to tell the police. It's the right thing."

"*God, Tori, just stop!* How could you accuse *Jenny*, who would never hurt *anyone*, of *that*? Do you even *hear yourself*? I told you I never meant anything by that. We never even talked about it after the Dunes. Not once, other than you bringing it up in the locker room that day, when I *told you, in front of Jenny,* that I didn't mean it. *Remember?*" Dalia stood up and paced around the room. "And the police are going to be here soon, so you better watch what you say."

"It's called doing the right thing, Dalia. I had *nothing* to do with this!"

"So *you* say. Look. I'm not trying to scare you. I'm just saying, I know a *little bit* more about the police than you do, and you do *not* want to have to deal with them. You want all that tuition money going toward legal fees? I'm sure your parents would *love* that!"

"Jenny?" Tori persisted.

"Tori, I swear to God, you better back the fuck off." Dalia put her hand squarely on Tori's chest.

Sarah grabbed Dalia's wrist and pulled her away from Tori. "You guys *stop*! It was me," she finally said.

"*What? What did you do?*" Tori cried out. Sarah couldn't bear to look at the shock and judgment that was surely painted across her face.

"I don't know, but it had to be. It's the only explanation. I was so, so angry with her that I must have tossed her up on an angle or something." She waited through their silent stares, hoping someone would tell her that there's no way it was her fault. But they didn't. Instead, they seemed to ponder it and possibly even accept it as a reasonable explanation. And then Carrie knocked on the door to let them know the police were ready to speak with them.

The girls filed down the stairs. As expected, Sarah's dad was making small talk with the officers.

"So, any leads on those Brown's Chicken murders? I have some theories if you're interested. I knew right away it wasn't that ex-employee. I'm leaning more toward thrill kill. Think about it. Some teenage punks, bored on a Friday night in the middle of winter . . . they just go in there and *pow*." He made a gun with his fingers and then sheepishly put it away. The tall, beefy officer glanced over at his short, skinny partner and shook his head. They looked exactly alike—dark eyes, wide noses, bushy eyebrows—like brothers. Brothers whose mom made them fight for their food, considering their size difference. Sarah envisioned one being raised on the other's scraps, which didn't make them seem very friendly, which wasn't helping her nerves.

"Hi ladies," the tall one said. "I'm Officer James, and this is my partner, Officer Dennison."

Officer Dennison took over the conversation, while Officer James took out his notepad.

"Do you need a pen?" Tori offered.

"Got one." He pulled a pen from his ear. "So why don't you all have a seat. I want everyone to know that there's nothing to worry about. We're just covering all the bases. There were reports of an argument before the show, and we need to make sure it wasn't a contributing factor to what happened. So, which one of you is Sarah?"

Sarah slowly raised her hand. Her parents both turned toward her with pleading, devastated, blindsided looks on their faces.

"Do you want to tell us what the argument was about? Some of the other girls mentioned you and Ella were fighting right before the performance. Is that right?"

"Fighting? No, I uh . . ." Sarah cleared her throat. "I told her she shouldn't be late. It was more like a lecture."

Officer James wrote something in his notebook and then turned the page.

"So, you thought it was important to lecture her, on the gym floor, right before you were supposed to perform? Is that when you said, 'I hope you die'?"

"*What? No!*" she cried out. Sarah hadn't decided whether she should come clean yet or not, but it was so far from *I can't believe I was ever friends with you* that she could legitimately, vehemently deny it. And then she just continued down that path, avoiding the hard stares of everyone around her.

"So you're denying that you said that."

"Sir, I promise you, I *never* said anything even *remotely* close to that."

Her dad's face turned purple. He stood up and moved to the center of the room.

"Officers, do either of you have any daughters? Teenagers? If you don't know, teenage girls get into disagreements with their friends *a lot*. Nasty ones."

"They sure do," Officer Dennison said.

"And the next day, they're best friends again. I actually get a kick out of it. But, for argument's sake, let's say there was some bickering. There is no reason to believe that it had anything to do with this *accident*. So I'm not sure where you're going with this."

"Well, it's the only one that's led to a death right afterward, at least in my experience." Officer Dennison picked up a chocolate eclair and took a bite. Despite the somber occasion, Jason nodded in the officer's direction and smiled at Sarah, understandably proud of himself for choosing the doughnuts.

"Okay, that's enough," Mr. Larson, the attorney, stepped in. "This was probably a bad idea." He handed Officer Dennison his card.

"If you have any other questions, call me, and we'll set up a formal interview at the station. It's best that you two head out now."

And just like that, they left. And Sarah never did have to speak with them again. Two weeks later, they ruled Ella's death an accident, and that was the end of that.

It was also the end of everything else because the moment everyone left, Sarah went into lockdown mode. She dropped out of Washington High and homeschooled the rest of the year. And despite everyone's repeated phone calls, she chose not to speak to anyone. Not friends, not Jake, not her family. She didn't want to have any follow-up conversations about what she'd confessed to, and whether she should have told the truth or not. She didn't want to hear Tori's lecture or Jenny's pity or *anything* Dalia had to say. And she didn't ever want to see or hear from Jake again. If he hadn't been with Ella that night, it would never have happened.

The Blakes were frantic with worry, dragging her to therapists, filling antidepressant prescriptions. The whole thing was a huge waste of time, as she could never be honest with any therapist. And she didn't deserve the luxury of a pill that would lessen her pain. Or their love. Or her friends' love. And the more everyone pushed, the more she retreated. Eventually, they stopped trying. All of them.

A fresh start in college was her only hope. She could reinvent herself and pretend her former life never existed. Her parents also decided a fresh start was in order, and the day she left for Pepperdine, they moved to Florida. And things were never the same.

49

I HOLD THE PIECE OF PURPLE stationery in front of me, staring blankly at Ella's handwriting. Nothing is registering other than the fact that it is Ella, speaking from the grave.

"What is it?" Tori casually rests her chin on her fist.

"I can't even . . . it's a letter. From Ella." I fold it shut and put it on the table. It sits there sending chills up my spine, begging to be read.

I turn toward Dalia. She interlocks her fingers into a prayer position and tucks her hands between her knees.

"Oh my god. What does it say?" Stacey pulls the wine bottle out of the bucket and turns it vertically, shaking the last drop into her glass.

"Someone else has to read it." I slide it to Tori.

She unfolds the letter and puts on her reading glasses. Her eyes move like a typewriter, scanning from left to right.

"You guys, this is . . . you'd think being a reporter nothing would shock me anymore, but . . ." Her hands fall to the table. Still gripping the letter, she fixes her eyes on Dalia.

"Dalia, is there something you want to tell us before I read it out loud?"

"I told you I'm here to make amends, Tori. I'll wait until after you read it."

A tornado of emotions swirls around me. I feel nervous, scared, suspicious, angry, yet hopeful that at a minimum, I'll get some sort of closure. But what could Ella have written before she died that could offer that.

"Just read it," I sigh, certain that whatever it says won't provide any solace.

"Okay." Tori takes a deep breath and waves the waiter over. "We're going to need another bottle." She picks up her phone and sends a quick text. "Tea is not happening today. Sorry, Chloe," she says as she clicks away. She turns her phone face down. "Okay, here we go."

Hello ladies,

Am I here with you today? I hope so. This is when you look over at me and laugh and ask me how I managed to sneak this into the time capsule. If you haven't figured it out, I really wanted to be part of this.

If I'm not here with you, it means my most important goal never came true. So, I'll just say what I have to say here and hope that you'll understand things from my side. Okay . . . here goes.

My 2015 goals:

1. You guys have forgiven me for being such an awful person, and we are all friends forever.

2. I live far away from my mother.

3. College out west somewhere—and settle down out there. Portland maybe? A city, but not a huge one.

4. Successful career as . . . I'm not sure yet. Maybe a lawyer? Something important that gives me interesting things to think about.

5. Zero kids. I know that seems like a weird goal. But if there's one thing I've learned over the past few years, it's this: I never want kids. They're too much to worry about, and the world can be kind of awful.

Anyway, when I moved back here, I hoped I would have my old life back. The life I had before my family fell apart in Tucson. I wanted to reconnect with Sarah—to my childhood, when life was fun. And I wanted to be friends with all of Sarah's friends, because we would have for sure had the same group of friends if I'd never moved. So, I thought I could just slip in and pick things up where they should have been, if that makes sense. I was so happy that first night at Stacey's party when everyone was so nice to me.

But instead of just being thankful for you guys, I went and ruined everything. And here's the only explanation I can come up with. Shawn was the guy in my life when everything was great. I know it was middle school, but I guess it was like the same thing with Sarah. When he started paying attention to me, everything just felt right. I felt happy, for the first time in years. And I wasn't strong enough to say no to that.

Please understand that I never realized how much it would mess things up. I know, Sarah, you told me. A hundred times.

But I guess I didn't really believe it. And I'm so sorry about that, because now I know that it wasn't just about Shawn and Dalia. It was everything . . . your whole group of friends, and I came and ruined it all. I started to realize what I was doing was wrong when I lied about being sick so Shawn would miss Jake's party. You were right, Dalia. That was terrible of me, and I'm so sorry to all of you.

Turns out I ruin a lot of things. I'm actually pregnant right now, which has made me think about everything. Here I am stuck, no friends to talk to, and not enough money for an abortion. I'm so scared right now. This is how scared I am. I actually stole my dad's blood thinners, hoping they'll cause a miscarriage—turns out they can do that. Crazy, right? Just add it to the list of terrible things I've done. But I'm keeping my fingers crossed it works, so I can put all this behind me and start over.

Okay. So, from this moment forward, I'm going to do everything I can to make things right with you guys, starting with Sarah's surprise party Sunday night. I just got back from shopping with Jake for the decorations, and I'm so excited for the party. And I'm so thankful Dalia included me. I can't wait to start fixing things. And Sarah, Jake is a super cool guy. I can totally see you two married, and I hope that that happens—add that to my goals. Are goals for someone else allowed in the time capsule?

So, tomorrow morning I'm taking Sarah's key from under her mat (Sarah, you guys really need a new hiding spot) after you leave for school and putting this letter in the time capsule. If I'm not with you right now (I really hope I am!), and if you do find it in your hearts to forgive me, look me up. I'll be so happy to hear from you. Don't make me wait too long though, please. I'll be anxiously waiting by the phone Oct. 28, 2015. God, we'll be like thirty-seven then. That's so old! I wonder what our lives will be like. Oh, and happy birthday, Sarah.

Love,

Ella

Without taking a breath or giving us a chance to digest what we just heard, Tori starts in on Dalia.

"So, what do you have to say for yourself?"

"Well, for starters, I told you guys something wasn't right about all that blood. She was taking *blood thinners* to try to kill her *baby?* Jesus. So, it wasn't *really* my fault." She shrugs, almost happily.

"You think that lets you off the *hook? What the hell is wrong with you?!*" A painful energy charges through me, lifting me off my seat.

"*Fuck*, I'm sorry. My shrink says I need to learn how to not be so 'me first.' It's like a reaction." She drums her fingers on the table. "I'm trying *so hard* to be better, you guys."

"Well then, here's your chance, Dalia. Are you going to make me drag it out of you or are you going to tell us the story?" Tori slams the letter on the table in front of her.

"No. I want to tell you everything. That's why I'm here. It's just that Jenny was supposed to be here with me, so it's kind of throwing me off not to have her here. Did I tell you she's in the program too? We were supposed to do this together."

"You and Jenny are AA buddies? I was right, wasn't I? You talked her into it. How'd you do it?" Tori challenges.

"It wasn't hard. I told her Sarah and Stacey were doing it, but that everyone promised not to talk about it because we wanted to make sure no one overheard anything."

"Are you serious? *How could you take advantage of her that way?* Really. I want to know," Tori demands. "You knew she wasn't smart enough to figure out what you were up to."

"Yes, Tori. That's why it worked. And *I don't know,*" Dalia says. "But I'm trying really hard to figure that out. If you want a diagnosis or something, my shrink says it's because I was neglected as a child. That I had to put myself first to survive. And I know it doesn't change anything, but it does make a little sense, right?" She suddenly looks like she hasn't slept in days. "And Jenny's been trying really hard to figure out her stuff, too, so please don't be upset with her. It was my fault, and no one else's."

"So, you've been friends this whole time?" Stacey asks with a clinical curiosity.

While Stacey and Tori are sidetracked by confirmation of Jenny's involvement, I am fixated on this surprise party bit, transported back in time to the night before my life was ruined. It all starts to make sense.

"*Of course!* I wouldn't just *desert* her after that. She did it for me."

"And *she* didn't desert *you?*" Tori asks aggressively. "How'd that work out for her?"

"Terrible. I ruined her life. She has a daughter who hates her too." Her voice starts to tremble. "That's what I do, I guess. I ruin people's lives." She picks up a cloth napkin and dabs beneath her eyes.

A firestorm ignites in me. There she goes, pulling from the same playbook she'd used to manipulate us for as long as I'd known her.

"Is this some fucking Dalia pity party? Is that why you're here? So we can make *you* feel better?" I stand up and yank the chair between us out of the way. Putting one arm on the table and the other on the back of her chair, I lean over her. I've had way too much wine at this point and am making a scene. But I don't care. "How about you explain whatever this *surprise party* was?"

"God, I was hoping that wouldn't come out. I can't believe it didn't come out *sooner*. I didn't even think it would work! That was really, really shitty of me. I don't know what to say, Sarah. I just remember feeling desperate, and it was like a different person took over," she says, not sounding anywhere near sorry enough to make this worth my while.

"*Are you making amends or not?*" I thrust my face within inches of hers.

"*Yes!* I . . . I don't know how to explain any of it, and I know that nothing I say will make it better. I look back at it now, and I . . . I . . . I just don't understand how I was so . . . *out of control!* But I didn't think it would work with just Jenny agreeing to not catch her. So, I wanted you guys to be mad at her—all of you—so you wouldn't pay that much attention to catching her."

"So, how did you arrange *that*?" I shout. The waiter comes over and asks if everything is okay. I sit back down.

"I took advantage of Jake in the worst way. I told him you love surprise parties, and he should help me throw one for you. And then at the last minute, I told him my car broke down and I couldn't get the decorations—and that they had to be done that night. I knew you'd be picking your jewelry, so I was pretty sure he'd be free. And when he didn't want to do it, I guilted him into it. I had already gotten Ella to agree to help—and once I got them in the car together,

I called you guys." She grips a fistful of her hair and twists it until she winces in pain. "And for the record, he *hated* lying to you about it. I shouldn't have done that to him. He didn't deserve that."

"*Jake didn't deserve that?* What about *me?* You *know* I've blamed myself . . . *this whole time!*"

"*I know, Sarah.* That's why I'm here. You, Jake, Ella, all of it. I'm sorry for *all* of it." She reaches for my hand. I pull it away. "Do you know how many times I've picked up the phone but was too chicken shit to call you? I was *so stupid.* But I was *seventeen* years old. Look at your kids. If they make a mistake, should they have to pay *forever?* Wouldn't you hope that they could be forgiven and get a second chance?"

"Maybe I would have forgiven you if you had reached out sooner. *Twenty years* I've been torturing myself. Had you called after two or three or even ten. *My god.* I lost Jake, my friends, my family . . . I *hardly* talk to them. The only person I still have in my life from what you did is Shawn. And now we're separated because we're both damaged. *Permanently.* And now our *kids* are damaged. And it goes on and on and on. So, to answer your question, first, my kids would *never* do anything like what you did, so I don't have to worry about them being forgiven for mistakes like *that.* And second, if you do something with forever consequences, sorry, but you pay *forever.*"

"So much for fucking amends," Dalia says. She grabs the bottle of wine and puts it to her mouth. And opens her own floodgate. The surrounding tables stare and whisper.

"Waiter . . ." She raises the nearly empty bottle in the air and points to it. She turns to Tori and Stacey. "So, you guys too? You're the *sober living expert,* Stacey. Is that what all your charity friends would say? That I have to pay forever? Because if that's the case, then *fuck it*. Why bother to make anything right? Why bother to even try to be a better person if no one is ever going to recognize you for it?"

Dalia's phone begins to buzz. She turns it over. "My fucking sponsor. Great." She hits decline.

"Look, Dalia. Obviously, Sarah suffered way more than we did. It's great that you came here today to get this off your chest. Long overdue, but still great," Stacey responds. "And Sarah might never forgive you. And you might just have to be okay with that. My personal opinion is that the only person whose forgiveness you really need is your own. And if you fall off the wagon now, you may never get that chance. Think about your daughter."

The waiter walks over with the new bottle. Stacey waves it away. "We'll just take the check."

Dalia's phone buzzes again.

"What the *fuck* does she want? Does she have some fucking radar or something? I have to grab this." She steps away and answers the phone.

"That's really good advice, Stacey," Tori says. "And Sarah, that goes for you too. I had *no idea* you were still carrying this around with you."

"How could I not? I thought it was my fault. All this time . . ."

"I know you said that, but none of *us* thought it was your fault. Had you answered your phone even one of the hundreds of times we called, you would have known that. I didn't get to talk to you for what. Twelve years? And you seemed fine when we reconnected. I had *no idea* we needed to talk about this. It seemed like it should just stay where it was. In the past."

"Well, now ya know." I smirk.

"I feel so bad." Tori covers her face.

"Don't feel bad, Tori," Stacey says. "We had no choice but to give up. Why does everyone feel like they have to feel bad all the time? Everyone makes mistakes. All that matters is that we learn something."

"Are you saying Dalia shouldn't feel bad?" I ask.

"That's between you two. But I feel like if we live in a world without forgiveness it's . . . well, that's a place I don't want to live." Stacey picks up her keys. "It's been great catching up with you guys, but I'm not sure I want to look at the time capsule now. Maybe we wait another five years. Same time, same place, 2020?"

"That's a good idea. I have to get back to the kids." Tori loops her scarf around her neck.

I don't know what to say, as I teeter between relief and regret. But I don't want this to end unfinished, not knowing if I'll ever speak to them again. And then Dalia comes slouching back to the table, her face pale, her eyes red.

"What now, Dalia?" I ask, and sigh.

"It's Jenny." She bites her bottom lip. A single tear runs down her cheek. "Her daughter found her this morning . . . on her bathroom floor."

50

I STEP OUT OF MY HEELS and sit on the couch. The corporate apartment feels more like a dentist's waiting room than living space, but I guess I should be happy that Shawn's company is letting us use it while we sort through this. The kids get to stay in the house while Shawn and I take turns here, though being in the city makes me feel far away from them.

I put my bare, reddened feet on the coffee table and look at the sparse walls, wondering how we got here, wondering where we go from here. I pick up the phone and call Shawn. After the earth-crumbling day I've had, it's good to hear his voice. I feel his warmth through the phone. I wonder why I haven't appreciated it.

"So how was the big reveal?" he asks.

"It was . . . revealing. Way too much to get into over the phone." I can't possibly get into it with him when I haven't even begun to process it myself. "How are the kids?"

"They're good. Maddie won her game. She scored two goals. She was a little upset you missed it, though. I told her—"

"She knows I would have been there if I hadn't had these plans for *twenty years*," I snap.

"I know, Sarah. If you would have let me finish, I would have said that that's exactly what I told her. And she's fine."

"I'm sorry. Thanks. And Jack?"

"He's great. He's at Timmy's house."

"Good. Hey Shawn, I'm glad we're doing it this way. I love that the kids aren't disrupted."

"Me too. I just don't want to keep them in limbo too long. Did you schedule the counselor yet?"

"That's what I wanted to talk to you about."

"Sarah, we agreed that we'd try, right?" He muffles the phone and says something to Maddie.

"Yes. One hundred percent. It's just that I know we're supposed to switch tomorrow, but I was wondering if I could have another week. I really think it will do me . . . do us . . . a lot of good."

"Another week? Well, are you going to come see the kids?"

"I really need to just get away and think for a bit. I'll call them every day, though."

"I don't know, Sarah. We haven't even started counseling yet. That doesn't feel like trying to me."

"It is trying. Please, Shawn, you just have to trust me on this. And I'll make the appointment for the following week."

"Promise?"

"I promise."

Shawn and I had a rule in our house that you never break a promise. He used to debate me on it, saying that sometimes things come up. But I would argue that if you're not one hundred percent sure that you can keep a promise, barring some act of God, then don't make it in the first place. This rule has served us well, especially lately.

I take off my coat and lie down. The couch is stiff and uncomfortable. I will myself to move into the bedroom, but a post-wine headache creeps in, and I decide to ride it out here. A few hours later, I'm awoken by the phone.

51

I WALK INTO THE BAR at the Peninsula Hotel. The door closes behind me, and the rest of life doesn't exist. It is the perfect place to be incognito. Other than illuminated liquor bottles and the soft glow of a fire, it is perfectly dark. My cynical side decides that it's designed for adulterers. Until I see Tori sitting by the fireplace and then I realize it's designed for celebrities. Tori's a celebrity. The fact that I haven't really grasped that is strange to me. I take a deep breath and go to her.

"Thanks for meeting me," she says softly. She's wearing black yoga pants and a gray wrap sweater. Her hair is pulled back, and she has no makeup on. No one would ever recognize her.

"I'm so glad you called," I say as I get situated on a burgundy leather chair. "Crazy day, huh."

"Crazy's a word. So, how are you?"

"I don't . . . I don't . . . *know.*" I lean in and rest my elbows on the table.

"Well, you have to be feeling a little better, right? Knowing it wasn't you?"

"Are we sure about that?"

Oddly, I find myself unable to let go of the notion that it *was* my fault. Because if it wasn't, it means I've got a whole lot of things to work through. And I'm not sure I have the energy.

The waitress finds us. I open my mouth to order wine, but somehow the words club soda come out. It feels like the slightest bit of progress, considering wine has been my best friend these days. Tori orders a Scotch straight up. She turns back to me and looks directly into my eyes.

"I need to know what happened to you. To us."

I drop my head and stare at the tiny bowl of wasabi peas on the table. I don't want to face her because I know where this is going. And I know she's right.

"Do you know why we haven't gotten close since we reconnected? It's because we never talked this out. We just . . . *left it.*" She flicks the backs of her hands at me. "And that is ridiculous. And I don't want to do that anymore, because I miss you. *What the fuck, Sarah.* Do you have *any idea* how much it hurt when you just shut me out like that?"

Her gestures are big. Full of a pain I never stopped to think she might be carrying.

"Do you have any idea how it felt to walk into my Syracuse dorm and meet a *stranger* freshman year when I was supposed to be there with my *best friend?*"

I don't know what to do with her words. For all the sympathy I'd spent on Dalia, somehow I'd never found any for the people who loved me, and I have no idea why. *Shame* enters my mind. I feel it so deeply, I can't bear to look at her as I respond.

"How could I go on with my *perfect life* after doing something like *that,* Tori? I caused the *death* of a *friend* of mine! Over a *guy!* I mean, the trauma alone was awful enough. But the shame, the guilt, the suffering that *I* caused *so many people.* I didn't see any option but to start over somewhere far away." I finally look at her. Her expression tells me I should have opened with I'm sorry. I quickly fix it. "I am *so so very sorry,* Tori."

"Even if you were careless or *whatever,* it still would *not* have been your fault. You didn't actively make a choice."

"Any way I dissected it, it was my fault. Whether it was consciously or unconsciously, allowing Dalia to plant an idea in my head, or even just *being friends* with her. Or just *not speaking up.* To Ella. Or my parents. It was *my* fault." I'm surprised at how fiercely I'm defending my self-inflicted guilty verdict. But my anger at myself suddenly pivots to Dalia. "But now . . . *what the fuck!* How could she let me suffer all these years when she knew I blamed myself? Why were we *ever* friends with her? Was she ever a good friend to *us?*"

"She was fun before Ella came along, and I did care about her. But a *good* friend? No. She was only there for us when it served her. That never seemed to bother you, though."

"I just always felt so bad for her. Even when she was being awful. She was just so . . . broken. Which is no excuse, by the way."

"More like shattered. I'm not even sure that what's happened to Jenny is enough to fix her."

"Jenny." I press my hands to my face and slide them down my cheeks. "I hope she's okay."

"Stacey pulled some strings and got an update. They said it was a miracle she survived. We need to go see her when she's allowed visitors."

"Absolutely. It's time we all do some healing. Together." I grab her hand and give it a squeeze. "So, did you see her much after the accident?"

"Not even once. She did exactly what you did. She dropped out of school immediately and wouldn't talk to anyone."

"I had no idea," I say with a sigh. The waitress returns with our drinks. I use the plastic stirrer to swirl my club soda. "Shawn told me she'd dropped out, but I didn't know you guys never talked to her again."

"That day at your house was the last time we saw her." Tori sniffs her Scotch and takes a small sip.

"And Dalia?"

"She kept trying to act like things were normal between us. And she *loved* the attention afterward. The victim part. The school constantly checking in, her crying in the halls, it was *gross*. That's why I wanted to leave after her sob story earlier. If she wants to forgive herself, fine. But she can go *fuck herself* as far as I'm concerned." She takes a generous swallow and sets her glass hard. "Stacey and I stayed in touch until she moved to St. Bart's. *Shit*." She glances over my shoulder. I turn around to see a couple staring at her. They recognize her. She shields her face with her hand.

"God, that must suck."

"You have no idea." She downs the rest of her Scotch and

waves the empty glass to the waitress. "So, what happened when you went to California?"

The fact that she even has to ask makes me realize we haven't talked about anything meaningful at all the few times we've spoken. That our relationship had been reduced to that of school mom acquaintances, running the gamut of small talk. Kids, activities, vacations, the "beautiful" or "love that" comments on social media. Which is how all of my adult friendships have been, I begin to realize. I'm suddenly able to define one of the giant holes in my soul. Lack of quality friendships. Until this very moment, I hadn't realized how shallow my current expectations of friendship had become. But just as quickly as the hole is defined, it starts to fill. Just sitting here with Tori, I catch a drip of my old self. And I dive in.

"It was hard. The only way I could start over was to pretend my old life never existed. But when I got there, it just felt so hollow. I thought about coming home, until I remembered there wasn't a home to come home to. Then one day I was wandering through campus, just staring at the ground, begging for a sign. And I looked up, and someone was holding a sign for a Catholic church."

"You asked for a sign, and you got a literal sign?" she says, laughing.

"A literal sign. Can you believe that church of all things got me over the hump? It made me feel like even if I couldn't forgive myself, maybe there was someone else who could. Like I could just hand it all over to something bigger than me."

She's absorbing my every word. It's so nice to feel heard. I wonder how I've survived without her.

"That sounds very freeing," she says. "I wish I could get into it."

"It was strange at first. In the beginning it was more like a distraction—from *me*. It made me less focused on *my* problems." It all starts coming back to me, and things begin to make sense more quickly than I would have expected. "And then something totally weird happened."

"Weirder than the literal sign?"

"Weirder than the literal sign. So, one day I noticed that I'd stopped worrying."

"*You?* Come on." She knits her perfectly sculpted brows together.

"Right? It was like once I'd lost everything, I didn't have to worry about losing anything. And *that* was liberating. Like this weight I'd carried around my entire life was just *gone*. Well, until the kids came along, and then it started all over again."

A memory surfaces of the day Jack was born. How the immense joy was immediately tainted with profound angst about my ability to keep him safe. And how much I hated that.

"I think that's one of the things that kept me from fixing things with everyone. If I didn't have anyone to care about, then I didn't have anything to worry about. And maybe I didn't reach out because I didn't want to give up that, I don't know, emotional freedom."

"What about Shawn?" she asks.

Leave it to Tori to immediately notice something I'd never noticed about myself. I shrug weakly as I realize that no, I hadn't worried about Shawn at all. And I wasn't really sure what that meant, other than the list of my things that needed exploring was growing.

"Wow. I need some time to process that one," she says.

The waitress hands her another Scotch. She takes another sip before setting it down. "Okay. I get the shutting down part, and the not deserving piece. And I forgive you, by the way. But your *parents* . . . they were *so great!* Why didn't you tell them?"

A jabbing pain in my gut jars me as my mind revisits a scene I'd tried desperately, unsuccessfully, to delete. I immediately want to drown it with Tori's drink, but I resist.

"Did you see their faces when the police asked for me? I can *still* see them. It is *burned on my brain.* We had so much love that I couldn't bear to disappoint them. You know," I tap the table, "if they hadn't been such amazing parents, it would have been easier to tell them."

"Fuckers . . . how *dare* they be such good parents." She sits back in her chair and laughs.

"*Yeah!* Fuck *them!*"

The laughter feels sublime. Genuine laughter, not new adult friend laughter. Not the *hope I didn't overshare* or *hope my joke didn't offend anyone* laughter. The laughter you share when you are one hundred percent yourself. It's what we should have been doing all these years. Going out into the world and living our lives but coming back to the safety of our coming-of-age friendship. I bask in the natural high for a moment before I go on.

"I just kept thinking about how upset they would be that I hadn't told them at the orchard. When you mentioned the *evil plan,* they asked what was going on, and I lied. And the night we saw Jake and Ella together, my mom practically begged me to tell her what had happened. If I'd told her, she would have sniffed Dalia out immediately. She would have told me to come clean with Jake, and Ella would still be alive. I disappointed everyone, including Ella. I just cut her off. And for what? For Dalia? When I go back over it in my mind, Dalia won my loyalty because I felt *worse* for her. And Ella lost because she was the big *disruptor*. *She* was disloyal. *She* broke a promise. But she deserved better. She was a good person, and I should have been there for her. I've gone over and over it. It's been a lot to carry."

"I guess I understand when you put it that way. Look, Sarah, you did the best you could with what you knew at the time. It's time to let that all go." Her eyes dart around as if she's gathering the remaining pieces of her mental puzzle. "So, how did your parents end up in Florida?"

"I think it was all just too much for them. My depression . . . and then Linda kept coming over, which was really tough on my mom. She couldn't put up any boundaries with her. And then my grandma broke her hip, so my mom went to Florida for a month. And I think she just felt better there, because when she came back, she was different toward me. Like I was just some girl who happened to live in the same house." I shake my head as I relive it in my mind. "And a couple of weeks later, they asked how I would feel about them moving. I said I'd be fine with it. And I was. I was relieved to not have to feel their pain anymore."

"Oh my god, Sarah. Well, I guess that makes sense. And Shawn? Any hope there?"

"Shawn." I stare off into the fire as I try to come up with the answer. "I'm going to have to get back to you on that. *God*, I miss you. I miss *this*. I want this back so much." I gesture back and forth between us.

"So do I. You know, for all the friends I've made since high school, even the really cool ones, of which there are *a lot*—by the way, you wouldn't believe the celebrity gossip I am privy to." Her eyes burst wide open, as if she wants to share something big but can't. "Those magazines we used to love? Some of them just make up whatever they want."

"*What?* No way." I smile.

"And those quizzes? Turns out Dalia was right. Total bullshit. I even wrote some of them myself."

"*Stop it!* You just ruined the hopes and dreams of teenage girls everywhere. This is *scandalous.*"

"I know. *Shhhhh!*" She tipsy-Tori laughs, just like she used to. "Anyway, none of them have even come close to what I had with you guys. There is nothing better than high school friendships."

"Amen to that." I raise my club soda. I look at Tori, and at the clear bubbles in my glass, and realize that I feel happy. And there is not a drop of alcohol deserving the credit.

52

THE NEXT MORNING, I shove a week's worth of clothes and a toothbrush into my overnight bag and take the elevator to the parking garage. I get in the car and think about where I should go. I have no idea, but I turn on the car anyway, hoping it will come to me. *Wherever I end up, they'd better have an iron*, I think as I pull out of the parking garage and onto Michigan Avenue.

It's so busy. I take in the hustle around me. People are laughing, happy. Some of them. Others are clearly unhappy. Some are in groups; many are alone. As I pass the Hancock building, there's one thing I'm sure of. All of them have their problems.

I turn right on Oak Street and snake around to inner Lakeshore Drive. I stop at a light outside of the Northwestern Hospital campus. There aren't a lot of smiles here. Even the pregnant woman and her husband look distressed. It makes me thankful that with everything I've gone through in my adult life, none has involved a hospital. And that makes me think that maybe my problems have been of my own making. Problems of the mind. And it starts to give me a sense of control.

I want to get as far away as possible from this hospital, so I hop on outer Lakeshore and head south. Habitually, I grab my phone and scroll to the Lakeshore Drive song. I remember the first time I played it for Shawn. I couldn't believe he'd never heard it. He thought it was cute that I had to hear it every time I drove on Lakeshore Drive. But some years went by, and he didn't think it was cute anymore. He thought it was annoying. Why did I *have* to listen to it *every time*? He was sick of it, and it became a fight. It happened after a nice dinner with friends, and he'd been in a bit of a mood, but we'd had fun, I'd thought.

I made that the defining moment of when things started to go south for us. After all, I hadn't done anything wrong. It was an unprovoked attack. And then there were more and more of them, from both of us. And then less and less of them as we stopped caring enough to bother. But he started it. Or did he? Maybe instead, what went wrong with us was a death by a thousand cuts of secret resentments and snide remarks. Of a lack of honesty and communication. Of neither of us actually asking for what we needed. Which was to be expected, I guess, of two trauma survivors.

Some days it was fine. Even great. But some days, I found myself cursing the day we bumped into each other on that San Diego beach, two years out of college. I'd been happily living my new life, my past far behind me. And there he was, picking up a Frisbee that had landed by my feet. It seemed like a sign, like the universe had brought us together to face our past and heal together. So, I didn't resist when, a year later, he asked me to move back to Chicago.

But we didn't heal together. Because I was never honest with him about the guilt I was carrying. And I resented him for bringing me back here where I was surrounded by memories. And that comment about the song probably had nothing to do with the song at all and everything to do with the fact that I couldn't let myself get close to him. But if the universe brought us together, was it the universe's fault we were falling apart, or ours, I wonder as I turn onto I-55.

My thoughts turn to the accident. How I've carried it around with me, using it as an excuse for everything I could. I drink too much? I killed my friend. Never established my career? I killed my friend. Marriage got me down? I killed my friend. It makes me start to think that perhaps there's a chance that it's not the accident holding onto me, but me holding onto the accident, conveniently pulling it out whenever it suits me. The fact that I'm doing this privately makes me even more suspicious about what, or who, is actually in charge.

As I leave more than one city landscape in my rearview mirror, I think about Dalia. Was what she did her fault? Of course it was. She made a choice, plain and simple. But then I start to think that maybe it wasn't, and instead it was simply a byproduct of the demons she'd encountered her whole life. Yet, if that's the case, is anyone ever responsible for anything? And if I was going to blame the accident for my mistakes, or blame Dalia, for that matter, wouldn't it only be fair for me to let Dalia blame her upbringing for her mistakes? And if I wasn't going to let her off the hook, how could I ever in good conscience let myself off the hook? There was no shortage of victims in my wake. Shawn, Jake, my kids, my parents. And then I think about Dalia making amends. And I realize she isn't the only one who needs to make them.

My planner sits open on the front seat. JAKE in block letters staring at me—and a phone number. I'd googled him last night and found a listing for Jake and Jacqueline Crenshaw, age thirty-five to forty-four. They live eight miles from me. All this time, and we've never run into each other. As I cross the border into Tennessee, I decide to dial his number. He answers on the third ring.

"Jake?"

"Yeah, who's this?"

"It's Sarah. Sarah Mat . . . Sarah Blake. From high school."

"Wow. Well, you're about the last person I thought would be calling me today. Or ever. So, how's it goin'?"

"Yeah, it was a surprise to me too. I'm good. Things are fine. You? Married? Kids? How's your life?"

"It's good. It's good. Married, four kids. They're great."

"Four kids? That's *crazy*. And the tattoo parlor?"

"Got six of them. Four in the city, two in Wisconsin. I don't do as many tattoos as I want because, you know, it's a lot of work running the business side, but it's cool."

"That's great, Jake. So, you're happy?"

"Yeah! No complaints. So, what's up, Sarah?" His friendly voice got a sudden edge to it. Like he just realized who he was talking to. "Why are you calling me after all this time?"

"Because there's something I need to tell you. And I'm sure you're not going to remember this, but the girls and I did this time capsule thing in high school, and it's twenty years later and—"

"Damn. I remember. Twenty years. That went fast."

"Right? So, this is totally weird, and I'm sure you're not even going to care, but Ella left a letter in it."

"Ella. I haven't thought about that in a long time. That was tough."

"Yeah. Well, she sneaked it in the time capsule on the morning she died. We just found it. And now everything I've thought for twenty years is just *wrong*... I think. So, she said something about you two planning a surprise party for me?"

"Yeah. Dalia talked me into it. I didn't want to do it, but—"

"I know. Dalia just told me. But there's something you don't know."

"What's that?"

"She set the whole thing up so I would catch you and Ella together and think something was going on between you guys. She told me you two had gone out together, when you had told me you were out to dinner with your mom, and then we spied on the two of you together at the restaurant. She wanted us to be mad at Ella."

"I *knew* something wasn't right about that. Dalia said her car broke down . . . and she needed help with the . . . and when I got there, it just didn't seem . . . but I was already there, so . . ."

He's not filling in the blanks. He's thinking out loud, each stage of grief manifesting itself through the tone of his voice as he revisits the events. Once he puts it together, he lands squarely on anger. But it's a soft anger. Almost pleasant. Just as I'd expect from him.

"Didn't I warn you about her, Sarah?" he asks gently.

"I know. I was so stupid."

"I was the stupid one. And you didn't do anything wrong. I just wish you would have answered my calls."

"I do too. I was a mess after the accident. I blamed myself, and I couldn't face anyone. I'm so sorry, Jake. I'm sorry I ever doubted you. I want you to know that. And I just hope that you're happy because you're a good person and you deserve that."

"Well, I don't know about that, but I am happy, Sarah. How about you? You doin' okay?"

"Yeah. I'm great." I hope he didn't notice the high pitch in my voice that precipitated the influx of tears.

"Well, that's good to hear. So it all worked out."

"Yeah."

"Well, it's been nice talking to you, Sarah, but I gotta run. It's our anniversary. Can't keep the wife waiting. But let me know if you ever want a tat."

"I will. And congrats on your anniversary. Your wife is a lucky woman."

"I'm the lucky one. I'm not sure how she puts up with me. All right, bye, Sarah."

I pull off to the shoulder. I can't see through the gut-curdling tears spilling down my face, each tear representing a loss I've never grieved. Losses I buried deep inside, putting meaningless hobby and wine Band-Aids on them every time they rose to the surface. How had I not trusted Jake? Why didn't I just ask him what they were doing? Why didn't I tell my parents about Dalia or what happened with Jake? They'd made me promise my entire life that I'd tell them if anything was ever weird. Why did I break *that* promise, of all things? I had so many chances to prevent events from unfolding the way they did, both before and after the accident, and I took none of them.

I think of all the downstream effects those decisions had. But then I wonder what would have happened if none of it had happened at all. What if *Jake* and I had ended up together? That's six kids who wouldn't exist. His four and my two. And if I wouldn't trade my kids for anything in the world, why have I ever, even for a moment, thought about what *could have been* or why I ended up with Shawn? Jake was right when he said everything worked out. Or was he?

The question fatigues me. I have nothing left to give it today. I google hotels nearby and settle on a two-star that boasts about their clean sheets. Between that and a shrink-wrapped 7-Eleven sandwich, I'm set for the night.

While the sheets are surprisingly clean, they are painfully scratchy. The mattress and pillow are equally as uncomfortable. I hope I'm tired enough to power through and get some rest. Instead, I am inundated with thoughts.

I think of our wedding. How Shawn's parents said they wouldn't come unless we married in a church, still upset that he'd left it. And how that was all the excuse I needed to tell him we should just run off by ourselves, proclaiming it our private moment, selling it as romantic. Which it was. Until I looked up at him smiling against a backdrop of lush Hawaiian mountains and crashing waves and realized I hadn't seen his telltale dimple since the last time I saw him with Ella. And I wondered if that meant I was his second choice.

But I shoved that feeling deep inside, and we turned our marriage into a family. We decorated, celebrated, raised, fed, taught, and traveled—together as a unit. To any outsider, it was a thing of beauty.

And as the reel of our life story plays in my mind, it seems we aren't much different from the other couples around us who *don't* have the complicating circumstances we have. In fact, as I'd listen to book club discussions, aka wine and husband-bitching sessions, I realized I didn't have a lot to contribute. We hadn't fought in years. None of the women could believe it. They declared ours the perfect marriage, fawned over us—how lucky we were.

But as I try to find one usable area of the rubbery pillow, I realize that maybe we should have. I was fighting harder to get comfortable in this bed than I'd ever fought for *us*. Instead of doing the work, we focused on maintaining our perfect exterior, hiding the fact that we were rotting away on the inside. Like the water spot on my parents' ceiling that grew and grew until one day, the ceiling collapsed. A consequence of neglect. We didn't even notice until one day our marriage came crashing down, sending shockwaves through our neighborhood, our kids. Shawn told me he'd slept with someone else.

He volunteered it, was sorry, wanted us to be better. Of course, instead of thinking about *my* contribution to our demise, I yelled with righteous indignation and kicked him out. But it was more for show. The fact that his infidelity didn't bother me *that* much told me a lot. But as I saw what our separation was doing to the kids, I agreed to counseling.

Of course, Shawn being the cheater put me in the power spot. To the rest of the world, he is the bad guy. Which is an easy train for me to ride, as it abdicates me from any responsibility. *Who wouldn't ride that train?* But maybe I'm being unfair, taking too much advantage of that. And then I realize that as long as I'm perched above him, pointing my finger down at him, we'll never get better. As sleep closes in, I wonder if I can get down from that perch.

Shawn is in a tuxedo, a white boutonniere pinned to his lapel. Behind him is a stained-glass window. To my left, a priest. And to my right, hundreds of family and friends sitting in pews. I see my parents. My dad looks like he's seen something funny and can't wait to tell me about it. My mom is smiling proudly. Shawn's parents are on the opposite side holding hands.

"You may kiss the bride," the priest says.

Shawn smiles at me. I see the telltale dimple coming at me. As our lips meet, I am overcome with joy. I feel someone lift the train of my dress. I turn around to see Ella smiling at me.

"I love you guys," she says.

I wake up happy. Until I realize where I am. I fumble for my phone and see that it's nine o'clock. I call home. The second I hear Shawn's voice, I break down. All he hears is his name and guttural cries.

"Sar, what's going on. Are you hurt? Talk to me . . . please." I can tell he's alarmed but trying to stay quiet so as not to alert the kids.

"I'm okay. I'm okay. I just . . . I'm just *so sorry*. For *everything*," I wail. "For not trusting us. For being too scared . . . scared to let myself love you in the way you deserve. And for not being honest with you."

"What are you talking about?"

I tell him everything. He can't believe it but agrees that it explains a lot . . . about us. Our problems. Especially when I relay my latest realization that marrying him made me feel like I took yet another thing from Ella. Though he calls bullshit on the dimple and says he has proof.

"Don't you remember our first Spin the Bottle game at camp, when I spun, and it landed on *you?*" he asks.

"*What?!*" I'm transported back to my first kiss. Dick Johnson, during a game of Spin the Bottle. Shawn spun. It landed on me. But he spun it so hard that the bottle also landed close to me. I nudged it with my toe, so it pointed to Ella. "*Shawn, Ella* wanted to kiss *you,* and *I* wanted to kiss *Dick Johnson,* so . . ." I laugh. It's not surprising we'd never talked about this, as we generally didn't talk about anything involving Ella. And then he reminds me that he asked me to Homecoming freshman year, and I said no.

"Well, that's because I wanted Craig Leitner to ask me, so . . ." I start to feel really stupid that I'd ever questioned his love for me when I knew deep down he'd liked me the whole time. He just tried at a time when I was rebelling against the clean-cut athletic type, the stereotypical image of who girls *should* like, and instead found myself irresistibly drawn to the artists and musicians around me.

"You *were* my first choice, but you kept pawning me off to your girlfriends! You know, part of the reason I liked Ella so much was because she reminded me of you," he says. "But you *were* my first choice, and you are *still* my first choice. I love you, Sarah. And I can't *believe* you put so much weight on this *dimple* that I'm sure never meant anything."

So, the dimple wasn't a thing? Could I really have imagined it? I start to laugh as I try to remember the first time I noticed it, but the tears come marching back. "I love you too. And I want to come home. To live. Together."

He is thrilled to hear this. And I am so sure about my decision that we get the kids on the line and deliver the news together.

"But there's something I have to do first," I tell them.

I pick open the plastic top of my coffee and put it to my lips. It is rich and full. Surprisingly satisfying. I feel around for the cup holder as I turn up the on ramp. And that's when I notice it.

Brilliant reds, fiery oranges, and gilded yellows bursting from the mountainsides like nature's fireworks. They are everywhere I look, as if fall's greatest gifts united in spectacular fashion to remind me they are there. That they've always been there.

As the glorious landscape passes me by, I wonder how just a day ago it had gone unnoticed. A bittersweet ache reminds me of all I've missed—the joys that went unfelt as I lived behind a protective moat of fear. I wonder how to be better. And then I *vow* to be better, fueled by a new fear. The fear of missing even one more magnificent moment. It feels like an obligation—not only to myself, but to Ella—to stop taking my life for granted when hers went unlived.

The roads start to flatten. The leaves are green again. With the fall behind me, I drive with a sense of urgency. Desperate to make things right, eager to try life without excuses.

After ten hours of driving, the Florida sun welcomes me. I open the window. The balmy air invigorates me. I feel peaceful, secure, excited. And it has nothing to do with the warmth, or a week without responsibility, or even my intact family.

It is because I finally understand that if everyone has problems, then the only difference between those of us who wither and die and those who come out stronger is how we react to them. It is the *only* thing we can control. And it is one hundred percent *in our control.*

And that is a wonderful thing, I think, as I pull in my parents' driveway. I get out of the car and sling my bag over my shoulder. I pick up the key from under the mat, unclick the bolt, and stick my head in the door.

"Mom, Dad?"

ACKNOWLEDGMENTS

First, I would like to thank my family: Max, for your endless encouragement and inspiration; Jake, for your robust vocabularic contributions; Kayla, for your incredibly kind and encouraging words; and Christian, for your love and support and for picking up the balls that I've dropped throughout this process.

A very special thank you goes out to my family and friends who were kind enough to act as my beta readers: Jill Leone, Nathan Leone, Cheryl Leone, Giulio Leone, Matthew Leone, Allison Leone, Caitlyn Light, Jamie Guerin, Lisa Ordway, and Jennifer Kane. I cannot thank you enough for your honest feedback and encouragement. And, of course, Alison Kulisek, Colleen Rolloff, and Jennifer Bernstein for all of your contributions, from pop culture references to funny memories to a lifetime of friendship. I am eternally grateful for you and everything we've shared.

I would also like to thank the My Word Publishing team: Polly Letofsky, Kirsten Jensen, and Donna Mazzitelli for your incredible constructive support and getting me over the finish line. I am so very thankful for you all.

ABOUT
THE AUTHOR

PAULA RIEHLE is a financial professional turned fiction writer from Chicago, a city near and dear to her heart. A fan of all things '80s, she will challenge anyone to prove to her why it wasn't the best decade ever. A voracious traveler, her passion is showing her children the world, especially those off-the-beaten-path finds like custom 3D cappuccinos and fake food-making classes in Japan.

In her downtime, you will find her playing Halo or Call of Duty with her family. Or wearing a mushroom costume at a Flaming Lips show. She currently lives in Downers Grove, Illinois, with her husband, three kids, and three cats.

For more information, or if you would like Paula to join your book club discussion, please go to www.paulariehle.com.

INVITE PAULA TO
YOUR BOOK CLUB!

As a special gift to readers of *Sarah's Fall,*
Paula would love to visit your book club either
via video conferencing or in person.

Please contact Paula directly to schedule her appearance at your next book club
meeting. Paula@PaulaRiehle.com

Made in the USA
Middletown, DE
23 November 2021

53194501R10246